Night Waking

Night Waking

SARAH MOSS

GRANTA

Granta Publications, 12 Addison Avenue, London W11 4QR

First published in Great Britain by Granta Books 2011

A CIP catalogue record for this book is available from the British Library.

1 3 5 7 9 10 8 6 4 2

ISBN 978 1 84708 215 2

Printed and bound in the UK by CPI Mackays, Chatham ME5 8TD

Night Waking

1

THE REALITY PRINCIPLE

It remains true that social behaviour cannot come about unless the individual has progressed from the pleasure principle to the reality principle. But the statement is not reversible in the sense that this advance itself guarantees socialization.

— Anna Freud, *Normality and Pathology in Childhood*
(London: Penguin, 1965), p. 145

The swans are by the shore, drifting bright as paper cut-outs against waves blurred by dusk. They spend the night murmuring oboe harmonies to each other, a woodwind of reassurance. Ordinary swans, the Queen's swans on the river where we feed the ducks at home, have faces apparently afflicted by some medieval disease, and sleep standing on one leg, heads under their wings like child-free passengers on long-haul flights who can summon night with a nylon blindfold. These sea swans seem to stay awake all night, sailing through the fading light like ships bound for far countries, and they have faces as smooth and neutral as the *corps de ballet*, faces that can't communicate any level of grief or pain. Perhaps this is an asset in species that mate for life.

I glance back at the house. Its façade, dark as the cliff-face at the other end of the island, turns away from the after-light shining over the sea, from where America is coming up for a new day as we turn away from the sun. One of the swans stretches towards the sky and cries out, wings threshing the water in sudden agitation like that of someone who has just remembered that a friend is dead. I saw a goose dying, once, a Canada goose that had flown all the way from the Arctic to end its life on the hard shoulder of the M40, and although one wing was still beating as if to music while the other lay across the rumble-strip, its face was impassive. I stood on the footbridge, watching, joggling the pram in which the baby would sleep only for as long as we kept moving, until some lorry driver, merciful or inattentive, left a flurry of feathers and red jam on the road. Our swans are safe from that, here. For a season. Like us, they will go south in the autumn, but for now there are no cars, no roads. No bridges, either. The stars are coming out in the darkening sky over the hill. I shiver; not cold, exactly, but time to go in.

The power was still off, which doesn't matter too much in summer as long as we keep our laptops charged. Giles had lit a candle.

'Look! Here we are.' He passed me a holiday brochure, folded back to show a stamp-sized picture of the blackhouse down by the beach, taken last summer before the building work began. The idea is that at some point the income generated by letting it as a holiday cottage will cover the cost of the restoration. The reality is that even if Giles stops telling our friends and, God help us, his family, that they'll be able to stay for free, the argon-filled triple glazing, grey water scheme (it flushes the loo with water previously used to wash your clothes) and reclaimed furniture (reclaimed from a shop in Bath and transported over land and sea at expense that surprised Giles) might be hoped to pay off in the lifetime of our grandchildren. If any. I held the brochure towards the light.

*

Spend a week or two on your very own island! A stunning new conversion of a traditional blackhouse dwelling with magnificent sea views from every window, set on the deserted island of Colsay. The house, newly restored by an award-winning architect, boasts slate floors with underfloor heating, rain-mist shower and a kitchen hand-made from local materials. No TV, but a thoughtful book collection and arts and crafts kits for rainy days. There are no roads or cars on the island; your host will collect you from the harbour at Colla and take you back at any time during your stay for shopping or days out, enjoying the walks, crafts and heritage of the Inversaigh area. Colsay itself has a wealth of bird life and historical remains to explore, or you may be happy to relax in the silence and beauty of this very special place.

'"Very special"?' I put the brochure down too fast and the candle on the table went out. 'And all those adjectives? Giles, you should have asked me to do it. You've even put an exclamation mark in, for God's sake. People can get silence at home, you know. In libraries.'

I miss the silence of libraries. Even whooper swans wouldn't talk in my favourite libraries.

'I couldn't have asked you.' Giles started trying to relight the candle from a tealight. Wax dripped predictably onto his papers. 'It was the week they both had that puking bug.'

The week Giles kept going to work because it was 'expected of him' and I stayed at home scrubbing sick out of carpets. I do, as Giles does not tire of pointing out, get paid whether I actually do any work or not. It's in my contract. 'The Research Fellow shall make such progress as might reasonably be expected with the research project outlined before taking up the Fellowship.' Apart from that I can discharge my contractual obligations by dining in college twenty-four times a year. Most of the Fellows (who are not fellows but ladies of a certain age and don't-mess-with-me demeanour) would not recognize me on the high street, although few people recognize me on the high street anyway because I am usually behind the pushchair. The pram in the hall may be the enemy of promise, but outside it would be the perfect cover for almost any kind of criminal act. You could strafe the high street with a machine gun and stroll away wearing nothing but high heels and a top hat, behind a pushchair, and nobody would remember you'd been there.

'Anyway,' said Giles. 'The anchorite enjoyed the silence. I mean, isn't that the whole idea? Ow.' Wax ran down his fingers.

'I expect the anchorite was far too busy looking for something to eat and hiding from the Vikings. Lighter? Matches?'

He shrugged and we both looked around as if we could see the children's books, half-eaten biscuits and papers awaiting filing that trickle from every orifice of the house.

'Oh well. At least we can't tidy up in the dark.' I moved my foot and encountered something squashy, either stuck to the floor or surprisingly heavy, perhaps a recalcitrant small mammal or my mother-in-law's fruit cake. 'I hope you know the on-call ferryman is you. I've got *Fair Seedtime* to finish. And who's assembling this book collection?'

Fair Seedtime: the invention of childhood and the rise of the institution in late eighteenth-century Britain was due at the publisher last month. In theory, I should be more employable with a book to my name. In practice, there will be no jobs in history for several decades to come and, if there were, they would go to people who haven't spent half of the last eight years changing nappies instead of buying drinks at the conference bar. Giles started picking the wax off the papers and rolling it into balls.

'Don't,' I said. 'Moth'll eat them.'

He dropped one into the tealight. 'Better than birdshit.'

I stood up. 'I wasn't claiming birdshit as the base line in infant nutrition. Anyway, that was why I gave up on the garden. I can't plant the sodding trees without looking away from him for the odd second or two. At least it wasn't foxgloves.'

Foxgloves contain digitalis, and will stop your toddler's heart

4

long before you can cross the Sound to the village surgery, which is open four mornings a week.

'I got to him in time. I made him spit them out. I told you.'

'Yeah. You said. I'm going to bed.' I burnt my fingers balancing the tealight on my palm and crossed the room as one might venture across a minefield in the dark, which is reasonable when many of the small objects you can't see have wheels.

I've stopped showering in the morning because Raph allows me three minutes and then stands on the bathmat with a stopwatch telling me how many millimetres of the polar ice cap have been melted by the energy used to heat the water and Moth, who still has vivid memories of what breasts are for, peers round the curtain, getting his clothes wet and gesturing unmistakably. Candlelit showers by night are awkward for obvious reasons, so I ran a bath hot and deep enough to drown polar bear cubs and stood at the bookcase wondering whether to drown my sorrows in *Marjorie Makes It at the Chalet School* or revive my intellect with the selected essays of Henry James. I picked up *Caring for Your Child* (1947) in the hope that I might have missed the solution to toddler insomnia last time I read it. Giles's family have been using this house as a repository for unreadable books since the War.

'You were asleep,' said Giles. He'd found matches and another candle, or maybe nipped outside with a couple of flints.

My neck was stiff and the water had cooled. I pulled myself up to sitting and yawned.

'So?' At least by candlelight I didn't need to pull my stomach in.

'One of these days you'll drown.'

I rubbed my neck and scooped water on to my face. 'I'm sure a lung full of water would wake me up. If it was that easy people wouldn't bother cutting their wrists. Anyway, it sounds a nice way to go.'

He started brushing his teeth. They can probably hear Giles brushing his teeth on the mainland. 'What about the children?'

'You're dribbling toothpaste on your jumper. They'd be your problem.' Which is probably one of my better reasons for staying alive.

I waited till he put the candle down on the bookcase by the door and then climbed out. The bathmat wasn't where I'd hoped it might be and I pretended to believe that what I'd stepped in was water, a regular pretence the alternative to which would be cleaning, which I decline on ideological grounds I cannot be bothered to specify, even to myself.

He spat toothpaste. 'Nice tits, missis.'

'Piss off. You can't even see them.' And they're not, haven't been for some years. My towel smelt faintly of fish. I walked through a curl of smoke as I found the door. 'I think you've just set the *Guardian* on fire.'

'Fuck.' He grabbed a flaming *Weekend* magazine from the top of an unsteady pile of clothes on the bookcase and dropped it in the bath. I caught a glimpse of a double-barrelled chef and a pig before they were consumed by green flames and then drowned. 'Oh well, I'd read that one.'

'I hadn't. I was saving it. For a bath with electric lights and all.'

'Read it online. Come on, it's gone midnight.' He ran his hand over my shoulder and down under the towel, tracing my spine with a fingertip.

I batted at his hand. 'If I get unmolested time on my computer I'm not wasting it reading the bloody *Guardian*, I'll write my book. I said, piss off.'

What I miss most when the electricity goes off is the steady gaze of my radio alarm clock. It's hard to navigate the night without the stations of the clock. I couldn't have been asleep long, because our west-facing bedroom was still as dark as a coffin when I swam up through sleep to Moth's shouting. The

6

floor was cold and gritty under my feet. As I crossed the landing, where the coming day was beginning to assert itself in the uncurtained window, something rustled and creaked in the attic upstairs. I picked Moth up and he clung to my hair and rubbed his slimy nose on my neck.

'Mummy.' There was food behind his ear but his hair still had the butter smell of babies. I kissed his salt cheek and felt the weight of him on my wrists. 'Mummy. Moth frightened.'

I paced, four steps across and four back, watching out for the nineteenth-century iron fender which juts out of the fireplace. Giles remembers his father putting in the electric heaters, not as a concession to modern ideas of comfort but in recognition of the fact that there was nobody left on the island to cut peat for him.

'Mummy sing a Gruffalo.'

'Later. Gruffalo in the morning.'

'Mummy sing a Gruffalo!'

I patted him. 'Night-night, Gruffalo. The Gruffalo is sleeping.'

'Want Gruffalo!'

If he screams, it wakes Raphael, who requires not the Gruffalo but lies about why there will probably still be a planet for him when he grows up. I murmured into Moth's ear.

'A mouse took a stroll through the deep dark wood. A fox saw the mouse and the mouse looked good. Where are you going to, little brown mouse? Come and have lunch in my log-pile house—'

He lifted his head. 'Unnerground house.'

I pushed his head back down. 'No, that's the snake.'

'Fox in unnerground house. More.'

'Well if you know it, why don't you—'

'More.'

'It's terribly kind of you, fox, but no, I'm going to have tea—'

'Lunch.'

'Lunch. With a gruffalo. A gruffalo, what's a gruffalo? A gruffalo? Why, don't you—'

'*Didn't* you know.'

I fear that I now know the works of Julia Donaldson better than those of Jean-Jacques Rousseau, but if that's true then Moth's commitment to accuracy suggests that I don't know anything very well. Which is plausible.

'Oh! But who is this creature with terrible claws and terrible teeth in his terrible jaws?'

Moth had gone soft and heavy on my chest again.

'His eyes are orange, his tongue is black; he has purple prickles all over his back.'

I crooned towards the vegan resolution – 'The mouse found a nut and the nut . . . was . . . good' – and his fingers stayed loose on my neck. I hummed the Skye Boat Song and, as if exploring the fifth arrondissement with no particular destination in mind, sauntered towards the cot and back towards the bookshelf. Reconnaissance successful. I made a second approach, heading for the window but pausing at the cot as if a jeweller's window display had caught my attention. Moth's breathing didn't change, and I'd eased him back down, risked putting a blanket over him, evaded the creaking floorboards and the rustling bin liner over the dinner jacket hanging from the door for reasons that presumably seem logical to Giles and was pushing Giles back onto his own side of our bed before Moth woke to find himself abandoned to what one of my parenting handbooks helpfully calls 'a barred cage far from you in the dark'. Not far enough. By the time Raphael required my services to evict the Somali child soldiers from last week's *Guardian* magazine from under his bed there was grey light in the sky over the mountains. I escorted the child soldiers all the way down the stairs and went to hide in the unfinished stunning modern eco-conversion with my laptop until morning forced itself upon me in the form of the builder's motor boat.

*

My book is about the relationship between the Romantic celebration of childhood as a time of joyful purity and the simultaneous increase in residential institutions for the young: boarding schools, orphanages, hospitals and prisons. At the same time as Wordsworth is rejoicing in the clouds of glory trailed by infants and Rousseau is telling us to learn from the instinctive wisdom of toddlers, other people – actually, sometimes the same people – are sponsoring establishments intended to take the children of the poor away from their families and make them into useful consumers and producers for the age of capitalism. Nothing changes; as in modern parenting books, either babies come with a beautiful inner self that we need to respect and liberate (bring your child into your bed when he wakes at night) or they come as a primitive set of desires and have to be socialized into humanity (leave him to scream until he learns not to be nocturnal). It's interesting that the era famed for its embrace of infant innocence is equally, and simultaneously, committed to the idea of taming the little savages in institutions. When I started the research I thought this was simply a conflict between idealism and pragmatism, indulgence and discipline, but the more I read their rules and manifestos the more I think that institutions have utopian agendas of their own. Institutions constitute an attempt to ratify a brighter future, to achieve what individual households cannot encompass. They exist in order to make things different or better, although it seems to be in the nature of either humans or institutions that they often end by reinforcing, or even fossilizing, the status quo and making things worse. Institutions, at least in the eighteenth century, are the incarnation of optimism, of a confidence in human capacity for change that we lost somewhere along the way. My editor has said she'll still take the manuscript if I get it in by September, and I think I'll make it. If the USB device proffered by Giles as the solution to my need for online databases on an island without broadband works more often than it has so far, I'll make it. If I can keep on behaving as if sleep were elective I'll make it.

I've finished the archival research, or even I wouldn't have been so stupid as to come to Giles's island. I've read the manuscript records of meals, accounts, expulsions and punishments in the boarding schools of the 1790s, plodded along lists of the benefactors of foundling hospitals across England, leafed my way through pages of yellowed instruction in uneven typeface: 'It is with great Pleasure that I see at last the Preservation of Children become the Care of Men of Sense ... this Business has been too long fatally left to the Management of Women, who cannot be supposed to have proper Knowledge to fit them for such a Task ...' (William Cadogan, *An Essay Upon Nursing* (London: 1753)). I'm more or less up to date on the secondary material, although I realized rather late in the day that the most important work on childhood and institutions was done by Anna Freud and her disciples in the aftermath of the Second World War. Freud himself has long been towards the top of the list of people I should have read, pretend to have read, but haven't. My understanding of Freud is that he shows that the realization of human potential depends upon the self-control of parents, while I find economic and political solutions to the problem of suffering more palatable and, frankly, more likely to be achieved. Peace in the Middle East and the end of poverty and famine would be easier to implement than perfect parenting for all, and so I prefer the prophets of the Left to those of the human heart, Marx to Freud; one is, after all, concerned with what is possible as well as what is right. Nevertheless, when I saw that the collected works of Sigmund and Anna hadn't been out of the college library in nine years I thought I might as well bring them here for the silence and fresh air. I've got the whole thing in draft so the idea, Giles's idea, is that the isolation of Colsay is perfect for drafting and polishing and meditating on psychoanalysis without feeling the Fellows breathing malodorously down my neck. He overestimates my capacity for abstract thought and hasn't really understood the extent to which the Fellows don't care.

I should have been trying to write the conclusion, which troubles me because I am not sure that the book is in any way conclusive. Behind my laptop, birds that might have been kittiwakes flickered across the sky and I watched some kind of gull dive-bombing the sea. From the boat, on a still day, you can see the other half of their lives, transmuted by water, bubbles streaming off their feathers as they glide and turn like seals after fish. I craned to see the swans but they were somewhere else. I opened the acknowledgements. Last but not least I thank Giles Cassingham, although for what I cannot say.

'Hey, you.' Giles sat at the table reading a gardening catalogue while Moth, frowning, concentrated on spooning porridge into an envelope which also contained a missive from the Child Tax Credit people, who wish alternately to shower us with rubies and to hold our oatmeal in security against what we owe them, depending on no factor that we have been able to isolate. 'The power's back. I made you some tea.'

'He boiled too much water.' Raph spoke from under the table.

'Mummy likes two cups in the morning.' Giles's gaze flicked over my off-off-white Victorian nightdress and cardigan outfit.

'But then she boils it again anyway so the second one is fresh. Do you know there are children in Africa dying because they haven't got any water? I bet their mummies don't drink cups of tea.'

Moth turned the envelope upside down and watched as porridge fell slowly to the floor, followed by a parachute of official communications. Giles actually packed these letters, a whole kitchen table's worth, and brought them from Oxford because he thought we might deal with them while on the island. Giles's sparkling career is founded on his ability to use observations about the present behaviour of puffins to predict their future

11

movements. I suppose it is necessary, if also delusional, to believe that people have more capacity for change.

'All splat,' said Moth. 'Again!'

Giles passed him another envelope.

I sipped the tea, which was tepid and stewed. 'There are also children in Africa who have air-conditioning and satellite television and chauffeurs, you know. It's a continent, not a refugee camp.'

'Why can't we have satellite television?'

Giles stood up. 'Because it's an instrument of late capitalist excess that rots the brain and promotes American cultural imperialism. Anna, if you can take over here, I'll go talk to Jake.'

'No deal,' I muttered. 'Oh, all right then. Raph, think of the carbon footprint of a television. You can't worry about global warming and want lots of big gadgets.'

He crawled out from under the table, through Moth's fallen porridge, and stood up. 'Why can't I?'

'Why?' added Moth. 'Moth wants jam.'

I sat down. 'Eat your porridge, Moth. Because making electronic equipment uses lots of energy and makes lots of toxic waste.'

'What kind of toxic waste?'

I had forgotten our new policy of not giving Raphael the basis of any further forebodings about the present and future state of the world.

'I don't know. Moth, love, don't put porridge in your hair. Or in your brother's hair.'

'Porridge in hair! Mummy clean it.'

I ran an old baby muslin over Moth's hair. He pushed it away. 'Peepo!'

I held it over my face and flapped it up on to my head.

'Peepo!'

'Mummy, you look really silly like that. Are you going to stay in that nightie all day?'

12

I ate some of Moth's rejected toast.

'No. In a minute I'm going to go upstairs and reappear in one of my fabulous designer porridge-scrubbing outfits.'

Moth started trying to brush his hair with a jammy knife.

'Do you want to wash the floor, Raph? I think you might just about be old enough to do it all by yourself if you're really careful.'

'What, with the big bucket?'

I lifted Moth out of his highchair and frisked him for concealed porridge.

'If you think you're grown-up enough not to spill it.'

The garden is Giles's idea. I've never seen much point in extending housework to cover parts of outside, especially now we've got the beach on the doorstep to give the children a nodding acquaintance with what Giles persists in calling the Natural World, as if the human habit of making shelters and arranging for people to buy food they haven't grown and read books they haven't written is in some way unnatural. Giles says I kept the children inside far too much in Oxford, wrapped round each other on the sofa, working our way like termites along the bookcases. Giles says Moth is far better off eating foxgloves and birdshit and getting wet in the great outdoors. Giles spends his days alone, working.

'Come on,' I said to Moth. 'Let's find some clothes for Mummy.'

It takes a long time for Moth to climb the stairs, and much longer if you try to hurry. I stay behind him, hands poised, and try to use the time to think about my book. In the hall below there are admirable Victorian tessellated tiles in white, black and a shade of red that reminds me of butchers' shops, of cut flesh, and the banisters are spaced for grandeur and not child safety.

'Raph?' I called. 'Raph, do you want to come into the garden?'

After a pause to greet the cracks between the floorboards on the landing, and another to poke all the flowers in the carving on the chest of drawers, we reached my bedroom. Moth climbed on to the bed, smearing porridge on the pillow. The jumper I'd been wearing all week had some soup on the sleeve but the chances of encountering anyone who would care were approximately the same as those of the swans turning into princesses and performing pirouettes along the beach. Moth handed me a sock.

'Moth in a garden too?'

I shook yesterday's knickers out of my jeans. It's not really a garden. We have crocuses and a few foolhardy and stunted daffodils in June. And Giles, who against most interpretations of the historical evidence believes in self-sufficiency with regard to fruit and vegetables up here, has found some hardy dwarf apple trees on the internet. When he finished the last of the four boat trips required to bring them from Colla, Jake came to consult him about roofing timbers and the Research Fellow in History found herself failing to dig holes for Icelandic trees while her offspring licked birdshit off pebbles.

'Moth eat worms in a garden,' said Moth, sitting down on my bare foot. I wriggled my toes under his bottom and he giggled. I didn't seem to have another sock.

'Raphael?' I shouted. Sometimes this house is too big, although mostly I enjoy the way the stone walls muffle infant rage. There were clean socks in Giles's sock drawer, folded into pairs, so I put one on and held out my hand to Moth. 'Come on. Let's go plant some trees.'

I'm working on what to do with Moth while I attempt anything other than interactive childcare. It never arose at home. In Oxford, I mean. If I was at work I was working and if I was at home I was attending to the children, performing constant triage to read to whichever one seemed likely to have a tantrum first. Finally the far shores of supper, bath and bed, a few curtain calls relating to misplaced teddies, drinks of water

14

and/or the necessity of reaching a clearer understanding of momentum and inertia before going to sleep and then intellectual life re-established itself, at least until Moth woke for the first time. No one expected me to plant trees. No one expected Moth to entertain himself. I'd never planted a tree. I could hear the rhythmic slap of Raphael's space hopper in the paved yard at the front of the house.

'Moth? Do you want to come and see how the trees grow?'

Moth continued to stagger across the tussocks, trampling nascent daffodils in the quest for birdshit. Perhaps it contains some nutrient crucial to toddler development that is inexcusably missing from my cooking.

'Moth? Shall we do some digging with Mummy's big spade?'

No response. I followed him.

'Mummy's big *sharp* spade?'

He looked round. 'Sharp spade?'

I nodded. 'Very sharp.'

'Very sharp spade.'

A pause.

'Moth very sharp spade.'

He turned back and trundled towards the sharp spade. Getting him away from the birdshit and towards my intended field of operations could only be progress. I yawned and stretched. Hours to go until bedtime. I tried to think about digging a hole in the ground.

Moth stalked around the trees, each muffled with a burlap sack, and seized the handle of the spade. He couldn't lift it.

'Moth very sharp spade!'

'Yes. Moth, love, do you want to help Mummy dig a hole? A nice deep hole for the trees to put their roots in?'

He began to drag the spade across the grass, a hunter so proud of his mammoth that he can't wait for back-up.

'No. Moth spade.'

'But the spade is for digging holes. Shall we dig a hole? Moth and Mummy?'

'No.'

'But Moth, look. This is how we use a spade.'

I took hold of it. He pulled it back.

'Mummy put it back. Moth spade.'

'But look, love—'

He cast himself to the ground and flung his arms out. The screaming suggested an innocent who had just seen Herod's minions coming his way.

'All right, all right. Moth spade.'

He had already drawn the next breath and eyed me as one might the minion being told that this particular child was in fact a girl.

'All right, Moth play with the spade. Mummy will find something else.'

'Moth spade.'

He sat up beside it and began to stroke the haft.

'Hush, little spa-ade, don't say a word, Mummy gonna buy you a mockin-bird.'

There was a trowel in a trug by the bundled trees. It had as little impact on the matted roots of the turf as one might have expected.

'If that mockin-bird don't sing, Mummy gonna buy you a diamond ring.' He leant forward and kissed the spade's handle. 'Moth's love. Sleeping now.'

I wondered whether, once the spade slept, I could reintegrate it to the adult world.

'Has the spade gone to sleep?'

'Shh.' He patted it. 'Quiet, Mummy. Spade sleeping.'

I knelt up to get more weight on the trowel. I might as well have been digging with a spoon. The space hopper had fallen suggestively silent.

We had a kind of potato omelette that I told Giles was frittata for lunch. It would have been better if I'd either boiled the potatoes first or started frying them about an hour earlier than

16

I did, but one advantage of a boarding-school childhood is that Giles can and will eat all but the worst misjudgements. In theory, I disapprove of cooking. It's not a coincidence that ready meals and supermarkets appeared at the same time as equal opportunities legislation. In practice cooking means that you can hide in the kitchen wielding knives and listening to Radio Four and still be a Good Mummy, thus achieving a variety of domestic servitude which is still not, I believe, what Mary Wollstonecraft, Emmeline Pankhurst or Betty Friedan had in mind. It's even less fun here, where I can't get Radio Four most of the time, vegetables come seasick from Colla once a week and the olive oil that Giles is accustomed to dribble over my more questionable creations like a kind of upper-class ketchup is probably more expensive than heroin. Which might in any case be more effective.

After the frittata I walked off while Giles was still making coffee. I learnt that from him. You don't say, do you mind if I go work for an hour or so and will you settle Moth for his nap and include Raph in whatever you're doing next? You don't even say, I'm just going to do a bit of work, if that's OK. Even this will be construed as a negotiating position. You just leave the room as if it has not occurred to you that someone will have to tidy up lunch, change Moth's nappy, spend half an hour hanging over the cot patting his back while Raph slides down the banisters yodelling as taught by his godfather Matthias, clean the loo, help Raph with the Lego that Moth will eat if he can and make a casserole before waking Moth, who will otherwise sleep all afternoon and stay awake all night as though he were a denizen of one of those vine-wreathed Mediterranean cultures in which adults appear to want no time at all to themselves. I sidled round the house, abstracted my laptop from the luxury green holiday cottage/building site, where I would be too easy to find, and headed along the shore towards the old village. It's barely a hamlet, really; the remains of twelve stone cottages, none larger than the kitchen in Colsay House. They were abandoned gradually from the late nineteenth century, and only the most recently inhabited one still has most of its roof. It's been a weak summer so far, and I've wondered if I might be able to light a small fire in the hearth, but the village is visible from the big house and the last thing the working mother should do is send smoke-signals revealing her whereabouts, so I make do with fingerless gloves and a coat, which gives me the regrettably accurate feeling that I am always on the point of leaving. The house also has a kitchen table, sheep droppings on the floor and a framed photo of a young man in a Second World War uniform on the wall, but I can usually get internet access from a room with an intact ceiling, which is all I really need.

I opened the introduction, which I usually avoid because it's not very good. I find it hard to justify beginning. I do it unoriginally, with the Wild Boy of Aveyron, who is the *amuse-bouche* of more than one other history of childhood. The Wild Boy was found sleeping rough in the woods around Aveyron, in the French Alps, in 1797. He was about twelve, had a deep scar from ear to ear, and had no clothes or words. He'd been stopping in at local farmhouses for food for several years, but no one knew, or admitted to knowing, where he'd come from and when he'd left. He became the perfect subject for philosophical experiment, a human being raised without society (they ignored the people who must have given birth to him, breastfed him, stopped him eating foxgloves and birdshit when he was too young to know better and, several years later, slit his throat and left him for dead in the woods). Jean-Marc Itard, who made it his life's work to civilize the Wild Boy, wrote:

How could he possibly be expected to have known the existence of God? Let him be shown the heavens, the green fields, the vast expanse of the earth, the works of Nature, he does not see anything in all that if there is nothing to eat; and there you have the sole route by which external objects penetrate into his consciousness.

– Harlan Lane, *The Wild Boy of Aveyron*
(Cambridge, Mass.: Harvard University Press, 1976), p. 39

I stared at it for a bit. God or food, which would you look for on a mountainside?

'Mummy?'

'Jesus Christ, Raph, what are you doing here?'

'Mummy, do you want me to make you a dynamo for your laptop? You could sit on it and bicycle the wheels and that would make the energy for the processor. Then you could get lots of exercise while you were writing.'

'No, I couldn't, because I don't get enough writing time to use up a grape. Supposing I could get a grape. Raph, please go find Daddy. Please let me write. Just while Moth sleeps.'

His hair was felted at the back where he sleeps on it and his top, bought two sizes too big three years ago, stopped short of his belly button.

'It would probably have to be fitted somewhere, it wouldn't be possible to move it around, but I could design it, quite easily. You'd have to go quite fast to power a game or something but for word-processing you could probably generate what you needed while you typed. I could even set it up so you could divert the power to the oven or an electric heater. I could look on the internet and find the materials . . .'

He was looking out of the window as he spoke, across to the untenanted henhouse and the roofless pigpen.

'Raph, please. I'm sure it would be lovely. Just let me look at the introduction.'

'We could put a gym in the blackhouse, couldn't we, so people could actually use their own energy. There could be a treadmill – that'd be quite easy to build, some kind of hamster-wheel like the Romans used to make slaves do to lift cranes.' He began to whirl his hands in circles, like those people who used to walk backwards in front of planes at departure gates. 'You could do it with a bench-press, actually, only the mechanism would be bulky, but that wouldn't matter.'

The juxtaposition of Romantic expectation and Lockean subsistence economics deomonstrated here lies at the heart of this book. The Wild Boy's wildness is shown to exist not, as the early nineteenth-century reader might expect, in his spiritual connection to land- and skyscape, but in its absence. This is not a child 'trailing clouds of glory' but an infant *homo economicus*, a being whose potential as consumer and producer must be liberated by a highly theorized syllabus. And it is *homo economicus* with which the more popular literature on childhood, and especially the new genre of parenting handbooks, is overwhelmingly concerned. Parenthood is no longer merely a biological state; it has become an undertaking in which it is possible to fail, and it is the possibility of failure that opens a space for the institutions that offered to replace failing families and communities.

All that we learn, I thought, all that we learn is that humanity is acquired from our parents, and can be lost, that people can be so badly damaged that they lose the capacity to be fully human. The Wild Boy never acquired language, never learnt to play or to love or even to sleep through the night. Because his parents threw him away. I deleted the first *homo economicus* and tried to think of a synonym.

'Mummy?'

'What?'

'Miss Towers at school said we should say pardon.'

'She was wrong. What is it?'

'When we get this eco-gym set up, yeah? Do you want it to power the TV over there as well?'

20

'There isn't a TV.'

'No, but there could be, yeah? Because if they were powering it themselves, it would kind of counteract the late capitalist cultural imperialism?'

'Raph, stop saying "yeah" all the time.'

The clock on my laptop is slow, but even so I'd been gone over an hour and it was time Moth was waking up. Giles leaves him to sleep, not so much, I hope, because he thinks the nights are my problem as because he is incapable of acting now to change something six hours in the future.

'Come on, let's go wake Moth.'

Dearest Allie,

I had hoped to find a letter from you at Inversaigh as I am told
that it may be some weeks before anyone finds it convenient to
cross the Sound again, but no matter. I hope all is well at home and
that Papa's Muses are behaving themselves? I keep imagining nine
little girls erupting from the studio in a state of undress and
Mama's ladies deciding to catch them and train them to be rational
women and then won't Miss Horton be cross! Do write soon,
darling, won't you? I had a very pleasant letter from Miss Emily,
assuring me of whatever supplies and advice I may need, and
enclosing one from Sir Hugo himself. He asks that I tell him my
impression of the community here on Colsay, attending especially
to those hardships that personal knowledge may allow small funds
to alleviate. Which hardly seems the sentiment of an oppressive
landlord!

My journey was largely uneventful, although you were right
that I should have kept more reading material about me, and I felt
so conspicuous in the Edinburgh hotel on my own that I was quite
unequal to the great dining room and found myself, for my
cowardice, subsisting on buns from a nearby cook-shop, which I
indulged myself by consuming in bed since there were no
witnesses! After a somewhat queasy passage, I arrived here two days
ago, and since then have passed my time in unpacking the big trunk,
walking around the hamlet and along the shore and attempting to
befriend the housekeeper. I suppose I must begin my work

tomorrow, somehow. I have only glimpsed the people and have had rather the impression that they have no desire for a closer encounter – the women had been talking together in the 'street' (a roughly cobbled area between the houses, quite unfit for wheeled traffic, which is of no consequence because there is, I think, no conveyance of any kind here) but somehow they sidled back to their houses at my coming. Perhaps that is just the impression of my fatigue during the first days in a new place.

I am to stay in the Big House (so called, though in fact it might just house the library and Papa's studio at home) and, comfortable though it appears by comparison with the dwellings in the village – can you believe some of the people are still living and eating with their animals? – I wonder if it won't prove a hindrance in the end. Everyone knows, I suppose, that Miss Emily brought me here and pays me, but none the less I wonder if my work wouldn't be easier if I could live among the people I am here to serve; the Big House is set away from the village and its fields, back from the sea, as if to show that its inhabitants have no need of field or net to stock their table. Although I must say that the feather beds and iron stoves of the Big House would be hard to leave, especially for what I have seen of the village dwellings! Do not picture to yourself an ancient castle such as to delight Papa's heart; if there are ghosts here, they must be those newly born of the poor and sick, for I gather that Sir Hugo's father tore down the old abode of Highland maidens and Prince Charlie's young henchmen when he bought the island, replacing it with a neat modern lodge that has no ideas above its station, room enough for either the family or a fishing party but nothing at all to compare to the Cassinghams' Edinburgh house. Don't tell Papa, but in truth I cannot much mourn a flagged floor and arrow-slits while I have a sash window and a nice little fender to toast my feet when the wind scrabbles under the eaves and rain pelts roof-slates brought across the sea for Cassingham comfort (though I would share his distaste for the tiled hall, which looks like a municipal baths and one would expect better of even a new-made aristocrat).

23

I have a small room at the side of the house, where the girls used to sleep when the Cassinghams spent their summers here before Sir Hugo remarried. I asked when the family had last visited the island; apparently there is a son, Hartley, who spent several weeks here in the Spring but seems to have won no favour by doing so – the hotel keeper at Inversaigh says 'the islanders are not accustomed to the ways of modern young people and there were many thought he should have been knowing better than to be causing such trouble for his father's tenants'. I observed that I should think the opportunities for sin on Colsay were few and far between and he replied in Johnsonian style that salvation is independent of one's residence, which is hard to contest! He showed a not unnatural curiosity about my own business here, for surely few enough English ladies show a disposition to visit Colsay, but when he understood that I am a trained nurse and no leisured lady commented only that it was a shame the Cassinghams had not felt able to do more earlier on. I pointed out that it is Sir Hugo and his sister who sent me here, out of pure philanthropy (in as much as philanthropy can ever be found to be pure), but this conversation is my first intimation of the bad feeling in these parts of which we read so much. It seems rather hard that politics must stain poor Miss Emily's charity.

I gathered from the innkeeper's more garrulous daughter that the second Lady Hugo has refused to come here, preferring Nice, and looking out of the window where I see precisely nothing because it is raining hard from cloud so low that the stone walls of the garden are obscured, it is not difficult to understand why. It's strange to think that Aubrey's paintings show the same place, but not even he could invent that light on the sea. I do hope I can do all that he hopes of me here. I wish I knew what Aubrey said when he recommended me to Sir Hugo, and sometimes I cannot help but wonder why he so wanted this post for me – it feels like a test, but whether of my affection for him or of my character or professional capacities I cannot say. In any case it seems that everyone has placed a great deal of faith in me and I admit I am a

24

little shaken by my reception so far. Miss Emily has charged a woman called Mrs Barwick, who comes from Colsay but was trained up as her personal maid and continued so until she married a childhood sweetheart and came back here to live, with the housekeeping and such services as I might require. I gather from her dress that Mrs Barwick is widowed, though for all I know it is merely the custom of the older women here to wear black, but Mrs Barwick's clothes do not appear of local manufacture. Apparently I may need to call on her services as an interpreter as well as cook/housekeeper for I gather that many of the women have very little English and of course will be even more inclined to use their native tongue at the moments of greatest importance!

I went down to the churchyard today (well wrapped indeed, with the mackintosh cape from Miss Emily over all), expecting to see too many little mounds, but when I got back Mrs Barwick, who must have watched my unsteady progress from a window, commented that it is 'not worth the work to make a new digging for every babe born' and that at the last burial there were two caskets in the grave already, not to mention old James McGillies. I did not enquire if Old James McGillies were the original occupant or the digger of this uneasy resting place!

Anyway, my candle is burning low and if I am to begin to earn my wages tomorrow I had best retire now. Do write to me soon, and tell Mama to do likewise – I won't ask Papa to leave his Muses, for who knows what they might do unsupervised (inspire poor Hettie, perhaps, or distract Cook into the production of sonnets instead of soufflés, and then wouldn't Papa be cross...).

Love to all, as ever,

May

2

NOT FOR THERAPEUTIC USE

It is even significant in which manner a small boy plays with his railway: whether his main pleasure is derived from staging crashes (as symbols of parental intercourse); whether he is predominantly concerned with building tunnels and underground lines (expressing interest in the inside of the body); whether his cars and buses have to be loaded heavily (as symbols of the pregnant mother); or whether speed and smooth performance are his main concern (as symbols of phallic efficiency) ... deductions of this kind are not for therapeutic use; or, to express it more forcefully even, they are useless therapeutically. To make them the basis of symbolic interpretation would equal ignoring the ego defences which are built up against the unconscious content ...

– Anna Freud, *Normality and Pathology in Childhood*, p. 26

Night Waking: 01:17

I remember the Pilates I used to do, back when the local population included Pilates teachers and many other middle-class mothers who had looked in the mirror once too often but couldn't quite summon up the self-loathing to go to the gym. Try to feel your vertebrae easing along the string of the spinal cord, the teacher used to say. (This is not, in fact, a comforting image, since surely we rely on the vertebrae to protect the spinal cord? Stiff shoulders seem a small price to pay for cognition and motor skills.) I have been bending over the cot, my index finger locked in Moth's sticky grasp, for thirty-six minutes, during which time I have made four escape attempts, sung 'Hush, Little Baby' end to end sixteen times and convinced myself that the pins and needles in my hands promise an early, if slow, release by mercy of a neurological degenerative disease. How many years of my life would I give for eight hours of uninterrupted sleep?

It depends on how long my life will be. Of a hundred years, I would give ten. I think about how much reading I might be able to do between being ninety and a hundred. I would be at liberty to live in what my mother used to call All This Mess and upon KitKats and salt and vinegar Hula Hoops. I've always fancied sheltered accommodation. I used to cycle past some flats when I took the children swimming or went to Pilates, and I'd peer in and see old ladies with flowery wing armchairs and kitchenettes reminiscent of the Barbie playhouse I never had, reading or watching television in the middle of the morning. When they were in those kitchens I bet they were baking cakes for themselves, and sometimes some of them gathered in a sitting room with panelling and occasional tables like a costume-drama eighteenth century, where there were flower arrangements and tins of chocolate biscuits and a piano. No, I'm not giving up a decade of sugar-fuelled self-indulgence, even for sleep. I try to move my finger and Moth snorts and opens one eye. OK, five years of a hundred. As long as the sleep is in solitude and somewhere soundproof and I know that Giles is on call for the children.

Moving to a global scale, what would I pawn for sleep? Would I, given the choice, have peace for Palestine or twelve hours in bed? Clean water for the children of Africa or a week off motherhood? The advent of carbon-neutral industrial processes or a month's unbroken nights? It's a good thing Satan doesn't come and chat to the mothers of sleepless toddlers in the middle of the night.

Moth's grasp loosens. Millimetre by casual millimetre, I pull my finger back and, holding my hand above his so as not to change the shape of the shadow on the cot or the current of his exhaled breath, I begin to straighten my back. He turns over.

'Mummy stay!'

I bend down again, offer the other hand so I can move the numbed shoulder.

'No. Unner hand.'

How many years would I give now? Right this racked moment? If I don't get to go back to bed and to sleep this instant I am going to walk out of the house and over the stones to the sea and I will keep going until the island is merely a blot on the shining waves and the cold water rises in my lungs.

I don't.

'You could leave him to it.' Giles, who must have asked Jake to bring him a copy of the *Guardian* from the end-point of the English newspaper network on the mainland, looked up over Sports. I caught sight of the front page, where a mother in a headscarf cradled a limp child.

'For goodness' sake don't let Raph see the news. We've been here. Moth can scream for longer than I can listen to it. He has an ultimate weapon and I don't. We've already established that he thinks it's quite funny if I sob and bang my head on the wall.'

Giles put his coffee down on an older but unopened letter from the Child Tax Credit people. 'I wish you wouldn't. It's not exactly setting a good example, is it?'

'For fuck's sake, Giles. You try hanging over the cot for three hours, staring into the dark and praying for death.'

'Fuck *sake*,' said Moth, banging his bowl on the table.

'Anna!' Giles hates it when the children swear.

'What? You're worried he's going to embarrass you in front of the neighbours? Shock the seagulls with profane language? Why don't you piss off to your homosocial bonding session in

28

the eco-conversion while I clear up breakfast and try to plant your bloody trees again.'

'Piss off,' said Moth to his spoon. 'Bloody trees.'

Giles stood up, not too distraught to remember to take the *Guardian* with him. 'It upsets me when you talk like that.'

I poured tea. 'Yeah, well. It upsets me when I'm awake all night and you pretend to sleep through it and then my day is consumed by housework and childcare and I'm not getting any time to write while you prance about counting birds and having tea with Jake.'

He began to retreat. 'Anna, I'm not counting birds. I'm trying to work out why the puffin population has dropped by twenty-five per cent in the last four years—'

'So you have counted them.'

'And as for housework, all I can say is, if your day is really consumed by housework then you're not doing a very efficient job.'

'I'm a historian, remember? I'm the Rackind Fellow at St Mary Hall? If you wanted housework you should have married one of those Clarissas your mother kept scattering at your feet. And you'd have to keep her in paddocks and rare-breed Labradors and probably parlourmaids as well.'

He went.

'Labbadores,' said Moth. 'Labbadores fierce?'

'Yes. Savage.' I drank some of the tea, which was cold. 'Come on, let's find your brother.'

Raph had gone back to his disaster games. He was lying on the floor of the playroom, a parlour with wedding-cake plasterwork on the ceiling, which had been, until Giles inherited Colsay, the dining room in which his parents replicated the napery, crested silver and gravy of their life in Sussex. It was not Giles's mother but his Italian girlfriend, the one for whose abandonment I consoled him, who taught him about food. Her risotti were without the charnel-house notes of my rare attempts at home-made stock, English tomatoes bloomed with flavour under her slim fingers, and after a while she was beamed back to the land of wild boar salami with fennel seeds and porcini. Probably. Giles is too chivalrous, to them as well as to me, to discuss his ex-girlfriends. Anyway, when Julia sees her dining room carpeted with acrylic rugs featuring urban plans with roundabouts and emergency services, adorned with Raph's diagrams of nuclear-powered popcorn makers and hydro-electric helicopters and furnished principally with Duplo, she will like me even less than she does.

'What are you making, Raph?'

'Trains!' said Moth, wriggling on my hip. 'Down.'

I tucked him more firmly against me. I can see that the last thing a person re-enacting apocalypse needs is a toddler making things worse. Raphael must have been up for hours. He'd used all our wooden train track in a system which left no extra pieces and no loose ends, without cheating by using the plastic links that convert female to male connections. This is a feat which has evaded several teams of Oxford academics towards the end of the third bottle of wine.

'Nothing.'

There was a particular arrangement of parallel tracks near a station, where a small train waited. A bigger one with InterCity livery was poised under the window.

'How do you know about the Paddington crash?'

'Crash!' said Moth. 'Big crash.'

'I'm not doing any harm. Please will you go away.'

'I know you're not doing any harm. I'm just surprised you know about it. Were you even born then?'

'Mummy, please take Moth away. He's going to knock it all over.'

I wondered about making a third assault on the trees, but it wasn't me who spent £500 and then left them in sacks. I looked at the landslide of paper threatening to engulf the half of the kitchen table that is, if not precisely clear, at least level enough

to form a resting place for abandoned cups of lapsang souchong, but I knew that at best I'd make the landslide into heaps
of rubble. Action this day, later, too late, compost, and file.
Then a dark river of new paper fills the valleys and we're back
where we started, except that this time I know there is archaeological evidence of human intelligence somewhere under
there. If I didn't take action regarding laundry I would not only
be reduced to knickers requiring a safety pin, but the stuff
washed two days earlier and still in the machine would develop
a mildew which does not come out in repeat washes, or at least
not in low-temperature repeat washes with environmentally
friendly detergent. I fantasize, sometimes, about the boil washes
and bleach of my childhood, the pink fabric softener that smelt
of hyacinths and blended with the Bisto fumes of my mother's
cooking as the clothes stayed damp on the airer that was always
in the way. She cannot understand why I, who could afford a
tumble dryer, choose not to have one. And nor, sometimes, can
I. I fantasize, alternately, about Joachim, whom I did not marry
and who is now a doctor in Copenhagen and who would give
me an apartment with beech floors and a steel kitchen and a
Baltic view relieved by the swoops and assertions of the Malmo
bridge which encourages thousands of people to surmount the
estranging sea in the name of civilization on a daily basis. I am,
I find, increasingly in favour of bridges.

'Mummy? Moth splash a forks! Moth helpful!'

'Splash' usually means 'throw into the toilet'. The cutlery
drawer was open. I went to investigate, relieved, at least, of the
decision about which bit of my contracted world I should
address first.

Giles came back late, his trees losing hope as they lay among
the budding daffodils. Moth had been asleep some time and I
had done about as much of the washing up as seemed necessary to tread the line between present martyrdom and the
promise of life-long domestic servitude.

'Good day at the office?' I flourished a tea-towel I had no intention of using.

He sat down. There was rain on his shoulders and his hair was slicked off his face in a way that gave a regrettable resemblance to Prince Charles in the early 1980s.

'I don't know. How's the home front?'

'Oh, a hotbed of intellectual productivity, obviously. Jesus, Giles, when precisely do you imagine I might write this book?'

He shrugged. 'You'll be fine. It's almost done. Can't you ever take a holiday?'

'If I were going to take a holiday, believe me, I wouldn't spend it doing wall-to-wall childcare in a house without central heating or a dishwasher, hundreds of miles from my friends.'

He put his head in his hands, which is all very well for people who have had the entire day to themselves.

'You agreed to come. Don't make it sound as if I kidnapped you and took you into slavery. You said it would be good for the children. You said you needed a break from the Fellows.'

'Yes, well. I was wrong. There's no supper. I gave the children beans and yoghurt.'

He looked up as if a strange smell had crossed the kitchen. 'What, together?'

'Yeah, it's the latest in molecular gastronomy. It was in the paper. Baked bean sorbet and strawberry yoghurt foam. What do you think?'

I left him in the kitchen. The sun was setting and the grass glowed in the slanting light, but Giles stayed with his back to the window.

'Raphael?'

He was in the playroom. The American city playmat that Giles brought back from a conference when Raph was young enough to be expected to play with these things, to play at parking in car parks and refuelling at petrol stations and stopping at red lights, was in the middle of the floor, and he'd built two

Lego towers nearly as tall as himself. I didn't even know we had that much Lego. The planes were on the windowsill.

'Raph.' I stroked his hair. 'Come on. It's past ten o'clock. You should go to bed.'

His glance flickered towards me. 'Not yet.'

I wondered when his hair had last been washed. Bruised knees poked through the holes in his tracksuit bottoms.

'Are you waiting for something? Is there some trigger for the – the impact?'

He positioned a small metal car near the base of one of the towers.

'Not yet, Mummy.'

'Can I watch?'

He froze.

'OK. I'm going to come back in five minutes and then I want you to go to bed, OK? When the sun goes down.'

I went back to the kitchen. Giles hadn't moved, so I went outside and picked my way down to the sea, where I sat on a rock with my back to the house and watched as the sun, smooth as a coffin gliding through the curtains in a crematorium, slid behind the sea. The swans came honking out of the sky, as if they were late for a sunset curfew, and rearranged themselves on the water, fussy as young children sitting down on a train, refolding their wings, shaking out their tails, changing places. The last rays picked out the pile of stones marking the alleged home of the anchorite on a ledge at the top of the cliff. She had decades of peace and quiet, the anchorite, a possibly mythical thirteenth-century hermit who roosted up there in holy resistance to wind and rain, which repaid her by coming at her call when raiders were seen in the Sound. The ability to invoke storms and drown people is an odd gift of God. She was also famed for living on water from the spring and an occasional crust, which was considered as further evidence of divine favour, though one might think a diet of mead and honeycake more convincing evidence of His special affections. I imagine her sitting quite still, watching the play of wind on the water and the passage of the sun across the sky, noting the comings and goings of birds and boats and the shapes of the clouds while her hair flutters around her face and her homespun robes pull against her body. She knew what she was doing when she answered her call to stay up there.

Light leached out of the cliff. The swans, calm now, drifted into their bay, and I went back to find Raph, to compensate by night for the constant attention exacted by Moth by day. He had already gone to bed, and when I followed him upstairs he was curled on the duvet under his window, reading an engineering textbook. I sat on his bed.

'Hello. I've just come to say good night.'

He didn't look up.

'Mummy, do you know how they tense the caissons on swing bridges?'

'No. Did you have a good day today?'

'I'm going to build us a bridge to Colla, but it can't be a high bridge and there's not much shipping here, so it won't be a swing bridge. Cable bridges need cables at the bottom as well so they don't swing, but I think we'd like one that swings.'

I stroked his shoulder. He wasn't wearing pyjamas.

'I think the swinging sounds fun, but I suppose it might swing a long way. We wouldn't want to get tipped off. Imagine, with all the shopping.'

I used to hate pushing the pram along the riverbank in Oxford. What if I misjudged the slope of the path, failed to engage the brake when we fed the ducks? What if a cyclist came round the corner too fast? Jump in, of course, but I don't think I could support the weight of our old-fashioned jumble-sale pram for very long, certainly not in a fast-flowing river with one hand while undoing the harness with the other. Send Raph for help, at least so he doesn't have to watch.

Raph's hands began to circle. 'I'd put a steel net to catch us. Like for those trapeze people. With special girders and pockets for food in case we had to wait a long time, but it would have lights and an emergency signal that went off if anything heavy fell in it. Not to be set off by birds.'

The sky stays light for so very long. Bedtime retreats like a parent's promise. It was still quite bright enough to plant trees.

'And you could have ladders up the girders and a boat at the bottom so we could still get ourselves home, but the boat will be self-righting in case it's stormy and you can seal up the cabin like a lifeboat so Moth would be safe even if it tipped over.'

'Raph, where are your pyjamas?'

'And some of those strobe lights, because none of us have epilepsy.'

'Raphael? Pyjamas?'

He made eye contact, briefly, but it was as if there was nobody there.

'I haven't got any pyjamas. I bet there are less carbon-heavy ways of designing lifeboats, especially the inflatable ones.'

I kissed his cheek.

'Raph, love, go to sleep. It's late. I'll leave the light so you can read a bit but one of us will be up in a few minutes to turn it off, OK? Get some rest.'

Giles wasn't at the kitchen table any more. I wondered about making him some supper, but a scan of the fridge suggested that any such effort was more likely to provoke anger than penitence. I thought about finishing the washing up but couldn't see why I should. I could have got my laptop out, sat at the kitchen table wondering how I had ever managed to weave paragraphs around quotations from the eighteenth century. I found some nasty chocolate in a variety box Giles had confiscated from Raphael on grounds of health and ideology, and stood at the window eating it.

'Anna?' Giles was in the playroom.

I shoved the chocolate into one of the paper avalanches.

'What?'

'Look. Raph's at it again.'

I went through. Giles was cross-legged on the floor, his head level with the Cantor Fitzgerald floors at the top of the second tower.

'I know. It was the Paddington rail crash earlier. I didn't even know he knew about it.'

Giles ran his finger down the lower floors, the restaurants and retail opportunities.

'Can't you stop him? Distract him somehow? Give him something else to do?'

Darkness had nearly fallen, but I could still see the sea rolling and glinting out there.

'He doesn't want to do anything else. I try. He just torments Moth. Anyway, why don't you distract him?'

'I'm working, Anna. It's a short season. I can't just do bits in the middle of the night or nip off for an hour, we need a proper statistical picture.'

'OK, but then don't criticize how I look after the children.'

He sighed and began to trace the one-way system with his finger. There was puffin shit on his shoes. He leant over and picked up the plane on the windowsill.

'Look. Here we go. Wheeee. And here comes the other one. Wheeee. Crash.'

I knelt down and took a fire engine in each hand.

'Nee-nah, nee-nah. Here they come.'

'No,' said Giles. He was still holding the planes, noses touching the Lego, leaving the real catastrophe for Raph to complete in the morning. 'Too fast. It took them a while to believe it was really happening.'

Colsay House,
Colsay

1st Oct., 1878

Dear Aubrey,

Only a line to tell you of my arrival. This place is so beautiful
that I know that whatever happens I will be glad I came. It is misty
and wet today and I watched the waves coming out of the fog and
breaking on the stones from which you brought Papa's rockery. I
have never seen quartzes so round and smooth before and only
wonder that you were able to resist sending half the beach! We see
winter coming closer day by day now and sometimes the dark days
seem to loom over me like the first intimation of a sickness, and as
with a sickness sometimes I doubt my own strength for the
struggle ahead. But after all, there is no fighting with the seasons;
my part is at worst to endure and I am certain of my capacity there.
For now, in any case, the cliffs are still great tenements of
shrieking birds and the beasts are passing their days in the fields –
well, on the hillside – for another week yet, though by night they
make bedfellows for the poor people! Mrs Barwick tells me that
there used to be a Holy Woman living up there on the cliffs, and I
thought such a figure would make a fine subject for you, but
whether she speaks of an early Celt, perhaps a female counterpart
to Cuthbert and Aidan, or some more recent eccentric, Mrs
Barwick cannot tell.

I have not made much progress with the islanders yet, but of
course it will take time to win their trust and learn their ways, and I
hope by the year's close to be able to send the news you are hoping
for and give you the satisfaction of having been the means of saving

37

not just the lives of individual innocents but the future of the community here. Think of me, won't you, and write if inspiration should spare you a few moments? I do not forget what was said that last afternoon at your house, with the sun coming down through the leaves. I hope I can be worthy of your trust.

Fond regards,

May

3

FEARING TO HANDLE A KNIFE

She retained a great affection for the child, at the same time even identifying the instrument that she would use to destroy it, fearing to handle a knife even at mealtimes.

– Mark Jackson, ed., *Infanticide: Historical Perspectives on Child Murder* (London: Ashgate, 2002), p. 177

On days when I was this tired on maternity leave, we used to go out. The advantages of out are that Mummy is unlikely to fall asleep on the job, and the presence of witnesses means that Mummy is not afraid that she might succumb to the urge to use one of the black-handled Sabatier knives in the beech block on the kitchen counter or a blunt object such as the playdough-stained rolling pin to bring about a few minutes' peace. There was always the chance of meeting another adult with whom I might be able to exchange complete sentences while the baby fretted in the pram. I used to feel, outside on those days, as if I'd come out of my burrow at the wrong time of day like a rabbit with myxomatosis, blinking in the glare of the intelligence of people who slept at night and did not think about infant bowel movements by day.

'I'm taking the children to the beach this morning,' I said.

Giles looked over the *Guardian*. Either the news had come

round again or he was re-reading, but in either case I didn't like the look of it.

'But we're on the beach.'

'We never go. I mean, do you take them? Paddling, exploring rock pools? Seal watching, for God's sake. Remember how much we paid to go seal watching in Vancouver Island?'

'Seal washing?' asked Moth.

Raph rejected a blackened crust. 'Watching, not washing. Even Daddy doesn't wash birds. Though sometimes people have to after an oil spill. Did you know they're developing bacteria that will eat spilt oil? Only no one knows what the side-effects will be yet.'

'That's good,' I said.

Raph pushed his chair back and stepped in the porridge. 'Mummy, I don't want to go to the beach.'

'Come on. You can enact disasters later. Only for the morning. I just want to get Moth really tired so I can do some work.'

He looked at a point above my head. 'Take Moth, then. I don't have to be tired so you can work.'

The tea I was pouring missed the mug, setting a bank statement afloat on the table. 'I thought you'd like it. We can look for crabs in the rock pools. I bet Daddy knows of lots of things we might find.'

I fear that this tone, this voice in which 'I would pay someone a five-figure sum to take you away for a week' comes out as 'Come and spend the morning on the beach with me,' will ring through everything I say for the rest of my life. I will say, 'I thought we could go have a lovely time at the tapas bar tonight' when I mean 'This marriage died years ago and I want a divorce.' 'Would you like a cup of tea?' will mean 'For some years I have spent every waking moment thinking of ways to die.'

Raph walked out, and a moment later I heard the space hopper begin its Morse code in the cobbled yard. SOS.

'Have you looked at the weather?' asked Giles.

I drank some tea. Toast was too much effort, and eating only means having to cook again.

'It's not been on the back page for years.'

I scooped some porridge into Moth's mouth when he wasn't looking.

'I mean the actual weather.'

The window was sequinned with rain.

'The sky's only white. It's not torrential. I thought you approved of outside.'

The *Guardian* flapped. 'No odds to me. I'm afraid I'll be at the rocks all day.'

When we got to the beach, after passing half the morning in negotiation about putting on shoes, Moth walked into the sea and then had a tantrum because it was wet, and Raph stood with his back to the waves talking about potential uses of hydroelectricity on oil rigs. I sat on a rough rock, my arms wrapped round Moth as he drummed his heels on my shins and tried to bite my arms, and remembered the staircase in the Bodleian Library, the ecclesiastical smell of dusty stone and furniture polish, the way the leading on the windows turns the quadrangle below into a watery mosaic, the thickening silence as you ascend towards the muffled door and the airless warmth, the opposite of fresh air, that waits to take readers into its chloroform embrace at the top. I decided that if I made Moth walk the whole five hundred metres back to the house he might take less than forty-five minutes to go to sleep after lunch and, if I didn't rush him at all, stopped to inspect every pebble and touch each flowering grass, it might almost be time to start putting together an early lunch when we arrived. I left Raph in situ, orating to the grass, which bent before him in the wind like the audience of a state-organized rally.

The wind was rising and the power went off again before I finished cooking the children's supper. Neither child likes eggs so the cooking was only symbolic in the first place. I poked at the pan, hoping residual heat would finish off the salmonella. Moth took one look and threw his plate on the floor.

'Mummy? Aren't you going to pick it up?'

Raphael had scraped off the egg as if he knew it was contaminated but was nibbling along the edge of the bread, my home-made soda bread. I could save myself a lot of time by buying raw ingredients, throwing them away and getting on with my book.

'In a minute.'

I put my head down on the table and took a deep breath. It's what the parenting handbooks, the modern ones, tell you to do. Breathing. If things are bad enough to require a more extreme response you are advised to leave the room and count to ten. A small, eggy finger was inserted into my ear. I sat up and administered plain yoghurt with some of Julia's plum jam, a combination that Giles finds morally preferable to the purchase of fruit-flavoured yoghurt.

Raph finished his yoghurt, got down from the table and took the dustpan and brush out of the cupboard. I watched, holding Moth's bowl, as Raphael swept up the egg, put it and the bread in the compost bin and Moth's plate in the sink. Then he came back and leant on my shoulder. I put my arm round him and kissed his yoghurt-smeared cheek. I thought I might ask Giles to clean the egg out of the brush, later.

The Wild Boy, here, is interested in use and not in amenity, and as such he is, oddly, the prototype of the hero of much didactic children's literature, particularly for boys, of this period. The childish concerns approved not merely by Thomas Day and Maria Edgeworth but, more surprisingly, by Mary Wollstonecraft and, later, Charles and Mary Lamb, are those of the nascent petite bourgeoisie. Good children are economically active; moral consciousness is matched by and sometimes subsumed into an understanding of the marketplace. Advice to parents often, but not always, mimics this preoccupation, as if what readers buy in the form of the handbook is shares in the literal and metaphorical future company of their children.

I glanced up, as if something had changed in the room. I had all the settings on low power to conserve the battery, and the light coming from the screen showed a few of the tea-stained papers on the table and the long shadow cast by my mug in the institutionally blue glow. No child's cry came rushing down the dark stairs.

And so the literary marketplace is implicated in both the literal marketplace and the fictional marketplaces within these texts. The handbook, more than most genres even in this period, is acutely aware of its commodity status in a way that, I hope to show, oddly mirrors that of the ostensibly unsocialized Wild Boy. Perhaps for the first time, childhood was for sale.

Too many adverbs. I deleted 'acutely' and 'oddly', then decided I'd rather lose 'ostensibly' and keep 'oddly'. Reading it through, I realized I had no citations and therefore no footnotes in the first three pages, which is in violation of academic codes of obscurity and arse-covering, so I opened a file of notes and began to skim through for quotes I could insert without changing the course of the argument.

The sound came again, a noise that could easily have been the wind finding a new crack to moan through or a seagull roused by whatever fears disturb seagull sleep. It occurred to me for the first time that while we imagine we have nothing here to fear but each other, in fact anyone with control of a small boat could land at any time and our only defence would be to locate an adequately charged mobile phone, stand on Raph's bed where the reception is usually good enough for the exchange of information and hope the wind was in the right direction and that there was somewhere to land a helicopter. As the locals found when the Vikings came this way, there's nowhere to run on an island. I began to wonder if we should assign a helipad before the visitors came, whether it is possible to call the emergency services using Skype, and then realized that I'd been assuming Giles was bonding with puffins until he could be quite sure I'd got the children to bed and washed up, but presumably puffins go to bed when it gets dark, and it was hard to imagine what even an ornithologist might wish to do with a cliff full of puffins asleep in their burrows. I heard the sound again. I saved my work and backed up. I turned the laptop towards the doorway, though the light barely illuminated the mulch under Moth's chair. The noise, like breathing, was clearer now, and I took comfort from the conviction that pirates do not storm islands and then hide in the parlour sobbing.

The sitting room was dark. Giles was sitting in a low early Victorian armchair, crying. I had thought I had the monopoly on emotional outbursts round here.

'Giles. What on earth are you doing?'

'Sitting in the dark, what does it look like?'

I went over and stood in front of him as if he was the teacher and I'd been caught. You'd expect that when men like Giles feel that things have gone so far as to justify tears they would do it properly, with runny noses and perhaps primal howling, but his grief seemed adequately absorbed by the linen handkerchief in his hand. I reached out towards him and then folded my arms.

'Has something gone wrong?'

He stood up, his shoulders cocked against the starlight. 'For fuck's sake. No, everything's lovely. Pa's been dead a year, that's all. And don't pretend you miss him. I'm going to bed.'

He stamped up the stairs.

'He hated me,' I shouted up. 'He tried to stop you marrying me. I'm not going to pretend I miss him.'

I went back into the kitchen and banged the door, which was built to last in the nineteenth century and is good for that kind of thing. Like counting to ten, banging doors doesn't change much unless the audience is already in the mood. Giles is right, I don't miss Hugo, who would have been prosecuted for inciting racial hatred had he aired some of his opinions in venues less exclusive than the drawing-rooms of West Sussex, who told me at our wedding reception how lucky I was that Giles's tastes were so catholic (as to encompass oiks as well as foreigners, I presume). He put Giles under some pressure to protect the Cassingham estate with a prenuptial agreement, the estate which in fact consists of a structurally compromised Tudor house that no one but a banker could afford to maintain and a collection of enormous antique furniture which is venerated with the kind of respect afforded to mummified ancestors in some parts of the world. Giles's first memory is of Hugo beating him with a belt for racing his toy cars across the mahogany dining table. I found some more of Raph's variety box, and ate it fast enough that the sugar surge carried me up the stairs for the last word, or at least another word. I heard Raph's voice and looked into his room. Giles was sitting on the bed with his arm round Raph's shoulders. They didn't see me, but sat talking about the best kind of solid fuel for the stove in the cottage considering the carbon costs of bringing pellets of recycled paper to Colsay. I went to bed.

Night Waking: 03:07

I am lifting Moth before I am awake enough to see. I cradle him against my shoulder, my ears ringing with his screams. He is still rigid, convulsing as if we are being tortured to death before his eyes.

'Moth, love. Mummy's here. It's all right, Mummy's here, Mummy's got you. Hush, love.'

I sway from side to side, rubbing his back, and begin to pace.

*

Giles reappeared mid-morning. Raphael, having dismantled the railway system with a series of explosions, had brought all the urban planning mats together and was building a town whose exquisite design boded ill for its imaginary inhabitants. I was sitting on the floor reading to Moth, hoping that my proximity might in Ralph's mind outweigh the disadvantages of Moth's premature assaults on civilization.

'Hi,' said Giles.

Moth pulled my hair, which I hadn't brushed. 'More reading! Mummy more reading!'

'One hot day Lucy and Tom and their mummy and daddy decided to go to the suicide. I mean, seaside.'

Giles squatted down. 'Are you OK?'

I glanced at Raphael, who was working on the lift-shaft of a multi-storey car park in Lego. 'Not particularly. You?'

He shrugged, the shrug of an Old Etonian and a gentleman undergoing the dark night of the soul.

'More *reading*!'

'Lucy is helping to pack up the picnic. There are sandwiches and biscuits and hard-boiled eggs and apples and a bottle of orange juice. There is also a lovely chocolate cake. Giles, Jake was looking for you. Something about the roof. Tom, reinforcing gender stereotypes, has gone to get the buckets and spades from the sandpit.'

'I'm sorry I didn't get up in the night.'

'You never do.'

He looked away. 'Don't be like that. Shall we talk later?'

I shrugged, the shrug of a woman who would say a great deal more if the children weren't listening.

'If you're not too busy with the puffins. I expect I'll be in. They go to the seaside in the train. Lucy wears her armbands so as to be all ready to swim when they arrive.'

'Moth swimming today?'

Giles and I looked out of the window as if there were ever any possibility of toddlers swimming in the North Atlantic in June.

'Not today. Too cold.'

I used to take him every week in Oxford, to a mother-and-baby class where the mothers stood with cold water lapping around post-natal stomachs, eyeing each other's stretch marks and chanting 'The Wheels on the Bus' while the babies stared at the lights and turned blue. 'Giles, if you could look after them for a minute I could make some more bread.'

He sighed. 'I thought you wanted me to go talk to Jake.'

There was a streak of something green above his left ear.

'Jake wants you to talk to Jake. I don't care. I don't particularly want to make bread. I don't even want to write my book any more, I just want to sleep. But if I don't, you'll have to go to Spar and buy Hovis in a plastic bag, which is fine by me.'

Raphael had gone very still, as if listening to something the rest of us couldn't hear.

'I don't like it when you talk to me like that.'

I hugged Moth tighter to me.

'And do you like it when there isn't any bread?'

Moth squirmed round and pressed his face into my shoulder.

'Fine. I'll mind the kids.'

I tried to put Moth down.

'Up! Come up! Moth coming too!'

He scrabbled at my knees. I picked him up and we went into the kitchen, where he clung to my jumper as I found flour, oatmeal, bicarb and yoghurt. I don't need to measure any more, so Moth could sit on my hip, silent, as I poured and mixed while Raphael and Giles sat silent in the panelled playroom. I wondered how Raph could bear to wait for the bombs to fall.

After lunch I took Moth upstairs and changed his nappy. We went into his bedroom and closed the curtains.

'Ready for you to have a little sleep, OK? Ready for you to

curl up in your cot with Duck and Bear and Baby and go fast asleep.'

'No,' said Moth.

I laid him down on his front and begin to sing 'Hush, Little Baby' and pat his back. He looked up.

'Come up! Cuddle Moth!'

'Not now. Time to sleep now.'

He pushed my hand away and struggled to sit up.

'More reading!'

I laid him down again. My head was aching.

'Not now. Reading when you wake up. Sleeping now. Hush, little baby—'

'Mummy more reading!'

I pushed him back down. In a few minutes I would be able to tidy up the kitchen, have a large drink of water and then either do some work or go sit on a rock and watch the sea until I felt better. Or try to play with Raphael.

'More reading! Now more reading!'

'Papa's gonna buy you a mocking-bird. If that mocking-bird don't sing—'

'No mocking-bird. Reading! Moth come up!'

I put one hand on his bottom and the other between his shoulders. He squirmed and I pressed down. I could feel his ribs flexing. I would listen to the news while tidying, I thought, and perhaps there would be ice to put in my water. I could try to check e-mail and see if any of my friends had remembered that I am here, maybe even take my phone up the hill to where I can sometimes get enough reception for text messages.

'Papa's gonna buy you a diamond ring. If that diamond ring turns brass, Papa's gonna buy you a looking glass.'

'More reading! Don't push!'

I stood up and slammed my hand into the mattress next to his head. He screamed. I shook his cot.

'Moth, for fuck's sake go to sleep right now. If you don't go

48

to sleep this minute, I'm going to kill myself. I'm going to take a knife and kill myself. Is that what you want? Mummy will be dead and then you'll be happy.'

My hands on the cot rail are shaking. I must not attack him. Must not touch him or I will put my hands round his neck and kill him. I cannot leave because I would never come back and I cannot stay because I am about to pick him up and ram his head into the wall until he stops making that intolerable noise.

'Anna, what the hell are you doing?'

Giles grabbed my shoulder. I stopped myself before my fist connected with his arm.

'I want three fucking minutes to myself. I want to pee. I want to have a drink of water. I want to brush my hair. I used to give lectures and write my book.'

Giles pulled me out of the room. Moth was shrieking louder and higher than usual, Mummy, Mummy.

'Go away, OK? Just go away and get control of yourself. And don't let Raphael see you like that.'

But Raphael was standing on the top step, looking at the floorboards as if he were reading them.

'I need to go to Moth.'

Giles stood in the doorway.

'You might need him but he certainly doesn't need you. Just go *away*, Anna.'

Raphael stood aside, looking at the wall as his mother stumbled down the stairs.

I went down to the shore. The sea was grey and opaque as milk, and drizzle greased the pebbles. The wind pushed at me as if checking I was still alive. I sat down and leant against a rock. I may have slept. After a while Giles was squatting next to me.

'Anna, did you hit Moth?'

'Where are the kids?'

'Did you hit him?'

'No,' I said. 'I didn't. Where are the kids?'

He sat down and stared out to sea.

'Moth is asleep and Raph's reading about bridges. I told him you are very tired and that when people are very tired they get upset, but he's not happy. You should go talk to him.'

I shifted away from him. 'Not now. I'm too tired. I need a break, Giles. I can't be with them all the time, I'm losing my mind.'

He sighed. 'Of course you're not losing your mind. Do you want me to play with Moth when he wakes up? So you can do something with Raph?'

'What about the puffins?'

He stood up. 'I can take an hour or so. I'm only charting their decline. It's probably already too late for the puffins. If I'm not going back to work, we'll get those trees in, shall we, before it's too late for them too? I'll get Raph to come and help.'

'No,' I said. 'I want to sleep.'

'Spend a bit of time with Raph first, OK?'

I don't know much about trees, but it seemed at least as probable that we were interring these as planting them. Burlap sacks seem unlikely to sustain trees for two weeks.

Raphael walked round the bare sticks. 'Are they still alive?'

Giles picked up the spade.

'Of course they are. They'll grow. We're a bit late planting, but next summer we might even get a fruit or two.'

He positioned the spade and pushed it down with his foot. It slid deep into the ground and he levered up grass and mud and half a frantic worm.

'Daddy, is that worm all right?'

I went over to Raph and put my arm around him. I could feel his shoulder blades like folded wings.

'Raph, are you cold? Shall I get you a jumper?'

He leant on me. 'No. But thank you, Mummy.'

I kissed his head and he looked up. He has the face of the young Venetian prince in one of those seventeenth-century portraits in the Ca' d'Oro.

'I'm sorry I shouted, Raph. I'm just very tired.'

He watched Giles turning earth. 'I could make Moth be quiet.'

'No. Toddlers do wake up, it's what they're like. You were, and you sleep at night now, don't you?'

'Sometimes. Can I try with the spade?'

We'd planted one tree by the time Moth needed to wake, or at least by the time we needed to wake him.

'I'll go,' said Giles. 'Raph, do you think you and Mummy can plant another one? And I'll bring Moth out to watch? I'll start the spade for you.'

'Giles, not there,' I said. 'It's too close to the wall.'

Giles rested his hand on my shoulder. 'It's fine. This is a dwarf apple, the roots don't go far at all.'

I watched him cross the grass. Giles is tall and slim-hipped, and after Raphael started to sleep through the night and before Moth was born we used to go to a tango class, after which we hustled the babysitter out and pulled each other's clothes off. I used to try not to wear tights, so hard to remove alluringly, on a Thursday. I still like the way he moves, I decided, but I would like it better on someone else. Someone who listens when I say I'm losing my mind.

'Mummy.' Raphael had turned over several inches of earth. 'I can't get the spade any deeper.'

I took it, pushed down and stood on it as if it were the pogo stick of my childhood. It slid down a little and I bounced. Raph laughed.

'There.' I stepped off and we pulled together on the handle. A clod of black earth, rich as chocolate cake, came up.

'Mummy—'

A small bone, rabbit or maybe cat – there are no rabbits on Colsay – was embedded in the loam.

51

'It's just a bone, Raph. Some animal that died long ago.'

'But Mummy.' He stepped forward and crouched down. 'Mummy, there are more. Look. And some cloth.'

I bent over. People do not bury animals in shrouds. Animals do not have hands.

'It looks like a rabbit. Do you want to run and get Daddy? He knows all about animal bones.'

'But animals don't wear cloth.'

He reached towards it. I stopped his hand.

'Best not to touch, love. Would you go get Daddy?'

He stood up. 'It's not a rabbit, Mummy. There aren't any, remember? Daddy said. And no mice.'

'It might be a badger. Or maybe someone had a cat here once. Daddy will know. Just go get him, OK?'

He looked back at me as he crossed the lawn. I waited until the back door closed and then dusted the earth away from the cloth with my fingers. It was knitted wool, stained brown. I scraped at the soil above Raphael's cut and there, where I expected it, was the eggshell arc of a very small human skull.

Colsay House,
Colsay

12th October

Dearest Allie,

Thank you so much for your last, which reached me yesterday
by a circuitous route that I don't pretend to understand! You can't
know how much it meant to me, especially the enclosure. I pictured
you going down to the postbox in your new hat (only I suppose
even so far south as Manchester it may be allowed to rain in
October enough that you would not chance the new hat) and
maybe meeting Pippa on the way back and being summoned in for
tea and helping the children set fire to the toast over the fire. I
cannot hope you will receive this as quickly as yours found its way
here (spirited by the Others, for all I know, for it turns out that
the Others, otherwise Trows or Grey People, still thrive on
Colsay), though Mrs Barwick undertakes to pass it into the right
hands at the right moment.

I cannot quite pretend to be delighted by your decision, for I
know how much you will be missed at home and I know (and you
don't, but you will) what a Scottish autumn is, but I know also that
we will all be so pleased and proud when you succeed, as you will. It
will be a hard fight for you, dearest Al. Not the work – believe me
that you are possessed of the necessary brilliance six times over –
but you have chosen hard ground to plough and I fear will
encounter much opposition. I hope you know how far some
doctors will go to prevent women joining their ranks, for they
know how poor feminine souls shrink before the very idea of their
ministrations, and how much of their practice they will lose as

women turn to their own kind for healing. I want to tell you both that you must not allow anyone to turn you from the road on which you have set your foot and that I would go far to protect you, my dearest sister, from the treatment meted out to those few brave women who precede you. Only be sure, Al, be very sure, that it is truly your own wish to become a doctor and not just the realization of Mama's hopes. And if so, God speed! Maybe some day, when you are all set up in practice and basking in fame and glory, you will let me come and work for you. I dare say the bodies of those poor beings who must content themselves with my services are not so different from the fashionable belles and anxious mamas who will call day and night on your expertise that I will be quite useless!

Though I fear that so far I have been little better than useless here. My lack of Gaelic is a far graver handicap than I had understood – had I known, I would have made some effort to learn before coming, at least enough to show willing. And yet Miss Emily says she has never addressed them in anything but English and has always been perfectly understood! Even so, there is one woman, Mrs Grice, whose child is expected, she says, at Christmas, although the most cursory visual inspection suggests to me an earlier date. I have not asked to examine her and learnt early that it is rarely wise to cast suspicion on a lady's interpretation of her dates (*nota bene* I do not suggest that in this case there is any reason for such delicacy). I went into Mrs Grice's house (a courtesy term; in truth they dwell like primitive Man in stone huts filled with smoke and paved with what I hope is not worse than animal ordure) and she allowed me to sit while she plucked fowl. Do not from this imagine a cosy domestic scene: her youngest child sat on the floor dabbling its fingers in what flowed apparently unstaunched from its lower clothes and the fowl, far from being a comfortably clucking barnyard creature, was some great white bird, a kind of goose-like swan, whose head trailed on the ground at one side of her lap and its feet near the fire on the other. Its neck and strange eyes seemed to glow in the firelight so that it looked quite alive, although from the angle of the head swinging off the neck it could not have been, and Allie, there was a tall heap of such birds beside her, and her pale hair hanging over her face and casting the strangest shadows in the firelight.

Not wishing to appear to pry, though I don't doubt they all know why I am here and what is my work, I began by asking her about the killing and preparation of these birds. She told me, in a hesitating English with the odd word I did not understand and a lilt that I found hard to follow, what Mrs Barwick had already explained: at certain seasons the men pass their time hanging off the cliffs at the north end of the island on ropes, catching such creatures in nets that they manufacture for that purpose. These birds, she added, gesturing, come from the sea and can be netted by night, and so are valued the more because the men do not chance their lives for them. I cannot, I confess, imagine it – how could anyone stand upright in the waves by dark while containing a great frightened bird in a net? Each wing was the size of the child on the floor, who was perhaps two years of age and well grown (Mrs Barwick later told me, the last infant to survive birth on the island and also the first in four years; something must have been done at this confinement that was not done, or done differently, at all the others). I gathered that the birds, like everything else here, which means principally fish and eggs, are boiled in a great pot suspended over the fire on a chain, and indeed there is no other means of preparing food except in the Big House, where I subsist tolerably well on gruel, oat and barley bannocks, and dark and fishy-tasting fowl about which I make no enquiries whatsoever. I ration myself to two pieces of Cook's fudge each evening, and, alas and alack, I finished her fruit cake last night. I pretend to believe another may yet reach me here, but it is in truth a hollow dream.

As Mrs Grice began to work on the bird's wings, I praised the child on the floor, hoping to lead up to the circumstances of its birth (for the matted hair and colourless clothes gave no indication of the child's sex). It came over and began to fondle the ribbon edging on my skirt with its blackened fingers, a liberty to which

55

you can imagine I took secret exception! It occurs to me that the Grey People may in fact be just what they are called. I said she was fortunate indeed to have such a fine baby and that in years of work in a great city I had rarely seen such a bonny one, and indeed he has his mother's great blue eyes and would doubtless look well enough after scrubbing and fine-combing. The look on her face suggested that I had perhaps gone a little too far, so I spoke to the child, asking if he liked to eat fowl such as his mother was plucking (a foolish question, for he might like it or starve). He began to cry and ran to his mother, and soon after that I made my excuses and departed into the rain.

When I told Mrs Barwick where I had been, she laughed and said aye, there was reason this should be the first Colsay child delivered by a stranger, but when I pressed her she said I must ask The Family about that. It is none of my business, of course; here as at home it is my part to deliver the babies and not to question their origins. You will say that it is not the lack of Gaelic but the lack of tact that hampers my work, and you are probably right, but how to engineer not merely presence but intervention at this most crucial moment in a woman's life? At home I have the work of the Society and the respect given to my training to ease the way, but Allie, these woman have no want of me, have never heard of Manchester, much less the Princess Alexandra Nursing School, and probably would not care if they had. And yet they must, surely, prefer living to dead children?

I am sorry to burden you with a letter of this length. I am so discouraged I seem to have more time for writing about life here than I do for living it! But I may yet have two months to ingratiate myself with Mrs Grice, and who knows but she will allow me the great honour of presenting her with a healthy baby like to live.

I'm sorry to be so gloomy. Pray send me an account of Mama's meetings and Papa's latest glory and Elsa and the Twiggses and Hettie's young man, oh and whether hats continue to grow like sunflowers and indeed what is happening in the world, for even at Inversaigh the papers I saw pre-dated my departure and here, for all we know, the monarchy has been overthrown and the Empire in open revolt and Europe aflame with revolution (and wouldn't Mama enjoy that). I suppose Mrs Barwick might be mildly interested but most of them know little and care less, just so long as there are birds in the sky and fish in the sea and peat on the ground. I am glooming again. Good night.

Love as ever,

May

4

THE CHILD'S CURIOSITY

In place of an emotionally charged, sometimes very stormy family atmosphere which stimulates the child's curiosity, the average institution confronts its inhabitants with a set routine.

– Dorothy Burlingham and Anna Freud, *Infants without Families: The Case For and Against Residential Nurseries* (London: Allen & Unwin, 1944, 2nd ed., 1965), p. 80

I will know next time I suspect the presence of pirate raiders that the police, even when assured that the victim has been dead some years are, at least during office hours and with favourable wind and tide, able to reach us with gratifying speed. We couldn't find a phone book and couldn't get online, so in the end Giles stood on Raph's bed to call our friend Dan in Oxford and got him to Google the Highlands and Islands Police phone numbers. We knew it wasn't an emergency, but I stayed with the baby as if it needed a companion until we heard their boat closing in on us and Raph came running to say that they had waders and were bringing the boat right up on to the beach. He stood at my shoulder and peered into the hole. The baby's face was turned away, into the earth, the way they turn away in sleep.

'Mummy, that's a baby, isn't it?'

We'd told him we thought they might be people bones from

long ago, and made reference to the Picts and the Romans. He knows perfectly well that there is no reason to involve the police in the discovery of long-deceased domestic animals.

I looked up at him. 'It looks small to me,' I agreed.

'What would you do if Moth died?'

He was looking towards the house, where a door banged and there were male voices.

'If either of you died it would be the worst thing in the whole world to me. I don't want to think about it because it makes me feel so sad.'

They were opening the back door, Giles with Moth on his hip and two men in uniforms with hats which would have blown off if they'd worn them on the boat.

'Would you cry for your whole life?'

I reached up to put my arm round his waist. 'Yes. Parents don't ever feel better if their children die.'

He pulled away from me. They were nearly with us.

'Even though you could sleep then?'

I stood up.

'Mrs Cassingham? Can you keep the child away from the scene, please?'

'I'm Dr Bennet. Or call me Anna. It was Raphael who found the bones and neither of us have touched it since we realized what it was.'

The taller one squatted down, gloved hands flat on the ground as if he were leaning in to smell the baby. The other one looked at Raph. 'Shouldn't the lad be at school?'

Raph clung on to my clothes as he used to when I took him to birthday parties.

'We're home-schooling for a few months.'

The tall one stood up and held out his hand.

'I'm Ian MacDonald and this is Rory Sutton. You were right to call us, Mrs Cassingham.'

I shook his hand. It was like holding a seal's flipper.

'They didn't look like animal bones. And the wrapping—'

I looked down at Raph, who had put an arm round my waist and was leaning heavily against me.

'The wrapping?'

'People don't knit for animals.'

Raph muttered into my ribcage. Ian MacDonald raised an eyebrow.

'Excuse me,' I said. I detached Raph and bent down. 'What is it, love?'

'Maybe the mummy knitted a blanket.'

The eyebrow stayed up.

'Maybe she did.' I stroked his hair.

'I gather you found the body, Mrs Cassingham. Perhaps we could go inside and you could tell me exactly what happened? And, Ralph, is it? Ralph, would you and your dad like to go with my friend Rory and look at a real police speedboat?'

Raph didn't move.

'Raphael,' I said. 'Raphael as in the archangel. Raph, I need to talk to Mr MacDonald. You could go do some bouncing or you could build some more of that town.'

'I couldn't. The town was raided by the Serbs when you went off to the beach and all the people got killed. Even the babies.'

I began to think it would be quicker, although perhaps only slightly quicker, to tell Ian MacDonald that I had delivered a baby, knitted it a blanket and then buried it in the back garden than to wait for Raph to incriminate me.

'Raph,' said Giles. 'Come on. Let's go and see how Jake's doing with that roof. He'll be going home any minute.'

Not, I thought, when he sees the police launch on the beach, and scents dirt on the lord of the manor.

Raph took Giles's hand. 'Daddy, if you could travel forwards or backwards in time, which would you choose?'

'Not now, love,' I murmured.

'Jake?' asked Ian MacDonald.

'Builder,' I said. 'We're doing up one of the old blackhouses for a holiday cottage. To rent to visitors.'

He smiled. 'Of course you are. Rory?'

Rory nodded. 'I'll just have a quick word with Jake myself, Mr Cassingham.'

Moth lurched into my arms and the three of them went off to give Jake the basis of many free drinks in the Black Sheep in Shepsay.

I made a pot of tea, deciding to raid the rose pouchong rather than expend my dwindling supply of Yorkshire Tea and advance the end of the milk. Ian MacDonald sat at the table. One might just as well give people access to our bank accounts, medical records and curricula vitae as sit them at our kitchen table (in fact, it may be the only place where it is possible to access much of this information). Moth sat on my hip, subdued, I hoped, by the sight of strangers rather than by the trauma of his mother's abuse.

'So, you were planting trees?'

I kept my back to him, adjusting the quantity of tealeaves in the strainer. Moth, who likes the tea strainer, leaned in to help.

'Timothy, this one, was asleep. I'd tried to plant the trees with him around but he kept wanting the spade or going off and licking stones and things—' I stopped, poured water. My inability to combine manual labour with childcare is a shame and a disgrace but not, yet, a police matter. 'Anyway, so yes, we were planting trees.'

'But you said it was your son who found the bones?'

Moth took a mouthful of my hair and leant away.

'Ow.' I tickled his chin. 'He was helping me dig. We both saw them, I suppose. He said first.'

'And then?'

'I tried to tell him they were animal bones. He looked properly and saw the blanket. I sent him to get Giles.'

'The blanket?'

61

'I looked, after he'd gone. It looked hand-knitted. And I knew the bones were small.'

I put the tea in front of him, translucent as amber, and waited to see if he knew not to ask for milk. Or sugar. Giles and I, in rebellion against opposite ends of the English social spectrum, meet over refusal to deploy a sugar bowl. I would, if asked, deny owning one, though there is one in each of the two silver coffee sets we were given as wedding presents. You should have had a list at John Lewis, my mother said, and I told her I'd rather have asked people to buy wells for Somali villages. I lied.

'Thank you, Mrs Cassingham. Anna. Now, Anna, as I expect you know, it's not uncommon for people to turn up human remains on the islands, and we nearly always find it's the archaeologists we need to call. But not, of course, in every instance. I need to ask you some questions.'

'Of course.'

I sat down, settled Moth on my lap. He pointed to my mug. 'Hot, hot tea. Mummy got a flower mug.'

He pointed to Ian MacDonald's tea but was unable to formulate words for a man in a suit given possession of one of our household gods in the form of the Bird Mug.

'You have just the two children?'

My stomach lurched.

'Yes. We used to think about a third one but—' Stop it. There is no legal obligation to have three children.

'But?'

'Just the two.' Oh, and the one I buried in the orchard, obviously.

'So you have had two pregnancies?'

I looked up at him. Moth pulled himself up by my hair and licked my chin like someone sampling a strange fruit.

'Is that necessary information, Mr MacDonald?'

'Old MacDonald,' said Moth. 'Old Macdonald had a farm.'

Ian MacDonald shrugged. 'I don't know, Mrs Cassingham, at this stage. I would be interested in your answer.'

My hand, gripping the straps on Moth's green cord dungarees to hold him when he overbalanced, was suddenly damp with sweat. Ian MacDonald's gaze rested on Moth's shoulder as if there were a rare butterfly there. I took a mouthful of tea. Moth turned and I gulped; it was too hot.

'It's not relevant,' I said. 'Everyone who needs to know my medical history knows it.'

Ian MacDonald watched the grass blowing in the wind outside and sipped his tea, but I didn't say anything more.

'Read a Gruffalo now?' asked Moth.

'You and Mr Cassingham have been here, what, a month now?'

'Giles has holidayed here all his life. I've been several times since we got married. Giles was coming and going through the spring, getting the house ready. He's researching the puffins, the effect of climate change and pollution on population levels.'

'I know a bit about Mr Cassingham's research.'

Dr Cassingham. Maybe Professor Cassingham, come October. He made it sound as if puffin-counting were a well-known front for drug-smuggling or terrorist plotting.

'The police take an interest in puffins?'

'I take an interest in ornithology. But you yourself came last month?'

I nodded. The mothers of young children are the obvious suspects for infanticide. I stroked Moth's hair and wound the long strands at his nape around my finger. He dribbled on my jeans.

'Sing a Gruffalo?'

'Later, Moth. When teaching was over. In Oxford.'

Sometimes the name of the city itself wields a certain power. Do you know who I am?

'Have you had visitors since then?'

'No.' Moth put his finger in my tea. 'No, love, hot!'

'Mummy kiss it better.'

I kissed it. 'Jake's been. Sometimes he works with a mate. Doug.'

Ian MacDonald nodded. I don't think Jake spends enough time with his children to develop murderous instincts; he has a wife for that kind of thing. I drank some tea.

'Surely it's been there a lot longer than a few weeks, though. Doesn't that kind of decomposition take years? In turf?'

'Does it?' He sipped his tea, his gaze on my Visa bill. £147 plus postage on clothes from a certain Swedish designer.

'I don't know, I'm a historian not an archaeologist. I didn't know anything about that burial, those bones, until I saw them. I mean, if I had, I wouldn't have been digging there and we wouldn't have called you, would we?'

I moved the Visa bill. He aligned the Bird Mug with the edge of a brown envelope on which I had drawn a number of cats for Moth.

'Mrs Cassingham – Anna –I am not accusing you of anything. As you suggest, it is probably a very old burial. But I am sure you understand that we need to rule out any more recent event before we notify Heritage Scotland. There is a team on the way. I trust they won't inconvenience you.'

I wondered what this was going to do for the cottage bookings. There are, God knows, far more dead than living people on this island. There is a whole graveyard down at the old village as well as a Neolithic mound which has not been excavated but looks, to those who can distinguish one grassy mound from another, a lot like the burial chambers on Shepsay. The island is thought to have been continuously inhabited for several thousand years and the inhabitants are unlikely to have gone somewhere else to die. Maybe the sort of people who think they'll like seclusion on an island prefer their company dead. Given the choice, I would prefer to holiday in Venice or Vienna or New York.

'I take it your husband is likely to know most of the people who have been here in the last few years?'

Moth stuck his hand in the tea again.

'Kiss it better!'

I kissed it and he dried it on my top.

'Well, anyone can come. Obviously. Giles's mother will know everyone who was invited if he doesn't. We can give you the number.'

'Anyone?'

I met his gaze. 'We haven't exactly ringed the place with barbed wire. Giles encourages visitors. As long they don't upset the birds.'

The wind rushed across the garden and rattled the window.

'It was last year his father died, wasn't it?'

'June.' I finished my tea. 'They got probate just before Christmas. The girls were cross that Giles has the island.'

'Your husband's sisters?'

Two unmarried women of child-bearing age with ready access to Colsay.

'Thea and Camilla. I think Thea spent a summer here a couple of years ago. She dropped out of law at Nottingham or Manchester or somewhere.'

'When would that have been?'

I thought about Thea, who irons her hair and clothes and washes her car and tucks her shirts into A-line beige skirts which make her stomach look as if it's encased in sausage-skin. I suppose it is possible that someone has had sex with Thea, but I do not think her capable of anything so bohemian as single motherhood. Though we were looking, of course, for someone who was not, in the event, capable of motherhood.

'A couple of years ago, I think. Before Moth was born. Giles will know.'

Moth wriggled on my lap. 'Down!'

He approached Ian MacDonald's jacket, paused to conduct what passes for risk assessment in the toddler mind, and then advanced to poke at one of the shiny buttons. He likes the glass lifts in Debenhams, especially the alarm bell which is glowing and red and within easy reach of the pushchair-bound.

'Moth pressing a button!' He ran back to me, glancing over his shoulder as if waiting for the siren to sound. I picked him up.

'Sorry,' I said. 'Not that kind of button. Moth, shall we find your toy phone if you want to press buttons?'

'No.'

Voices approached the back door. Ian MacDonald stood up.

'Right. Well, thank you for your help, Mrs Cassingham. We'll go have another look at the site, if that's all right. As I said, some of our colleagues are on their way but there's nothing further that need trouble you for now. We'll hope to be off the island before dark. We'll put a tent over the site but we must ask you not to touch anything until we've finished here. Is that all right?'

'Of course.'

'Bye bye,' said Moth. 'Bye bye, man. Off a go. All gone tea.'

Ian MacDonald turned. 'Bye bye, Timothy. I'll let myself out, Mrs Cassingham. And – ah – I'll be back to talk to you again.'

Later, much later, after Raph had spent the afternoon watching from his window as men in white overalls put up a tent and carried things out of it, and Giles had not played with Moth but gone off to see the puffins while I tried to cook a debased spaghetti alla carbonara with toddler help and improbable substitutions for vital ingredients, and I had stared at my computer screen as if the words were in Inuktitut or Japanese while Giles washed up as if he were starring in a film about a dad doing housework, he came to find me in the bath. Especially with electric lighting, it would not have been my preferred venue for conversation. He put the lid down and sat on the loo, regarding the droops of my body as if contemplating a purchase.

'So what happened earlier?'

'Earlier as in discovering a body in the garden or earlier as in shouting at Moth? Or maybe earlier as in not shouting at Moth most of last night while you were asleep?'

He frowned at his shoe.

'Earlier as in shouting at Moth.'

I sat up and drew up my knees. The water was cooling.

'I shouldn't have lost my temper but I have had less than five hours' sleep in the last three days and I was very thirsty and I needed the loo. Not to mention the destruction of my mind and the ruin of my career. And mostly I'm too busy and tired but I do worry about Raph.'

'Raph will be OK. He's bright. Are you bothered about the bones?'

I was too tired to be bothered about anything.

'I don't like them being taken away. She looked almost asleep there. In the blanket.'

'She?'

I shrugged. The wind reaching through the old window frame ran its nails down my naked back.

'Just how I thought about it. Giles, that policeman was asking about Thea. That time she stayed here on her own.'

He looked up and smiled. It was as if the room had got warmer.

'I know. He asked me. I mean, Thea. Honestly.'

'You don't think – I mean, if she had got pregnant, she's not exactly one to organize a quick abortion or decide that single parenthood has advantages, is she? Wouldn't she just freeze and hope it would go away?'

'Anna! She is my sister.'

I wanted to get out of the bath but didn't want him looking at me unfolded.

'Whoever did it was someone's sister.'

'I know you don't like her but you can't accuse my sister of infanticide. I don't know why you're assuming it is infanticide, anyway.'

I wrapped my arms more tightly round my knees.

'I don't dislike her. I'm not accusing anyone. Ian MacDonald was asking. As far as I know, Thea dropped out of wherever it was and came here on her own and stayed for quite a while, a few months, and then went off back to London as if nothing had happened.'

He picked birdshit off his shoe and crumbled it on to the bathmat.

'What do you mean, as if nothing had happened? Nothing had happened. I always thought she'd been dumped.'

'Maybe she had. Giles, I'm freezing here, I need to get some sleep.'

He passed me a damp towel and left. When I came to bed he was there and he curled around me in the dark, but after he fell asleep the emptiness of the grave lay strange as the vacant belly after birth. I pictured the baby unwrapped, laid on a slab under lights, her bones probed. I was almost grateful when Moth woke, a real child with real needs and warm skin and the vanilla smell of baby sweat. I paced him to sleep through the smothering scent of the hothouses in the Botanic Gardens and the clouds of fallen leaves in the University Parks when the year has turned and it is dark before the library closes, and even when his head rolled on my shoulder and his hands hung like dead flowers against my body I wanted him to breathe in my arms until morning came.

Colsay House,
Colsay

15th October, 1878

Dear Miss Emily,

I write, as promised, to offer you a report of Colsay and my work here. I must thank you again for employing me here; the people's need and thus my opportunity to do good are great indeed. I only hope I may achieve what we all hope for; I have learnt already that the path is hard.

As I know that you will pass this on to Sir Hugo, I begin with the account he requested of the villagers' welfare. Sir, I cannot say that all is well. I know it is some years since you were last able to visit the island and assure you that, whatever life was like then for these people, it is worse now. I scarcely know where to begin, for the truth is that these 'blackhouses' are insanitary, overcrowded and unventilated, such as must break down the best constitution; the people's diet is coarse and unvaried, entirely lacking in fruits and vegetables, low in both quality and quantity; if they have been spared serious infection until now it is as a result of climate and natural hardihood, for drainage and sewerage are non-existent and, if you will pardon an indelicate subject which it is too often part of my calling to consider, I have reason to believe that, especially in inclement weather, people perform their natural functions on the floors of their dwellings. It is hard to speak to the welfare of the children because there is but one child under the age of seven, though I am endeavouring to gain access to the next childbed where I am sure that normal modern precautions and practices may at least prevent the babe's fall to the 'eight-day sickness' – although I cannot, of course, guarantee life to any child, much less one beginning its days in this place.

I must add that of the eleven children between the ages of eight and fourteen, not one is able to speak any English or read or write its own name, and I am told that there has been no resident schoolmaster these five years; I believe this to be a violation of the new Education Act (with which my work in Manchester has necessitated some acquaintance) and in any case it is clear that the provision of basic education is the *sine qua non* of any improvement in these people's lives. I would almost say, better to educate the children (supposing we can bring any children to school age) than to provide potable water and ventilated houses.

The people are living not so much as they did in the last century but as they must have done eight or even ten centuries ago, barring only the partial introduction of leaf tea and shoe leather, although the older men and women yet sport footwear made of birds with the feathers still on them. The men gather birds and fish (or die in the attempt, which I am assured is all too frequent) and the women, twice a day in all weathers, walk near three miles across the hill to milk the cows and then back, bearing the milk in wooden pails on great yokes and, more remarkable yet, knitting as they go. The food is then distributed in strict accordance with the needs of each household, regardless of the contribution of labour, in the same way as such services as burial and – at least until my arrival – nursing are provided by each according to ability and to each according to need. It is no doubt a noble principle from which many of us have much to learn, but the result, here, is a people endemically hungry, endemically dirty, endemically sick, in which no one has reason or opportunity to improve. Such change is necessary to raise them even to the standards of all but the poorest slum dwellers of Manchester that I find it hard to see how such change might be brought about; at least in Gorton and Cheetham Hill there is the sight and hope of better things to inspire effort, not to mention the work of the schools and societies such as my own. I do not see where the people of Colsay are to find that hope which must be the prerequisite of improvement.

For my own work, I believe I am making progress, although of course the final test will be the result of Mrs Grice's confinement in December. Eschewing the examinations one would normally conduct, which are likely to cause needless alarm in one to whom the idea of such procedures is alien, I have been visiting her and endeavouring to befriend her and her family. In the course of these conversations, I learnt that the 'knee-woman' who has attended all births on the island these thirty years was sick in her bed at the time of Mrs Grice's last confinement, and also that the child was delivered so quickly that her husband had barely time to call on the village women before the delivery of the afterbirth (you will pardon me these details, but I know you are not without familiarity with whatever affects the health of poor women). I asked who cut the cord, but perhaps I asked too eagerly, for she gave the impression of not understanding my question and I judged it expedient to turn the conversation into other channels. But this part of the tale certainly seems to confirm our view that something done by the 'knee-woman' at the time of birth is responsible for these deaths. I asked, of course, for the 'knee-woman's' name but 'She is just an old body who will be helping us when we are needing her'. Of course it will not be difficult to discover this person's identity in time. Everything I have heard so far would tend to confirm that the disease is neonatal tetanus contracted through the umbilical cord, either as a result of unclean practices in cutting the cord or through the application of unclean substances to the cut end, such as I have read of among an uncivilized African tribe (where, oddly, it did not have the same disastrous result). Diagnosis, however, may be the easy part of this undertaking; the difficulty is in persuading the people to accept the aid of the modern world, to which they appear to feel a fierce resistance.

I will, of course, continue to inform you of my progress here. Yours most sincerely,

May Moberley

5

A SNAKE, HARMLESS

A snake, harmless and about 2ft long, was placed in a box sufficiently deep to ensure that it could not immediately climb out when the top was removed. In the box was placed a small coloured toy. The child's attention is directed to the box, the lid is uncovered, and the child is allowed to look in; if he raises any questions the experimenter simply says 'It is a snake,' and then points to the toy and asks the child to reach in and get the toy.

— John Bowlby, *Attachment and Loss*, Vol. 2, *Separation* (London: Penguin, 1973), p. 139

The police didn't come back the next day. The tent sat there, candy-striped as if round the other side there might be a window and a Punch and Judy show, but none of us went to look. Rain fell, and Giles went into Colla and came back with a treasure haul in cardboard boxes so damp we brought the wheelbarrow we use to bring them back from the landing stage right into the kitchen. Moth ran around helping to unpack, and twenty feet away the grave lay empty as an old cradle.

Moth put a tin of tomatoes in the washing machine. 'Thank you, Moth, Moth very helpful!'

'Giles,' I said. 'That last family. The couple your father remembered, in the village. Did they have children?'

Giles was kneeling by the freezer, trying to push cartons of milk into irregular spaces.

'I have no idea.' Moth handed him a bottle of shampoo. 'Thank you, Moth. Anna, it could have been there centuries.'

I opened the child-lock on the flour cupboard and Moth came running. There are sometimes, when I haven't eaten them late at night, chocolate chips in there.

'Not that one, love, it would make a horrible mess. It hasn't been there centuries, not with a knitted blanket like that. I saw it.' I offered Moth a sealed pot of baking powder in exchange for an open bag of couscous. No deal. 'Giles, can Thea knit?'

He slammed the freezer door. 'Anna, stop it.' The freezer door popped open and he leant on it. 'Moth, not on the floor, please. There must have been hundreds of women on this island in the last two hundred years and they could all knit. More importantly, I had an e-mail this morning from someone asking about booking the cottage for next month, so let's concentrate on that. I mean, even one booking this summer might start things rolling next year. You can't worry about all the burials on the island.'

Moth poured couscous on to my foot. 'Bugger, couscous on a floor! Mummy sweep it!'

Giles looked as if I'd peed on his shoe. 'And please stop swearing in front of Moth.'

I caught the packet from Moth, who stamped on my foot. 'No snatching, Mummy!'

'Moth, is it still raining out there? The police aren't worried about all the burials on the island. When they start asking me how many babies I've had I think I'm allowed to take an interest.'

Giles paused in his assaults on the freezer. 'They think you did it?'

'You haven't read enough detective fiction. They always suspect the person who found the body. And you don't know enough women's history. It's young mums who commit infanticide.' Women who can see no way forward and cannot undo the multiplication of cells and go back.

73

He stood up and the door stayed closed. 'You're not that young.'

'Thanks. But Thea was, you see. It's also mostly single women with unplanned pregnancies.' Mostly.

Raph spoke from the door.

'What's an unplanned pregnancy?'

I deployed the 'walking off without explanation' technique after inveigling Giles into changing Moth's dirty nappy after lunch ('That nappy needs changing. I'm just going to the loo'). I had used the last of the baby wipes on yesterday's poo and forgotten to tell Giles to buy more, Raphael was on the space hopper and not monitoring my movements, and so I reckoned I could probably be settled in the village and a hundred words in before they realized I'd left the house.

Case studies reveal the vulnerability of the most utopian institutional projects to entropy and abuse, although they also attest to the possibility of subsequent redemption. Christ's Hospital is an obvious example of this trajectory: a foundation for the rescue and nurture of indigent urban children, intended to provide the skills and self-discipline necessary to independence and a measure of social mobility, which became, according to some of the more lurid accounts of Coleridge's contemporaries, a place where de Sade's fantasies were reified and realized at the cost of children who had forfeited all protection when the institution took over their care. I hope to show in the following studies how the twin possibilities of salvation and destruction are worked out in other, more obscure institutional histories.

It's always good to get 'reification' in. It's a word I encountered late and have only recently begun to use in print. I deleted 'entropy' as outworn and put it back as a formality that might counteract the personal note of 'I hope'. Only the more daring academics risk an occasional use of the first person and it is still considered by the Fellows to be bad form. One is supposed to pretend that academic prose is written by an omniscient and nameless consciousness like God himself.

I looked up at the young man in uniform, sepia and blotched with damp. For my grandfather, the war brought liberation from the confines of working-class Newcastle. He volunteered before he could be conscripted, and the navy put him through his accountancy exams, taught him to ski (for reasons that continued to elude the rest of us) and flew him round the world, although he'd made the mistake of marrying before he left and therefore spent his life with a woman whose horizons were comfortably contained by her postcode. Maybe the sepia man had gone to London for the first time, met people who didn't believe it was a sin to laugh on a Sunday, eaten ice cream and drunk red wine. Maybe he'd seen terraces of olive trees rustling in a summer breeze, touched the bloom on dark grapes and tasted oranges warm from the sun. As well as learning again the precise extent of human inhumanity. Maybe he'd met a French girl and fallen in love, realized that subsistence farming in some places is a matter of peaches glowing under dark leaves and cows with long eyelashes in a cool stone dairy (we will ignore the water shortages and insects). Maybe the old couple left not for a few years of porridge and saving money on the gas in Inverness but for dark-eyed grandchildren in white cotton and siestas with the shutters closed against the sun. I skimmed chapter three, which attempts to present the new forms of writing for children as cognate with the late eighteenth-century interest in institutionalization.

The parental status of children's authors takes surprisingly literal form in the trope of text-as-milk, where the (female) writer compares herself to the nursing mother, nurturing the reader on the most wholesome moral fare. This metaphor works to legitimize the work of these women writers in moral terms, appearing to collapse the distinction between intellectual and reproductive labour which continues to vex our own culture in relation to motherhood, but it also, less obviously, reconfigures both reproductive and domestic labour in economic terms. In the eighteenth century, mothers' milk, like books, was for sale.

I deleted 'which continues to vex . . .'. It was true, but I could hear the voice of Dr Marjorie Owdon: 'One is not writing for the *Daily Mail*, my dear. There is no need to appeal to the housewives.' As if being mindful of the housewives revealed one's own dirty secret of domesticity. The Fellows nearly all 'lived in', adult lives distilled into bed-sitting rooms, with shared kitchens and bathrooms distinguished from those of the undergraduates only by coloured paint on the walls and less food but better wines in the fridges. The Fellows took their meals in Hall and elections to the Food Committee were fought with a fervour born of routine subjection to boiled ox tongue. Members of the Food Committee – who were usually, like most of their kin, given to factionalism and wars waged for years over the placement of a biscuit tin or folding of a napkin – collaborated gleefully in the occasional treat of planning the dinner given as part of the interview of candidates to join the Fellowship. The point was to devise an obstacle course of etiquette that would weed out any undesirables sufficiently adept at disguise to penetrate the British class system as far as shortlisting for an Oxford Fellowship. Cherry pie with the stones left in, as traditionally practised by All Souls, had long been a cliché. Olives would have been an obvious substitute had the chef been willing or able to venture so far towards the Mediterranean. The Bursar would never have countenanced the expense of shellfish – being a former women's college, St Mary Hall had to count its pennies as the more generously endowed foundations did not – and in any case I think the required impedimenta were considered bourgeois. Spaghetti was too bohemian a challenge, one that would have been proudly failed by the majority of the Fellows themselves, and so they were reduced to placing large discs of hard caramel on top of blancmange and presenting small fish whole. It was possible to avoid both of these by declaring oneself vegetarian and preferring fruit to pudding, in which case an apple appeared on a plate, followed, enough minutes later to trap the unwary, by a fruit knife and fork on a salver and napkin. I should, really, be more grateful to the Cassinghams for training me in matters of fish-knives and eating apples with a fork, since I may owe them my Fellowship for it.

'Mummy?'

Raphael, again. I would have to inspect the other cottages for a new secret office, although I knew none of them had such a complete roof.

'What? I'm working.'

He came in and stood rubbing the floor with his shoe.

'You weren't writing.'

I straightened my shoulders.

'Raph, I'm allowed to think as well, OK? Writing isn't just typing.'

He looked at the photo above my head. There was ink on his hands and black dirt, like the soil we had been digging, under his fingernails.

'Sorry.'

I reached towards him and stroked his shoulder.

'Sorry, Raph. It's just I get so little time. And if I don't get this book finished I won't get another job.'

He watched his foot scraping the floor.

'Mummy?'

'Yes.'

'Mummy?'

I sighed. 'What is it, Raph?'

'Mummy, why did the baby die? In the ground?'

I saved my work and closed the file.

'Come here.' I put my arm around him. 'You know that long ago, the people who lived here couldn't always find healthy food? And they didn't always have clean water?'

His face cleared a little, recognising a familiar narrative.

'Like children in Africa?'

Rain hit the window like a handful of stones.

'Like some children in some parts of Africa. And in some parts of the US, actually. When people don't have healthy food, their bodies can't deal with illnesses. And when they don't have clean water, they get ill. Babies' bodies haven't had any practice at getting better so babies get more ill than other people and sometimes they died. Now we've got good food and clean water and if babies do get ill there are lots of ways of helping them to get better.'

'In hospitals?'

He was remembering someone in his class in Oxford, whose very premature sister died in hospital.

'Sometimes. Sometimes, if babies come long before they are ready, even in hospital people can't make them better.'

Raphael is not readily distracted. We had a well-rehearsed story about baby Olivia's birth and death and he'd heard it before.

He ran the hem of his T-shirt through his fingers.

'Why did they bury the baby by the house? Why not in the graveyard? With a stone with her name on it?'

'I don't know,' I said.

'Tell me what you think.'

'I don't know, Raph. It was long ago. Things would have seemed different then. People thought differently.'

'Tell me what you think.'

I shut my laptop and put it in the plastic bag from Blackwell's of Broad Street that I use as computer rainwear and talisman.

'It might have been buried there before the house was built, you know. Our house is the newest building on the island.

Come on, shall we go make some supper? Daddy brought lettuce, we can have a salad.'

Moving here has made both children, and indeed their parents, come to view salad as a treat. We could, Giles says, if we were more organized, grow our own. We could do a lot of things if we were more organized.

Raphael began gesturing to his invisible planes.

'If I had a baby I would put it in a special tank and I would filter the air and I would feed it with a special tube that was sterilized and I would have machines to tell me it was breathing properly and then it wouldn't die—'

'Raph?'

'And there would be a machine to keep it warm and the mummy and daddy could pedal on a sort of exercise bike to make the energy for it—'

'Raph? That's just for when they're early—'

'And if it was somewhere hot I'd make a machine to keep it cool, but it's harder to do that without using lots of energy because you have to convert heat into coldness—'

'Raphael, I'm going to go make supper. Come and help. You can spin the lettuce.'

Night Waking: 03:11

I surface, this time, a moment before the screaming begins. The house is silent, and there is enough moonlight to show the lines of our four-poster bed, a movement in the voile panels with which I have replaced Julia's unwashable Victorian drapes, and the outline of Giles cocooned in more than his share of the duvet. The wind wails around the corner of the house, scudding past the Punch and Judy tent. There is no preliminary whimpering. Moth screams as if the skeleton's mother, her hands still shaking from wringing her own baby's neck, is reaching into his cot. I find myself beside him and snatch him from her grasp. He clings to my hair and claws at my shoulder and

I stroke his warm back. I kiss tears from his temple and he curls up so I can hold him the way I held him when he was new and we were not separate.

'It's all right, Moth. Mummy's here. Go to sleep.'

We walk. Down Parks Road, where Keble glows like a lava lamp in the setting sun and I have a sudden vision of what the Victorians might have done with neon. The leaves are turning and they eddy around my feet as we pass the University Museum, within whose portals dinosaurs sleep, and behind which lurk the shrunken heads and colonial guilt of the Pitt Rivers. Visitors may open all the little drawers under the display cases but risk their dreams in doing so. Over the scuffed stone kerb, watching for bicycles, and past the high walls of Rhodes House. Roses swarm over the stones, and behind them the library drifts like an upturned boat. Moth's breath catches and I begin to rub and pat his back. The wind howls again, rain spatters, and out in the dark the tent flaps over a shallow bed. If I take Moth back to our room, where I would like him to be, Giles will go to the sofa as if I persist in introducing toads to the marital bed. Across the road under the gaze of Hertford and in through the hobbit hole cut into the wooden door of the Bodleian quadrangle. We approach the cot and pause. Moth's breathing changes as I lower him.

'Mummy!'

I put him back on my shoulder and we saunter across the quad in the sun, taking the last breaths of sunlight before leaning on the heavy glass doors which grant provisional admittance. Through the shop, where visitors buy things to confirm that their feet have also touched the stones where Oxford scholars tread. At the side of the cot, I listen again to the house. Nothing stirs, which is not to say that it is not there. I lower him as if he were a Grecian urn. He murmurs, turns over, reaches for my hand. I am tethered. I rest my head on my arm along the top of the cot. After a few minutes my hand goes numb.

*

The police came back in the morning, six of them in two boats. Giles had gone off to the puffins, I was trying to hang the laundry on a clothes airer positioned over a turned-off heater in the superstitious belief that the ghost of winter's warmth might dry the clothes, and Moth was helping by taking the clothes off and putting them back in the washing machine. Ian MacDonald appeared at the back door.

'Mr MacDonald. Did you find out how old the burial is?'

He looked around. Raphael hadn't had breakfast yet so I hadn't cleared the table, and the deposits of yoghurt around Moth's chair made it look as if birds had been roosting there. It is not a criminal offence not to have brushed your hair.

'It can take a while, Mrs Cassingham. We'd like to have another look at the site, if that's all right.'

And if it isn't, I presumed, they return with warrants.

'Of course. When do we get the garden back? We need to finish planting the trees.'

Although I suspected that the trees were already dead.

'We'll let you know, Mrs Cassingham. It's only the parts we've cordoned off that we'd ask you not to touch. And perhaps I could have another word with you, later?'

Moth pottered over and offered him one of my less appetizing pairs of knickers.

'Moth! No, bring that back to Mummy.' I grabbed it, and then caught Moth's head as he flung himself at the floor. I lowered him and stood back. There are times when it feels as if he is lying on the ground screaming and kicking on my behalf. The police watched. I used be area representative for Youth CND, an easy way of annoying my mother that came with the possible bonus of saving the world from nuclear holocaust, and we went to workshops on Non Violent Direct Action where we exchanged ideas about raising public consciousness and winding up the authorities that none of us was prepared to implement, I because I was scared of the police and most of the others because they were planning to do law and didn't

81

want a criminal record. So instead of blocking motorways with stolen police cones in the middle of the night we performed home-made plays about nuclear winter in the High Street. Enter Cockroach, stage left. Toddlers, clearly, would have been the solution. A campaign of co-ordinated tantrums in the corridors of power would effect political change faster than any more traditional protest.

'Mummy, is Moth all right?'

Raphael, wearing his favourite pink flowery pyjama bottoms and nothing else, with a green bruise on his shoulder. I picked Moth up and he hit my face and drummed his feet on my ribcage.

'No hitting, love. Raph, do you want to get some clothes on? You must be cold.'

He scratched his bottom. 'No.'

The police were still standing there.

'Feel free to get on whenever you're ready,' I said.

'How did the lad get that bruise?' asked Rory.

'Raph?'

Moth relaxed against my chest and waved. 'Hello, man!'

'I don't know. He bruises easily. Raph, did you fall off the space hopper?'

'No.' He wandered off.

'Right,' I said. 'Well. I'm going upstairs. The back door's open.'

One can, I presume, trust the police in one's kitchen, and I was rather hoping they might go through the papers on the table and learn that we are, in theory, innocent.

The police were still there when Moth went to sleep after lunch. I hadn't checked e-mail for several days and was beginning to need internet access more than I needed sleep. I wasn't waiting for anything in particular, exactly, but there were a couple of articles under review and there is always the theoretical chance of an e-mail that will change one's life, although the exact form of such a missive is unclear to me, especially since we all delete without opening the news that we have won a million pounds in much the same way as we section people claiming to be the Messiah.

'Raph?' He was building what looked like an airport. 'Raph, I'm just going to pop over to the blackhouse. I want to check e-mail. Do you want to come? See how the roof's going?'

He looked at the window, as if I were standing in the garden. 'What about Moth?'

I glanced up the stairs. Moth never wakes at lunchtime until I wake him. He would like nothing better than to sleep all afternoon, refreshing himself for the night ahead. The garden was full of custodians of the law.

'He's got half the Highlands and Islands Police on duty. I'm only going for a minute.'

Raph fitted the sails from a Lego windmill that I'd bought in an attempt to interest him in heritage domesticity to the top of the control tower. Radar.

'What if there's a fire?'

'Nothing's switched on. There's no reason for a fire. Raph, come on, decide, I've not got long.'

Seconds dripped away. He looked at me.

'I think I'll stay here and mind Moth. Thank you.'

Jake was, as I had known he would be, having lunch, smoking and ogling the twin engines on the police launch down on the beach. I perched on the stairs and the computer found the network and connected immediately. Messages to All Fellows about porters' annual leave and the need to submit library requests before the beginning of term, a bulletin from the British Association for Eighteenth Century Studies, notice of a conference in Boulder, Colorado, that the organizers thought I might like to pay several hundred dollars to attend. I have been to only one conference since Moth was born. I stopped breastfeeding so I could go, thinking to relaunch my career after maternity leave, and then spent most of my time asleep, in the hotel pool or reading Canadian newspapers in cafés on the harbourfront. I bought slices of pizza and pots of ice cream and lay on the bed eating them and reading detective stories. I did give a paper, one I'd cut-and-pasted from my book during the flight on my usual assumption that no one listens to my papers with more attention than I listen to theirs, which means that most of the audience most of the time is wondering what to have for lunch or deciding whom they would choose if they had to have sex with one of the people in the room. If it's a keynote speech, or I'm not hungry, I decide which of the men in the room I would sleep with in exchange for tenure and/or a book contract with Yale University Press (although, it occurred to me last time, if the men I'm ogling are playing the same game they will observe a lot of very toned female graduate students at American conferences. I am no longer sure that access to my person, so thoroughly rummaged by five midwives, a registrar and a sequence of metal implements, has much exchange value on the open market). I deleted the e-mails and had thirteen minutes in hand before I needed to wake Moth. I stood up to look out of the window. No plumes of smoke. I logged into J-Stor and searched for articles containing the key words 'infanticide' and 'Scotland', glanced out of the window again and saved the more promising titles, mostly relating to Neolithic archaeology and nineteenth-century legal proceedings, to the hard drive.

'What've you done with your lads?'

Jake stood in the doorway, dressed as usual in tattered tracksuit bottoms and a tight black T-shirt with a washed-out picture of something aggressive across his belly and a scattering of dandruff on the shoulders. He seems impervious to cold. Jake's wife does a little secretarial work at the school during term now the youngest child is six.

'Hi, Jake. How's it going?'

'Well enough. Where are your lads? Not with their dad, I saw him go.'

I looked back at the screen. I employ Jake, I reminded myself, and not as my conscience. 'I've settled Moth for his nap and left Raph doing Lego. I needed to check e-mail and you know the signal over there is crap.'

His glance fell on the computer as if he'd caught me downloading pornography.

'And download some articles to read next time I get the chance.'

He reached up and held on to the lintel, blocking the doorway with the light coming through his red hair as if he were an avenging angel.

'I'd gi'e my wife the back of my hand if she treated ours the way you treat those little lads.'

The wind flattened the grass at his feet.

'What?'

'I've work to do.' He picked up a tool and started to make a noise with it.

I turned back to the window, feeling as if he had indeed hit me. Does he abuse his wife? My instinct for argument wrestled with the desire to call the police and have him arrested for making threats, though I could imagine whose side the police would be on and in any case he was not threatening his wife, who had not left her children while she checked her e-mail, nor me, since I am not his wife.

'Jake?' I shouted.

The noise stopped. 'Well?'

'I'm doing my job, Jake. What I get paid for. Imagine if you had to finish this job and your wife was out eleven hours a day looking at puffins. What would you do with your kids?'

'She's not, though, is she? I wouldn't let her.' He started the noise again. There is no point in arguing with people who want to make a noise.

Moth should have been woken three minutes earlier. I ran back across the rough ground to rescue my evening's work from jeopardy.

'Mrs Cassingham.' Ian MacDonald was sitting at the kitchen table, his hat balanced on one of the piles of paper. He didn't appear to be doing anything.

'You made me jump,' I said. There was no sound from upstairs, nor any indication of where Raph might be.

'Mrs Cassingham, are you in the habit of leaving your children alone?'

I started to twist my fingers and stopped myself. Oh yes, I leave them alone and I swear at them and I push their faces into the mattress when they won't go to sleep, but for all that I don't want you take them away.

'You were here,' I said. 'You were here, and anyway Moth was asleep. Raph knew where I was. It's an island, for Christ's sake. It's not exactly crawling with heroin addicts and sex traffickers.' I stopped. My stomach turned. 'Why? Where are they?'

Ian MacDonald waited, and there was no sound from the space hopper or from Moth's room. He spoke, at last, to Moth's bowl of congealed porridge on the table in front of him.

'There are sensitivities on these islands, Mrs Cassingham, to profane language. If you prefer not to cause offence, you might find other ways of expressing yourself. And I would imagine that I know more than you do about the levels of criminal activity here, wouldn't you agree?'

'The children are all right,' I said. I bit my lip.

'Yes. I looked at Timothy a few minutes ago and my colleague has taken Raphael to see our boat. But Mrs Cassingham, the Highlands and Islands Police are not here to provide you with childcare, and while I cannot say what view Social Services might take of your leaving them, I'm sure we can agree that it would be better if there were no need to involve other agencies. Whatever your professional commitments, I suggest that you and your husband arrange care for your children as the first priority. You are not the first English family to come here with the idea that the islands are a refuge from your responsibilities.'

'I didn't—' I stopped. 'I was only gone a few minutes. I just needed—' I took a breath. 'I'm going to go find Moth now.'

I hope I got far enough up the stairs that Ian MacDonald couldn't hear me crying. I picked Moth up and held him tightly, still fast asleep, feeling the warmth of him and the reverberations of his heartbeat while I wept into his hair. I cannot do this, motherhood. I should not have had children.

I took notes, I don't know why. I opened a new file and called it 'Orchard Baby', and sat curled on the sofa with my laptop on a cushion and a glass of the claret Hugo left in the cellar at my side. At a Neolithic chambered tomb in Westray

> four neonates are among the latest burials at the site and are concentrated in the first two compartments. Two further separate burials of neonates in the cairn matrix occurred at a time when the monument was in an advanced state of decay and collapse. It has been suggested that the use of this somewhat derelict site for the disposal of neonates may indicate that some of these infants are, in fact, infanticide victims and that such sites were used for the burial of a specific category of 'unwanted dead'.
> – Nyree Finlay, 'Outside of Life: Traditions of Infant Burial in Ireland from Cillin to Cist', *World Archaeology*, Vol. 31, no. 3, pp. 407–22

I found I had not only electricity but a flicker of internet access. I lifted the laptop on to the sofa's arm and the signal strengthened enough for me to follow the citations. Excavations of Neolithic and Bronze Age tombs across the islands, from Skye to Orkney, are ongoing. There is the tomb here, out on the headland at the other end of the island, over the crest of the hill where it is not visible from anywhere except the beach below. Even the anchorite took up her station along the cliff, where her view of the sea was uninterrupted by matters of life and death. I took Raphael to our barrow two summers ago, when I was pregnant with Moth and content to have a holiday somewhere cooler than Oxford that didn't require flying, and we had a picnic and listened to the waves and the wind. It was a sunny day, so warm that we went paddling later, and we sat on the turf mound and talked about death while Moth pushed his feet into my hip joints and jabbed at my pubic bone.

I sipped my wine. The house was quiet and the police had taken the tent down, leaving a much bigger hole. Don't fill it, I told Ian MacDonald. We'll go ahead and plant a tree for her. We don't get the baby back for a proper burial, he told me when I asked. Not unless we turn out to be her closest living relations, he added thoughtfully. There are nothing like as many bodies in tombs on these islands as there were living inhabitants, suggesting that many of the dead are somewhere else, out to sea or lost, but it seems that Neolithic babies were mostly buried in the 'liminal spaces', at the edges and in the passageways, of tombs which served the whole community. Sixty per cent of the bodies in the one on Westray were new-born babies. They were stuffed vertically into gaps in the rubble that loosely covered the bodies of adults, which were bound in the foetal position and showed signs of having been subject to a series of rituals over several decades between death and what became, but perhaps was not meant to be, their final inhumation. The lead archaeologist commented in print that 'the place must have stunk when it was in use. With all those dead bodies, decomposing under loose coverings of stone and rubble' (Orkney Archaeological Trust, *Annual Report 2006*). There is speculation that such a high percentage of neonates among the dead indicates the widespread practice of infanticide. Several of the Neolithic tombs have staircases leading down into the earth, at the bottom of which there are signs of feasting, as if people used to go there to share their festivities with the dead. There were photos of the stairs, one with a cramped archaeologist in raingear peering up from the bottom. Our broch has never been excavated, although it is on Heritage Scotland's register. I remembered only curving turf and scattered pebbles, but I guessed that, if there had been a staircase, later residents would probably have blocked it. They go both ways, staircases, and who would want things creeping up and out into the night?

More wine. Darkness had fallen and I got up to draw the curtains. I used to mock Julia for the curtains, wholly unnecessary in rooms where no one sleeps and one can place absolute confidence in the absence of passers-by, but seeing myself and my electric light wavering over the wind-whipped orchard I saw the appeal of lined velvet. I went and stood in the hall, listening, repressed the urge to bolt the doors, and went back to the sofa. Bronze Age islanders, after the people who built the chambered tombs, lived in roundhouses. The things they left on the floors suggest that the occupants of roundhouses moved round them through the day, sleeping on platform beds of turf and heather in the northern half where small children's pee left traces that endure to this day, and working with food and leather goods and textiles in the south during the day. They seemed to have left the north-east quadrants empty, which made a kind of sense when human bodies, mostly those of babies and small children, were found under floor level in this section of each house. The Bronze Age people were not burying their children under the floor but building them into their houses; the bodies were interred after the walls were built but before the floors were laid. I thought again about the rough ground and scattered stones of the orchard, the stones in the wall that marks its edge. Building materials get reused all the time on these islands. Any of those stones might have been used in any number of dwellings over the centuries,

89

handled by any number of long-gone hands. Maybe we had come upon the rearranged remains of a Bronze Age round-house. Some of the children's bodies found under roundhouses seemed to have been stored in bags between death and burial, as if their families were keeping the body until they needed it for a new house, but others, particularly newborns, were buried immediately after death. Not, perhaps, so much the unwanted dead as the usefully dead.

Something fell, somewhere in the house. A stone down the chimney, one of the rubber ducks which have recently moved into Moth's cot on to the floor. I looked over my shoulder and then wished I hadn't, although there was nothing there, nothing even in the heavy Victorian mirror over the mantelpiece which meant that anything standing in the dark hall might see me before I saw it. I pulled my cardigan around me. I was sure the police must by now have some idea about the age of the bones, but I supposed there was no reason for them to confide in us. The problem with the Bronze Age idea was the blanket. None of the articles explicitly excluded knitting from a list of roundhouse activities, but I was fairly sure that if we'd found a Bronze Age knitted blanket we had reconfigured prehistoric archaeology at a stroke.

There were footsteps on the path and the front door opened.
'Giles?'

'No, a door-to-door mop salesman. Of course it's me, who were you expecting?'

Small wraiths from prehistory, of course. It had been raining for hours but his waxed jacket was almost dry.

'Giles, you haven't been with the puffins, have you? Where do you go?'

He stood in the doorway and looked at me as if he were an MP and I were a journalist.

'What do you mean, where do I go? Where do you think I'm going, to the pub?'

'Somewhere dry. Somewhere, at a wild guess, with lights.

Either you've found a cave and you've got a secret stash of candles or it's the cottage. Jesus, Giles, what are you doing in there?'

He sat down in the armchair as if someone had cut his string.

'It's only been a couple of evenings. I'm working on it.'

He was talking to the hearth rug, which still had dog hair on it from Julia and Hugo's last visit. I stroked the stem of my glass.

'On it or in it?'

'Does it matter?'

My head began to hurt. We have had this conversation too often. 'It matters to me.'

He stuck his chest out. 'So you want me to stop doing my job? You are writing your book, aren't you?'

He tilted his chin at the laptop.

'I'm trying to. I've been awake for nineteen hours and I'm still bloody working because it's the only chance I get, even though I know Moth's going to wake up any time now and that's it for another day. I can't do this, Giles, I can't keep going.'

I keep saying that, meanwhile providing evidence that I can. Giles paused by the door but did not turn round.

'I'm going to bed. I had another e-mail from that woman. Judith Fairchild. She's asking for three weeks at a fifty per cent discount. Says it's called a soft opening, or something. So they can tell us what needs improving for people paying full price.'

'Sounds a bit of a cheek.'

He shrugged. 'It's not as if anyone else wants it. And she might be right, at least this way she can't complain if we have overlooked something. Anyway, if she takes it they'll be here in two weeks.'

Dear Aubrey,

I know you will forgive my writing again when I say that,
without any postal deliveries these three weeks, I cannot tell if you
have answered mine or not, but in any case the illusion of your
paper company is a comfort to me as I sit here, wrapped in a blanket
at the fireside, my feet almost too hot on the fender. I have a peat
fire, a clear glow without the tricksy flickering of coal and wood,
which is perhaps as well, for Mrs Barwick has been entertaining me
with weird tales of selkies and the Grey People. Did you know
about the selkies? Sometimes at the full moon, men have seen
women dancing naked on the skerries (so far as I am aware, there is
no still on the island and I have certainly witnessed no drunkenness
but since I am, I fear, considered a Cassingham emissary it is not
likely I would know if there were). If you were to approach these
visions, you would find sealskins shed on the beach, and if you
were to take one of these skins, one of the dancing women would
become yours and would clean your house and bear your children
and obey your every word (this seems to be the extent of feminine
glory in Mrs Barwick's mind, but don't tell Mama), but if ever you
were to be so careless as to leave her skin where she might find it
she would creep back to the beach, perhaps leaving her human
infants crawling the stones and crying for her, and return to her
natural husband and children in the deep. Don't tell me your
imagination is unaroused by this tale. Do you not long to paint the
dancers, perhaps with the Northern Lights (which remain
obstinately invisible) providing discreet illumination?

Colsay must have been a very different place when you were here; the sea is dark and angry now and it is a mere article of faith that the heavens above Scotland are blue, for Colsay has been swaddled in grey since my arrival so that it is not even possible to see across the Sound, which is, I believe, a scant two miles across. For all I know we are quite alone in the world here, me and this people who do not want me. Forgive me, Aubrey, I am tired and a little discouraged, for it is a greater challenge to help these fiercely independent islanders, who seem to have no aspiration to anything different or better than the hardest of my work at home. I would not want you to think I find no pleasure in the task you have set me, however; there is beauty here, if not the beauty of sunlight and heather in bloom, and I know that when I succeed the pleasure will be in proportion to the endeavour. I remember that you have faith in me.

Think of me here, won't you, as you go about your life? I hope the new colours for the St John window are as we hoped and that Mrs Henderson likes herself as Penelope! What do you think of Alethea's decision? I am sure Mama is delighted but I will confide to you that if they all knew more of hospital life I believe they would at least reflect seriously on the step she is about to take.

Yours in faith,

May

6

ANXIOUSLY PREOCCUPIED
WITH OTHER MATTERS

When compared with the children in a control group, more of the injured children are found to be unwanted and unloved and/or to have a mother who, currently, is anxiously preoccupied with other matters, e.g. illness in herself or in others in the household, younger siblings, elderly relatives, or her own pregnancy. Similar findings for children who sustain burns are reported by Martin.

– John Bowlby, *Separation*, p. 175

There was a film of mist between the window and the sea, and the garden wall was dark with damp, the moss between the stones a rainforest shade of green.

'Mummy read it tiger!' Moth pushed the tiger book into my hand.

A seagull made wartime siren noises close by. My eyes closed.

'Mummy read it tiger!'

'One day,' I said. 'A little girl and her mummy were eating cake, because in those days you were allowed to give children cake every day and it helped to pass the time. Suddenly there was a knock on the door—'

'Big furry stripy tiger!' Moth wriggled with glee.

'Mummy, that's not what it says. Mummy, when I build the

system so the visitors can store their own energy from the gym, yeah, do you think I should make a meter that tells them how kilojoules convert into kilowatts?'

My head began to tip and I sat up. The seagull screamed of Messerschmidts over the white cliffs.

'What?' Warmth and darkness settled around me like a shawl.

'Mummy! Stop going to sleep. Would you like a meter that shows you how kilojoules make kilowatts?'

'More tiger!'

'"Good morning," said the Tiger. "I'm here to symbolize the excitement and danger that is missing from your life of mindless domesticity. May I have some of your cake?" "Please do," said the little girl's mummy. "Sit down."'

'Mummeee! You're getting it wrong, that's not what it says. I've worked out how to make the meter, only it's going to have quite a big carbon footprint, yeah, but I could set it so the first people have to make enough energy to offset that before they start being able to use it.'

'More tiger! Straight now!'

'And when everyone's got one, they can switch off the National Grid, yeah?'

'More tiger! Turn a page! Now!'

'Mummy, would you rather go forwards in time or back?'

Warmth again, and the womb-like pink behind my eyelids.

'Mummy! Stop sleeping like that. I can hear a phone.'

'More TI-GER!'

'Shh, Moth, it's all right. So the tiger came in and sat in Daddy's chair—'

'Mummy, there is a phone.'

'And the little girl's mummy said, "Take me, now." No there isn't. Not for about five miles.'

'Mummy, I can hear it.'

He was right.

'Never mind, it's only Daddy's mobile. They'll leave a message.'

Raphael looked around as if we'd heard a mosquito.

'It's on the dresser.' Giles's phone has better reception than mine. Raph climbed on to a wooden multi-storey garage to reach it. 'Hello, this is Raphael Cassingham. Oh. Hello. Sometimes she goes out to do her work but she's here now. Mummy, it's that policeman you don't like.'

He passed me the phone, which was sticky.

'Moth press a buttons! Moth phoning!'

'Mrs Cassingham, this is Ian MacDonald. I'd like to talk to you and your husband this afternoon, please. Around two o' clock.'

'Moth press a buttons!'

I leant away from Moth. 'I have no engagements. I'll do my best to locate Giles.'

'We'd be grateful, Mrs Cassingham.'

Surely they don't tell you if they're coming to arrest you? Wouldn't they just show up, probably in the middle of the night when they may imagine we'd be asleep?

I put Moth down and stood up. 'Come on, we'd better go find Daddy.'

'Moth done a poo.'

I changed Moth's nappy, compelled Raphael to put on his shoes and socks, persuaded Moth into his waterproofs by ceasing to sing a customized version of 'Puff the Magic Dragon' every time he stopped co-operating and told Raphael that I recommended a cagoule and waterproof trousers but he was at liberty to get wet if he preferred, which he did. The puffin colonies are at the other end of the island, between the village and the headland, where even our *Vorsprung durch Technik* pushchair can't handle the terrain. I went back into the kitchen and sacrificed a private hoard of chocolate biscuits against the moment Moth, who had used most of his breakfast to paint the table, recognized that hill-walking in heavy rain is a violation of the toddler's charter.

By the time we got there I was carrying Moth, whose crying

was muffled by wind and rain, and hoping Giles would come straight back with us. The village women, like my eighteenth-century subjects, could go only where they could carry their children, a limitation that seemed less outrageous as cold water seeped down my boots and shoulders and Moth's face reddened with rage. There would be advantages to being house-bound.

'Come *on*, Raph. The slower you go, the longer we have to be out here.'

The village women would have had no waterproofs, either. No Gore-Tex, no Velcro, no zips, just woollen skirts becoming steadily heavier and woollen shawls wet around their faces. Moth's fingers on my collar were turning blue.

'Raph, will you hurry *up*. Moth's freezing here.' I shifted Moth and pushed Raph forward. He stumbled against the heather and twisted away.

Then I saw Giles. He was lying on the ground at the edge of the cliff as if he'd already fallen from a height. I hadn't brought his phone, would have to leave him there and get the children back to the house, and once Raph saw him he wouldn't want to leave. We should have made wills. The island in trust to Raphael, the house in Oxford mine, back to nursery, sleep, the end of the war, I the only grown-up left standing. A life of single parenthood, of evenings of silence and hot chocolate, beckoned. We could eat fish fingers and tinned peaches without sin. How could I ever remarry with body and mind destroyed by small children?

'Daddy!'

Giles moved his head, waved like someone uninjured. An English gentleman to the end.

Raphael ran past me. 'Daddy! The police want you! And Mummy!'

Giles rolled over and stood up. 'What?'

I made lunch, cheese on toast, tomatoes and the end of the cucumber, apple slices and yoghurt. We were at least going to go to prison well nourished.

'Giles?' I tried to pick the skin off an apple slice. 'What would happen if we just got in the boat and went away? Over to Shepsay, I mean, or somewhere, and then when they'd gone we could get to the airport or go home or something.'

He frowned and looked at Raph, who was reading *Alternative Technologies for Family Homes* and crumbling his bread with the other hand.

'They'd think we'd done something that was worrying us, I presume. Are you going to get that child to sleep?'

Moth buried his head in my lap. 'Moth tired. Mummy's love.'

I picked him up and felt him soften against me. I stroked his cheek, still pink from the wind and rain, and he pressed my hand against his face. I'd been intending to ask Giles to settle him so I could brush my hair and find a top without baby snot and tomato seeds stuck to it to impress Ian MacDonald. I carried him upstairs.

Ian MacDonald was at the table by the time I came down. Giles had found the cafetiere and made coffee, and decanted milk into Julia's milk jug. I wondered if he also had access to her sugar crystal mine.

'Sorry to trouble you again, Mrs Cassingham. I was just explaining to your husband that we'd like to hear all that you know about who's been on this island.' He sipped his coffee. I heard the space hopper slapping on the wet flags outside.

I sat down. 'When? There've been people here for three millennia.'

He exchanged glances with Giles as if they were the grown-ups.

'We don't usually concern ourselves with anything over seventy years old, Mrs Cassingham.'

'I'm not Mrs Cassingham.' I'd meant not to antagonize him, not to be taken away from my children in the back of a police motor launch. Which, come to think of it, would be relatively easy to capsize once we got out into Colla Sound.

Giles looked out of the window, where Raphael's hair flew in and out of shot. The rain had nearly stopped.

'The head of my family bought it in the middle of the nineteenth century. I can check the exact date if you want. The McColls had to sell it to cover some debt and my' – he counted on his fingers – 'great-great-great-great-grandfather had just made a lot of money on the railways. It should have gone into another branch – my grandfather was a younger son – but his brothers were both killed in the war. I think the younger one maybe owned it for about a year, but he was somewhere in north Africa and I doubt he ever saw it. Then towards the end of the war I think it was used for children's holiday camps or evacuees or something, and then it came down to my grandfather and then to Pa and now me.'

Giles makes good coffee. My thoughts were beginning to lose the underwater quality of extreme tiredness. 'Children's holiday camps?' I asked.

It seemed unlikely. Even in peacetime, getting the huddled masses of Glasgow out to Colsay would be almost as difficult as feeding them once they were here, and in any case the journey would pass a great many more suitable locations for fresh air and communal jollity where bombs were no more likely than here. The North Atlantic was no haven.

Giles frowned. Ian MacDonald's pen waited.

'I really don't know any more about it. Only that the house needed some work after they left. The evacuees, or whatever.'

'I take it your grandparents have passed away?' Ian MacDonald rolled the pen between his fingers.

'Thirty years ago. My father and his father both had children late in life.'

Ian MacDonald made a note. Admits to being a late baby.

'Institutions have records,' I said. 'Always.'

Institutions have also sometimes allowed people to dispose of inconvenient individuals, even – or especially – small ones.

'I could find out.' I slid my fingers into the handle of my

99

cup. Julia's cup, actually, bone china, so thin you can see the coffee from the outside, the ornate handle a tight fit for two plebeian fingers. 'Giles, do you know anything more about it? Where they were from? How long they stayed? Who let them stay?'

'Thank you, Mrs Cassingham, we will make our own enquiries. And after the war, Mr Cassingham? Your family used the island as a holiday home, is that right? After the local people left.'

Ian MacDonald was looking at his notebook. His shoulders were set. I sipped my coffee.

'Local people, Mr MacDonald?'

His shoulders twitched. 'Those who were born here.'

As opposed to Giles, presented to the world under sterile drapes in a private maternity home in Sussex. Giles gulped coffee. It would be interesting to see the Old Boys of Eton lined up and held to account for their ancestral sins of colonialism. There would be a trove of vacant Oxford Fellowships.

'Yes,' said Giles. 'We used it for holidays.' His face reddened. 'There is still no mains gas, sewerage or telephone here, Mr MacDonald. The younger people had been leaving since the nineteenth century. There were only a couple of households left by the end of the war, weren't there? That's no way to live. And one family went to Australia – paid for, I might add, by my grandfather – and my father remembered the last couple here. He liked them. He thought they liked him. And he didn't take any rent. And of course when the husband died in the early '70s his wife went to live with relatives. She didn't want to be here alone. My father *discussed* it with her. Made sure she knew she could stay on if she wanted to. And her children, if they wanted to come back.'

She wouldn't have been alone, not with the chambered cairns and the churchyard with its names and dates and the baby in the orchard. She could have stood out on the hillside and heard the wind singing and looked across to the nearest living people in the matchbox houses at Colla. She could have slept as if she were dead.

'I know that, Mr Cassingham. The lady was Mrs McAlpin and the family who went to Australia now own a catering business in Melbourne. The daughter was back here last year. And then?'

'You'd have to ask my mother for the detail. My parents married in 1969. There are photos of them here, before I was born, and we came at least once a year from when I can remember.'

'You were born in 1971? And you're the first child?'

Giles leant back in his chair. 'As your informants have told you, clearly.'

The bouncing outside stopped. I waited for the front door. Julia? Could Julia, who had not allowed us to share a bedroom under her roof until we were married, have slipped up? If she had, it would be in character that she would give birth silently and equally silently dispatch evidence of the offence. But, unless I went for a complex scenario in which Julia was secretly pregnant by someone other than Hugo before marriage and managed to conceal the fact until delivering and silencing the baby on honeymoon, the time during which it would have been disastrous for her to be pregnant was the time before she had access to her husband's island. Raph had still not appeared.

'Excuse me. I just want to check what Raphael is doing.'

Ian MacDonald lifted his coffee cup. 'I am glad to hear it.'

I stood on the doorstep. The air was clear and smelt of sea. The space hopper was rolling in the wind, incongruous as a party balloon against the stones and wind-bent trees.

'Raphael?'

I went round the corner. He was sitting at the edge of the grave site.

'Raph, what are you doing?'

He looked round. 'Thinking about death.'

I squatted down next to him. 'And what were you thinking?'

'Nothing. Like being dead.'

'Oh.' The burlap from around the saplings, come from Iceland on our promise, blew across the field. I remembered what the good mother is meant to say to elicit further confidences. 'How does that make you feel?'

He shrugged. 'Probably not dead, because dead doesn't feel like anything, does it?'

Alas, poor Yorick. Raph's wrists, sticking out from his favourite pink and blue striped top, were mottled purple.

'Raph?' I touched his shoulder. 'I'm sorry I pushed you. When we went to get Daddy. I shouldn't have done that.'

'You hurt me,' he said.

The wind lifted my hair and rain began to spatter the apple trees, which still looked like dead sticks.

'I'm sorry. I was tired and anxious but I should have controlled myself.' I say this kind of thing as if it makes me a better parent than my mother, who did not – does not – apologize or admit weakness or error. But I fear it only makes me a different kind of bad parent, a weak and apologetic kind.

I hesitated. My mother told me, when I asked, that dead people turned into angels and celebrated with God in Heaven. I imagined a kind of soft-focus birthday party taking place on a cloud, where winged blonds dangled their feet over the abyss like the lunching construction workers in the poster and ate cheese and pineapple cubes and chocolate fingers under the gaze of God the albino Santa Claus. We are not parents who have been able to be convincing about Santa Claus, and Raph – perhaps as a result – is less gullible than I was. It was probably too late to attempt such a tale about death, even if I thought I could be convincing.

'Raph, you know some people think being dead is another kind of being alive, don't you?

He looked up. 'Yeah. But they're wrong. You said there aren't any ghosts.'

'No. They're just in stories.' Raph doesn't like stories, doesn't

102

see the point of fiction. Rain dripped off my hair onto my eyelids.

'Why don't you come inside and do some more work on that generator? The carbon-neutral gym?'

He stood up. 'It's not carbon-neutral because of the manufacture. You can't actually make something like that carbon-neutral, you just have to design it so it puts back more than it takes out over a certain number of years. Is that policeman going to take you away?'

He sounded almost hopeful. We made for the back door. 'No,' I said. 'Of course not. Whatever made you think that?'

If Ian MacDonald took me away, it would be to somewhere I could sleep. I could lie on a pallet under a fluorescent light and sleep, or on a concrete bunk beside a toilet and sleep. Ian MacDonald had gone. It was time to wake Moth and change his nappy and read simple tales of women brought to inanity by the systematic denial of economic independence and hang out the laundry if the rain stopped and hear a monologue about fuel-injection systems and change Moth's nappy and wipe down the kitchen counters and cook a meal and throw most of it away and wash everyone's hands and wipe the counters. There were five hours and three minutes before I could take Moth for his bath, six hours and thirty-three minutes until Raphael could legitimately be denied any further conversational opportunities until morning.

'Giles? Is there any chance at all you could look after the kids for an hour and let me sleep? Just an hour? I'm so tired I keep cutting myself, look, and I was dropping off on the floor this morning, wasn't I, Raph?'

Raph wasn't there. I showed Giles the cuts on my fingers where I'd kept missing the tomatoes before lunch. He raised an eyebrow, ran his glance down my jeans. He looked round for Raph.

'Only if you'll have sex with me later.'

'I need to work. You know I do.'

'OK. No deal.'

'Giles! I shouldn't have to bargain with you to look after your own bloody children for one hour.'

Raphael put his head round the door. 'We're not bloody children.'

'No, love, you're lovely. Sorry. I'm tired.'

'I should think so.' He disappeared again.

I yawned. Sleep closed in on me.

'All right,' I said to Giles. 'Fine. If you want bought sex you can have it. Wake Moth now. Don't wake me before half-past three and hang the laundry up or you won't have any clean pants. And I reserve the right to lie still and think of the Bodleian Library while you do all the work.'

He stood up and patted my bottom as I went by. 'Excellent news.'

I will sell myself, it turns out, not for tenure but for an hour's sleep.

It was dark when I woke, and the house was silent. The sea was breaking rocks on the beach, audible even over the rain on the windows, and there was a warm hump at the other side of the bed. I turned my head cautiously, hoping the night might still be young with many more hours of potential sleep ahead. 11:57. I stretched out and lay watching the voile panels wavering like ghosts. No one was asking me to do anything and it was possible that no one would ask me to do anything for several hours. I arranged my hair more comfortably off my neck. The idea that Giles had managed to feed and bathe both children and put them to bed was like discovering that a house plant (which we do not have, I do enough damage to my children without having plants to neglect as well) had made a cake while I was at work. It had potential. Unless, of course, he had not fed them, bathed them and put them to bed. I slid out from under the duvet, managed not to moan at the shock of the cold floor under my feet. Giles had forgotten to wrap whichever item of clothing came to hand around the doorhandles to muffle the latch, which can wake Moth. At least if he woke I'd know he was alive. I eased our door open, stepped over the creaky floorboard and sidled up to Moth's room. Yes. A small shape under the blanket, a fan of dark hair on the pillow. I went in and rested a hand on his shoulder. He snuffled and shifted and I froze until his breathing lapped gently on the shore. I unbent slowly and followed the choreography for leaving the room.

Light fell on the wall of the landing in a way I couldn't remember having seen before. I shivered, managed not to glance behind me despite the sudden certainty that I was being watched. The stairs gaped into the darkness of the hall. I wanted to go back, to guard Moth.

Raphael used to sleep through engineering works carried out on the railway line outside his open window in the small hours of the morning. I went in and sat on the bed. He lay as if he'd been dropped on top of the duvet, the array of engineering textbooks around him counter-evidence of a gentler passage to sleep. There was food around his mouth, something red, and garlic on the air. Fed, if not washed. I stroked his hair and shoulder, surprisingly warm, and sat there watching him breathe, the curve of his cheek against the pink trelliswork of the pillowcase, his ribcage, the bones formed in my body, rising and falling. I lifted his hair and kissed his forehead, rested my cheek against his face. I am never sure about the legitimacy of these stolen caresses, taken like sexual harassment for my pleasure rather than his. I touched the back of his neck, where there is a seam of red-gold hair that women will, in later years, want to kiss. It is a pity that by the time our children wake up we love them less.

I crept back along the hall. A board creaked in the floor above. The bedroom door snicked as I closed it.

'Hey, you.'

Damn.

'Thanks for letting me sleep.' I got back in and huddled in a ball.

'Cold? Come here. Did Moth wake?'

'No. I was just checking on them. Did you lock up?'

He folded himself round me. I shivered again.

He stroked my shoulder, muffled by an anachronistic fabric known as flannelette. 'I am capable of putting them to bed, you know.'

I straightened out, and regretted it as my feet dipped into the half-frozen pond that seems to form in the lower half of the bed. 'How on earth would I know? You never do.'

He ran his hand down to my waist. 'When you went to Montreal I did. Hell, Anna, it's not gravitational physics, putting children to bed.'

'No,' I said. 'Well, it wouldn't be, would it? I mean, women have been doing it for centuries. It can't possibly be hard.'

His hand moved down. 'Don't start that.'

I pushed it back. 'Don't start that.'

'You said we could have sex.'

I pulled my nightdress down and wrapped my feet in it. 'I changed my mind.'

He started to kiss the back of my neck. I had forgotten about that. He lifted my hair and blew on my ear. I shivered. His fingers traced my collarbone and I turned my head.

'So why should I believe you next time?'

His hand came round and began to work on the buttons, of which there are many.

'Next time I might not change my mind.'

He spoke into my belly. 'Not when you remember this time.'

Night Waking: 03:11

Moth is screaming. The ten steps to his room pass too slowly, the hall still dark as the grave. He is standing, rigid, grasping the bars. I pick him up but he is too stiff to cuddle and his sleeping bag is damp with sweat. Maybe he has a fever. Maybe he has meningitis. We'll need the helicopter. I can't go to a hospital in a helicopter wearing a stained nightdress. Pack his teddy. And lots of books. I pat his back.

'Come on, love. You're all hot. Let's have your bag off. Sit on Mummy's lap.'

The room is full of grey light and colours are coming back. Freed from his sleeping bag, he wraps his arms and legs round me and snuffles into my neck.

'Mummy sing a Gruffalo.'

Maybe not meningitis. I stroke his hair.

'Gruffalo sleeping. Night time.'

'Mummy sing a Gruffalo!'

Maybe not even spectres.

'Not now. Moth sleeping.'

His face is cooler.

'Bag off. Morning time!'

I could, actually, get up, having had more time asleep, or at least in bed, than I have since before Raphael was born. What time would Giles have put them to bed? If I get him up now, he will sleep later and I will be able to work. On the other hand, if I get him up now he will want to get up at four for the next three months.

'Come on, love. Back in your bed. Night time.'

'Gruffalo!'

I lean over the cot and begin again. 'A mouse took a stroll through the deep, dark wood . . .'

I remember earlier and certain muscles contract. I had forgotten what it is like with Giles. We should do that more often. And he should put the children to bed more often. I would win on both counts.

'Owl, Mummy. Owl but no.'

'I'm going to have tea with a gruffalo. A gruffalo, what's a gruffalo? A gruffalo, why, didn't you know? He has . . .'

Do I love Giles? A question, I have thought for some time,

best not asked once there are children at stake. What am I going to do, leave? With my fixed-term contract and a salary that barely covers childcare? I once defined love as meaning that you would die for the beloved. Not a chance. The children would cope better without him than without me. Do, in fact, cope without him. We all know that sex and love are not the same, although in marriage, it occurs to me, sex might be an adequate if unusual substitute. I used to know I loved him because I spent time on things – fresh figs with Parma ham from his preferred delicatessen, removing hair from my big toes, getting his photographs of Colsay framed – intended to please him and, giving no thought to reward, was happy that he was happy. He used, come to think of it, to bring me flowers on Fridays and maintain a supply of my preferred, expensive bath salts, the last of which ran out some time before Moth was born. I don't do things for him any more and if I did it would be by prior negotiation and I would want to be paid back in childcare. Would I cry for the rest of my life if he died? (It is almost light enough to read now, but Moth is pretending, perhaps to himself, to be asleep.) No. No, I wouldn't. I murmur my way through *The Gruffalo* one more time and make my way downstairs.

The wind had fallen, but waves were still lumbering on to the beach and water that was not quite rain hung in the air. The sun stood over the horizon, papery and provisional, as if it had not yet been glued in place. My laptop case banged on my legs as I tried not to spill my tea on the wet grass. The cottage, at least on the inside, was beginning to look like something out of one of my mother's magazines, and I could see that we would have to ban the children from its glossy floors and white curved walls. I settled on the floor in front of the full-height corner window from which we were encouraging visitors to 'watch the wild Atlantic rolling on to the beach at your doorstep'. The satellites, or whatever they are, were auspicious and the computer had connected before I'd got bored of watching the column of seagulls over the village. I was planning to read through chapter three for the last time, but first I went to EBSCO and searched 'Colsay + World War Two'. Nothing. I tried again with 'Colsay + wartime'. Something about naval charts. 'Colsay + evacuees'. Nothing. And surprisingly little about evacuees in general. I put the laptop down and straightened my legs. Outside, a sparrow-sized bird with black and white Finnish designer plumage pecked an invisible breakfast from the stones, its legs so thin that they must be made of something finer than bone. I wondered if evacuees were under-researched, whether anyone would fund the kind of project a historian of childhood might undertake. I could travel around the country on my own and interview old ladies over cups of tea and cake, and maybe some of them, in between extolling the re-use of dripping and the moral benefits of aerial bombardment, would tell me how to raise functional children and sustain marriage without resentment. The bird hopped closer to the window and peered in like someone with doubts about a restaurant. I'd need a tape recorder, of course, or the hi-tech equivalent, which meant it was really a sociology project. Historians are people who are more comfortable in the company of the dead.

Colsay House

1st Nov.

Dear Miss Emily,

I write in some excitement, having just heard from Mrs Grice
an extraordinary tale. I went to her house this afternoon as I have
been doing from time to time, and found her somewhat
distracted with three children under her feet, her house in greater
disarray than usual and what had no doubt before the children
seized on them been careful piles of dead birds about the place,
each with its neck broken and the heads swinging crazily as the
two older ones, who are, I think, her sister's children, tossed
them about. I have often found at home that help at such times
can elicit confidences sturdily withheld by mothers over weeks
and months of visiting at more orderly moments, so I scolded
the children and asked if they were not ashamed to treat their
mother so in her condition, assuring them that in the civilized
world any child who behaved so would be soundly punished. I do
not know if they understood my words, but they certainly
received the general import and slunk out into the rain, no doubt
in search of further mischief. 'They have done their work,' Mrs
Grice said sullenly, as if I had chided her. 'It's not so bad if the
bairns have high spirits sometimes.' I took the bird from the
youngest child, who was fingering its eyes and opening and
shutting its beak while the tail draggled excrement on to what
one might hesitate to call his clothing, and offered him instead a
pasteboard book of the sort that I often give to the slum
children at home. Mrs Grice sat down, appearing, as much as I
could tell in the low light, drawn and grey. She allowed me to

110

take her pulse, which was fast, and to bring her a drink of water. I asked her to instruct me in the plucking of fowl, which is not, as you may well believe, a task in which I have any expertise! It was of course uncongenial work, but worth the result.

She disclosed under careful questioning that the 'knee-woman', whose name she still refuses to confide, has certain rituals or tricks carried out both before and after the birth. Neither mother nor child may be left alone until after the infant is baptized, for the 'trows' or – but I may have misheard – 'hildufolk' will cause the mother to die and exchange the baby for one of their own if they find them unguarded (apparently the hildufolk have particular need of young mothers to suckle both trow and changeling children). A 'trowie' child is hard to feed, cries incessantly, may have strange features or physical peculiarities and, if not returned to its natural parents, will usually die in the first year of life (God knows I have seen enough such in Manchester – would that the Grey People were the only cause of such infant misery!). I asked if those who died from the eight-day sickness were trowie babies and she shrugged; some might be, some not – it is still possible for carefully guarded infants to die. I asked what is done to prevent these exchanges and she showed me a knife or dagger stuck into the wooden lintel over the door; trows will not pass an iron blade, and, for extra security given their particular predilection for the new-born, the 'knee-woman' brings with her an effigy of a child, which the mother nurses while her neighbours care for the real infant in the days after delivery, the idea being that the trows (who are clearly not possessed of much intelligence despite their startling powers) will take the doll. Before confinement, the pregnancy must not be spoken of or referred to in any way lest the Grey People overhear. It is unfortunate that I did not know this earlier, for it is a rule that I have inevitably broken in the course of my work, and it seems cruel indeed, especially to women awaiting their first confinement who suffer greatly from the denial of experienced advice (I have several times assisted at childbeds where it became clear that the young mother did not understand how the child would leave her

111

body until the process was complete). I gather this is also one of the reasons why it is not customary for the expectant mother to prepare little clothes, lest the hildufolk see her at work and understand what she awaits, but then surely it should devolve on the neighbours to make these preparations on her behalf?

I took up another bird, she having taken the first from me after plucking six or seven herself, and asked if the need to keep the child from the Grey People required any particular treatment of the cord. No, she said. The knee-woman will be doing nothing but what is natural and necessary and now it is time to be preparing the meal for the men will be cold and hungry when they return. I took the hint (!) and made my way back here, where indeed Mrs Barwick had my supper on the table – it is dark so early now that one quite forgets the time, but I suppose that must be just the same with you in Edinburgh as here, though at least you have the gaslights and of course the city clocks. I believe the clock on the mantelshelf here to be the only one on Colsay, and would you believe when I arrived it had been stopped for years, with no one knowing the time at all!

I am not sure quite how to take these tales of 'trows' (trolls?). Can it possibly be the case that, while we can govern an empire on which the sun never sets and bring education and rational thinking to poor people from India to the New Zealand savages, there are still British subjects going in fear of elves? But I suppose that as long as they live in dark, unventilated stone huts and remain illiterate there are no depths of superstition that should surprise us, and truly, the conditions of life here are distressing to observe.

I remain yours most sincerely,

May Moberley

112

7

THE ABILITY TO DEFEND ONESELF

It is a known fact, though perhaps not sufficiently stressed, that the ability to defend oneself develops later than the ability to attack.

– Anna Freud, *Infants Without Families: Reports on the Hampstead Nurseries, 1939–1945* (New York: International Universities Press, 1973), p. 570

The kitchen seemed brighter than usual, as if someone had adjusted the resolution of my screen, and I thought I would deal with the piles of paper after Giles had gone out. And phone the library and local archive centre in Colla to arrange a visit, and maybe clean the fridge, especially the salad drawer, whose contents had reached a stage where they could be emptied straight into a flowerbed without need for an interlude on the compost heap. And cook something proper for supper, maybe even the kind of thing normally accompanied by potatoes, and then some child-centred project of the sort that I used to pay nursery to do, papier mâché (out of Giles's *Guardian* archive), or a collage of leaves and feathers, or gingerbread men, though the first and last time we tried gingerbread (ecologically sound Christmas tree decorations) it

113

stuck so resolutely to the baking sheets that I hid the whole lot in next door's bin and bought new baking sheets on my way home from work the next day. We could make paper dragons out of Julia's hoard of used wrapping paper, or accelerate the next trip to Colla by printing with the potatoes, or – the rain being not quite heavy enough to fall – I could take the children round the village and explain eighteenth-century life, or even to the headland and pass on my new-found knowledge of Neolithic burial practices. Not being tired was almost like not having children, or like taking recreational drugs, in terms of imagining creative and educational experiences we might share. I began to stack papers, as if aligning the edges were the first step towards order.

'What would you like to do today?' I asked.

Raph looked up. 'Can I play on your computer?'

Moth handed me *Lucy and Tom's Day*. 'Mummy read it.'

I took the book. 'No, Raph.'

'Why?'

I put the book down and picked up another pile of paper. It would, I thought, be much quicker to recycle them all than to make the usual subsidiary piles, which after all only sit very slowly decomposing on the kitchen table.

'Mummy read it!'

'Why, Mummy?'

I thought about why. Because I don't want you to. Because I don't want your grubby fingers on my nice clean keyboard, adorned so far with the detritus of chocolate stolen from you and the odd drop of claret. Because I think of my laptop as part of my mind and you do quite enough buggering around in there. I opened one of the big recycling bags provided by Oxford City Council.

'Because I'd like to do something with you, and because those games encourage you not to think about other people.'

'Moth in a bag?'

'No, love. Absolutely not.'

114

'Read *Lucy and Tom*!'

I dumped an armful of bureaucracy into the bag.

'But I don't like thinking about other people.'

'Mummy read it!'

'Just a minute.'

I held the bag open under the table and swept all the papers off the edge. A cup in which islands of blue mould floated on what was once tea rolled off the edge of the table.

'Oh Mummy! Bugger a tea.'

I picked up the cup, and on second thoughts added it to the bag. When it's my turn to take the rubbish over, I sometimes dump the recycling bag in landfill anyway, just for the thrill.

'That's why it's good for you. All right, Moth. Once upon a time there were two little children called Lucy and Tom. This is a picture of them in the early morning.'

'You said we could choose what to do and now you're doing Moth's thing and not mine! It's not fair.'

'Lucy is big enough to get out of bed and put on her slippers and her red dressing gown. Tom sleeps in a cot. He throws all his toys out, one by one – bump – on to the floor. I didn't say you could choose, I asked what you'd like. Three people usually call at Lucy and Tom's house before breakfast, the paper boy, the milkman and the postman. Lucy is scraping the last bit of porridge out of her bowl.'

'But now you're doing what Moth chose and you won't let me do what I chose.'

A better mother would have them cutting out dragon scales by now.

'Raphael, for goodness' sake stop whining like that. I'm offering to play with you. Think of something we'll all enjoy. After breakfast, Lucy is very busy helping her mother about the house.'

'You just keep reading that stupid book and tidying up and you won't ever do what I want.'

Moth pointed at Raphael. 'No shouting at Mummy! Raph being very boring.'

'I am not being boring! Mummy, he called me boring!'

'No shouting at Moth!'

'He's not shouting at you, darling. And I really don't spend all my time tidying up. Raph, you're just wasting time we could be spending doing something fun. We could do potato printing, or make a dragon collage, or we can go look at the village.'

I picked up a tea-towel with brown stains and discovered that it was concealing a pile of Giles's smug organic lifestyle magazines, which even he doesn't actually read, although I suspect him of leaving them in the kitchen in the hope that I will follow the recipes. I added them to the bag.

'I don't want to look at the bloody village. If they'd built it properly it wouldn't have fallen down.'

I made a final effort.

'We can go look and see if we can work out why it fell down.'

'I want to play on your computer.'

'More reading!'

The sink was surrounded by empty jars awaiting recycling, some of which had been there since we were here last summer and none of which had been properly rinsed. I tumbled them on top of the magazines, and was then inspired to remove from the cupboard several jars which we appeared to be keeping out of a superstition – originated, I feared, by Julia – that minute scrapings of Marmite and mustard might be capable of parthenogenesis if left to themselves for long enough.

'Mummy read it!'

'I said, I want to play on your computer.'

I knotted the bag.

'At half-past ten, the children have a drink and a biscuit. If it is fine, they go into the garden.'

'Mummy, I said I want to play on your computer!'

'And I said you can't. Why don't we make a card for Daddy's birthday?'

Moth waved his arms. 'Cake an' candles! Pick Moth up!'

Giles's birthday wasn't for another month, but I could imagine the manufacture of a card taking that long.

Raph slammed his book on to the floor. 'Because it would be crap.'

'Raph, come on. We've talked about this. It's better if you don't use words like that.'

'You do.'

I put Moth down and he sat on the floor and leafed through *Building Bridges*. 'I know I do sometimes, but people get offended when children swear.'

'Why?'

'Oh, Raph, I don't know, they just do. Because they like thinking children are innocent.'

'What's innocent?'

I like this kind of conversation. Conversationally, sometimes, I'm a good mother.

'It means either you haven't done anything wrong or you haven't meant to do anything wrong. It's the opposite of guilty. I think it comes from Latin. Daddy would know.'

'What does that have to do with saying "crap"?'

There was the sound of tearing paper. I grabbed Raphael as he lunged.

Raph pounced, fists raised. 'Mummy, he's torn my book! Mummy, I hate him, I don't want a little brother any more! I'm going to hit him!'

Moth looked up, half a page waving in a damp hand and apparently unmoved by his brother's onslaught. 'Oh dear, Raph being very boring again.'

'No, Moth, no tearing. No tearing books. Poor Raphael. Give me that page, Moth. Raph, I know you're very angry but we don't hit people, do we?'

117

Moth waved the page at the window and giggled. I wedged Raphael under my arm and he kicked at the Cassingham ancestral armchair. Just under eleven hours until bedtime and no papier mâché or gingerbread in sight.

When Giles came back I was stirring yoghurt into Moth's soup so it contained some calories. Giles put his arm round my waist and kissed me.

Raph watched. 'Daddy, why did you do that?'

'What?'

'Kiss Mummy.'

'I always kiss Mummy. Shall I kiss you too?'

'Kiss Moth! Lunch nearly ready!' shouted Moth.

'No, you don't kiss Mummy.'

Moth's soup was now too liquid for him to manage and I was already behind on the laundry. I crumbled some bread into it, making the kind of mess that no one over the age of three would be asked to eat, even by me. Raphael was right, Giles doesn't kiss Mummy.

Giles sat down. There was no birdshit on his shoes or clothes.

'Anna, are you remembering that the Fairchilds are coming at the end of the week? I've ordered extra soap and loo paper but we still need some books over there and I'm afraid some-one's going to have to make up the beds and put out towels and such. And I told her we'd supply the basic groceries, salt and oil and so on.'

I put his bowl in front of him. Vegetable soup, made with vegetables and water. Heinz do these things better, because that's what they get paid for. 'By "someone" and "we" do you by any chance mean "Anna"? And would "and so on" happen to take out any stray hours of research time?'

'I'm pretty busy, you know. And it is in your interest as well to make this work, now we've sunk all that money. Jake says the painting will be done and dry in time but there are bound to be snags.'

118

I put my own bowl down and took a deep breath. Moth was putting handfuls of soup on his face. I felt like eating about as much as I felt like putting on a frilly pinny and skipping about with a feather duster.

'Oh, so this is about the destiny of the son and heir, is it? And my obligation to sacrifice my foolish little ideas about writing for the greater glory of the Cassingham dynasty.'

He put his head in his hands like a husband in a 1930s farce. 'No. It's just about us making our project work, that's all. You and me, remember? Our project for our island. That we worked on all year. That was, actually, your idea. That's all it's about.'

'Oh.'

There was a silence.

Raphael took the last spoonful of his soup and left the room with his bread and butter. Blue sky showed through a hole high in the mounds of cloud outside, and I could see Jake's boat cutting a white furrow across the sea. Off to the mainland for supplies. Again.

I turned my spoon over in the bowl. 'I'm sorry. I shouldn't have said that. I'm just so worried I'm going to lose everything.'

'Not everything. Not, for example, me or the kids. You just might not get another academic job straight away.'

Moth yawned and looked surprised.

'Come on, love. Let's have that top off. And we'll find you a clean one and then time to go have a sleep, OK?'

I rolled his top off so the soup didn't transfer to his hair, wiped his hands and face and picked him up. He patted my face. 'Mummy very sweet.'

I kissed him.

Giles watched us for a moment. 'I'll take him up, if you like. Have your lunch. Then maybe we could go over together and talk about what we need to do before Saturday.'

'OK,' I said. I sat down.

'Mummy,' said Moth.

'It's all right, love. Daddy take you up.'

'Daddy?' Moth held my gaze over Giles's shoulder as he went off down the hall. I should have gone to find Raphael, but I sat at the table, gazing at the patterns of the children's spilt soup and listening intently to the note of guilt twanging somewhere at the back of my mind. I have sinned, yes, I have put not just the recycling but the charity bags in landfill, because it's easier than taking them to the shop. I have never cleaned a fridge. I have twice slapped Raph and once put newborn Moth down to sleep on his front in the half-hope that he would not wake up. I have kept an extra ten pound note when given too much change in a perfectly pleasant restaurant. But there were other things too, reverberating just out of sight. I shook my head, as if to get water out of my ear, and started to stack the plates.

While the influence of Rousseau on literary treatments of childhood in this period is obvious and well documented, it is interesting that there is little evidence of his work having any effect on the lives of children. Children's experience is notoriously difficult to reconstruct, but the childcare manuals studied in this chapter, taken together with accounts of the foundling hospitals and boarding schools, suggest an era in which, contrary to prevailing Romantic ideology and the practice of a very few experimental childcare practitioners such as Dorothy Wordsworth, the days of children living away from their birth families were assiduously managed to conform to immovable routines, with very limited variation or stimulus beyond prescribed and authorized activities. As ever, it seems that the relationship between the theory and practice of parenthood may be inverse.

The middle sentence was too complicated. I sat for too long looking at 'suggest an era in which' and then stretched until my shoulders cracked. Darkness peered in through the window. I could hear Giles reading to Raphael upstairs, something about space travel and computers with gold lettering on the front, and I could hear the sea, which was beginning to calm down. I needed a footnote for 'well documented', even though anyone who had read anything at all on the subject would know it was true. A footnote, at least, would push me closer to the word limit, which was more of a word goal. I typed 'See, for example' and then gazed at the screen. I use a photo of the children as my wallpaper, not because I like looking at it but to remind me that my time is limited and I mustn't mess around, and Moth's feet stuck out from under the footnote. I wondered about making a cup of tea or, better, finding another bottle of Hugo's claret. And maybe some chocolate. Though if Giles found me foraging in the kitchen he might reasonably conclude that work was less pressing than I had claimed. There was a cluster of lights out at sea, signifying a container ship making its stately way to or from America, a great floating car park carrying plastic toys in their impenetrable packaging and new shoes nesting in tissue paper, the frozen corpses of lambs from the green hills of New Zealand and tuna fish that had nosed the seaweed of the tropics, a cornucopia of the unnecessary topped by small cabins where men had distilled their possessions down to the truly essential and lived, like the hermit, without the tangles of objects and demands that snare most of us. I let my chair thud forward and Googled 'ww2 Colsay evacuees'. Google is no way to conduct academic research.

People have been generating history on purpose. The archive held more than five thousand first-person accounts of evacuated children, which are either oxygen for the next generation of historians or an obfuscation of the historical record. History is a retrospective that needs to be partial and fragmentary if we are to make any sense of it. There is no story in the muddle and pain of real life, rolling from century to century in births, couplings and deaths distinguished only by the settings and costumes in which we enact them, only a twisted familiarity. I tried and failed to imagine the mess that would

121

result if every Pict had tweeted an account of Roman occupation, every Roman his or her own personal narrative of the decline and fall, every Saxon peasant a full and frank account of conversion to Christianity, every Viking farmer the detail of the theft of every Saxon cow. If every human presence on this planet left a story. A written record that is a mere simulacrum of real life in all its trivia and futility is worse than nothing; it seemed suddenly possible that social networking sites are in fact the end of History. Which is not of immediate concern to an eighteenth-century specialist. Two clicks later I had found what I was looking for.

The Castle School's wartime location was even more beautiful than our usual abode. The owners of Colsay House on the island of Colsay off the north-west coast of Scotland offered their house to Miss Leach for the duration (it was only years later that it occurred to me that they might have thought it better to offer it to a genteel girls' school than have their house requisitioned for military training or some such). Getting there was such an adventure for us! Most of us had never been so far north, and of course the trains were just a joke during the war – there wasn't really a timetable at all and they were so slow and you could never ever get a seat. There was blackout by then and I remember me and my friend Mabel sitting on my suitcase telling ghost stories and getting sillier and sillier as we got more tired, until in the end a man told Miss Leach that if she couldn't keep us quiet he was going to pull the cord and stop the train. And then we were in some kind of hostel in Edinburgh, and then another train and I think we walked the last bit, because petrol was so hard to get, and then at the end a boat. I've grandchildren of my own now and it makes me shiver to think of those two poor women shepherding thirty girls on that journey, but it was wartime and you just did what you had to do.

Anyway, I still remember that first morning. It had been dark when we arrived but we woke up and you could just tell from the light that we were by the sea, and we all ran out in our pyjamas! It was only September, of course, and such a bright day – we didn't know then that it would be the last time we saw the sun for weeks. The house was lovely, solid stone, but even so it was a terrible winter and we all had chilblains. We used to sit in lessons wrapped in blankets sometimes, but of course if anyone complained they got told to think about what our fathers and brothers were enduring and that shut you up pretty quickly. We'd always had quite a lot of freedom at school, children were more independent in those days anyway and Miss Leach didn't believe in too many rules, but on Colsay we could do pretty much whatever we wanted as long as we went to lessons and behaved like civilized human beings and stayed away from the cliffs at the north end. I don't think there's anyone living on the island now, which always makes me feel sad to think of it, but there were a few families still farming then and because the house wasn't big enough for all of us some were boarded out. They were so kind to us, considering. I mean, it wasn't an easy life at all up there and most of the men were away, although farming was meant to be a reserved occupation, and then they got given all these silly English girls and there wasn't much room in the houses to start with. They were lovely people. I think actually they felt sorry for us, coming from London as most of us did. They even let me milk a sheep! I'd never heard of anyone using sheep's milk before.

Miss Leach had the idea that we should be trying to grow our own vegetables, same as everywhere else in the country. The locals told her it wouldn't work, and of course they'd have been doing it themselves if they could – the food wasn't exactly luxurious for them at the best of times – but she thought maybe they hadn't tried the right varieties and she had us all out there digging and planting. We enjoyed ourselves, but I can't say the results justified the outlay! We kept hens, which was more successful, and goats, though I'm sure we didn't milk or eat those so I don't know exactly how it was helping the war effort. Miss Leach and Miss Bower used to take it in turns to go over to the shop at Colla on Saturdays and we'd give lists of what we wanted with our sweet rations, though in practice you had to take what you could get, which was sometimes nothing! Of course there was no gymnasium, and nowhere really where we could play tennis or netball, so after a while Miss Bower decided we would have football instead, which was unheard of for girls but we rather enjoyed it, and some people tried to swim at the end of the summer term but it really was too cold.

I remember hearing about Dunkirk, but somehow where we were none of it seemed real, not until a few of the girls started to get bad news about their families. We had one girl, Esther, who'd come out of Germany on the *Kindertransport*, and she used to wake the others in her room with nightmares and crying for her mother, though of course we didn't know then what was happening to the Jews in Germany, and someone else whose mother was in a house that got bombed out, and so on. The worst thing was one of the younger girls had an accident. She'd been boarded out with a lady called Mrs Buchan until Mrs Buchan had her baby, and then she had some bad news from home and she was in such a state she got the week off lessons. She took the baby off for a walk and went over the cliff – a terrible time. I remember them bringing her body back with a blanket over it and we weren't even crying, we didn't know what to do. It must have been very bad for her mother. I think we all had someone to grieve for, by the end, but it really was a happy time for me. I always meant to go back to Colsay but I don't think it's going to happen now!

You hear some terrible things about evacuation, it seems especially now we're all so much older and maybe less busy and you start to remember things you haven't thought about in years, but for some of us it shaped our lives in the best ways.

And the baby? I re-read. Was the baby implicitly included in the 'going over' or does the silence about its death mean it was somehow saved? There would be no need to bury a baby killed by a distraught or suicidal schoolgirl in the back garden. Did she have the mother's permission, I wondered, to take the baby for a walk? Even in the era of babies left outside shops in prams and parked at the bottom of the garden for four hours to cry, surely people had more common sense than to wave off a baby in the arms of a disturbed child heading towards a cliff. Perhaps the mother came down from putting the laundry away to find the baby gone, or went to investigate after an unusually long nap and found the pram empty. You would search, heart pounding and hands shaking, first the kitchen and then the other rooms. You'd run into the garden and look and look, willing yourself to wake up, and back into the house and look again, and still it would be real. Would it be worse to lose a child through negligence or through bad luck, to know that you betrayed the only thing that really matters or to know that everything that really matters can fall and smash for no reason at all? In neither case could I see any reason to remain alive.

'How's it going?'

Would it be more suspicious to minimize the window or to leave it and hope he didn't come and look? Gentlemen, after all, don't read their wives' letters. He came over and began to massage my shoulders. 'I thought I might go back over to the cottage. I told Jake I'd get the second coat on to the bathroom walls if I had time.'

'OK,' I said. 'I'm working anyway.'

The massage stopped. He'd seen the screen.

'Are you? On World War Two evacuees?'

'I've been thinking about psychoanalytic theory again. Anna Freud did a lot of work with evacuees.'

'What, on Colsay?'

His hands had left my shoulders.

'I've been working too.'

'Yeah, right. Jesus, Anna. What are you looking for, someone remembering that once when they were sleepwalking they came across someone burying a baby? Lots of people round here find ancient human remains, you know that. They're not accusing us of anything, you don't have to find an alibi.'

I tipped back to look up at him.

'You want to be careful, using that kind of language round here. Ian MacDonald said.'

'Said what?'

'"There are sensitivities to profane language on these islands, Mrs Cassingham."'

'Only if you're the bloody vicar. Come on. Jake swears even more than Connor.' Connor is one of Raph's Oxford classmates.

'Maybe it's just women who aren't allowed to swear.' I swirled the cursor around with the mousepad. 'Giles, he says there's "local concern" about the kids' welfare.'

'He says *what*?'

'You heard. Local concern. Emphasis on "local".'

'Are you sure? I mean, you do tend to think people are judging you. I know he'd rather there was a commune of Gaelic-speaking crofters here, but he's hardly alone there. He's been perfectly correct with me.'

The screensaver appeared.

'Oh, he's always perfectly correct. Nothing I could take down and hold in evidence against him. It's just – I sometimes wish we hadn't come here. Or I wish I had your sense of entitlement. Or maybe I just wish there hadn't been a dead baby in the garden.'

He put his hand back on my shoulder.

'I know. But you know, I feel entitled because I am. This is my island. And there are lots of burials. You don't need me to tell you about dead children. Think about your foundlings.'

One of the foundling hospitals in London tried a three-year experiment of 'hand-rearing' the babies in the late 1790s, feeding them on mixtures of cow's milk, sugar and flour instead of getting in wet-nurses. The milk was carried through the streets of London in open pails and the bottles they used for feeding had long leather teats which there was no attempt to wash. The mortality rate varied, year on year, between 97 and 99.5 per cent. Having collected the evidence, the trustees sent the next few years' worth of abandoned infants out to wet-nurses in the country and compiled statistics noting which women had the lowest death rates, which were around 30 per cent.

'There are so many of the foundlings I can't really think of them as individuals. And they're not in my garden.'

The massaging began again. 'I know. But get your book finished, OK? I think we'll all be much happier when it's gone off to the publisher.'

So I should finish it to make you happy, to get it out of the way so I can get on with *Kinder, Küche und Kirche*? I didn't say it. 'I'm trying, Giles. I get very tired.'

He stroked my hair. 'I know you do. Look, if we can make the cottage work maybe next year we'll get an *au pair* or something, someone to have the children during the day.'

I tipped my chair back again and looked up. He was smiling at my laptop as if Mary Poppins would bound out of it at his command. I was an *au pair* for a few months when I was eighteen, for a Parisian family who seemed to think the British were still painting themselves with woad and sacrificing people in bogs, but they had a house by the Parc Monceau with a swimming pool, the children were at school all day and it never occurred to them to expect an English girl to produce food.

'Giles, if you seriously think any teenage girl with whom we would contemplate leaving the children is going to spurn the metropolises of Europe to live with a family of mad academics on an island with no shop, no television and no way out, where it rains about three hundred and sixty-two days a year, you need – you need a weekend in Paris to remind yourself what life is really like.'

He lifted my hair off my neck and ran his fingers lightly around my nape.

'Let's do it. We'll park the kids with my mother.'

I tipped the chair forward again and maximized the window with chapter four in it. 'What, and leave the Fairchilds to their fate? Anyway, I'd as soon leave the children in the monkey enclosure at the zoo as with your mother. Animal instinct is probably a better bet than class war for childcare.'

'It takes two sides for a war, you know. She means well.'

'I dare say George Bush meant well. Go on, do your painting. Paris can wait.'

He left. I woke up the computer and he came back.

'Anna?'

'What?'

'What's in this bag?'

'Which bag?'

'Oh fuck, Anna!'

I sighed and went not particularly fast to investigate. He had tried to pick up the bag of bureaucracy and it had burst. Brown envelopes and bills which Giles opens but puts back in their envelopes slid across the floor, followed by nearly empty jars and the mug, to which mould still adhered although most of the ex-tea had been absorbed by the smug lifestyle magazines.

'What were you *doing*?' he demanded, in tones more appropriate to fish under the pillow or toothbrushes down the toilet than recycling in a bag labelled recycling.

'Tidying,' I said. 'I'm going to bed.'

As I climbed the stairs, Moth began to cry. Behind me I could hear the rustle of plastic and paper as Giles resurrected the heaps.

Night Waking: 01:42

It would be much easier just to sleep in here, to lie on the floor and put my hand through the bars. If Moth would let me lie down. Instead, I pick him up and we set off to the window and back, up Walton Street, glimpsing the green and pleasant land of Worcester's gardens behind the tangle of bicycles. Past the end of Little Clarendon Street where, giggling to the point of incontinence late one night, my nineteen-year-old self stood on the periphery of a group rearranging some roadworks for reasons which have long eluded me. Past the cocktail bar that provided a series of unsuitable young men the year I was twenty-three, two of whom subsequently got together and seemed to be in every café and library I entered for the next two years. Moth droops on my shoulder and we near the cot.

'Mummy sing a Gruffalo.'

'A mouse took a stroll through the deep dark wood . . .'

My eyes are closing. We set off again, not to fall asleep and fall down. If I had known then what I know now, would I have had children? I think about childless, child-free, friends, who not only go to see plays in New York and attend weddings in Singapore and must not be phoned until eleven o'clock at weekends and are always out, that mysterious 'out' of childless people who can afford to live in Zone Two, when the children are in bed and I could phone them to hear about plays and galleries and new restaurants, who read the weekend papers at the weekend and cook using both hands. They keep up with their publishing schedules and get the jobs we all apply for. Would I do it again, understanding as I do now and didn't then, that failure at motherhood is for life and beyond, that everything that happens to my children and my children's children is my fault? That my meanness and bad temper are going to trickle into the future like nuclear waste into the Irish Sea? No. Not because I don't love my children – everyone loves their children, child abusers love their children – but because I don't like motherhood and you don't find that out until it's too late. Love is not enough, when it comes to children. Bad luck.

Dearest Allie,

Thank you for your letter! It made me feel very far away,
somehow, to understand that you and Mama had been in London
and I still fancying you at home. You might go, of course, to Paris
or Rome or back to Lausanne and be home before I knew of the
journey. It seems, though, that you did not receive my last? I must
ask Mrs Barwick again about the postal arrangements, but you
know there is no road closer than Inversaigh (for all the islanders
pay the road tax! I sometimes begin to doubt Lord Hugo's
philanthropy, and no school either), and so everything must be
carried on someone's back, as if the poor people were just beasts of
burden. It is no uncommon sight to see the women especially doing
the work of animals here; apparently in the Spring they harness
themselves like oxen and drag the plough and harrow themselves. I
do not look forward to seeing this. Aubrey and Papa would say it is
no different from factory work, but it is – to drag a plough
requires not even the manual dexterity of the boys at the looms
and somehow it troubles me particularly to see the women reduced
to mere brutes. They are not fair ladies, to be sure, though one or
two are comely enough on Sundays when they remove their
weekday headdresses and take clean aprons, but I think even Mama
would agree that it is a painful thing to see a woman's body strain
under a weight a man could lift. Although one of the things that
has been upsetting me rather is the way they do treat their
animals – all the dogs (and there are many) spend their days
hobbling around with one paw tied up to their necks so they can't

131

run away or trouble children or sheep and of course sometimes the bindings get caught and the dog strangles. And sheep going to market are marked by the simple expedient of cutting a piece off the ear with a knife. The worst, somehow, is what Mrs Barwick told me when she saw my distress at the method used to dispose of a litter of unwanted puppies, which I will not harrow my soul by committing to paper nor yours by communicating, but suffice it to say that nothing in man's inhumanity to man should surprise us when we think what children are sometimes allowed to do to animals. She told me also that when the lambs are born, it is the custom to force a stick or stone too large to be swallowed into the lamb's mouth in the evening and tie its jaw hard, so that in the morning the ewe's milk can be taken for the children before the lamb is able to suckle again. Is this not horrible?

I will not pretend, to you, that all is well here (though please keep this letter quite to yourself, I would not have it known even in the family that I may be betraying Aubrey's faith in me). I have made some progress with Mrs Grice, who expects her child in the next month, but I am far from confident that she will allow my presence at the delivery, much less that she will dispense with the services of the 'knee-woman' in my favour, so that the most I might hope is to witness the child contract the poison. I hear that the wood for its coffin is already set to steam, coffins being now the sole item in the layette here. Truly, there are no baby clothes on this island. In late years, when a child is born they wrap it in rags and wait to see if it will live before going to the bother of sewing, and of course in all cases but one this economy has been quite justified by events. I watch Mrs Grice. Her cheeks are hollow now, as the unborn babe takes more of her overtasked strength. Sometimes you can see the child's limbs pushing under her gown (for I do not think women here are burdened with the manufacture and maintenance of many petticoats) and she knows and they all know that before Christmas it will be cold in the ground. There is nothing I can do.

I tried, last week, to start a small school for the children, thinking that at least I might teach them the alphabet and perhaps some rudiments of English. I knew, of course, that without Gaelic myself I had no right to expect much progress, but someone must do something or they will grow up with no hope beyond the filth and hardship of what they already know. Education or emigration seem the only possibilities for improvement, although the people themselves, so far as I can see, express no dissatisfaction with their lot beyond the universal belief that rents and other expenses are too high in relation to income (on which topic, if you were able somehow to send me six pairs of new stockings, whatever you have been reading this Autumn and please, dearest Allie, another fruit cake and perhaps one of those boxes from Kendal Milne?). I asked Mrs Barwick to tell all the parents, and I made up an alphabet myself, trying to find objects that would be familiar to the children in place of the apples, balls, elephants etc. (cats, dogs and fish are familiar – in the case of the two former, too familiar for my liking!). Lacking slates, I prepared to sacrifice some of this paper and my own supplies of ink, planning to ask the boys to make pens from the feathers which are after all available in unlimited number in every household. Nobody came.

Mrs Barwick has been teaching me to knit. Often, after serving my supper (only don't imagine soup, or Welsh rarebit, or omelette – dried fish and gruel, or, very occasionally, a barley bannock with the suspicion of butter on it), she goes off to the villagers, but of late, with the weather so bad and food, I fear, becoming scant, I believe most of them are retiring very early and I found that she sits at the kitchen range with her needles going faster than the clock ticks. The women knit not to clothe their families, who are mostly wrapped in a kind of rough tweed that would bring you out in hives, but because the shawls and jerseys can be taken off to Inversaigh, where someone calls once or twice a year to take them 'away'. The payment for this labour is made not to the women but to the shop in Colla, minus the expenses of transport, where it reduces the debt run up by each household against their supply of meal and tea. The mystery to me is why

Mrs Barwick, who has after all worked in Edinburgh and travelled even to London with Miss Emily in the days of her youth, should choose to remain here, but I suppose she is well housed and clothed and her own knitting is certainly not to pay off debts for oatmeal. I am making a sort of blanket or shawl, which has the advantage of being straight and not rendered structurally unsound by the odd dropped stitch!

I am also hoping that these evenings around the fire will give me a chance to find out more about the islanders and what can be done to help them, although so far Mrs Barwick prefers to tell old tales of supernatural happenings that make it difficult for even such a hardened rationalist as myself to go calmly up the dark stairs and to bed by candlelight afterwards! I wish the Grey People were less in the habit of jumping out from cupboards and chests with their menaces and unreasonable demands!

Anyway, my fire is dying and I must go to bed before I lose its little glow. Already the shadows seem to crowd close around my chair.

Fondest love as always,

May

8

THE CAPACITY OF AN ADULT

The difficulty in using reality as a criterion lies, not in there
being no reality, but in our imperfect capacity to comprehend it. That a child has an imperfect capacity to
comprehend what is or may be truly dangerous is usually
taken for granted. That the capacity of an adult is greater
often by only a small margin tends to be forgotten.

– John Bowlby, *Separation*, p. 186

Two days later, we all went over to the cottage. There was sun
bright on our faces and when Moth rolled on the turf he found
it was warm, so we all sat there for a while, watching a trawler
pull across the sea, black against the sparkling water. I looked
back at Colsay House; on the bluest summer day with the air
smelling of honey from the sun-baked grass, it still looked as if
it had been built by Calvin to remind sinners of the tomb.
Moth was eating grass. A raven flew gleaming overhead and
landed on the roof.

'Mummy?' said Raph. 'Have you ever seen a baby raven?'

'They nest on the cliffs.' Giles lay back, hands behind his head,
and closed his eyes. The Cassingham nose in all its splendour
shone in the sun. 'They don't want people to see their babies.'

'I found a worm,' said Moth. He held it up, squirming. 'I eat
it. In my mouth.'

I stood up and held out my hand to him. 'Put it down, love. The worm wants to wriggle in the ground. They don't like the sun. And we don't eat them, do we? Shall we go see the cottage?'

The painting was finished and it was the first time I'd been there without feeling Jake potentially or actually peering over my shoulder. Telling me what I deserved. Giles had been right about the white paint. Sunlight spilt across the floors and the walls glowed like tanned skin. It was almost hot; perhaps we should have thought about blinds. Raph lifted his face as if there were a nice smell.

'I like it in here.'

He lay down in the middle of the floor, his copper hair spreading across the boards. He looked like an installation in the Tate. Fallen Angel. Moth pattered over.

'No standing on Raph, no not.'

'No, love, that's right, no standing on Raph. Come and see the seagulls.'

Raph flung his arms wide. 'Can we live here?'

I looked at Giles. We'd discussed it, of course, all those evenings when we spread the architect's drawings in the two-up, two-down behind the station where we could hear the neighbours closing the cupboards in their kitchen, built for Victorian navvies and now inhabited by City lawyers and academics with hereditary wealth, and graced with organic paint and a hanging basket of (long-dead) geraniums.

'Instead of the big house, or instead of Oxford?'

He rolled over and lay propped on his elbows as though reading. 'Instead of Oxford of course. Could we, and never go back to school? Please?'

Giles turned back from the window. 'Raph, there's a difference between moving to Colsay and not going to St Peter's, you know. You have to go to school wherever you are, it's the law.'

'No, it's not. Paul's home-schooled. He doesn't go.'

'Moth, come away from the stove, please,' I called. 'Paul's

136

mother doesn't have anything else to do. No, Raph, absolutely not. We're about a hundred miles and four hours from the nearest copyright library. Moth, leave that alone, please, love. Moth!'

'You wouldn't need a library if we lived here,' said Raph. 'You wouldn't need to work. You could look after me and Moth like Jessica's mummy. And Marcus's mummy. And Edward's mummy.'

'Stop it,' I said. 'No. I'm not that kind of mummy.'

I am the kind of mummy whose absence, at least some of the time, is good for you. Giles turned back to the window. The views are better from the cottage, closer to the beach and built for seeing rather than being seen. There's a research group at the University of the Highlands and Islands that has been courting him, and he'd make enough money for food and books. We'd need a much better boat to get the children over to Colla for school, and we'd need a better internet connection and a more reliable electricity supply, which it would no doubt be Raph's pleasure to design. Maybe I could commute weekly to Oxford, pick up the sleeper at Inverness. The sale of the Oxford house would fund a few years of that. Assuming, of course, I had anything to commute to Oxford for.

'Anyway, we'd all miss our friends,' I said. 'There was a reason why everyone left Colsay, you know. But we're lucky to have it for summers. Come on, let's get it ready. They're arriving in a few days.'

'Yeah,' said Giles. 'You know, maybe some of those reasons have changed. With the internet.'

'When the Bodleian Library is on the internet and you can get internet childcare we'll talk about it. Meanwhile, I expect the Fairchilds would like sheets.'

Raph didn't move. Moth poked his ear.

'Fairchildren,' said Raph. 'I'd like to live here.'

'There are universities closer than Oxford, you know.' Giles opened a drawer, which contained knives and forks gleaming

137

like mirrors and heavy as guns, and watched it slide silently closed. 'You'd be able to pick up sessional teaching. Make some contacts.'

Raph rolled over. 'I thought you hated college anyway.'

'Mummy likes institutions,' said Giles.

I felt as if I was being circled by wolves.

'I think they're interesting, that's all. Go on. You and Daddy do the beds. And no, OK? No.'

Giles took the sheets, which were only slightly damp, up the open-tread stairs. It's one advantage of having been sent away to prep school at six: he can make beds the way he thinks they ought to be made, with linen sheets that should be ironed and hospital corners. After some experiment, I engaged the child-lock on the washing machine and stopped bothering to convince Moth that it wasn't hungry and didn't want a banana. I started trying to break into the parcel of books I'd ordered, which soon became interesting enough for Moth to abandon his passionate interaction with the pedal bin.

'Ow! Bloody Amazon.'

'Bugger amazons,' agreed Moth.

'No, no, not a good idea. Damn. Giles? Giles! Have we equipped this place with scissors?'

'Kitchen drawer,' he called.

Moth ran ahead of me. 'Sharp, Mummy. Careful.'

It was hard to choose the books. We'd agreed that I wasn't just going to buy what I wanted to read and then borrow it, but I was determined to offer something more local than people were likely to bring with them. I'd provided Walter Scott in deference to the Heritage Experience approach to holidays, George Mackay Brown for those who like their islands whimsical, and a selection of the more accessible literature on the Clearances so that liberals could have the pleasures of indignation and conservatives could be reminded how they got here. Then I'd realized we had no women, and actually nothing I particularly wanted to read myself, so I'd added Margaret

138

Oliphant's ghost stories and rather more contemporary Scottish women's poetry than perhaps took account of ordinary reading habits.

'Stand back, Moth. This is very sharp.'

I took the bread knife to the carapace of glued cardboard. He came over to investigate the result of all this knife-wielding and strong language.

'More books.'

'Books for the visitors,' I told him. 'Moth, we're going to have visitors. People coming to the cottage.'

He prodded the bubble wrap. 'Go away people. Moth not like visitors.'

Giles went back to the puffin colonies after lunch. Moth wasn't particularly tired but I was particularly determined and eventually he went to sleep. Violating the bad news blackout for the sake of my work, I'd given Raph a graphic account of the end of Pompeii over lunch and suggested that, if he worked outside, he could collect some of the darker sand from the far end of the beach to represent lava. I tried to connect to the internet from the sofa and found again that I could, so I settled there where I could see Raphael building Pompeii out of Lego while consulting *Life in Roman Towns*.

I logged into J-Stor and ran a search on 'women's history' and 'infanticide'. Bones might outlast history but I've never heard of a prehistoric textile. Wet wool rots fast. But a baby dead even as much as a hundred years would be relatively tolerable, and there was a lot of infanticide in the nineteenth century, when 'funeral clubs' in the most deprived areas paid out on the death of a child. The clubs were meant to provide insurance against children's funeral expenses for parents who could barely afford to eat, and so, in practice, paid desperate families to neglect or even kill their youngest members. You had to provide a death certificate to get the money, but you didn't have to have a funeral. I skimmed the results. All the infanticides that make it as far as the secondary literature – a subset which necessarily excludes all that were successfully concealed, which this might have been – were carried out by unmarried girls who denied their pregnancies, delivered alone and subsequently claimed that the baby was stillborn. Which, as juries tended to agree, they could have been. The bodies were usually found under the bed or in the privy, and it seemed that in the cases of most of those buried outside the house the mother had had what the courts took to be an accomplice, although it seemed to me that he was more likely to be the killer. Newly delivered women are rarely capable of going outside and digging a grave. Those were also the babies who tended to have had their throats cut – I remembered the Wild Boy of Aveyron – or been hit on the head. Mothers acting alone usually went for suffocation, or sometimes strangulation with the umbilical cord. Raph's cord was cut before I saw it because, without my consent, they'd injected me as he was born with drugs that shouldn't cross the placenta, but I remembered Moth's, disconcertingly alive, a grey snake throbbing with blood, and my dismay when the midwife held it out to be severed. It should have hurt, that cut. The bloody ends looked like eighteenth- century images of guillotined necks.

'Mummy! Look, I'm putting under-floor heating in the baths!'

I opened the window. It wasn't exactly sunny outside, but you could see where the shadows would be when the clouds moved.

'That's lovely, darling. The baths had lots of rooms, didn't they?'

I found a table showing the ages of infanticide victims at death. More than 80 per cent were under one week, the rest divided between those killed by fathers and childminders who couldn't stand another minute of screaming – odd, but perhaps in evolutionary terms not surprising, that mothers, who are after all exposed to more noise with less sleep than anyone else, in fact rarely resort to this means of procuring a moment's peace – and those suffocated by mothers who couldn't feed them and didn't want to watch them starve. One such woman told the judge, 'My husband left me with five under ten. I knew the baby was like to die anyway, having lost three already, and I couldn't find food for all. He'd been crying three days with hunger. The two older boys are already working and need what we can give them. I couldn't find it in me to watch him die so slow.' The judge drew the jury's attention to the defendant's extreme thinness.

'Mummy, did they have some kind of air-conditioning for the caldarium? It's hot in Naples.'

The wind ruffled his hair. There were more freckles on his face, but I cannot bear to subject Raph to the physical force necessary to apply sunscreen.

'I expect they were just good at designing buildings to be cool. With lots of marble.'

He sat back on his heels. 'How?'

'I don't know, love. Let me get this work done, OK?'

'Sorry, Mummy.'

I tried to remember the size of the orchard baby, and the size of newborns. I could hold Moth against me on one arm, his head in my hand and his feet tucked under my elbow, and he was a kilo heavier than Raphael at birth. I looked out at Raph, who was waving his feet in the grass as he attempted a curved archway. He's probably as tall as a lot of nineteenth-century Scottish adults already, although the islanders fared better on fish and oats than the teeming poor of Glasgow on adulterated bread and jam made with sawdust. What we saw of her skull was small, more of a shell than a coconut, but the long bones were at least big enough to be recognizable. I remembered newborn arms and legs as largely decorative appendages to the twin spheres of head and stomach, seeming to be there more as signs of human form to come than for any present use. Whereas the orchard baby – call her, like so many female skeletons, Eve – had bones that looked functional. Maybe all bones look functional. I'd rather, on balance, that she'd barely taken a breath, not adapted to light, never left the daze of surprise at air on her skin and sounds not muffled by water in her ears. Never quite come to life. Moth was born in his bag of waters, asleep, and when the midwife told me to pick him up from between my legs he hadn't started breathing, didn't know he'd been born. He's not breathing, I said in panic, he's not alive, and Jane said, wait, it hasn't been a minute yet, the cord's still pulsing. I took another deep breath for him, to oxygenate our blood. And then he opened his eyes, eyelashes still filmed with amniotic fluid, looked into my face, and started to breathe. He began his life in my arms. It wasn't yet time to wake him, but I closed my files and went up to watch Moth sleep.

'Mummy,' said Raphael.

'What? Look, Moth, what's that?'

'Elephant,' said Moth. He giggled. 'Elephant jumps on a garage!' The elephant from the Noah's Ark leapt on to the second floor of the wooden multi-storey car park ('complete with helipad and functioning lift for hours of imaginative play!').

'Mummy?'

The elephant was followed by a giraffe, which had to go in sideways.

'Yes.'

'Cows going in a lift!' exclaimed Moth.

'Mummy, I think there's something you should know.'

He sounded as if he was about to tell me he was gay, or had decided to join the army, or both. I don't think I would mind not having grandchildren – it would in some ways be a relief to know that the rot stops here – certainly not as much as I would mind a child of mine being paid to kill people. He came to stand in front of me.

'Go on.'

'You might be frightened.'

I dropped the rhinoceros.

'Crash rhinoceros!' said Moth.

Raph twisted his hands. 'It's – I don't like saying it.' He hid his face.

'What? Raph, love. Come here.'

Moth sat pink-cheeked and giggling. I pulled Raph towards me and held him. He ground his forehead against my collarbone.

'Cuddle Moth too!' Moth crawled over and tried to push between us. I moved Raph round.

'There! Raph, tell me. I won't be frightened. It's my job to stop things frightening you.'

He pulled back and Moth seized his opportunity. 'I thought it was your job to write your book?'

I felt slightly sick. 'That too. Go on.'

Raph went over to the window. 'There's something in the attic. Something that moves about and makes a noise. I keep hearing it. I thought it was a burglar.'

'Raph—' I said. 'Raph, it's not—'

He turned and went out, turning his face away as he walked past. Moth pulled my top forward and peered down the neck. 'There Mummy's tummy.'

Raph spoke from the stairs. 'It's that baby. It's that dead baby.'

I picked Moth up, took *Mog and the Baby* to distract him, and followed Raph up the stairs. He had got into bed and pulled the duvet over his head.

'Raph hiding,' said Moth. 'Peepo Raph!' He pulled the duvet back and Raph growled.

I sat on the bed. 'Leave him be, Moth. Look! Here's *Mog and the Baby*!'

Moth sat on the floor, in the perfect straight-legged, straight-backed yoga position of the person who has never sat at a desk, and began to leaf through a faux-naïve account of post-natal depression encoding a thinly veiled warning about what will happen if you leave your screaming baby with a motherly neighbour for an hour in order to go shopping (it will crawl into the path of oncoming traffic and survive only by grace of an improbably positioned cat, to which you will then owe a lifetime of gratitude and service). I stroked Raph's shoulder.

'Raph, there's nothing in the attic. Really. How many times have we been up there, and never seen anything? There's nothing scary here. That baby probably died hundreds of years ago, maybe even before the Vikings. Lots of people used to die when they were babies and now we've got so good at making sure people have enough food and clean water and doctors to help when they're ill that nearly everyone lives a long time.'

He pushed the duvet back from his face. 'Lots of babies still die because of dirty water. It gives them diarrhoea and they get dehydratated and people won't give them a bit of sugar and salt to make them better.'

'Dehydrated. I know. But at least we do know, so we can do something about it.'

'Do we do something about it?'

No. We spend our money doing up the blackhouse and buying olive oil and books and designer clothes from Swedish catalogues which cheer us up and we don't, once we're grown up, give the dehydrated babies a moment's thought from one week to the next.

'We can give money to charities who do something about it. But Raph, the baby isn't in the attic. The police are looking after her bones and the rest of her is gone.'

'There's something up there,' he said. 'I keep hearing it.'

'Come on,' I said. 'Sit up. Look, next time you hear it, come and find me and we'll go look together.'

He flinched.

'Or I'll go, and tell you what's there. And now, shall we go down and make some popcorn?'

'In a minute.'

I gave him a hug. 'All right. Moth, shall we come down and make popcorn?'

'Moth have some hotcorn too!'

Popcorn offers a uniquely consoling combination of snack and controlled explosion, which I emphasize by making it in a Pyrex bowl, which burns the bottom layer but allows the children, standing on chairs pulled irresponsibly close to the stove, to watch things blow up as they are not allowed to do in any more conventional setting.

Raph took another handful and I burnt my fingers trying to pick the blackened ones from the bottom of the bowl.

'Mummy, if you put oil in would they not stick?'

'More hotcorn!' said Moth.

'The only time I put oil in, it caught fire, remember?'

A small fire, easily extinguished with a pan lid and a wet tea-towel. Another secret from Giles.

'Anyway,' I said. 'We're going to Colla this afternoon. To the library.'

Raph stopped with popcorn half way to his mouth.

'I don't want to go to the library.'

'You'll like it,' I said. 'Come on, it's full of books. We'll get you a ticket and you can borrow engineering textbooks.'

'I want to stay here and read.'

So do I, I thought.

Moth reached for his bowl and spat his popcorn into it. 'Moth want to stay here too.'

'Nonsense. We'll go in the boat and you can see the birds and the waves going splosh, splosh, and there might be seals, maybe a mummy seal and a baby seal!'

Though I think that for seals maternity is merely seasonal.

Raph stood up. 'I want to stay here and read and I'm going to.'

'Raph?' I followed him. He was deploying his father's tactic and hiding behind the *Guardian*, which was full of unsuitable tales in which evil is rewarded and good people come to bad ends. 'Raph, you can bring a book. OK? You don't have to stop reading. And they've probably got a whole section on bridge-building. Come on.'

'No.'

I sighed. 'All right then. If you're not outside the door in your shoes and coat by the time I've got Moth ready I'm going to take away your Lego until the weekend.'

The library is a low brick building on the edge of the village, recently built with EU money. Inside, there was a 'pushchair park', posters of the characters from children's books and a purple carpet with red dots. It reminded me of the children's ward in our hospital in Oxford, effervescent with plastic toys, as if books were a manifestation of the mortality from which the general public, and children in particular, must always be distracted.

Raph rubbed birdshit from the edge of his shoe on to the carpet. 'It looks like a bloody playgroup.'

I was unpeeling Moth from his waterproof jacket and trousers, which won't pull over his shoes. 'I know. But don't swear. They've got lots of books.'

Moth tried to run off and fell over his trousers.

Raph grabbed him. 'Shut up! Shut up! This is a *library*.'

I once took Raph to the History Faculty Library when I had to return some books and he was off school. The memory was apparently still vivid for him. 'It's all right, Raph. It's not that kind of library.'

I hoisted Moth on to my hip and held Raph's hand. There was someone behind a counter in the children's section.

Moth wriggled. 'There's a Gruffalo!'

'Mummy, can I use those computers?' asked Raph.

'Yes. If you must. Why not find some new books?'

The woman at the counter was wearing the kind of understated tailoring last seen on women with BlackBerrys and expensive glasses on the 19.10 out of Paddington. She looked up. 'Good morning. He'll need a username and password for the computer,' she said. 'Are you wanting to join the library?'

'If we can,' I said. 'Do we count as local residents?'

'You don't have to,' she said. 'Visitors use the library too.'

'Oh.'

She's right, of course, nothing in Giles's stone-by-stone knowledge of Colsay makes him – or me – less of a visitor. I straightened my back.

'And I was also wondering about the archives. I'm Anna Bennet, Giles Cassingham's wife. We're staying on Colsay for the summer and letting out the blackhouse. I thought I might try to write a booklet for the visitors.'

She typed something into her computer. 'You know there's a very good local history. Thomas MacFarland – he was our rector here – when he retired he took a PhD and wrote his book. Published by Birlinn.'

'I'd like to see that,' I said. 'Raph and I have been talking about World War Two, haven't we, love?'

She pushed her hair back and smiled a teacher's smile at Raph, who ducked behind me. 'You know we had an exhibition about wartime here in the winter? The schoolchildren did a bit of an oral history project and we had lots of old photos up.'

I breathed in and out carefully. 'I didn't know. Do you still have them, the photos and recordings? Raph would love to see them, wouldn't you?'

He ground his head against my back.

'And maybe we could sort out computer access for him?'

She kept her gaze on my face, as if Raph were doing something obscene which she was too well bred to acknowledge.

'I'm sure we could do that.'

'Mummy!' called Moth. 'Mummy, look! A baby gruffalo! Mummy read it.'

'I'm sorry,' I said. 'Raph's just shy. And of course we don't see many people at the moment.'

'Not to worry. When you're ready I'll show you and the lads the exhibition, all right? Some of the old ones gave us their photos at the end and we've the recordings.' She paused. 'I'll show you something else as well, you might be interested for your booklet. We had a grant to digitize the local paper right back to the 1920s. It's all there, every word. And I couldn't honestly say it's been much used. I'm Fiona Firth, by the way. The archivist.'

'Thank you,' I said. 'Really. Thank you.'

The photos had the strangely jovial quality that seems to mark most amateur wartime photography, at least in Britain. Women with shiny curls laughed up at the camera as if the medieval agricultural implements in their hands were cocktails and the wind-scoured fields Californian swimming pools. There were some more serious pictures of men, facing away from the camera and getting on with manual labour with faces shadowed by tweed caps and beards.

'Mummy? If it was the war, why are they smiling?'

Fiona Firth put a picture of some children down in front of him. I craned to look. Girls and boys together, so probably not the Castle School.

'Maybe they were enjoying themselves,' she said. 'You can listen to some of the people who remember it, if you like. People got to do lots of things they wouldn't have done without the war, especially the children.'

Raph looked through the window. There were rabbits cropping the grass, and a build-up of cloud to the north. Time to go home soon. 'There were lots of people dying in Germany. And Poland. I've seen pictures. And children and babies.'

Fiona Firth looked round at me.

'Not here,' I reminded him. 'Here children were just going

to school and playing and helping on the land the same as always.'

His gaze moved to the gathering clouds. 'And people holding hands waiting to be shot and all the houses falling apart.'

Moth placed a sticky hand in mine. 'Moth and Mummy holding hands. Up and see more rabbits!'

I picked him up. 'We'd better go,' I said. 'I don't like the look of those clouds. Would it be OK to come back, maybe tomorrow, or – or—' Or the next day, which might be Wednesday or Thursday but I would not be very surprised if it were Friday or Saturday. And on one of those days, the Fairchilds were coming.

Fiona looked at Raph as if he might tear down all the Disney on the way out and replace it with multiple copies of *If This Be Man*.

'Oh,' she said slowly. 'Oh, whenever you want. Of course.'

She followed us towards the soft play area. 'Were you wanting the newspaper? If you've got the internet out there I'll give you a password.'

'Giles? Is there a copy of your family tree here?'

He was washing up, and I was pottering around the kitchen trying to look busy.

'Almost certainly. Why?'

'I was just wondering who was around before the war. Who lent the house to that school. That article just says "the owner".'

His face, reflected in the window behind the sink, was blank.

'What, before the war? Or during? Because I told Ian MacDonald, remember, it got passed on several times when people were killed.'

'Before, probably. Or at the beginning.' I looked into one of the covered bowls in the fridge and looked away again.

'Those two cousins, they were called Edwin and Nigel—'

'Of course.'

'Who inherited but were killed in action in quick succession. There was my Great Aunt Edith—'

'Every household needs one.'

'Shut up. Who lived a blameless if anachronistic life in Bath for most of the twentieth century. I think she might have owned it after Nigel died, but that was 1942 or '43. You probably want earlier than that.'

So she would have been roughly the right age to have a baby late enough for the knitting not to have rotted; well into the twentieth century, but before living memory. Before Giles's parents would have had to have been involved.

'Tell me about Great Aunt Edith.'

He turned round, water dripping from the popcorn bowl.

'Are you planning to impress the Fairchildren with family history, or are you about to accuse Great Aunt Edith of pre-marital sex, secret pregnancy and infanticide?'

I reopened the fridge, as if the covered bowls might have moved on.

'I was just thinking, if that burial is pre-war it's much more likely that she was buried by someone who was living in the big house than one of the villagers. I mean, why would you risk carrying a dead baby to someone else's house? It'd be quite a walk for someone who'd just given birth. So I'm just thinking about who was around earlier in the century.'

He put the pan down and came and stood with his hands on my shoulders as if he'd like to shake me, which Old Etonians don't do.

'Anna, stop it. Write your book. Start getting some job applications out, if you've got spare time. Teach Raph Latin, or something. But stop accusing people of killing babies, OK?'

'I don't know any Latin. State education, remember? Someone did kill a baby.'

His grasp tightened and then he stepped back and returned to the sink.

'Either someone did, or the child died of something. I don't know why you're so sure it was murder. The police might find out, though it seems a lot more likely that they'll dismiss it as historical. In either case, it's not your problem. Jesus, Anna, if you want to join the police get a job and make some money out of it.'

'I have a job, remember? Research Fellow, St Mary Hall?'

'Yeah,' he said. 'I remember. Will you go write your book now, please, and let me get on in here.'

I wandered towards the sofa, as if I had time to spare. I don't know why I'm so sure it was murder, either.

While the brief lives of foundlings and abandoned children are in general beyond the scope of this kind of cultural history [insert footnote – ?Levine book], most of the images of urban life from the late eighteenth and early nineteenth centuries attest to the constant presence of the destitute. The children in Hogarth's satires (see figs. 29 and 30) are well known, but even the painting opposite (fig. 31), commissioned by Lady Alicia Chevalier when her marriage to the Duke of Dorset removed her from her much-loved London home, shows very young children begging in the most glamorous parts of the city. Their presence in this deliberately romanticized image of London suggests the ubiquity of malnourished and homeless infants in cities across Europe, and it has been estimated that approximately 120,000 babies in the first year of life were abandoned each year in western Europe in the first half of the nineteenth century. Where, then, are these children in the conduct and didactic literatures for the young which boomed during precisely these decades?

I heard the voice of Antonia Rivett. 'Save rhetorical questions for rhetoric, please, Anna.' Ten years later and I still couldn't brook her disapproval. I deleted 'Where, then, are' and inserted 'are missing from' after 'children'. The wind howled along the beach and through the orchard, throwing rain against the windows. Those eighteenth-century children must not have seemed fully human to the people coming out of Sheridan's new sell-out success and heading for vol-au-vents and hothouse grapes in rooms the size of swimming pools. They would have been feared a little, small people but, like child soldiers, small people with nothing to lose, children who would do anything at all, and allow anything to be done to them, for money. Or food. I got up to close the curtains. If we did move here, Moth and Raph would be spared all that. The conviction that children are up to no good, guilty until proven innocent, loitering with intent. I shivered. I watch Raph growing up in England with the parallel fears that some less educated child who can spot a naïve geek across the park will knife him because he doesn't have a mobile phone to hand over, and that he will be arrested and taken away from us for anti-social behaviour because he bares his teeth and growls at strangers. We could keep him safe, here. If Ian MacDonald and the local concern didn't get to him first.

These children are not, in fact, erased from cultural memory, but they figure exclusively as objects. Objects of charity, fear or scorn, often – like the misbehaving children on today's 'reality TV' programmes – objects of comparison against which the most impatient middle-ranking mother can feel adequate, their subjectivity remains inadmissible, an idea that is almost never entertained. It is a situation that casts a glancing light on the Wild Boy of Aveyron, who may have been distinguished from these most familiar children not by his destitution or even by his unsocialized mind but by his habitat. European cities of the later eighteenth century were littered with children believed never to have learnt to be human. The USP of the Wild Boy, the basis of philosophers' belief in his possible redemption, was his Alpine backdrop.

152

It was good, but I wasn't sure it was true. I could see the Fellows' red pens scoring through the reality TV and the USP. I ran my hands through my hair, which needed washing, and maximized the Colsay evacuees' story. I still couldn't really make it fit the orchard baby, although two tragically dead infants on one small island seemed too much of a coincidence. Or maybe not. Maybe the planet is in fact sown with broken babies. Or maybe Giles was right, the baby was a stillbirth that hadn't qualified for burial in consecrated ground and had been quietly interred in the orchard. In England at least there was no obligation to register stillbirths until the twentieth century, which I suppose means that, like the result of a miscarriage now, you could bury one anywhere you wanted. Somewhere you could watch over it from your window, where the sea would sound until the world ends. If I had to bury either of mine I would—

I pushed the chair back and went to find Giles. He appeared to be cleaning the sink.

'What you are doing?'

He turned round.

'Look, Anna, I can't keep doing this any more.' He was going to leave me. He had a secret boat, had been having an affair with someone who is not obsessed with her children and her career. Someone who cares when he is depressed. He looked at the wall above my head. 'I know what happened. At college. With Moth. And I know you haven't been back.'

I shouldn't have been surprised. Secrets at Oxford are about as common as students from the inner city.

'And?'

'Oh, Anna.' He came over to where I stood in the doorway, tried to put his arms round me. I stood stiff. 'I'm sorry. But I don't know why you stopped going to college. You must have known they'd notice in the end.'

'No,' I said. 'No, I suppose you don't. And if you ever mention it again I'll – I'll take the kids and leave.'

'Back to Oxford?' he asked.

'I'm going to bed. I'm tired.'

The bathroom door locks with a key, which we hid high up after Raph locked himself in for the third time and had to be rescued by Jake with his ladder. I scaled the bookcase, raising swirls of dust, and then gave up and wedged the ancestral mahogany towel rail, which stains the towels and regularly falls over on Moth, under the door handle. I ran a bath. I brushed my teeth. I read *Happy Babies and Children* and concentrated on feeling guilty ('all that your child really needs, now and later, is the absolute certainty that you love and approve of him, that your affection is not in any way conditional'). The bath came out well, just short of the overflow and hot enough to remind me of the point where pain and pleasure merge. I could stay in it a long time and the towel rail would, at least temporarily, frustrate any rescue attempts on the part of Giles.

What happened in college was that a student complained to the Principal that I had failed to turn up to a tutorial, which I had, because I'd had a phone call from St Peter's saying that Raphael had been involved in an altercation in the playground an hour earlier and had been hiding under a desk, refusing to speak, ever since. A phone call I'd missed because I'd been in the library with the phone, as it should have been, silenced, and when I came out to cycle up Keble Road to the tutorial I checked the messages, phoned school to find that he was still unresponsive and that they had been unable to contact Giles (subsequently found to have been taking a potential college benefactor out to lunch). 'A family emergency,' I told the porter. People miss tutorials all the time, usually because they've been asked to speak at something in London, have lost their cat or are hungover, but the Principal was disposed to take this more seriously because he felt that, after a promising start (before the morning sickness kicked in and I began to decline the port), my commitment to the college had been questionable for some time and I needed to understand that a Research Fellowship was not simply a gift from the college to a fortunate individual but a contract between the Fellows and the scholar holding the Fellowship, an invitation, in effect, to join them for a number of years. That my formal obligations were limited not because the College wished to underwrite my domestic interests but because they hoped that the scholar who received the Fellowship would benefit from the freedom to carry out the most demanding research. The Principal hoped he would not find it necessary to repeat this interview and looked forward to seeing me at more of those events where the Fellows gathered, which were the cornerstone of college life.

The water had made a red tidemark above my breasts, which were, I was interested to note, leaking milk which drifted away like smoke from a cigarette. I turned on to my stomach so that my pelvic bones, missing in action since morning sickness wore off two years ago, grated on the enamel. I took a breath and pushed my face under the water. Victorian plumbing noises gurgled in my ears. If Giles came, if Moth cried, if Raphael had a nightmare or an urgent question about bridge pilings, I would not know. I should spend more time with my head underwater.

There was a Formal Hall three days later. Gowns will be worn. MA gowns (the doctoral gown is worn so rarely that it is usually hired) cost more than cashmere cardigans and since for babysitting reasons we never needed one at the same time we shared one that was short for Giles and long for me. As several elderly male professors of our acquaintance would attest, a gown covers a multitude of sins with regard to soup and, much less commonly, baby snot and sicked-up milk. Formal Hall begins at 7 p.m., sherry from 6.30 in the Senior Common Room. Moth, then seven months old, had supper at 6 p.m., bath at about 6.30, followed by a breastfeed which finished when he fell off the nipple so deeply asleep that the last gulp ran out of his open mouth. The ceaseless arithmetic of parenthood; I asked nursery not to let him nap so I could put him to bed early and leave Giles with a small warm bundle anaesthetized by milk, and hoped that by skipping dessert (which is not pudding, oh dear no, what do you think you're living in, the post-imperial age?) and cycling really fast I could get home before his distress at the breast having unaccountably missed its 10 p.m. appointment annoyed the philosophy don next door.

Moth went to sleep in the pushchair on the way back from nursery at 4.30, a catastrophe. I lifted him out, sang songs about bouncy rabbits, tickled him, put him back, and he slept so deeply I kept touching his eyelids to make sure he wasn't in a coma. We collected Raphael who, once convinced that he really was being encouraged to make a loud noise and wake the baby, produced more decibels than I had thought the human voice capable of generating. Moth's eyelids flickered and he sank back into the stupor of an overstimulated seven-month-old who has found peace at last. Then I hoped he might sleep on into the evening so we could do the supper-bath-bed tarantella when I got back.

He woke at six, screaming as if he had just understood that we are all bound for death. Puréed avocado and baby-rice were ineffectual, but he scrabbled at my top as if I kept the elixir of eternal youth in there.

'I can't not feed him,' I said, opening my shirt.

'He's going to want it again before you get back,' warned Giles, who was trying to convince Raphael that an odd number of fish fingers on the plate is not a widely recognized harbinger of doom.

Moth grabbed a handful of the padding over my once visible ribcage and pulled my breast into his mouth. Silence, for a moment, filled the room, followed by gulping. Giles passed me a glass of water. It was 6:25.

'OK,' said Giles. 'I'll get the gown. You haven't time to change.'

'I need some make-up,' I said. 'Spotted bag in the bathroom cupboard. I'll do it in the loo at college.'

'Mummy,' said Raphael. 'Mummy, what happens if submarines run out of compressed air?'

'Giles, can you put my phone in the sleeve of the gown? On silent?'

The only thing I was looking forward to was leaving the house without a bag.

Moth went on and on. At 6:40 I pushed my little finger into his mouth and pulled away. Milk spurted in jets. Moth rooted for a minute and then remembered mortality.

'Fuck, fuck, fuck. I can't leave him like this.'

'Mummy, what if a submarine runs out of compressed air before it gets to the top?'

'OK,' said Giles. 'Look, go now. At least show your face. If he doesn't calm down in an hour I'll bring him in a taxi, you can feed him somewhere and then I'll take him away again. But you need to go now.'

I remembered the Principal's pointing finger, his gaze on the rain outside. My Oxford career was probably already beyond redemption.

'Anna, come on. You can't lose your Fellowship over one breastfeed. He won't starve in three hours.'

I poked my finger into his mouth again. Milk trickled. I pushed some kitchen paper into my bra, settled the gown over the whole sorry mess and ran for my bike. Moth's screams curled round my legs to the end of the road.

The bath was cooling, becoming comfortable. I sat up, let some water out and added more hot. The house was silent, as if Giles had gone to bed. I lay down again and wriggled back until, by tilting my head, only my nose and mouth were above water.

I'd arrived at college with wild hair and my skirt soaked. The Fellows were filing in, meaning that I was too late to engage in the SCR dance where you try to make sure you finish the sherry in close proximity to someone whose company you can tolerate for the rest of the evening. It is not all right to swap places when the Principal rings the bell. I added myself to the procession and found myself next to the Bursar, who would have made an excellent prison warden or doctor's receptionist. The Principal banged the table three times with the silver gavel, required the Almighty's blessing in Latin, and the students sat down. As the noise level rose I remembered Moth's open mouth and felt milk for him beginning to trickle into my bra.

'Have we seen you since you took all that maternity leave?' asked the Bursar.

'Early evenings are difficult with small children. I've been back at work for eight weeks.' Because maternity leave makes me want to chew my feet off. Because there were days when Raph was at school and Moth cried if I tried to put him down – so I could dial a phone number, for example, or butter a piece of toast – when I ended up walking up and down the road with him in my arms because I couldn't actually go anywhere in case he needed feeding (which I did too badly to attempt in public) but I couldn't stay in the house any longer because I didn't trust myself not to hurt him.

'Hmph,' said the Bursar. 'Of course in my day we had to choose. And if you chose to have children, you looked after them yourself. Better all round.'

A small white plate supporting an arrangement of fish and beetroot descended over my shoulder. You are not supposed to make eye contact with the butler. If you do, you will see in his eyes that he has decided which knife he would use and how long he would take over it. My phone banged against the table as I moved my arm.

'It must have been hard,' I said.

She forked beetroot. 'Not in the slightest.'

There are four courses, not including dessert, which is a more or less optional extra. You converse with the person on your left until the plates are removed and then change sides, like one of those 1940s breastfeeding regimes. The senior Fellow should initiate the change. I was trying to drop casual remarks about recent progress with my research into conversation with the Fellow in Engineering when my phone began to whirr. I excused myself and ran for the corridor.

'Anna, I'm sorry. He screamed until he was sick. We're in a taxi.'

I could hear Raph singing 'Old MacDonald' and Moth moaning and hiccupping.

'You mean he didn't stop at all?'

'We're at the gates. I'll come and find you.'

I heard the howls coming down the corridor. Hall has double doors lined with green baize. Oxbridge colleges are probably the last refuge of the green baize door, but I don't know that they keep baby hysteria from the unsullied ears of the Fellows. Moth's face was beetroot pink, his mouth cavernous with woe.

'Oh Christ, quick. Give him to me. Raph, Daddy will take you to see something.'

'But Mummy, what if a submarine runs out of compressed air?'

I ducked into the SCR, which was quiet and to hand, leaving Giles to address submarine contingency plans in the corridor, or perhaps to take Raph into Hall and make enquiries of the Fellow in Engineering. Moth's howls rose. Death is certain and God is not in the world, suffering is inevitable and we had brought him into a vale of tears. I sat in the nearest seat, a low gold brocade which was probably meant by its eighteenth-century maker as a nursing chair, tucked the gown under my chin and latched him on. He pulled off again, screaming. I bared the other breast, leaving the first one waving in the wind, dribbling milk on to the brocade and the Persian rug below, and that was when the Principal came in.

Giles is right. I haven't set foot in the place since, haven't opened their letters. My salary keeps coming in, but if there is a mechanism for sacking Oxford Fellows it is so arcane that even other Oxford Fellows can't invoke it. My contract ends in a few weeks and my career is effectively over.

What Giles doesn't know, what nobody knows except the doctor at the Family Planning Clinic and perhaps, now, Ian MacDonald, is that the following week I unplanned our family. The sickness and tiredness I'd put down to Moth's sleeplessness and constant breastfeeding, which I held also responsible for my lack of periods. But when the vomiting started and the soreness spread across my breasts, it occurred to me to check. I abandoned research to cycle out to Bicester to buy a pregnancy test where there was no risk of encountering an old student or one of Giles's colleagues. I dithered in the chemist's, briefly convinced that some kits must be for women who want a baby and some for women sickened by the idea and that if I bought the right one it would give me the right result. Is Clear Blue the clear blue line of a (male?) baby or the clear blue skies of freedom? Is the worm promised by Early Bird a writhing infant or the security of a long, free day ahead? The sales assistant began to watch me and I picked up an unbranded box, hoping that economy and (Giles's) anti-capitalist principles would buy me peace.

They didn't. I peed on the stick in the ladies' at the public library in Bicester and watched two lines appear as swiftly as skin blistering after a burn. I wrapped the test in the chemist's bag, poked it into the bin, washed my hands and cycled back into town and straight to the clinic. Giles has always wanted a daughter. Given my history, it was not hard to persuade two doctors that my mental health would be jeopardized by a third child. I turned over quickly, slopping water on to the floor, and kept my face under until the plumbing went quiet and stars exploded under my eyelids.

Colsay House

18th November

Dear Aubrey,

I make bold to write again; although I have received nothing from you the postal service here is such that the absence of letters tells me nothing about my friends' intentions – as you perhaps noted on your travels in the summer, there is no post road closer than Inversaigh. I have been making progress here, I believe; it is slow work but the best prizes are not easily won and I have reason to be more hopeful than when I last wrote.

The great news here is that Lord Dumfermline has decided to offer all the residents of Shepsay free passage to Canada at the same time as raising the rents of those left behind. Apparently the people have been for some years crowded on to subdivided crofts at the northern end of the island, where the land is poorer and the water not so good, and, after an outbreak of sickness, it has been decided that they must be better and happier where there is land for the asking, with fine trees and rivers and a climate which means that they will never have to borrow for meal again. Mrs Grice tells me there is great unhappiness at the announcement, but Mrs Barwick says most sensible folk are glad at the chance so it is hard to say who might be right, but in any case it seems to me that it would be a great thing for the people of Colsay to do likewise. Do you think it would be objectionable if I were to write to Miss Emily about this? I imagine it would be cheaper than building and maintaining a schoolhouse and paying a schoolmaster for the rest of the century, which after all the new Education Act will oblige Lord Hugo to do if the people remain, and I am very sure that it

161

would be in every way better for them to build new houses in a new land than to drag on in the filth and smoke and dampness of their current abodes, however competent such a schoolmaster might be (which is, is it not, highly doubtful, considering the situation here and probable remuneration?).

I hope to be able to send you good news of Mrs Grice later this month, and am happy to say that I am in expectation of another patient in the Spring, although she is not a woman with whom I have been able to have any conversation so far! I do hope you will find a moment to write soon. I recall what was said under the tree in August and wonder how much was truly meant ...

Fond regards,

May

9

COMMON KNOWLEDGE

It is common knowledge that only love for children will prevent their continual demands, the continual noise caused by
them, and the continual damage done by them from being
considered a nuisance.

Foster mothers, i.e., householders, are expected to suffer
children whom they neither love nor overestimate.

– Anna Freud, *Infants Without Families: Reports on the Hampstead
Nurseries, 1939–1945*, p. 175

Night Waking: 02:08

Someone is tapping softly on our bedroom door, someone who
is already between us and the children. It comes again, low
down, not the rapping of someone who needs to wake us but
something signalling its presence.

'Giles!' I hiss. 'Giles! Wake up.'

I shake his shoulder but there is no response. The knocking
ceases and there are steps on the landing. Moth begins to
whimper. I throw back the duvet, not waking Giles, and hurry.
Whatever it is, it's now in Moth's room and he's scared.

It's Raphael.

'Raph! What on earth are you doing? Shh, go out there.'

I push Raph back out to the landing and pat Moth's back.
'Hush, love. It's all right. Shh, Mummy's here.'

163

Moth wasn't fully awake, and after a few minutes I can sidle out of the room.

Raph is sitting at the top of the stairs, hugging his knees. He's not wearing a pyjama top and I can see each rib in his back. I go and sit next to him, and as I sit down I freeze. There is something moving in the attic.

'Mummy,' he whispers. 'Mummy!'

I put my arm round him. His skin is cold to the touch. 'Shh. I heard it.'

The tapper on the door? I don't want to ask Raph in case it wasn't him.

There is rustling and bumping above us. Moth sighs and turns in his cot, shaking the Cow Rattle, of which he is still fond.

'That was Moth,' I whisper.

The thing upstairs moves again, and there is indistinct speech. Not the cry of a baby. Raph shivers and burrows against my flannelette.

'OK. Raph, look, I think there's something there too, OK? I can hear it.'

He whimpers. I abandon my feminist principles. Spectre-hunting, like checking the tyre pressure and peeing standing up, requires a Y chromosome.

'Come in my room and we'll get Daddy to go look, all right?'

It is no moment for courtesy. I pull the duvet off and Raph tugs Giles's feet.

'Daddy! There's something in the attic and me and Mummy are frightened.'

I'm listening for steps on the stairs, for it to come down and get Moth while we're all in here.

'Giles, for God's sake wake up. I'm worried about Moth.'

'What? What's wrong with him?'

'Daddy, please just go upstairs and – and – Daddy, I'm frightened!'

Raph, who does not cry, is crying. I can't cope with Moth being on his own any more, and I go back, treading quietly

164

across the landing, and work my hands under his back so I can scoop him up without changing his position. He settles against my neck, warm as new bread and damp and heavy. Back in our room, Giles is pulling on clothes, as if going out to rescue sailors from the rocks, and Raph is sniffing and shivering in the middle of the bed.

'This is ridiculous,' says Giles. 'There better bloody had be something there. You do realize I have to get up in three hours for the puffins?'

'Mummy heard it too,' says Raph.

I sit down beside him, trying not to shift Moth's weight about too much, but it is futile.

'Hello, Raph. Morning now. Porridge!' He is, none the less, uncertain about this gathering in the yellow light of my bedside lamp. The four-poster throws towering shadows up the wall.

'All right,' says Giles. 'This better be good.'

We huddle together while he goes upstairs. I feel as if we are in *Little House on the Prairie* (which I have seen here somewhere and should find for Raph, as a counterpoint to the military hardware porn), waiting for Pa to come back having prevailed against a hungry bear in hand-to-hand combat.

'What if it gets Daddy?' asks Raph. Then I get the house, I think, and enough life insurance for a damn good nanny.

'Where Daddy gone?'

'Daddy's just gone upstairs. Raph, I'm sure there's nothing there really. It's probably just – just the wind or something.'

He is staring at the door, waiting for it to open. 'You heard it, Mummy. Wind doesn't walk about on the floor.'

He grabs my arm. There are steps coming down the stairs. 'Mummy! It's hurt Daddy and now it's coming down! Mummy!'

He burrows under the duvet. Moth giggles. 'Raph down a hole. Peepo!'

Giles flings the door open. Whatever is up there clearly has no intention of exposing itself to a sceptical gaze.

165

'There's nothing there. I told you. Absolutely bloody nothing. Go look. Now for God's sake let me get some sleep.' He strips his clothes off.

Raph emerges and we exchange glances. There was something. Probably.

'Raph?' I stroke his shoulder. 'We'll go up and look in the morning, OK? So you can see Daddy's right.'

Raph looks away. Moth launches himself at Giles, who is showing signs of going back to sleep, and pokes his eyes.

'Come on,' I say. 'Everyone back to bed now.'

Moth looks round, indignant as if I'd given him a new toy and then taken it away.

'Porridge, Mummy!'

'More sleeping first.'

'Mummy?' Raph is standing by the door as if there is a fast-flowing river on the landing. 'Mummy, can I sleep in here? Just for tonight?'

Giles stops pretending to be asleep. 'No,' he says. 'Sorry but no. Setting a precedent.'

And reinforcing fear, I think. All the parenting books, eighteenth-century and modern, warn against appearing to take your children's irrational anxieties too seriously. I have, myself, yet to experience a fear assuaged by the brisk application of common sense.

Raph looks into my face, as if in a mute plea to be pulled from the current.

'OK,' I say. 'Come on. Moth and I will sleep in your room.'

I am wrong, of course. Raph sits up in bed keeping watch and Moth potters about messing up Raph's Lego and singing an approximation of 'Baa Baa, Black Sheep' until the sun rises and I give up. Prisoners awaiting execution, I am sure, greet sunrise with less enthusiasm than I do, but most days I would put myself forward with some confidence against people facing dental treatment or driving tests.

*

Later, we went over to make a final check on Black Rock House while Giles took the boat to Colla to collect the Fairchilds. There were clouds, but high and white. Innocuous, although moving faster than I would have liked, their shadows sailing across the hillside behind the house. The waves had turned white since breakfast and we watched as Giles reached the open water and began to lurch from one crest to the next. The boat would be sitting lower with three extra bodies and groceries for six, and I hoped the Fairchilds were as beguiled by the great outdoors as by the rain-mist shower.

'Put Moth down!'

He landed as awkwardly as a seagull.

'OK, but we have to walk to the cottage.'

'Moth go a beach!'

Raphael ran after him.

'No, Raph, don't grab him. Moth, we need to go to the cottage now. Beach later.'

'Later' is a concept with about as much meaning to your average toddler as 'new historicism' or 'neurophysics'.

'Go a beach, now!'

'Later. Cottage now.'

'Come *on*, Mummy.'

I picked him up again. 'Come on. Mummy will be a horse. A-gallop, a-gallop.'

'Do you think we should put some flowers?' I asked Raphael. 'Well, some grasses or something? In a vase with some pebbles.'

He looked at me as if I'd suggested a pleasing arrangement of socks or tin openers.

'Why?'

Moth was playing with the washing machine again.

'Oh, never mind.'

I wandered around, half listening to Moth's conversations with domestic appliances. The 'arts and crafts packs' were inadequately represented by some pencil crayons in which

Raph had never shown any interest and some watercolour paint and a block of artist's paper acquired by me in a rare moment of optimism before Moth was born. But there was a home-made soda loaf charmingly wrapped in one of Julia's linen cloths (technical purpose unknown), and a basket of soap made by a woman whose husband farms sheep outside Colla. There is some connection between the sheep and the soap which I do not wish to contemplate in any detail.

There were now roller-blinds with child-strangling cords which didn't matter because the house is officially unsuitable for children anyway, and I'd come over the previous night when the goblins that control Giles's USB thing weren't in the mood at home to check e-mail and wipe the fingerprints off the full-height windows. There was loo paper and cold-pressed olive oil and green tea. Giles, briefly distracted from the puffins by the vicarious gratification of gastronomic fantasy, had ordered smoked salt from the smokery at Shepsay and two kinds of pepper. When they came I could see him salivating over imaginary menus, although I have never seen a recipe calling for smoked salt. There were tea-towels with birds on them from the website of a shop on Marylebone High Street and there were plates in two sizes and mugs and bowls from the pottery at Eynvik where Giles once bought a vase for my birthday. We could send the children to boarding school and step straight into a new life.

'Oh dear, soon dry Moth. Never mind.'

'Moth?' I said. 'Mummy just needs to go to the loo, all right? Just for a minute.' I did, but mostly I was succumbing to a sudden longing to be the first person to use a pristine bathroom, to sit on a toilet seat that not merely by good fortune but by definition hadn't been peed on by anyone else, to wash my hands with new soap and dry them on a new towel.

'No.' Moth reappeared. There was water all down his dungarees. 'No. Mummy not go a loo.'

'I'll only be a minute.' I set off into the hall.

'Mummy! Moth come too!'

'Mummy, what are you doing?' Raph called from upstairs. 'You can't leave Moth here.'

'I'm not bloody leaving him, I'm trying to pee, for Christ's sake.'

Raph put his head over the banisters. 'Why do you need to swear about peeing?'

'Oh, bloody hell.' I strode down the hall. If I'd been able to get the door shut before Moth joined me, I'd have locked it and left him banging and screaming outside.

'Moth helping,' he said happily, placing a cold hand on my upper thigh. The underfloor heating was off, but the slate tiles were clean and smooth and the walls gleamed. A panoply of towels hung at right-angles from the heated towel rail. I got up. Giles had bought nicer loo paper than we use ourselves, whether through ignorance or romance I didn't know. I helped myself lavishly, with only the briefest thought for the small luxuries of my past, in which toilet paper played no part.

'Mummy.' Moth was standing in front of me, peering up as if I were performing an interesting surgical procedure he wanted to learn. 'Mummy, where Mummy's penis? Where it gone?'

He was younger than Freud says boys should be when they ask this question (though I doubted, somehow, that Freud had personally been called upon to answer it). I wondered about anticipating subsequent acts of psychological destruction, which are after all what parenthood is for, by telling him Daddy had cut it off. Raph put his head round the door.

'Mummies don't have penises. Mummies are women and women have vaginas.'

They both stared at me. I pulled my knickers up.

'What, in there?' Moth pointed.

'Yes,' said Raph. 'And daddies put their penises in to make babies.'

169

Moth looked from me to his brother and back. I thought Raph had forgotten this unlikely tale before Moth was born.

I ran the tap. 'Right. Time to go home.'

The wind was too high for us to hear the boat's engine. There were voices in the hall. Having flicked through some of Giles's holiday magazines ('Penelope, Rupert's wife, came to greet us in a waft of cinnamon and a pristine apron'), I'd decided to be found in the kitchen doing something rustic with the children about my feet. I'd had to settle for assaulting a lump of frozen soup which I'd forgotten to get out of the freezer the night before, while trying to explain to Raphael why the *Titanic* ended up in two pieces.

'Hello,' I said. 'I hope you had a good trip. I'm Anna.'

Three of them. A large woman with dyed mahogany hair and the kind of orange make-up that makes you want to scratch it to see what's underneath, wearing a small but high-spec waterproof jacket; a man in aggressively trendy glasses with grey hair razor cut in a manner unknown to Oxford academics; and a teenage girl in damp jeans, hiding behind her pale hair and hollow as the people in Raph's book about the liberation of Amsterdam in 1944.

The woman stuck out her hand. There was a drop on the end of her nose.

'I'm Judith. I must say, I hadn't thought the boat would be quite that small. I mean, not so small that people's luggage gets wet. But I suppose it's an unusual place, isn't it?'

'It is,' I said. 'I'm sorry your luggage got wet. I'm afraid we hadn't thought of that.'

'Oh, it doesn't matter. I mean, my husband was a bit worried about his laptop but I'm sure it's fine. Those cases are very good, aren't they?'

The husband cleared his throat. 'It's not a problem. Good to be on the water after all that time in the car. The way things have always been round here, isn't it? Brian, by the way.'

Moth peered from behind my jeans. 'Mummy not got a penis.'

I hoped this remark was so extraordinary as to be incomprehensible. The corners of Judith Fairchild's lips twitched.

'This is Timothy.' I patted him. 'And Raphael.'

'Hello, Timothy. And how old are you, Raphael?'

'Mind your own business.' Raph disappeared back into the kitchen.

'Raphael!' I said. 'Sorry, we've been here all summer, they're not used to visitors.'

'It was perfectly reasonable,' said the girl. She shook her hair back. 'Mum, you wouldn't like if it the first thing someone said to you was "How old are you?".'

'Don't be so aggressive, Zoe. I expect he's shy.'

Zoe slouched. 'You'd have smacked me if I'd spoken to someone like that. You never let me be shy.'

Giles rubbed his hands together. 'Parenting fashions change, don't they? We had a nanny who used to hit us with a garden cane. Anna's working on children's history, you know.'

Judith looked me up and down. 'Are you? You're lucky to find the time, with two boys.' She smiled at Moth. 'I expect you keep Mummy on her toes, don't you?'

He looked at my feet, puzzled.

'Why doesn't Giles take you over to the house?' I asked. 'I do hope you'll like it.'

The drop fell on to her stomach and rolled down the white Gore-Tex. 'Thanks. Would you like me to keep a list of snags?'

'We stayed in a cottage in the Lake District last year.' Zoe fiddled with a yoghurt-smeared bowl on the table. 'And it didn't have a coffee grinder. Mum had to improvise.'

Giles did not meet my gaze. The nearest coffee grinder in private hands is probably in Glasgow, along with the nearest coffee beans. 'Oh well,' he said. 'If you need anything that's not there you can always come and find us and we'll do what we can.'

'We will,' said Judith. 'Best to find out now, isn't it?'

We were finishing lunch when Giles came back. The soup seemed to be mostly cabbage and was worse than usual. I felt sorry for him for the first time in years.

'Jesus, Giles, how did you manage not to push them into the sea?'

He sat down, looking as if a mink had eaten all the puffins.

'The real question is why that girl has come on holiday with her mother. They hate each other. Not one civil word. Poor bloke.'

I passed him a bowl. 'Makes me feel like a decent human being.'

He looked up. 'You are a decent human being.'

I buttered bread for him. 'Not always.'

Giles went back to the puffins when Moth went to sleep, taking a well-earned break from human beings. I set Raph up in the bathroom with a sequence of plastic pots and toy boats and asked him to write down which ones were most seaworthy and why, which I thought I could probably count as part of home education if the parenting police ever stopped by. I took my tea into the sitting room and woke up my computer. The bibliography was still not in alphabetical order and the simplicity of the job appealed to me. I scrolled through and began to cut and paste from a document entitled 'Books to Find'. Many of my colleagues will look only at the bibliography and the index and will be content with the book if they find their own names there. I wondered if I could be bothered to check the publishers' guidelines about alphabetizing anonymous publications – by title or under 'Anon' – and then thought I might just glance at the *Colla and Inversaigh Free Press Observer*.

172

Fiona Firth must have got a major grant for the project, the kind of grant that would put my CV on to the smaller pile when I apply for jobs. I searched for 'Colsay + Castle School + accident' between 1940 and 1945 and was immediately rewarded. On 10 June 1943, 'On Thursday, the body of Mary Homerton, a pupil at the Castle School, was pulled from the water under the cliffs at Eyness Howe. A Fatal Accident Inquiry will follow.' No more? What about the baby? I clicked the next link, to an issue five months later.

MARY HOMERTON CASE: FATAL ACCIDENT INQUIRY OPENED
The Fatal Accident Inquiry into the death of Mary Margaret Homerton, whose body was found in the water below the cliffs of Colsay in June of last year, opened at Inversaigh Parish Hall yesterday. Mr Robert Webb is Acting Sheriff. The dead girl's father died on active service last year and her mother, who remarried shortly after the accident, has not travelled north to attend the inquiry.

Mr Webb began by hearing from Miss Leach of the Castle School, who explained that Mary Homerton had stayed on the Buchan croft last year because Colsay House was not big enough for all the girls. Asked if it was wise to billet out the younger children in this way, especially when it was known that Mary had recently lost her father under distressing circumstances, she replied that on the contrary, she had thought it better for the child to be in a family environment and that in fact it seemed that leaving Mrs Buchan had caused Mary more upset than going there. She had left when Mrs Buchan's condition made it advisable for her to do so, but had remained fond of both Mrs Buchan and the baby and visited them often.

Miss Leach was asked why Mary had not been in lessons on 7 June, and replied that Mary had been much upset by a letter from her mother received earlier in the week and had been unable to apply herself and sometimes distracting to other girls. Miss Leach and Miss Bower, in accordance with the principles on which the school is run, decided to 'respect her feelings' rather than requiring the child to conform to the usual rule. Miss Leach agreed that since they were two adults in charge of thirty girls this meant that Mary was effectively unsupervised during the day, although she added that the girls had been told to keep away from the cliffs and that there had been no previous difficulties relating to their licence to wander the island.

Asked if she knew the contents of the letter, Miss Leach produced the original, which was found among Mary's possessions, and read aloud the pertinent part, to the effect that Mrs Homerton intended to remarry, had sold the family home and would be living in her new husband's residence when Mary returned from school for the summer holidays. It appeared that Mary had had no previous intimations of her mother's intentions and was particularly unhappy with her mother's choice, alleging that Mr Barker had been her mother's companion before her father's death and that he did not like Mary and resented her claims on her mother.

Mary had received permission to go visit Mrs Buchan and had agreed that she would return to the school for four o'clock tea. When she did not do so, Miss Leach was irritated but assumed that Mary had been offered tea by Mrs Buchan. It was only when Mrs Buchan herself appeared shortly after four o'clock, saying that Mary had taken baby Alexander for a walk two hours previously, that the alarm was raised.

Mr Webb asked Miss Leach to consider whether, in retrospect, she felt that anything could and should have been done differently. Miss Leach said that naturally she and Miss Bower had given this question a great deal of thought and discussion, usually concluding that the only way they would have been aware of the extent of Mary's unhappiness, since she was not a confiding child, would have been to read her letters, and that even in retrospect they could not regret allowing the girls their privacy.

Mr Webb pointed out that at most English schools it is customary to read the pupils' letters, if not the parents' replies. Miss Leach said that this was precisely not the kind of school she aspired to run, adding that she and her partner have always held that children treated as intelligent and sensible beings are likely to behave as such.

Mr Webb adjourned the inquiry until tomorrow, when he will hear the evidence of Mrs Buchan.

I listened for Raph upstairs, wanting to go and make sure that Moth was still there, that he hadn't been quietly removed by Mary's ghost, but also wanting to finish the story. I went and stood in the hall. Water swished in the bath. John Bowlby describes an experiment called 'the glass cliff' in the 1960s. The psychologist arranged a room on two levels, using wooden boards and fabric to make a vertical drop of a few feet look much longer, and covered the apparent chasm with clear, non-reflective glass. Then he placed a sequence of newly mobile babies at one side of the chasm and asked their mothers to call them from the other side. Three of the babies under one crawled over the edge of the 'cliff' without a flicker of concern. Young toddlers were more likely to pause and cry, but could be persuaded to keep going. The two-year-olds refused outright (I wondered if the experimenters had allowed for the tendency of two-year-olds arbitrarily to refuse outright any request on grounds that have nothing to do with judgement. I wondered also if they had given any thought to the fact that the experiment, while acceptable to the ethics committee of the day, taught its subjects that crawling over the edges of cliffs brought no alarming consequences). I was not sure this experiment meant that Mrs Buchan's baby had died without fear; young babies may be immune to the fear of heights but they have some self-preserving instinct, albeit one that comes by definition too late, in the form of a grasping reflex which any careless parent can trigger in the course of a bath or nappy change. His final seconds would have been filled with terror, and then pain.

MARY HOMERTON CASE: FATAL ACCIDENT INQUIRY CONTINUES
Mrs Buchan gave evidence today at the inquiry into the death of ten-year-old Mary Homerton on Colsay last June. Mr Webb, Acting Sheriff in the absence on active service of Douglas Henryson, began by thanking Mrs Buchan for attending and reminding herself of highly distressing circumstances. He asked her to give her account of 7 June.

Mrs Buchan said that until teatime the day was quite ordinary. She assumed the court had no interest in the earlier part of her day, before Mary's arrival at the cottage, but the baby had been awake a great deal of the previous night, perhaps troubled by teething, and although she had risen at the usual time to feed the hens and get the washing out, she had been exceedingly tired all that day. Mary arrived while she was giving the baby his lunch and asked if she could feed him. Baby Alexander was fond of Mary and Mrs Buchan was happy to sit and eat her own meal, so Mary gave him some pease pudding and then an egg custard. Mary had had her own lunch at school, the teachers being good about making sure the girls were no burden on the islanders' ration books. Afterwards Mary helped to tidy the house and wash up the meal, and then asked if she could take Alexander for a walk, suggesting that Mrs Buchan could sleep for an hour or so.

Mr Webb asked if Mary had shown any signs of being upset or unhappy. Mrs Buchan said that she knew Mary didn't like her new stepfather and was angry about her mother remarrying so soon after her father's death, but nothing had been said on this occasion. Mary had shown

Mrs Buchan her mother's letter earlier in the week and 'had a good cry' but seemed quite absorbed in the baby on this occasion and had in fact said little directly to Mrs Buchan. Mary had often played with Alexander while Mrs Buchan was busy about the croft, but had never taken him out before and at first Mrs Buchan was reluctant to let him go. However, she was very tired and expecting more teething troubles in the evening, and she knew Mary to be a sensible girl, so she said Mary could take him down to the shore and back, knowing that she could easily carry him there and be home in three-quarters of an hour. She helped Mary wrap up the baby and went to lie down, and when she awoke it was nearly four o'clock. She knew at once that Alexander was not in the house and ran down to the beach to find them. When they were not there, she ran to the school and the search began.

Mrs Buchan had been composed until this moment. Mr Webb assured her that there was no need to recall the rest of the day. He said he must ask her a difficult question and asked if she would like a moment to prepare her mind first. Mrs Buchan said she would prefer to continue, and he asked if she felt anything should have been done differently to avoid the tragedy. Mrs Buchan looked up and spoke clearly, saying that of course she regretted having let Mary go and would never forgive herself for putting herself ahead of the children's safety, but she did not think the school had done anything wrong and, having spent a great deal of time remembering Mary's behaviour that afternoon, could not see any sign that the balance of her mind was disturbed. It was her belief that the fall was an accident, although she could not say why the children had been at that end of the island in the first place.

Mr Webb again thanked Mrs Buchan, and said that the inquiry would hear from Jamie Norman and John Peterson in the afternoon.

I pushed the laptop back and went quietly up the stairs. Moth was in his cot, bottom up, face down, breathing evenly. I held the back of my hand against his cheek, which was slightly sticky, and he sighed and murmured. Warm but not feverish, breathing deeply but without pauses, sleeping and not unconscious. I half closed the door and tiptoed across the landing. Raph was lying on a heap of dirty laundry reading *Raising Happy Children: A Parent's Guide to the New Generation*. Shipwrecked Tupperware drifted in the bath, which was fit to be seen only by candlelight. I went back downstairs and re-read the page.

I couldn't believe Mrs Buchan's was the testimony of a woman whose baby had been taken away and killed. How could she care about Mary if Alexander were dead? But if he was not dead, why would she need to be spared the recollection of the rest of the day? Maybe he had been injured, found smashed on a ledge, and died in her arms before bedtime. Mrs Buchan's story was a parable for mothers: the price of rest and solitude, even for forty-five minutes, is your child's life. She seemed too collected, too clear-voiced, too 'composed' for Alexander to be dead. If someone did that to Moth, took him away from me and— I went back upstairs. I could have had ten more minutes to myself, but I picked him up still sleeping, eased myself into the armchair and leant back while he slept on my chest.

'Mummy! That policeman's coming over the field.'

Raph appeared over the banisters. I was trying to make a casserole with some meat from the bottom of the freezer, of unknown vintage and provenance and thus, I thought, best subjected to high heat for a long time. The onions had sprouted, the stock cubes were out of date and I was increasingly sure that everyone would be better off if I spent the rest of the afternoon in meaningful interaction with the children and served beans on toast for dinner, except that we were low on bread and I didn't think even Moth would eat beans on crispbread.

Moth pushed a plastic sheep on to the chopping board. 'Policeman say baa in a field. Sheep wants a onion.'

'More than anyone else does,' I said. 'But it would probably prefer carrot.' I handed Moth the sheep and a bendy carrot and washed my hands, although Ian MacDonald would probably be pleased to find me with fingers soiled by honest toil.

'Raph? Do you want to go read upstairs? I expect this is going to be very boring.'

I looked out. The sky was hurrying east and Ian MacDonald was passing the gap in the wall. I reckoned the chances of Judith Fairchild failing to observe the presence of the police were remote.

'No,' said Raph. 'Of course not. I expect it's going to be rather interesting.'

I went to the door and opened it before he could knock.

'Mrs Cassingham. Is your husband around? We have some news about the remains.'

'Come in,' I said. 'I was just starting some supper. Giles is at the puffin colony. Our first visitors have arrived, at the cottage.'

'The Fairchilds.' He stood in the hall. 'I know. The boys are OK?'

'Come in and see,' I said. 'Do you want some tea?'

Come and see how normal I am. He looked up the stairs as if Lady Macbeth were standing at the top waiting to confess.

'Thank you.'

I wiped soup off the table and sat him in Giles's chair, hoping he'd notice the signs of domestic labour.

'That Daddy's chair,' said Moth.

'Hello, Timothy. Hello, Raphael.'

'Daddy's chair.'

Raph didn't look up from *Discovering Earthquakes*.

'So.' I was conscious of him watching me fill the kettle. Surely even Victorian physiognomists didn't think there was a criminal way of filling a kettle? I wanted proper tea enough to share it. He waited until I'd turned round.

179

He looked at me. 'You're quite sure there's nothing you can tell me?'

'About what?'

He looked round. 'Raphael, I brought you one of the maintenance guides for the police boat, but I think I must have put it down when I stopped to put my jacket on in your field. Would you go get it? It's in a clear plastic bag.'

Raph stood up. 'Go on, love,' I said. 'Put your coat on.'

We watched until the door closed behind him.

'About anything you might consider relevant to the discovery of a baby's remains in your garden. Anything at all you might have heard, or wondered about.'

I turned round to pour the water into the teapot. The teabags rose and bobbed like overturned boats. The grass outside bent in the wind. What if a storm came up and Ian MacDonald got stuck on the island? I suppose he'd get the helicopter out. Provide Raph with the thrill of the year.

'I was wondering – I mean, I'm sure you've thought if it – and it wouldn't be, really – but – it's not the one that – that went over the cliff, is it?'

I went over to the fridge. The milk bottle was stuck to the shelf. Giles, who never cleans anything, quotes a tabloid statistic about people cleaning the fridge less often than the toilet, which seems to me perfectly intelligent since, even in our house, people do not poo in the fridge. Ian MacDonald was waiting.

'The one that went over the cliff?'

I passed him the tea. 'The wartime one. Mrs Buchan's baby.' My hand shook. Mrs Buchan, it occurred to me, could still be alive.

'I see. No, we don't believe it was Alexander Buchan.'

'Oh.' I squashed my tea-bag against the side of the Star Mug. Giles likes it so weak he reuses them. 'So she's a girl?'

'Is she?'

'I presume that's how you know it isn't the Buchan baby?

180

Though I suppose the skeleton of a newborn doesn't tell you the sex.'

He watched me. 'It seems to have told you. A newborn?'

'A small baby. I don't know.' I filled my mouth with tea to stop myself talking. He watched me swallow. 'I can't stop thinking about it. The mother. How she could have kept going. I want to know the story, that's all. I know it wasn't me. I know you don't but I do. Or maybe you do. And if it wasn't Alexander Buchan and it wasn't me and we're discounting the idea that anybody could have landed at any time and buried anyone or anything here, then it's almost certainly pre-war and certainly not so far pre-war that the knitting wouldn't have lasted, and I don't know much at all about textiles and rates of decay but I'd have thought that made it no earlier than the late nineteenth century.'

He sighed and moved his cup. There is a border between criminal and historical investigation but I don't know where it is.

'Do you know when it first became obligatory to register a stillbirth? Because I did think that someone could have perfectly legitimately buried a stillbirth there, or a late miscarriage.'

'That would not be legitimate, Mrs Cassingham. Do you have experience of miscarriage?'

I could feel my face reddening.

'No,' I said. 'I don't. There was no obligation to register nineteenth-century stillbirths. It was a loophole that a lot of infanticides were accused of exploiting. I don't know when the law changed.'

He drank some tea. 'Indeed. I'm going to go see your husband in a minute and I suppose you're wanting to get back to your children. Or your work. Can you give me a copy of your husband's family tree?'

'No,' I said. 'But he will. He can probably draw it on a rock if you take him some chalk.'

It seemed that the police were on the trail of the Cassinghams.

*

I have never taken much interest in the Cassingham dynasty. The first thing Giles does in a hotel room in a new city is look for Cassinghams in the phone book, hoping for a long-lost cousin or branch of the family who thought they'd escaped, although he is embarrassed when people ask, as they do, if he is related to whatever Cabinet position Guy holds now. A distant cousin, he says, and political affiliations are not genetic. Liar. In each pregnancy I have enjoyed suggesting to Hugo and Julia that the baby will have my surname. Giles brought the Family Bible with us up here, a leather-bound Victorian folio wrapped in another of the linen cloths. Maybe they're shrouds. Small shrouds. That Bible probably exists in a category other than 'books' for him, 'ritual and votive objects' for example, or 'ancestral gods', so I started looking in the carved oak chest at his side of the bed rather than on the bookshelves. Giles's old toy cat, the one that his dormitory prefect threw out of the window on his first night at prep school, was at the top, and I handed it to Moth.

'Mummy cat. Mummy cat got a penis?'

'Shouldn't think so,' I said. 'Have a look.'

The chest is where he'd keep his secrets, if he had any, but I was so sure that Giles's secrets leave no evidence that I felt no shame when Raph came in.

'What are you doing?'

'There's a mummy cat. Where's a baby cat?' asked Moth, poking Giles's cat into my lap.

'Looking for the Family Bible.' Some ivory collar-points fell out of a blue leather box. 'I thought you could draw a family tree. And then we'll see what we can find out about your ancestors.'

'Oh.'

Spare shoe-trees, wrapped in crimson felt. A piece of heavy fabric wrapped in tissue paper so old it was disintegrating.

'Baby cat in a box?'

'What's that?'

I unrolled it. It was a flag with the Cassingham family crest in yellow on a blue background, with yellowed white toggles and loops. Raph craned out of the window to see the flagpole on the roof.

'Oh, for fuck's sake,' I muttered. The family flag.

'Some people don't like it if you use words like that. Can I hoist it?'

'No,' I said. 'The Queen's not in residence. And you might fall out of the window.'

'Mummy find a baby cat!'

Though it might be worth it to annoy Judith Fairchild. First the police and then a family flag. It was beginning to look as if Giles's secret fantasy was being a Victorian paterfamilias.

'Are these Daddy's?' asked Raph.

A pair of worn crimson velvet slippers, embroidered with the Cassingham crest in gold. I realized what this collection meant.

'No. These are Grandpa Hugo's, aren't they? Grandma Julia must have given them to Daddy. This is all Grandpa Hugo's. I haven't got a baby cat, love. Isn't there one in the toybox downstairs?'

'But he's dead,' said Raph.

'I know. I suppose that's why Daddy likes having his things. To remind him of his daddy.'

'And a daddy cat?'

Had Giles been poring over them, Grendel fingering his treasure, while I was working, or when I got up early with Moth? There was a flat package at the bottom wrapped in modern tissue and sealed with the sticker of the bookbinder on St Michael's Street.

'Was Grandpa Hugo Daddy's daddy?'

'Daddy cat gone to work.'

I looked up. 'Oh Raph, you knew that. Moth, maybe that is the daddy cat, and the mummy cat's gone to work.'

Moth clasped the cat to his stomach. 'Mummy cat not go to work. Mummy cat look after a baby cat. Where baby cat?'

I tore the tissue around the seal.

'Ought you to do that?'

'I'm part of the Cassingham family too, you know.' No.

Inside was a blue cardboard folder, the sort used in libraries to protect rare books. I unwound the strings and there it was, the red leather binding I remembered Hugo showing me in his panelled study when he added our marriage and then the birth of each child. Giles Hugo Fitzwilliam Cassingham, m. Anna Louise Bennet, 1) Raphael James Bennet Cassingham, Oxford, 2) Timothy Miles Bennet Cassingham, Oxford. He'd left space for several more children.

'There's me!'

'There you are.'

Moth came to see. 'And me. And Moth.'

Raph leant on my shoulder. Thea Clementine and Camilla Beatrix. There was a line leading off the page and some extra sheets of paper, but at the top of our tree was the marriage of the first Hugo Giles Cassingham, b. Bringham Hall 1820, to Esme Fitzwilliam, b. Chatton Hall 1833 and d. Bringham Hall 1854, younger than me and leaving a three-year-old son, Hartley, and a daughter born three days before Esme's death. Hartley grew up, and eventually married Adeline James, b. 1879, leading to issue in the form of the prematurely deceased Edwin and Nigel, two daughters, Violet and Clementina, and another son, who had issue 1) Giles's grandfather (also Hugo) and 2) Great Aunt Edith of Bath. At least I didn't let them name Raph, Hugo. They weren't as bothered about Moth; I think Julia still thinks of him as the 'spare'. I put my arm round Raph's shoulder. The tree in the garden rustled and sighed in the wind.

It could have been any of them, Great Aunt Edith in a youthful indiscretion that left her unmarriageable; either of her aunts, both of whom married young; or indeed any of the men, sowing their wild oats in their feudal island. A seduced or violated local girl hiding her shame, or maybe a daughter of

184

the aristocracy dispatched to a remote island to conclude her scandalous pregnancy, who dies in the course of delivering a stillborn infant. Standard fodder for sensational fiction, although usually the infant survives and, disowned by the aristocratic family, grows up beautiful and virtuous amid the wilds of Romantic Scotland and eventually saves the fortunes of the fallen house of Cassingham, after which it turns out that the parents were secretly married after all and our heroine is, in fact, the legitimate heir. Whereupon she marries a cousin and they all live happily ever after, shame about the dead mother.

'They have funny names,' said Raph.

'Most of them have the same names. Anyway, yours might sound funny in a hundred years.' My son is not the only Raphael at St Peter's Primary School, Oxford.

'What does the "d" mean?'

'It tells you when they died.'

He stood up. 'You mean they're all dead?'

'Raph, they lived long ago. The dead ones.'

'Grandpa Hugo didn't live long ago.'

Giles had added the date of Hugo's death. The King is dead; long live the King.

'He did. When he was born there were no computers and very few people even had cars.'

'There were still steam trains.'

'That's right.'

Raph began to direct 757s again. 'All you really need to make steam an environmentally friendly technology is a way of burning things you might put in landfill without making the toxins go into the air in smoke. There's a train in Sweden that burns rubbish, but the problem is you still can't use plastics.'

I turned over the pages in the Bible. Inside the rubbed edges, it was pristine. Votive object, not for reading. I wasn't sure I had learnt anything. I began to put things back in the chest.

'Mummy?'

'Yes, love.'

'Mummy?'

I closed the chest.

'What?'

'Mummy, if Grandpa Hugo died and he was Daddy's daddy, does that mean Daddy will die too?'

The presence of the Fairchilds, I realized, left Giles with a choice between spending his evenings outside in the dark with sleeping puffins or in our house with me. It meant he would probably wash up but also made it harder for me to be asleep by the time he came to bed.

'What did Ian MacDonald want?' I asked. He was washing dishes and I was moving wet clothes from the washing machine to the clothes airer as if I thought they would dry there.

Washing up stopped. His reflection in the window above the sink stared out into the night.

'Ah.'

'What?' I flapped the creases out of a T-shirt.

'Well, he was – ah. He was, I suppose, telling me about the DNA test. On the baby.'

Our eyes met in the reflection, faces deformed by the waves in Victorian glass.

'And?'

He picked up a pan and began to scrub it.

'It seems to be a Cassingham.'

I dropped a handful of mismatched socks.

'What do you mean, "seems to be"?'

'It has our DNA. My DNA.'

I bent down to pick up the socks, feeling sick. Giles? Giles's DNA? Giles's baby?

'Yours?'

He put the pan down and turned round. 'Not mine, obviously. I mean, not my personal DNA. The family. Cassinghams.'

'Date? They must be able to tell.'

He shrugged. 'He didn't say. He was asking about the post-war years. He's not stupid, that man. Realizes it's much more likely that the child never made it on to the family tree.'

I thought about the apple trees, innocent of branches. I have a family tree, too, though no one has ever felt the need to sketch it on the endpapers of a bible or raise a flag in its honour. There were five of Moth's socks, not one of which matched another. If they had reason to suspect it was Giles's baby, presumably he would not be washing up but answering for himself in an interrogation room in Inversaigh. I think he has been faithful. I have never harboured suspicions, though I can imagine that discretion in these matters runs deep in his genes. They may even teach it at Eton. But Giles had fifteen years of fertility before he met me. I stretched the socks out one by one. The next size up were still in a box in the loft in Oxford.

'Is there anything I should know?'

He put the pan on the draining board. I could see tinned tomato stuck to the outside.

'What do you mean by that?'

'Oh, you know. Ruined maidens in the closet. It's a staple of Victorian fiction: the squire gets the serving-wench into trouble and then runs back to London.'

'Anna, stop it. That's tasteless even by your standards.'

I thought about Moth upstairs, breathing quietly in his cot with his bottom sticking up, and Raph leaning on his pillow, intent on *Ships and Shipbuilding*. We were both scared to hold Raphael when he was first born, a red alien with a head that threatened to fall off, but Giles put Moth into his first clothes on the bedroom floor while I delivered the placenta. I didn't think about the cells that would have multiplied into another baby.

'Are you asking me if I have a dead baby I never told you about?'

'Of course not.' Yes.

'So?'

'Don't you mind? I mean, doesn't it worry you? It could be

187

your – your cousin or something.' Your sister. Your niece. Your aunt.

He swished tomato-stained water around a wineglass and then put it on the draining board.

'Let's wait and see, shall we? It's much more likely to be a lot older than that.'

I don't understand how he can do this, put his emotions on hold pending incoming data. Though I can see that it must make life more comfortable.

'But don't you care? I mean, the earliest it could be is about 1860, because your lot didn't buy the island until then, did you?'

He picked up another glass. '1860 is a long time ago. If I worried about everything my family's done since 1860 – well, I wouldn't have time for much else.'

He's right, of course. A few hungry winters on Colsay, a few mistakes in the Great War which had significant consequences for other ranks, some cousins who seemed perfectly happy in South Africa throughout the apartheid years and in fact rather less so thereafter. Not to mention a lot of voting.

'You mean there's so much blood on the family tree that an extra baby doesn't make any difference?'

'Oh, stop it, Anna. All I said is that we'll have to wait and see. If the police thought it was recent, I wouldn't be here, would I?'

Feet came up the path and someone hammered the knocker on the door.

'Oh, bloody hell.'

Moth shrieked upstairs and Raph came thundering down as Giles went to the door.

'Mummy, it's that Fairchild woman.'

I heard her in the hall. I preferred it when the only people who came calling at night were imaginary.

Giles came back. 'No nutcrackers,' he said.

She appeared in the doorway. There was a new drip on her nose and whisky in the air.

'Good Lord, your children are still up.'

'They are now,' I said. 'Excuse me, I need to reassure Moth.'

She stayed in the doorway.

'They only scream for attention, you know.'

'That's why I attend.'

She didn't move.

'They have to learn that they can't always have what they want when they want it. He'll be calling for you all night if you go every time, you'll never get any sleep.'

I didn't meet Giles's eyes.

'Why can't we have what we want?' demanded Raphael. He was wearing a pink T-shirt of mine which I hadn't seen for some time and his swimming trunks, which have fish on them and cannot be passed off as pyjamas to any kind of police.

'Because sometimes the grown-ups have other things to do. Anyway, life's not like that, and the sooner you accept it, the better.'

'Oh,' said Raph. 'Mine is.'

'Come on,' I said. 'Bed. And we'll settle Moth again.'

'We saw you had a visitor, earlier,' I heard her say as we went upstairs. 'Nothing wrong, I hope?'

Night Waking: 02:11

I wake to hiccupping sobs. I've been back in bed for twenty-eight minutes. It's Giles's turn, it's been Giles's turn for weeks. I shake his shoulder and he snorts and turns over. 'Giles! Wake up.'

He pulls the duvet up around his ears. Moth's dismay rises a tone. 'Giles, Moth's crying.'

I could kick him, I think. I could squeeze a flannel of cold water on to his face. I could beat him up with a mahogany dining chair. But meanwhile Moth is crying. The floor is still cold and still gritty. I wrap myself in Giles's striped silk dressing gown, which trails behind me. I keep my eyes on the floor as I pass the stairs, and the crying rises. There are wars over oil that will never end, nuclear material in the wrong hands and asteroids the size of Belgium raining into the atmosphere. I pick him up.

'Mummy!' He snuffles into my neck and rubs his nose on my collarbone. The crying stops. Mummy is magical, Mummy takes away the sins of the world. Everyone should have a mummy.

'Shh, love. It's all right. Mummy's here.'

I cradle him.

'Mummy's love.'

'Hush, little baby, don't say a word. Papa's gonna buy you a mocking-bird.'

We walk. The island lies quiet outside, holding the Fairchilds in their teak and stone cocoon, the villagers in the graveyard and those older, stranger beings in their stone barrows. And beyond that there is the sea where there are lights that shine all night, automated lights which hold on whether the people wake or sleep, and ships under way for the Far North and for America, and the ships are talking to each other and to the satellites, a web of conversation across the dark water. We are not alone.

'Mummy sing a Gruffalo.'

'No, love. Sleeping now.'

I stroke his hair. Above his ear, it is matted with soup.

'Not pull Moth's hair.'

'Sorry. Sleeping now.'

'A mouse took a stroll. Mummy sing it.'

'Sleeping now.'

'Mouse in a deep dark wood!'

'A mouse took a stroll through the deep dark wood. A fox saw the mouse and the mouse looked good.'

There is a light in Black Rock House, where someone is moving in the full height window with panoramic sea view. Zoe? I can't see Judith indulging in insomnia. If I were going to run a business devoted to making people happy, to meeting their every whim before it is expressed, if I were, in short, planning to mother adults for money, I wouldn't try to make Judith Fairchild's dream kitchen (and anyone who dreams of kitchens should be traumatized until their dreams are more interesting). No, I'd open a refuge for mothers. A retreat. Concrete 1970s brutalism, an anti-domestic architecture without flounces. Something low with big windows and wide corridors, carpets to deaden sound. There will be five or six rooms off the corridor, each with a wall of glass and sliding doors looking on to a cold, grey beach. Each room has a single bed in the corner, a table and chair. You may bring your laptop but there is no internet access and no telephone. There are books with a body count of zero and no suffering for anyone under the age of eight. A cinema where everything you wanted to see in the last eight years is shown at a time that allows you to have an early night afterwards. And the food, the kind of food you're pleased to have eaten as well as pleased to eat, is made by a chef, a childless male chef, and brought to your room. You may ask him for biscuits at any moment of the day or night, send your mug back because you dislike the shape of the handle, and change your mind after ordering dinner. And there is a swimming pool, lit from below in a warm, low-ceilinged room without windows, which may be used by one mummy at a time to swim herself into dream. Oh, fuck it, I am composing a business plan for a womb with a view. So what? I'll call it Hôtel de la Mère and the only real problem is childcare. Absent, children cause guilt and anxiety incompatible with the mission of the Hôtel; present, they prevent thought or sleep, much more swimming and the consumption of biscuits. We need to turn them off for a few days, suspend them like computers. Make them hibernate. You can't uninvent children any more than you can uninvent the bomb.

191

Dear Papa,

Your turn, I thought, for a letter all your own! I saw the women's knitting today and was reminded of your Penelope's weaving, the soft browns and greys and perhaps also the expression on her face, for the women here have also reason to think of the perils of the sea while their hands are busy, although I cannot think that anyone will compose an epic from the terrible grind of Colsay life.

I had prepared a short lecture on home nursing which I meant to give today to the women of the village, not that I think they have the means nor perhaps even the understanding to put into practice what I might say to them – and I had greatly modified the proceedings I suggest at home, which include such impossibilities as beef tea and clean linen. But I meant to begin a programme of these little talks, hoping to lead from home nursing to hygiene, hygiene to weaning, weaning to infant care and so towards the conduct of confinements. I have tried to be subtle! But of course that way too is blocked; I had offered to speak in the dining room here, thinking that they would find the church no fit venue for such allusions as I would necessarily wish to make and that it would be too much to suggest using one of their homes for this purpose, which in any case have scarce room enough for the beasts and people who must sleep there, and perhaps hoping also that curiosity to see the Big House might tempt those immune, as most of them seem to be, to the appeal of longer and healthier lives. I had specified two o'clock, and knowing that they have no way to know the time did not concern myself that no one came. Half an hour later there was still no one, and at three I betook myself in search of my audience. The street stood empty – no surprise with the rain blowing out of the puddles – so I steeled my nerves and began knocking on doors. I think it is not the custom here, I think they enter each other's houses without ceremony, but it seems too much for me to adopt local manners in this regard – after all, I would not have them enter my bedroom without warning! No answer at the first two dwellings, not even the tell-tale scuttle away from the window, but at the third I found four women standing huddled, the needles always flashing in their hands around the fire, where foul-smelling steam rolled from a pot suspended on a chain.

I wished them good day, complimented she whom I took for the lady of the house on the rough carving of her dresser, and asked if I might visit with them a little while. I had to take silence for consent and there followed the most awkward afternoon call of my life, myself making all the conversation on both sides so that you would have laughed to hear May discussing the weather with herself, but the knitting proceeded apace the while and so while my mouth gabbled of rain, seasons and the blessings of the harvest or some such nonsense, images of your struggles with Penelope's work drifted through my mind. Did anyone finish the weaving in the end? I remember Mama saying it would be a waste if the unfinished work were disposed of and that you had no need to make such outlay on wool. I am finding that I miss the sense of things being made here, which is foolish since the women are about nothing else from before dawn to after dusk, but you know what I mean, Papa. I miss your work, miss living in a place where there is always some project in hand, some new object of beauty, and friends coming by to comment and discuss. I wonder how Aubrey's Icarus is coming along? I should like to see the colours of it, the blue and flame, for Colsay is a scene done all in brown and grey.

Fondest love as ever,

May

10

THE MORE HIGHLY ORGANIZED FORMS OF LOVE

> One important instinctual need, that for early attachment to
> the mother, remains as we know more or less unsatisfied;
> consequently it may become blunted, which means that the
> child after a while ceases to search for a mother substitute
> and fails to develop all the more highly organised forms of
> love which should be modelled on this first pattern.
>
> – Dorothy Burlingham and Anna Freud, *Infants Without Families:*
> *The Case For and Against Residential Nurseries*, p. 22

Judith Fairchild appeared again while we were having breakfast. She had painted a line in a darker shade of orange across
each cheek.

'Oh, I'm sorry, I didn't think you'd still be having breakfast.
Routines slip, don't they, when there's no school? You're lucky
you get such long holidays from the university, though. Must be
a huge perk.'

I offered Moth a spoonful of porridge, which he spat out.

'Go away that woman.'

'Hush, Moth,' said Giles. 'We don't say that. Can we help
you, Judith?'

'There's a difference between a holiday and a vacation,' said
Raph. His mouth was full of toast and peanut butter. 'There

wouldn't be anything to teach the students if people didn't get time to do their research.'

She looked at me as if she'd been the recipient of the porridge. 'Shh, Raph,' I said. 'Eat your breakfast.'

'But you always say that!'

'I hope you had a comfortable night,' I said to Judith.

'Why?' asked Raph.

Moth drew in the spat-out porridge with his finger, which was blotched with what on closer inspection turned out to be red jam.

'Oh, well, we were a bit warm. It's funny, isn't it, you come to the Hebrides and even with all the windows open all night it gets hot – and those duvets are very cosy, aren't they, for summer?'

'There's a special condenser boiler,' said Raph. 'It's meant to maintain a steady temperature. And there's triple glazing.'

Giles stood up. 'I'll come over now and reset the thermostat for you. Easily done. Was there anything else?'

'We were hoping to do the circular walk from Rothkinnick. Only we'd need a lift over there.'

'Sure,' said Giles. 'When did you want to go?'

'We should make the most of the weather, really, shouldn't we?' She looked pointedly at the sky. 'While it's bright. It's meant to rain later.'

'Whenever you're ready.' Giles finished his tea and held the door for her. I could see the puffins flying sadly across his mind.

I lifted Moth out of his chair and began to tidy up breakfast. It would, I knew, be sensible to stop looking for the baby. She wasn't Alexander Buchan, not unless his mother had had both a wartime affair with Nigel or Edwin and some unimaginable reason for burying him in the wrong place, which was hardly plausible after all the official involvement in Mary's death. I didn't really think Julia or Thea would secrete even a stillborn baby on Colsay. Why should they? She could be anyone, any small human, wanted or reviled, lost to anger or accident or despair, any of those brief and unrecorded lives that never got as far as the baptismal font, let alone a first-person narrative on the internet or a journal held in cold storage in a city archive. The Cassingham DNA didn't really change anything; a late miscarriage, a stillbirth, common enough now and more so in the nineteenth century. I wondered how the world would be different if the accidents of infant mortality had fallen in slightly different places, erasing, for example, Einstein, Freud and Stalin while leaving for articulate adulthood the contemporaries mourned only by mothers and those whom infant mortality deprived of motherhood. Instead of psychoanalysis and general relativity and the gulags, with their own harvest of human potential, what?

'Moth done a poo.'

I picked him up and held him at the shoulders and knee. Never squash a full nappy.

'Raph? I'm going to change Moth's nappy and then we're going down to the headland, OK? I want to show you something there.'

'What?'

'Surprise project. You'll see when we get there.' Unless I thought of something better in the meantime, an interactive lecture on Colsay Burial Practices Through the Ages.

We could see showers moving across the sea, blurring the horizon like grease on a lens, but the sky over Colsay was silver and the grass was dry. The air smelt of seaweed and peat. I shifted Moth on to the other hip and unfastened my cagoule; the house is so cold that I often find myself overdressed when I get outside. Raphael had run ahead and then been arrested by something on a dry stone wall.

'What is there?' I called.

'Moth down. Moth go see.'

I put him down and watched him diminish across the grass.

I don't usually see Moth from a distance greater than I might cross between him losing his balance and hitting the floor, I don't go too far to be able to smell the food in his hair and the poo in his nappy. He's so small I could lose him in an open field.

There were patches of blue sky by the time we came to the ruins of the church, and a hesitant reflection of the pale sun in the sea. The church is at the end of the 'street', the worn stones between the two rows of houses. I don't know if there were never any pews or if they were taken out, but there is one small window high in the eastern wall and even I have to duck in the doorway. It would have been a dark place to spend summer Sundays, with the birds calling and swooping outside, the sea blue and the grass rippling in the sunlight.

'Careful, Raph. We don't know the walls are safe. It was the graveyard I wanted to look at.'

He came out. 'Why?'

'I thought it might be interesting to see if we can read any of the inscriptions. Moth, love, don't go through there.'

'Why?'

'Moth, come here!' I crouched behind a stone. 'Peepo!'

He came running. 'Peepo!'

'Why, Mummy?' repeated Raph.

'Because then we can find out about the people who lived here. That's history.'

He stroked the top of a gravestone, worn and tilting.

'Are the bones still here?'

'Probably. Bones take a long time to – to disappear.' To rot.

'Peepo!' shouted Moth.

Raph fingered his own eye sockets. Shadows flickered across the grass, a brighter green here than anywhere else on the island. Two ravens glided over our heads, squawked and tumbled up the sky, turning like stunt planes.

'Come on. Let's see if we can find any we can read.'

197

Most of the stones had been hammered by rain and scoured by wind until it was hard to tell that they had ever been pulled from the ground and chiselled into words. There were people there whose only legacies were posterity, and perhaps the ghosts of their impatience, their bad temper, the way they never recognized their children's achievements and were incapable of admitting error, were still whispering in the ears of parents in Colla and Newfoundland and Sydney.

'Look, Raph, can you see? Even rock gets worn away by wind and rain in the end. Look how they're so much rougher on this side where the wind comes off the sea.'

'Down,' said Moth. 'Moth want a biscuit.'

I pulled a foil package out of my pocket and offered him an oatcake.

'No oatcake. Biscuit.'

'OK. Biscuit while Mummy looks at some more stones, all right?'

'Stones biscuit.'

I gave him the ginger biscuit from under the oatcakes, which left me without a bribe for the way home.

The newer graves are further from the church, towards the rocks.

'I still can't really read any letters.' Raph was kneeling at one of the stones, tracing grooves with his finger.

'I think this might say "Mary",' I said. 'I doubt they bothered with long inscriptions. Everyone must have known who was where anyway.'

It was seeming less and less likely that we were going to find Alexander Buchan or any other story lying in a rough grave behind a drystone wall. There were lots of mounds in all sizes, and it was hard to tell which were man-made and which natural, let alone the size of the bones underneath. I like the churchyards in Sussex, where you get names and relationships and causes of death and how the survivors wanted people to think they felt about it, but perhaps that's just another way of denying mortality. Perhaps it would be better for the living to accept that the narrative inside our heads is finite and probably inconclusive, not to be chiselled on to stone and cast out into the future.

Raph stroked a fallen stone. 'This one's broken.'

'It's probably been there a long time. The graveyard might pre-date the church.'

I stooped over a small mound with a knee-high stone. Under the lichen, three letters were engraved, probably initials, as if passers-by might need reminding who lay there. If even the majority of those born on Colsay had died here over the centuries, there must be a lot more bodies somewhere. The ravens landed on the church roof, and one of them shouted something down to us.

'Mummy? Where's Moth?'

My heart turned. Where?

'Moth! Moth, where are you?'

Small head bouncing off the rocks, little fingers scrabbling on falling stone. I had always deserved this.

'Moth!'

'Mummy, where is he?'

'I don't know. Help me look. Look behind all the stones.' But he'd have come out by now.

'Moth!'

Where would he go? Not, usually, away from me, not voluntarily. 'Moth!'

Raphael was running from stone to stone, as if Moth would really cower there while he called him. I climbed up the dry stone wall. This is the beginning of it, this is what it feels like to become one of those stories. Alexander Buchan's story.

'Mummy, don't, it'll fall.'

He wasn't there.

'Moth!'

In the church. No. I ran around the outside wall. I knew what came next.

'Moth!'

He was gone. Moth was gone. No sign of him on the rocks, no body bobbling like discarded plastic on the waves. No – no blood.

'Moth! Moth, come back! Moth!'

Raph let out a wail. I looked at him and had nothing to say.

'Moth!'

I didn't know what to do next. Run for Giles and his phone, but I didn't want to leave the place we'd last seen Moth. Keep looking, but we knew he wasn't there. Find him.

I heard a shout. Not Moth.

'Anna! He's all right. I've got him.'

Zoe. Zoe coming up the street, holding Moth's hand as he trotted beside her. I ran to him.

'There's my mummy.' He sounded as if I was expected.

I picked him up and held him so tightly I could feel his ribs flexing. My eyes filled. Never out of my sight, never again. He wriggled.

'He was just pottering in the houses,' said Zoe. 'He was totally safe. He's been chatting away.'

I buried my nose in his hair. Zoe's mouth made the shape of a smile.

'He does. But I was frightened. I looked up and he wasn't there.'

She pushed her hair back. 'He was there. Just not where you thought.'

'Bad enough. Believe me.'

Raph came up. There were tears on his face. 'Can I cuddle him too?'

'Of course you can.'

I knelt down, Moth on my hip, and put the other arm round Raphael.

'Don't squeeze him too hard.'

Raph stroked my hair. 'You did.'

'Moth pulling Raph's hair,' said Moth. I disentangled his fingers and stood up. 'Moth down!'

'Not yet.' My hands were shaking. I tried to take a deep breath and failed.

Zoe looked at Raph. 'Hello. I'm Zoe. I was just exploring your village.'

He studied her clothes. All fashions have always looked convincing on thin eighteen-year-olds, from balloon sleeves and Leghorn hats to tight jeans and the kind of top I vaguely associate with American ball games, but she was obviously cold, her hands mottled and lips pale. Her lollipop-stick legs ended in those canvas ankle boots they all wear, which were wet and muddy. Her mother should have made her put her wellies on, I found myself thinking, as if I didn't myself allow Raph out without a coat most of the winter. Her hair, the caramel colour often adopted by women in their later thirties but rarely seen in nature, hung in tangles around her face. I had an uncharacteristic urge to wrap her up, warm her, feed her.

'Why are you exploring it?' Raph asked.

She smiled. 'Because I think a deserted village is cool, and because I didn't have anything else to do.'

'I think it's warm. The Romans could make buildings that stayed cool even in Naples in summer. I took my coat off.'

I glanced around. Took it off and left it somewhere, but there are worse things to lose than coats.

'Down!' said Moth. I put him down but kept hold of his hand.

'It is bright,' Zoe agreed. 'Can you tell me about your village?'

The sun was on his face and he squinted up at her. I should have tried to inflict sunscreen. There is a rule that babies and children should not be in direct sunlight at all between 11 a.m. and 3 p.m. and it applies in Scotland as well as on the beaches of the Mediterranean.

Moth pulled my hand. 'Mummy come!'

'I can tell you a bit,' said Raph. 'People lived in it until after the war, but not many, and then they went away and died. And we can't read the gravestones.'

'No,' she said. 'I expect they're pretty worn out by now.'

I followed Moth towards one of the houses and stood watching outside the door when he went in. The island children must have roamed freely, but some of them must also have fallen off the rocks. And in winter they'd have been corralled inside like animals in a byre.

'You didn't feel like a walk?' I asked Zoe.

'I felt like a walk. That's why I came here. I just didn't feel like spending the day with my mother.'

I nearly said that I wouldn't either. 'Sometimes it's nice to have some time to yourself,' I substituted.

Moth came back to the doorway. 'Up! More biscuit!'

'All gone biscuits,' I told him. 'Oatcakes.'

'No oatcakes!'

'All gone biscuits.'

He rolled on the ground. 'Moth wants a biscuit! No oatcakes! No!' His feet drummed my boot and I moved.

'That's pretty cool,' said Zoe.

'Yeah. I always think that.' I looked at her. I had no hope of achieving anything until after lunch anyway. 'Would you like to come back to the house and have some tea or something? Stay for lunch if you like, though we're not a gourmet establishment.'

'OK. Thanks. Only I'm vegetarian.'

'Oh, we don't have meat for lunch. I'm no cook.' I scooped up Moth and clasped him as he kicked at my pubic bone. 'Ow, Moth, no kicking Mummy. Raph! Come on, love, I think we'd better go home and make lunch.'

He poked his finger into a hole in the wall. 'Can I stay here? I won't do anything silly.'

No. Because the Neolithic wraiths will come up their stairs and drag you in. Because the sky might fall on you. Because one day those walls will collapse and therefore I don't want you anywhere near them ever. 'I can't see a good reason why not. But Zoe's coming back with us.'

His shoulders relaxed. 'OK. I'll come too.'

Moth stopped kicking. 'Raph come too and have a biscuit.'

It is occasionally clear to me that they as well as I would prefer a wider world.

'Should I take my shoes off?' asked Zoe.

I stared at her. 'Why? Your feet would probably freeze to the floor.'

She shrugged. 'Mum insists, at home. She says she won't have whatever people have stepped in on the pavement walked all over her carpets.'

I put Moth down and he stood holding my hand and looking up at Zoe.

'But there aren't any pavements. I even reckon the birdshit has probably worn off Giles's shoes by the time he's walked back here. Not that there's much carpet either. Don't worry.'

'Zoe,' said Raphael. 'Do you like bridges?'

She smiled at him through her hair. 'I like standing on them watching the water. Do you play pooh-sticks?'

He went into the playroom. 'I like them because of the building. Do you know how they tense the caissons?'

He held out the bridge-building book and she went over to him.

'I'll make you some tea,' I said.

Alone in the kitchen, I ate a dried apricot and sniffed at some out-of-date cream cheese which I was hoping to feed Zoe. It was too far gone, but there were eggs only a couple of days past the date stamped on their shells.

'Do you like scrambled eggs?' I asked.

'I don't,' said Raph.

'Yucky eggs,' Moth added.

'I wasn't asking you. There's enough soup for two.'

'Sure,' said Zoe. She was sitting on the floor between them,

203

helping Moth push the animals into the ark. 'But I'm not very hungry.' She had the body of someone who had been very hungry for a very long time.

I went back into the kitchen and broke the eggs, which seemed to be all right. I didn't have to persuade Moth to be put down while I stirred in milk and pepper, and I didn't have to step over Raph and his book to get to the fridge. Toy cars were not being pushed under my feet and no one demanded to play with the milk carton and its lid or push down the lever on the toaster. I could have put the radio on and heard the news or – I glanced at the clock – maybe even the Afternoon Play without concern for developing young minds. I went and looked into the playroom.

'Are you OK here, Zoe? Don't feel you have to entertain the children.'

She looked up. Mrs Noah (doesn't that woman have a name of her own?) was standing on the roof of the ark as if reasoning with the elephant threatening to jump off the second floor of the garage.

'One, two, three, jump!' said Moth. 'Oh bugger ark.'

Zoe grinned. 'I'm having a great time. Best for weeks.'

'Zoe's been in a rainforest,' said Raph. 'A temperate rainforest in Canada. With bears. Not the Amazon rainforest. People keep cutting down the Amazon rainforest and it makes half of the oxygen on Earth so if they don't stop we won't have any oxygen to breathe and we'll all die.'

I stroked his hair. 'I'm sure they'll work something out. Someone will work something out. Was it fun, Zoe, in Canada? Where were you, on the West coast?'

Her hair swung down. 'Vancouver Island. It was fun for a little while. Then I came home.'

'Lunch nearly ready?' asked Moth.

'Soon, Moth. I'll get back to the eggs. I'd love to hear about Canada, I haven't been anywhere for years.'

*

204

'That's far too much for me,' said Zoe. I tipped most of her egg back on to my plate.

'Like so?'

She shrugged. I am entirely willing to waste food in exchange for childcare.

'So you're just back from Vancouver?' I wanted to hear about a different ocean, the smell of different trees, the sound of other accents. I put some cheese on Moth's fork in the hope that experiments with cutlery would lead him to eat it. 'Are you having a gap year?'

Zoe pushed her egg around, watched by Raphael as if eating disorders were a form of avant-garde performance art.

'What's a gap year?' he asked.

'When people finish school and before they go to university they spend a year travelling on their own or with friends.'

Zoe's hair came down.

'Oh. Why?'

'Because it's interesting,' I said. 'To see bears.' Or Save the Rainforest.

'Yeah,' said Zoe. 'Only I dropped out of mine.'

'Dropped splat,' said Moth.

'You dropped out of your gap year?'

'My mother doesn't think it's funny. She's, like, shadowing me in case I try to drop out of Cambridge as well.'

'Are you going to Cambridge?'

She cut up some toast and pushed it under the egg. 'I'm meant to be starting next year. She says if I can't cope with a gap year I should go in October instead. I think she thinks they should throw someone else out so I can change my mind. Or she can change it for me.'

'What are you going to read?' I put some more butter on my bread.

'Law.'

Law didn't seem like a mother-hater's choice. English literature, perhaps, populated by malevolent parents (why do children tell all the stories?), or a modern language involving many months far away. The impenetrable realms of physics, or the secret kingdom of mathematics.

'Are you looking forward to that?'

She shrugged. 'It seems too far away.'

In fifteen months, Raph would be nine and Moth would be a person with bowel control, the beginnings of altruism and a haircut. He squeezed a piece of cheese on toast until it extruded like toothpaste through the gaps in his fingers.

'Don't do that,' said Raph. 'There are children in Africa who don't have anything to eat at all.'

I sat up straight. 'There are also children in Africa who are too full for a second helping of ice cream. It's a continent, not a refugee camp, Raph.'

Moth began to rub the squashed cheese into the table.

'Moth like some ice cream.'

'I haven't got any ice cream. We were just talking about it.'

'More ice cream?'

'There isn't any ice cream.'

He banged his plate on the table.

'Moth wants ice cream!'

'I know Moth wants ice cream but there isn't any. What about a biscuit?'

'No biscuit. Not like biscuit.'

'Yes, you do,' said Raph. 'You're always wanting biscuits.'

Moth's plate and cup swept on to the floor as if a tornado had passed over the table. His feet drummed and his arms lifted as if he were about to speak in tongues.

'Moth wants ice cream *now*! Now!'

I hauled Moth out of his chair so he didn't bang his head on it. Raph put his fingers in his ears.

'Zoe,' I shouted, 'you and Raph finish lunch.'

She nodded. I took Moth into the playroom, where I passed the time by thinking about my book until the storm cleared.

*

Zoe helped me tidy up lunch and congratulated Moth on putting wooden animals into animal-shaped holes in a wooden cube while I loaded the washing machine and put away some dishes which had been air-drying for several days. She offered to play with Raph so I could work when Moth went to sleep, and when the ensuing silence made me peer over the banisters I could see them lying on their stomachs building another doomed Lego metropolis. I went back to my laptop, which was sitting on the bed, expectant as a dog.

Although it was, in theory, possible to reclaim abandoned children from the Hospital, in fact barely 1 per cent of those given into its care returned to the wider community. The numbers are so small that it is hard to generalize (and it should be borne in mind that 70 per cent of foundlings did not survive their first year in the Hospital during this decade), but in general those who were reclaimed were under six months old, had been at the Hospital for less than three months and were returned to their mothers, many of whom had been forcibly deprived of their babies as a result of sickness, indigence or drunkenness.

I rolled off the bed and went to the door to listen. I could hear Raphael saying something about fire engines and Zoe laughing. I went along the hall, setting my feet down carefully and avoiding the creaking boards, and sidled down the outside edges of the stairs. When I was little, I used to get out of bed and sneak downstairs to make sure my parents weren't arguing, which they were. It seemed somehow that by providing an audience I made a boundary for their conflict, ensured that the knots in my stomach and the rawness of my bitten fingers were the manifestations of nothing more cataclysmic than my own fear. As long as I was crouching on the stairs, neither of them would leave. Zoe was building something rectangular with a tower at one end, like a Saxon church, and Raph was readying the fire brigade on the other side of the room. There are places in the world where people have been herded into churches which are then locked and set on fire, but they are not usually places and times for the emergency services. I went back to my room, leaving the door wide open.

It is, of course, impossible to follow the subsequent lives of these babies in any detail, although study of parish registers (see Kenton and Johnson, 2002, pp. 112–18) suggests that, as one would expect, mortality rates after return were disproportionately high. Whether this is a result of enduring physical problems consequent upon time spent in the care of the Hospital or a reflection of the economic and social problems that caused their admission in the first place is now beyond investigation; the lives and deaths of poor children from this era often appear to elude the most basic records.

The sky was grey. No particular weather, no birds. I could hear Zoe making fire-engine noises with an edge of self-consciousness in her voice, like a primary school teacher singing hymns *pour encourager les autres*. I reopened the 'Orchard Baby' folder.

Mr Webb again thanked Mrs Buchan, and said that the inquiry would hear from Jamie Norman and John Peterson in the afternoon.

Mr Norman and Mr Peterson confirmed that they had lifted Mary Homerton's body from the water. They had taken their twenty-foot dayboat out to the north end of the island when they heard that the children were missing and that Mary had been seen carrying Alexander past the church in the afternoon, thinking that 'You've a better view of the cliffs from the bottom than the top.' They saw the searchers on the headland and began to survey the water, following the current where it sweeps round towards Inversaigh. There was a slight easterly wind and no waves to speak of, and they followed the cliff round towards the cave, where they saw something bobbing in the water. They guessed at once what it was. Mr Peterson raised the body with the boathook and both men pulled it in. It had been face-down in the water so they knew there was no point in trying to revive her, but they tried anyway. There was no pulse and they were unable to start respiration. They did not wave and shout to the searchers for fear of conveying the message that Mary was alive. When they were sure she was dead, they spent some time looking for Alexander, but being so much smaller he was harder to find and after an hour or so decided they should return the body to land.

Dr Welling appeared next. He had been among the searchers and was summoned as soon as the boat was seen. He confirmed that the cause of death was probably head injuries almost certainly incurred in falling down the cliff, followed by drowning; at the time it had been hard to say whether death had occurred before or after entry to the water, although the post-mortem has since indicated that Mary drowned. Grazes on her hands and arms suggested some attempt to arrest her fall, although he did not like to say that this indicated an accident; instinct or perhaps second thoughts had been known to lead suicides who had left quite explicit notes to incur severe lacerations under similar circumstances.

Mr Webb asked Dr Welling if he felt anything could or should have been done differently to prevent the tragedy. He replied that a secure fence would prevent accidents, and incidentally reduce the loss of livestock on the island, but under present conditions it was clear that such a project would be practically impossible, and no physical impediment will prevent a determined suicide. At this point someone arrived with a message that Dr Welling was urgently required elsewhere; Mr Webb confirmed that he had nothing further to say and the case was adjourned.

Mr Webb concluded the Mary Homerton case today, reminding the court that it is not the role of a Fatal Accident Inquiry to apportion blame in the moral or legal sense but only to make recommendations with regard to what might be done to avoid or reduce the risk of any repetition of a fatal accident. It is in the nature of accidents that they need not have happened and that had events unrolled differently they would not have happened; it was clear in this case, for example, that had the person who saw Mary leaving the village with Alexander asked her where she was going and why, the outcome might have been very different. But perhaps she would have given a plausible answer – perhaps, indeed, she had a plausible reason – and continued on her way. We will never know, and several of those involved have testified to their self-doubt and questionings. These are natural but not useful preoccupations.

Mr Webb suggested that the Castle School should reconsider the amount of unsupervised free time allowed to girls known to be unhappy or fragile, but accepted that, within reasonable bounds, every institution must find its own balance between the freedom of the many and the safety of the few, and he did not believe that the Castle School's unusual ethos had been outwith the bounds of reason on this occasion. He would communicate with the Cassingham family with regard to the possibility of fencing the cliffs, but felt there were no grounds for an urgent or formal recommendation at the present time.

The baby must have survived then, somehow. Mustn't it? There was a patch of sunlight out to sea and brightness behind the clouds outside the window. A raven came gliding past, and out across the weed-stained stones on the beach, each feather of its wings clear against the pale sky. The cliffs, of course, are still not fenced, and I find it hard to imagine that

210

any barrier would withstand the winter winds. There are traces of a dry stone wall along the section above the church, which means that someone must have balanced there, hefting stones with the sea exploding against the rock face so far below that you can tell a drifting lifebuoy only by its shape (Giles waited for it to follow the tide round into the bay and then went out to check the ship's name so he could report it to the coastguard, as if Colsay were a fellow traveller subject to the codices of seamanship). Raph and I once saw a lamb fall down the cliffs when they were rounding up the sheep on Shepsay, bounding and leaping vertically in a fast-forward parody of springtime gambols until it lay broken on a ledge. The lambs were being taken to the mainland for slaughter and we knew that, had eaten lamb chops for supper the previous night, and I knew, but did not tell Raph, that that jolting flight was a better death than the one awaiting it two days later. Still it figures in my dreams sometimes, the way a misstep leads to death. The babies who crawl across the glass cliff into their mothers' embrace are perhaps right after all: we pass our days on that glass, all of us, and if we looked down we could not move at all. I heard Moth begin to stir and went to him; children need the mother on the other side of the chasm or they stop, suspended between past and future like the Wild Boy of Aveyron.

I picked him up. He put his arms round my neck and rubbed his face on my shoulder.

'Hello, love. Mummy just needs to finish with her computer.'

He raised his head. 'Pooter. Moth press buttons.'

'Not just now.'

I carried him back into our bedroom. The sun had gone in and the sky was dark over the sea. I closed the computer and took him downstairs, to where Zoe was determinedly rescuing Raph's Lego churchgoers with a wind-up fire engine driven by a grinning plastic cat.

While theories about the historical specificity of emotional bonds between parents and children have become deeply unfashionable in recent years, it is hard to find a fully satisfactory alternative account of the rise of boarding schools during this period. The advent of paved roads and the stagecoach network made people of middling rank much more mobile than they had been in the previous century, while the kinds of knowledge that were valued, especially for boys but also to a lesser extent for girls and especially girls from socially aspirant families, were less compatible with the daily occupations of most parents. It is relatively easy to teach a child what you are doing while you do it, but harder, and often economically inefficient, to stop what you are doing in order to teach a child double-entry book-keeping or French grammar. The increased value placed upon these skills in the context of the urbanizing and industrializing world of the mid- to late eighteenth century was in itself a reason for sending children to institutions where such things were known and could be efficiently passed on, while the mechanics of this 'sending' were ever easier, but neither seems quite sufficient to explain a shift in what we would now call 'parenting culture' of which contemporary observers seem to have been fully aware.

I was teetering on the edges of an inversion of the outdated view that children became more precious to their parents as their economic use declined. Does it betoken greater affection to keep your children with you, illiterate and limited to a life of manual labour like your own, or to send them away at considerable cost to learn another way of being? It was far from clear to me that parental love is reliably manifest in action anyway, and once you find yourself trying to write the history of love you would probably be better occupied tilling the fields yourself. I deleted the double-entry book-keeping, on the uncharacteristically honest grounds that I do not really know what it is.

'Anna?' Giles calling from upstairs, where he was reading to Raph.

'What? I'm working.'

Footsteps along the landing. 'Can you get the door?'

I looked up. The grass on the hill was glowing in the light of the low sun, and there was probably a photogenic sunset in progress over the sea. Someone knocked on the door, and regrettably there was no possibility that it was a pizza delivery or even Jehovah's Witnesses. I saved my work and went down the hall. There was indeed molten pink sky etching the clouds and reflecting off the sea and I felt that, having come so far for the Great Outdoors, Judith could reasonably have been expected to give it her attention.

'Judith. No further problems, I hope?'

She was wearing a Liberty peacock skirt. I once gave my father a tie in that print, bought on my first excursion to London, but he never wore it and when we went through his clothes after the funeral it was not there.

'No,' she said. 'No' with the cottage. I've been enjoying the view.' Whisky, again, and her diction blurred.

'Good.'

She took a breath. 'Anna. Can I talk to you? I mean, please could I come in? It's abou' Zoe.'

'Oh.' It is in contravention of the spirit of the Hôtel de la Mère to take on other people's distress. I was willing to exchange houseroom and meals for *ad hoc* childcare, but coun-selling was not part of the deal.

'Of course,' I said. 'I'll make some tea.'

She followed me down the hall, bumping once against the wall. 'Do you have mint? Or anything else without caffeine? It stops me sleeping.'

I stood in front of my glass of claret and put it behind the toaster. My experience is that alcohol will prevail over caffeine, but since she wanted tea I was very willing to give her Giles's rather than mine.

'Here,' I said. 'Giles has a cupboard full of infusions.'

I gave her the Bird Mug. I leant against the counter and she stood in the middle of the room, legs planted apart, like an estate agent sizing it up.

'You had Zoe with you most of the day.'

I warmed my hands around my mug. 'Most of the afternoon, anyway.'

'Was she – was she OK?'

We both know the extent to which Zoe is not OK.

'Judith, I don't know her. She seemed happy enough.' The balance of her mind was not disturbed.

'It's just – well, I don't know if you noticed how thin she is.'

'I did. I'm afraid I've seen quite a few anorexic students.'

'So I worry about her.'

I waited, sipped some caffeine. I wondered if she would regret this in the morning.

'And she doesn't talk to me. We got her to the doctor but she said she wasn't interested in any treatment and Brian says she's not sick enough to be sectioned and anyway sectioning people keeps them alive but it doesn't make them better.' She looked up and some of the tea jerked on to the floor. 'Only – you know – she's my child. I'd settle for keeping her alive. Sorry. I'll wipe that if you show me where the cloths are.'

'Don't bother,' I said. 'These days I count that kind of spill as cleaning. Come on, sit down. Would you like a biscuit with that?'

There was half a packet of the ginger bribes at the back of the cupboard. I think Giles thinks the children snack on rice cakes and carrot sticks.

She nodded. 'Thanks. I shouldn't really. I don't have them in the house, at home.'

And you and your daughter are models to us all. 'Surely the point is that neither your doctor nor your husband think Zoe's in immediate danger?'

214

She shrugged. 'It just seems so pointless to wait until she is. In danger. You wouldn't, would you, if you saw Timothy going towards a river or trying to get the top off a bottle of pills. I'm her mother. And I've read about it: sometimes people collapse quite suddenly and it just seems – Anna, it's such a waste. I mean, they've always done so well. Will, my son, you know he's reading medicine. At King's.' She took a slug of tea as if it were gin. 'And she's so pretty when she's not so thin and she got such good A-levels and she was always so polite. All my friends used to be envious, their children were getting into drugs and drinking and not doing their homework and all I had to worry about was that she was working too hard. And then she started going running on the streets, which was a worry, but she let me drive her to the gym instead, every day after school, and then that stupid, stupid idea about going off to Canada. I knew she wouldn't cope on her own, I told her over and over and she just said I was being controlling and I wouldn't let her live her own life. And now I'm just having to watch while her whole life goes down the toilet. All those years. Just when we were expecting – I mean, just when you think you've done the job.'

Tears slid down her face. The make-up was waterproof. 'Maybe she wanted to try it without help,' I suggested. Maybe she doesn't like being someone's job.

'Her! I don't think she knows how to use a washing machine or fry an egg. The idea of flying off to Canada . . .'

'Oh, we all work out eggs and washing machines. I mean, Moth can do the washing machine, he just doesn't always put clothes in the drum. And you know, she'd do some of that at Cambridge anyway.'

Unless Judith was planning to book herself into the Hilton for the duration of term. We had one parent who did that, though what really astonished me was that her son accepted it, as if it was entirely natural that his mother had no life of her own, as if he hadn't noticed that other people's parents had gone back to their own worlds.

Judith began to stack our unopened bills. 'Yes, in college, with people to look after her and me at the end of the phone. I did most of Will's washing in his first term anyway, and then I think he found a girlfriend.'

I bit my lip. It was too late for Will anyway.

'Don't you think if he's going to practise medicine, domestic appliances shouldn't be beyond him?'

She met my eyes for the first time. 'They appear to be beyond his father, who specializes in cardiothoracic surgery.'

We heard Giles coming down the stairs.

'I'd better go,' she said. 'Sorry. I only wanted to ask you how Zoe seemed. Since I can't – can't get through to her these days. Did she eat anything?'

I finished my tea and brushed the biscuit crumbs on to the floor before Giles saw them. 'A bit of lunch. Not much.'

'Oh,' said Giles. 'Good evening, Judith. Everything OK over at the house?'

'Yes. Thank you. I'm just going back over there. Thanks, Anna. Good night.'

She saw herself out, banging the door. Giles sat down. 'Didn't you have a bottle open? Anna, was she drunk?'

I retrieved it and poured him a glass. 'Yup. Cheers.'

'Cheers. And what did she want? No fish forks? Shortage of cappuccino whisks?'

'Oh,' I said. 'Nothing much. Nothing to worry about.'

He drank some wine and began to turn the glass by its stem. 'Listen, Anna?'

I yawned. I wasn't sure I'd be able to stay awake if I tried to keep working. 'What?'

'I had an e-mail from Sam.'

I leant back in the chair. My eyes were closing. 'How is he?'

'Fine. Says hi. Anna, are you awake?'

I opened my eyes. The room blurred and they closed again. 'More or less.'

'There's a job in Glasgow.'

I sat up. He'd stopped turning the glass and was looking at me.

'Glasgow?' I said. Too far for even Giles to think he could commute from here. Unless he was planning to abandon me with the kids on Colsay while he holed up in some pristine new-build flat all week, somewhere with wooden floors and a shiny kitchen. 'What about me?'

He took another drink. 'It's for you. A history job. Eighteenth or nineteenth century, interest in family studies, gender or childhood particularly welcome. Rather a plum, I'd say, especially at the moment. God knows how they got the funding.'

'Oh.' I ran my finger round the rim of my glass. Another invitation to chip away another piece of my self-esteem. I negotiate not getting jobs that aren't a perfect fit by saying that they probably found someone who really knows about the Grand Tour or the Napoleonic Wars or whatever it is, but not getting the job Giles was describing would mean there is someone else who does exactly what I do better than I do it. Or perhaps just more than I do it, which would not be hard.

'I thought you'd be interested. Sam said he thought of you as soon as he saw it.'

I wouldn't get it. There are too many men and childless women who go to the bar after seminars and work through the weekends. I like Glasgow, though. Scottish schools are meant to be good. If we sold the Oxford house – but I have been 'at Oxford' all my adult life and I think I might be a different person without that word on my lapel badge, neither the eighteen-year-old who left home by walking down the street to the bus under a rucksack so heavy it was like learning to walk for the first time, ignoring my mother who stood waving in the curved window of the front room, nor the person who is able to hold her institutional affiliation like a secret pregnancy or an invisible comfort blanket. *Affiliation*, a word holding both *filament* and *filial*, the ties that bind. The comfort blanket, which neither of my children could be persuaded to accept as a substitute for my nocturnal attentions, is what I have recently learnt to identify as a 'transitional object', a material substitute for or reminder of the absent mother. The university as transitional object for adults whose need for Mummy was never satisfied: discuss. Giles, whose mother sent him to boarding school before he could tie his own shoelaces, flicked his hair.

'So. You should apply.'

'So you can take that professorship at the Highlands and Islands place? You realize everyone in Oxford would think you were mad?'

He shrugged. I think being that posh equips people with such an implacable sense of self-worth that they can take down struggling democracies, thunder downstairs while the children are asleep and send the lower orders over the top at Ypres without feeling in the least implicated. It should come as no surprise that this also makes it possible to resign from the jobs for which other people would sell their bodies in order to become the saviour of puffins.

'Why would I care? I wouldn't be there. Come on, Anna. It would be good for all of us. Think about it, OK?' He stood up. 'And if you got that job and we moved, you'd be earning as much as I would.'

I yawned again. Maybe I could just put my head down on the table and sleep here, further from the children. 'Would you like that?' I asked.

'You would. Come on, bedtime. You're falling asleep there.'

Yes, I would.

Colsay House,
Colsay

24th Nov., 1878

Dear Miss Emily,

No news of the new inhabitant yet! Mrs Grice appears well
enough, and though I have forborn to exact a promise I do believe
that she may trust me enough to allow my presence when her crisis
comes, and I know you will believe me when I say that if I am
present I will not allow anything to be done that will harm her
child no matter what the superstitions and customs may be here.

No, I write on a matter perhaps yet more momentous. You have
perhaps read or heard of the proposed emigration of the people of
Shepsay to Canada. You and Lord Hugo asked me to inform you
of what I thought best for the welfare of the population of Colsay,
and I would be failing in that promise if I did not say now, before
there is thought of the Spring planting, that it is my opinion that
the people of this island should receive, and be encouraged to
accept, a similar offer. Truly, they are living like savages, like
animals, and the sufferings of the women in particular are what no
subject of a civilized nation should be asked to witness, let alone
endure, in the present century. Emigration of course is not an easy
choice, particularly for a people so deeply attached to familiar
terrain as the islanders are known to be, but, the first hurdles over, I
am convinced that the women who spend their days eviscerating
birds and trudging like beasts of burden through the rain and the
men who daily risk their lives in the primitive pursuit of seafowl
would live to thank you for transplanting them to a place of
sunshine and wheat-fields. I know the expense would be great,

perhaps even compared to that of erecting and maintaining a school, but, knowing also of your family's commitment to the best interests of the people entrusted to your management, I am emboldened to explain my views.

Naturally I have not mentioned this to anyone on Colsay, and if you see fit to investigate my suggestion it would surely be better not to mention my name in this connection, for to do so must jeopardize my work here and thus the lives of those who may yet see a brighter future, for the islanders have that prejudice against the idea of emigration which ignorance and superstition must lead one to expect.

I will, of course, write again as soon as there is news.

Yours most sincerely,

May Moberley

11

WATCHING BUT NOT STARING

In each test the tester, who was well known to the animals, stood close to the cage. In one he offered them pieces of banana; in another he stood quietly watching but not staring; and in a third he dressed up in the mask and cloak and made slight movements.

– John Bowlby, *Separation*, p. 163

'It's very uplifting, isn't it, all this sky.' said Judith. She sniffed, but the drip fell anyway. DNA on the wet grass. 'It must be a real contrast to Oxford. I'm afraid I've never liked it, down south. All those hordes of people everywhere. And nowhere to park. Zoe, do you remember driving round and round Cambridge? I thought we'd run out of petrol.'

'You're a member of the human race as well, you know. One of those hordes. And you keep going on about wanting me to go to Cambridge. Down south,' said Zoe. 'Oops, Moth.'

Judith stopped short. 'Zoe, I won't have this rudeness. You shouldn't be speaking to anyone like that.'

'I like Oxford,' I said. 'I miss it. Especially the libraries.'

Judith set off again. We were walking down to the landing stage because Judith had arranged for herself to be shown around the distillery at Inversaigh and I'd arranged for myself to go back to the archive, in search, this time, of all three lost children: Mary, Alexander and Eve. What could Mary's mother have written to make her daughter jump off the cliff? I had been back up to the cliff the previous evening, telling Giles I'd been inside most of the day and wanted to feel the wind on my face before going back to my footnotes, which is the kind of thing Giles finds plausible, even after nine years of marriage during which he has had ample opportunity to observe that I am more likely to refresh myself with DVDs of French films in which nothing whatsoever happens in enviable Parisian apartments. I'd stood closer to the edge than I would consider advisable for anyone else and looked down on white birds mingling and chatting, a few of Giles's puffins blundering through the air like overloaded planes about to crash and, below them, below the turfs of waving grass and the heather which a falling hand might vainly grasp and the sharp edges which would crack your head and tear your skin on the way down, the sea sparkled in the evening light. I wondered if it would be possible to jump out far enough to go straight into the sea like a plummeting gull, and if so whether I would have to wait for the waves to batter me to death against the rocks or whether some more graceful death would embrace me as I entered the water. I do not think falling is in itself a mode of death, not without a landing, and the water is deep enough that a human body could dive far down and still rise again. (At what stage do the people pushed out of aeroplanes die?) I was not feeling particularly suicidal, but the drop was mesmerizing and there are some opportunities that are in themselves almost sufficient motive for various sins. Maybe especially so for a child with a limited sense of death's finality. Maybe Mary just wanted to see what would happen if she went closer, and closer again, and maybe then Alexander wriggled in her arms. Maybe she died trying to save him. None of which explained what she was doing up there with the baby in the first place.

'Of course, we're rather spoilt in Cheshire, aren't we, Zoe?

So much quieter than the South. You know, I really don't think I could bear to live in Oxford.'

Brian was staying behind to work, probably unaware that Giles was similarly excused, as if Colsay were a gentlemen's club. Hôtel du Père, except that I am not sure that Giles or Brian would find the Hôtel du Père noticeably different from daily life. All meals and childcare provided, laundry done, ample opportunity for private pursuits. Why do we do it, Judith and I?

'Maybe southerners couldn't bear you either,' muttered Zoe. 'Maybe you're so toxic you ought to be banned from anywhere with a population density of more than about two per square mile.'

'Mummy, look, there's a caterpillar. It's all furry.'

'Where a caterpillar? Caterpillar ate one apple.'

'Zoe, really. How can you say these things? Do you know how that makes me feel?'

'They don't really eat apples, that's just a story.'

'And one slice of salami and one pickle and one slice of Swiss cheese. Moth have a pickle?'

'And if you say one more passive-aggressive sentence before we get to Colla I'm going to e-mail Trinity and say I don't want my place.'

There are libraries where no one is allowed to talk. Where, once through the door, anyone may sit in silence and read and think as slowly as she likes. Raph took my other hand.

'Boat!' Moth ran ahead.

'Mind the stone, Moth.' I called. He tripped and fell on to the turf, glanced back and began to wail. I ran to pick him up.

'Poor Moth. What a shock. Mummy kiss it better.'

I made a loud kiss on his red corduroy knee and he giggled. 'And the other one.' I lifted him high in front of me and kissed the other one.

Judith blew out air like a surprised horse. 'You weren't looking where you were going, were you, Timothy?'

'That's because he's a toddler,' Raphael explained. 'They learn by experience.'

'Only if they're allowed to have any experience,' said Zoe. Her face was very pale, and blue about the mouth. I caught sight of Judith's gaze and looked away.

I pretended I couldn't hear Judith and Zoe over the noise of the engine. Raph sat in the boat's nose, where he likes the bouncing and the salt that blows on to his skin, and Zoe held Moth for me. He is not resigned to his lifejacket. As with driving on the motorway, I enjoy the boat as long as I can pretend my children are not in jeopardy. The South, or in this case the Atlantic, calls from far away. You could just keep going, except that people will need biscuits and nappies and a drink of water and, very soon thereafter, will scream until you let them out. I went a bit faster and Raph turned to beam at me. Judith said something.

'Anna, sorry, dear, but you are trained to handle this boat, aren't you?' We had come into the lee of the little headland, where cows were artfully scattered.

'Fully certified,' I said. What was she going to do, insist on evidence?

'Well.' She pushed her hood down. 'Only I'm sure it was smoother when we came over with Giles.'

'Less windy then,' I lied. 'He's busy. We both work. I've got some research to do in the archives today.'

The water sparkled in the sun and the grass above us was bright green. The hill on Colsay was purple with heather, and I could see the cliffs where I knew Giles was working.

'Off lifejacket!' Moth pulled at the collar, designed to cradle a little head in the water. Assuming he was on his back to start with.

'Soon,' I said. 'Soon on land.'

Zoe took Raph and Moth to the children's section in the library, so that Raph could play with computers without destroying anyone's work and Moth could enjoy books where polar bears chat to penguins untrammelled by geography.

'You're sure you're OK with them?' I asked. 'I don't want to exploit our guests as childcare.'

'I'm enjoying it. It's fine. They're fun kids. Look, if there's a problem we can come and find you straight away, can't we? If it's much of a problem you'll probably hear, anyway.'

I squatted down to talk to Moth. 'Mummy's just going to do some work in there, OK?' I pointed. 'I won't be long.'

'Mummy not go away.'

Raph was already at one of the computer terminals.

'I'm not going away. Just a few minutes' work.'

He took hold of my arm. 'No. Moth come too.'

I looked at Zoe.

'Look, Moth.' She held out her hand to him. 'Here's a book with tigers in. Grrr, says the tiger. Here's a baby tiger. Can you see?'

He let go of my arm.

'And here's the mummy tiger, up in a tree.'

He looked at me and walked over to Zoe.

'And here's a baby lion and a daddy lion.'

Moth leant on her arm and looked at the book. His hair, I noticed, had at last grown down to his neckline. It feels like stealing, cutting children's hair. Come back, I thought. I've changed my mind. I'm going to renounce thinking. I won't read another book until you're five. I walked over to the counter, and was pleased to find that Fiona Firth, although attired in a shiny asymmetric skirt that could not have come from any shop nearer than Glasgow, was absorbed in comparing food processors on Amazon.

'Hello,' I said. 'Sorry to interrupt—'

She started and minimized the window. Windows move more slowly when you have something to hide. 'Anna. Dr Bennet. Sorry. We were so quiet.'

'Of course,' I said. 'I do too much of that. I was wondering if I might be able to see the Parish Record for the wartime years. On Colsay, I mean.'

She looked past my shoulder. 'And the children will be all right here while you do that?'

Surely I am not the worst mother in the Colla and Inversaigh area. There must, statistically speaking, be several children within ten miles of here, within the library's catchment area, who are beaten and ill-nourished and verbally as well as emotionally abused, which are at least in legal terms worse offences than wishing they would shut up and go away so I can read.

'Zoe's with them,' I said. 'She's staying with her parents in the cottage.'

'Well, as long as you think it's all right.'

She came round the desk and I followed her towards the Local History Resource Room.

I craned back over my shoulder. Raph was, I guessed, back on the NASA website and wouldn't have noticed if Zoe had started ritually disembowelling goats on the Little Farm rug behind him, and Moth was still leaning against her and following a story about a family of giraffes who appeared to live in a rainforest.

'The Parish Record, you said?' Fiona Firth was busy in a filing cabinet. 'Are you looking for anything in particular? Because you know the parishes were merged in 1918, don't you, so it's the Colla record you want?'

'Yes,' I said. No. Rain began to patter against the window. It is particularly difficult to find out things you should already know. 'And after that, burials were over here?'

She looked up. 'No. We've a couple of people here who'll be buried on the island where they were born.' She opened another drawer. 'With the landlord's permission, of course.'

Because Giles obviously makes a habit of interfering with the births, marriages and deaths of people he's never met.

'I thought my husband had made it clear that he expects

everyone local to come and go as freely on the island as they do everywhere else. Has he ever suggested that anyone should ask permission to go anywhere?'

She shut the drawer and handed me a blue document box, secured with tapes. 'Very kind of him. Look, have a seat. I hope you find what you're looking for.'

Rain blurred the hillside only a few metres away.

I didn't really know what I was looking for. For Alexander, as always. Maybe for Mary, for a sidelight on her life and death that might make sense of the story, at least in my imagination. Perhaps for details of how Miss Bower and Miss Leach felt afterwards, although it seemed unlikely that they would have confided in the Rector. The notebook was bound in crimson leather which had not been properly stored and felt too soft, almost furry, in my hands. The pages were yellow and rough as dry skin.

The first entries gestured towards the rhythm of life on the island:

December 1903: Great storms have wrought such damage to the church roof that it was necessary to conduct services at Colsay House, Lady Cassingham having kindly sent permission ... March 1904: There is grave anxiety for the crew of the *Lady Jane*, last seen in difficulties in the Sound last Tuesday before the fog came down ... April 1904: Lady Cassingham sent books, ten slates and maps for the school. Baptism of Alison Petrie, b. 26 Mar, on Easter Day ...

Two of the crew of the *Lady Jane* had swum ashore near Inversaigh, the boat having been smashed on the rocks in the fog, and the bodies of two of the remaining four washed ashore near Rothkinnick a few days later. Occasional acts of charity by Lady Cassingham, who must have been Giles's great-grand-mother. Her finely judged contributions suggested a careful use of resources which in no way reflected my understanding of

life at Bringham Hall in the closing days of Edwardian splendour. In Julia's attic there are hats almost airborne on the
feathers of birds now poised on the edge of extinction, and a
handwritten book of family recipes which typically begin 'Take
5 pints of best cream' and progress to sponge cakes, best sherry
and candied rose petals. Early photographs show family groups
so large that the women must have fallen on the first publications of Marie Stopes a few years later with cries of inarticulate
gratitude – mothers, nannies, governesses and children of both
sexes decked with lace and parasols and intricate tucks and
piping. It was not a household that concerned itself with the
price of school slates.

I glanced at my watch and flicked through World War I.
The Rector had noted when each family received the news
they were dreading, six young men 'killed in action' and four
'missing believed dead'. Colsay must have lost more than half
its young men. One more wrecked fishing boat and the next
generation would have disappeared. One wedding, in that war,
and the groom killed six months later, two births, and four
people between the ages of fifty-nine and eight-two died on the
island. After 1918, in the new book, the notes contracted to
brief *aides-mémoire* about births (four between 1918 and 1940),
deaths (eleven) and marriages (two). I read more carefully.
During the second war, there were three deaths recorded:
George Petrie, aged seventy-nine, Margaret Maclean, aged
seventy-six, Hannah Grice, aged sixty-two, and one birth,
Alexander Buchan, November 1942. So he was seven months
old. Probably sitting, certainly smiling and babbling and pointing, probably not crawling. Not, these days, old enough for egg
custard (risk of salmonella, since if you boil what Giles calls
'real custard', as if Birds' lovely stripy tins were imaginary, it
curdles), but old enough to play with a little girl. Able to point
and clap and show a range of feeling far richer than the newborn's distraught/not distraught. One of the things I liked least
about small babies was the impossibility that one's most

Herculean labours would result in any greater reward than the baby not being furious for a few minutes, but by seven months they are well on the way to humanity. And young enough to crawl over the glass cliff without the slightest intimation of mortality. There was no mention of Alexander's death, and no reference at all to Mary Homerton. I looked up. The rain melted the hillside and sky in the window and the wind pushed at the walls. I remembered the boat, the passage back across the Sound whose sandy floor is littered with the bones of people who knew the wind was rising but wanted to get home for supper and reckoned their luck would hold. Time to go.

'So,' said Fiona. 'You found what you wanted?'

I was kneeling on the floor, trying to persuade Moth to let me put his coat back on. 'No, Moth, arm through. No. Or at least, I found that it wasn't there. Moth, put your arm through, please.'

Moth shook his coat off the arm I'd just threaded through. 'No coat. Hot sunny day.'

'Moth, it's not. It's cold.'

'No coat.'

'You have to wear a coat, it's raining.'

He wriggled away and turned to face me. 'Mummy stop it raining.'

'I can't stop it raining. Believe me, if I had supernatural powers the world would be a very different place. Moth, please put your coat on.'

'No coat.'

We eyed each other. The theory that I am in charge is undermined by his readiness to lie screaming on the floor in a public place in a town where I am believed to make Medea look like the most diligent follower of Penelope Leach.

'Oh, all right then. Suit yourself.'

'So you found an answer, anyway?'

'No.' I stood up and held out my hand to Moth. 'I think I'm

going to have to rephrase the question. But it was useful. Come on, love. Let's see what those waves are doing.'

Raph came back from the door, where he'd been waiting. 'Waving, I expect. Come on, Mummy. Or I might as well go back on the computer.'

Fiona held out a book. 'Will you take this, then? Help you in your enquiries?'

I lifted Moth on to my hip. 'I haven't got a library card.'

'It's my copy,' she said. *Colla, Inversaigh and Colsay from Settlement to the Present Day.* 'Bring it back when you're ready. And you know if it's births and deaths you're after you should try the Scotland's People website.'

'Mummy, come on.'

'OK,' I said. 'Scotland's People. Thanks. And Fiona, thanks for the book. I'll bring it back soon.'

The boat was bobbing against the landing stage, the fenders rolling like eggs along the sides. I felt queasy.

Raph watched a fishing boat lurching at its mooring. 'It's going to be very bouncy, isn't it?'

'Moth go swimming?'

I picked him up as he made for the edge. 'Not today. Too cold. Yes, the wind's rising. If Judith doesn't come soon I think we shouldn't risk it.'

'What, stay here?' asked Raphael.

This conversation is how people's bodies get washed up in the cove at Rothkinnick.

Zoe frowned at the horizon. 'I'm not sharing a hotel room with my mother.'

'There isn't a hotel,' I pointed out. 'Anyway, isn't that your car?'

A red Volvo was snaking along the shore road like a tank approaching an undefended village.

'Yes,' said Zoe. 'I'm just going to buy something. I'll be back in a minute.'

'But, Zoe!'

The waves inside the headland were beginning to break. Judith's whisky might have to wait in her car. Maybe Judith, who must have weighed as much as Zoe and the children put together, ought to wait in her car.

'Moth tired.' He rested his head on my shoulder.

'I know, love. Soon home.'

'Biscuit?'

I had a cottage cheese pot in one pocket and a proper Tupperware one (Julia's) in the other. The cottage cheese pot turned out to contain an unidentifiable biological hazard.

'Can I have that?' asked Raph.

'No.' I dropped it in a bin. KEEP SCOTLAND SMILING. 'This one's got biscuits, Moth.'

'Mummy, now that pot's going to go to landfill and take thousands of years to decompose and release PCBs into the soil.'

'Oh well,' I said. 'Never mind. Look, here's Judith. And Zoe's coming.'

I felt like a small state caught between two superpowers. Zoe had a large plastic bag from Spar.

'What have you been buying?' asked Judith.

'Mind your own business.' Zoe's hair blew across her face as the wind came over the water.

'Judith,' I said. 'I'm concerned about the weather. The wind's coming up. I think we need to go immediately and be ready to turn back if it's too rough out in the Sound. And I'm sorry, but if those boxes are whisky I think we should leave them for next time. I don't want any extra weight in the boat.'

She held a box with a plastic carrying handle in each hand. No one needs eight bottles of whisky, not even to guarantee the effectiveness of an overdose. If Zoe were mine I don't think I'd want eight bottles of whisky in the house.

'Really?' she said. 'Only with no shop on the island, you know, people will want to be able to take their groceries over.'

231

'I know,' I said. 'But we have to put safety first. And you can manage, can't you, for a day or two, if we just take one or two bottles?'

Zoe sniggered.

'Of course I can. But it's hardly putting safety first to leave bottles of whisky in full view in the car, is it?'

This woman's presence was making Giles believe his project was viable. It was feeding his vision of the role of hereditary landownership in the twenty-first century. I took a deep breath, which was wetter than I would have liked.

'Put them in the boot if you're worried,' I said. 'We don't even lock our car here. Come on. Raph, Moth, let's get your lifejackets on. Zoe, do you mind holding Moth again?'

I made Raph as well as Moth wear a safety harness and clipped them to the boat. If it sinks, they sink, but boats sink more slowly than prams and if it doesn't sink they will be easier to find. Judith was climbing down the ladder when the librarian came hurrying along the harbour. I held the boat against the wall.

'Did I forget something?' I called. 'We're in a bit of a hurry.'

She was breathless. 'I've been watching. It's too rough out there. With the little lads. I've phoned to Alec. My cousin. He'll take you out in his boat. We'll get yours aboard. We'll not watch you sink.'

Judith stopped with a foot on the boat. 'I don't think we've met?'

The librarian smiled under her hood, her skirt and hair whipping in the wind. 'Fiona Firth.'

'Thank you very much,' I called. I began to secure the ropes again. 'No, sit down, Raph. I was worried. I'd be very grateful to buy a safer passage.'

'You'll need to talk about that with Alec,' she said. 'Here, I'll help with the children. And then I must get back. There's Alec now.'

A white-haired man in yellow salopettes came along the

wall. I remembered reading somewhere that fishermen still don't like having women on their boats, although I think that was in the Greek islands or maybe Brittany.

'You'll be Anna? Right, let's get her tied down then.'

I passed Moth back to Zoe and climbed down into the boat to secure the oars and fenders.

'Who tied down?' asked Raph, looking at Judith.

I held on to him as he stepped on to the ladder.

'Your boat,' said Zoe. 'Boats are always called she.'

'Why?'

'Tradition.' I said. 'It's ready.'

'There you go,' said Alec. His body swayed with the boat as if he were gimballed like the compass and the stove in the cabin. 'We didn't want to watch you floundering out here. The cliffs are no good in an east wind.'

I looked at him. 'You're very kind, Mr . . .?'

'Buchan. Alec Buchan. You call me Alec, Anna, we don't use titles round here.'

Ian MacDonald does. A handful of spray blew into my face. 'Alexander Buchan?' My stomach swooped as if we were driving too fast over a hilly road.

'Alec. I told you, Alec.'

A white bird flew between waves. I tightened my grasp on Moth.

'And you were born in 1942?'

His gaze flickered away from the boat's prow, ploughing into the sea, and met mine. 'As a matter of fact. Why?'

I swallowed. 'I've been doing some research. Colsay in wartime. Fiona'll tell you, I thought I might write a little booklet for the visitors.'

'And you found poor little Mary Homerton.'

The boat lurched more as we came round the headland. He moved his feet and began to sway again, as if to slow music.

233

'Yes. And it sounded as if – as if— Well, I didn't expect to meet you.'

'They found me asleep in a field. Well back from the cliff. Not until they'd found Mary's body, mind, and you can just imagine the state of my mother.'

I worked my hand through one of the straps on Moth's life-jacket.

'Were you crawling?'

'What? Crawling? Shuffling, my mother said. That's what they do, isn't it?'

Raph did, a seal-like gait with one foot trailing which didn't work at all on carpet. Moth crawled like a bear, a fast bear who could get down the hall and halfway up the stairs in the time it took me to answer the phone.

Alec Buchan slowed the engine as we came into the bay. 'My mother thought it was the shuffling that saved me. I couldn't get over the rough grass. Gave up and went to sleep in the end.'

'What happened?' asked Judith. 'What are you talking about?'

'Ancient history,' he said. 'Nothing but ancient history.'

His gaze rested on the horizon as the boat rose and fell.

'I know,' I said. 'But do you mind – is your mother . . .'

'Died ten years back. Cancer. And here we are now.'

Did your father come back, I wanted to ask. Do you have siblings? Did she tell your story often or did you have to force her to return to those hours when she had lost her baby? Could she read about the ones who stayed lost, or worse? How many months did it take her to let you out of her arms, to stop smelling your hair and touching your apple cheeks for long enough to go to the loo or hang up the laundry? Did she ever take another nap? I rummaged in my bag. 'You're very kind. Please tell me what I owe you.'

'Ah.' He turned in towards the landing stage. 'You send me a copy of that book when it's done.'

'What, my book? On eighteenth-century childhood? Or the pamphlet?'

'I'd like to see your book. I reckon I know about Colsay.'

'I'd be delighted. Are you interested in eighteenth-century cultural history?'

'Aye,' he said. 'I am.'

He probably had a coffee grinder too, down in the cabin with the minutes of the Colla and Inversaigh Post-Colonial Theory Research Group. I kissed Moth's cheek, which was cold as stone, and stroked his red fingers. In two hours the children might be in bed and Judith and Zoe would have gone away and I could lie in a hot bath and close my eyes.

'Anna?' Zoe had her arm round Raph, who was kneeling on the seat watching the waves run past. 'I'll come back with you and mind the children while you make the tea if you like. I bought some ice cream for them.'

With her hair blown off her face I could see the bones working at her temples.

'Oh, thank you,' I said. 'That's a very sweet thought, but you must be tired. I think Giles is back anyway – look, there's a light on. We'll just need to feed them and get them to bed.'

Moth looked up. 'And supper.'

'And supper.'

'You're coming back to the house with me,' said Judith. 'I'm sure Anna could do with a break.'

'Oh, stop it, Mum. You concentrate on your whisky.'

Raph looked from one to the other as if he were watching tennis.

'Zoe's been very helpful,' I said. 'I wouldn't have been able to do my work without her.'

Judith looked at her daughter. If Zoe had closed her eyes, and loosed her hold on my son, she would have looked dead. 'I'm glad she's helping someone.'

Alexander Buchan glanced at the shore where the waves scribbled white on the rocks.

'Still getting up. This'll be worse before it's better.'

*

I took a packet of Maltesers into the bath with me, and though the water was hot enough to redden my skin the air stayed cold enough for them not to melt. I lay back with my ears underwater, listening to the amplified sounds of sugar bubbles crushed against my palate. When I'd finished I sat up, arranged my towel over the packet in case Giles came in and rinsed my hands. I, who once rode pillion on a motorbike from Cambridge to wildest West Wales for a party, who at Zoe's age used to cycle home in the early hours from nightclubs through parts of town where there were boards instead of net curtains in the windows and burnt-out cars on the streets, now regard eating chocolate while reading borrowed books in the bath as foolhardy.

I skimmed through the early chapters of *Colla, Inversaigh and Colsay from Settlement to the Present Day*. Geology is a noble science; Wordsworth and Darwin and many other great minds of the nineteenth and for all I know the twentieth century were fascinated by prehistory written in stone, but for me it is like going on holiday in countries where the currency has been inflated until six figures barely covers an ice cream; I cannot think in numbers larger than the historical record. The Norman Conquest and the birth of Christ are my decimals, even though I regard the latter as fictional. The Fall of Troy is a waymark seen through shifting fog, from which I am sometimes able to discern the Bronze Age, and earlier (alleged) events are beyond my horizon. You need a different language, I think, for worlds known only by their physical remains. The first person to leave a written account of Colsay was William Tabb, who spent three weeks here in 1637 as part of a journey up the West Coast, taken for no apparent reason other than to write *A Narrative of a Journey up the West Coast of Scotland*. He reached the island on the third attempt, after the skipper of his hired boat twice turned back 'on Account of the Highnesse and Whitenesse of the Waves which is they say in those Parts an infalliable Prognostication of Storm'. At last the wind fell and 'such Tribes

236

of Fowles were seen in Flight as Promise Calmnesse from the West'.

William Tabb, the Rev. MacFarland recounts, was greeted with 'what I took for a Kind of Quiet Pleasure' and shown to 'a Bed of Straw' where he was offered 'Eggs and Fowles, both longer cooked and more advanced in Yeares than they are eaten elsewhere'. He reported that the people were living in 'most extreame Poverty, having barely Roofs to their Heads in these most inclement Conditions, their Nourishment obtained at the Mercy of a raging Sea'. The men of the island 'perforce pass their Days upon these fearsome Cliffes, where with the utmost Diligence and Skill they doe worke at gathering Eggs and Fowles, all the while Hanging above that raging Sea by a mere Thread of Rope, which often breaks and sendes hime to a tumbling Deathe'. Even drinking water came from 'a Springe to which no Stranger would venture to ascend, forbye the Boys judged too younge for the cliffes must risk themselves in that Place'.

I sat up, put the book carefully down on the towel, and added more hot water. There is a well above the church, almost certainly later than the seventeenth century, but there is also a spring by the anchorite's cave and several patches of luminous green velvet moss where fresh water can't be far to seek. How would little boys bring water down from a steep rock in any useful quantity, unless they spent most of their time going backwards and forwards with goatskin bottles (not, I reflected, a bad idea at all, but not particularly probable either). It seemed possible that Tabb's informants were enjoying his credulity.

I lay down again. William Tabb found the women of Colsay 'most ill-favoured and dirty, for indeed they have but few Opportunities of washing Themselves or their Cloathes, and the great Hardnesse of their Life must necessarily make them old before their Time'. Neither he nor the Reverend MacFarland showed any interest in how the women spent their time or what they thought about their way of life. They alleged that the children 'live in such a State of Filthe that it

237

is impossible to discern Faces, and are allowed to perform their Natural Functions upon the Floor or Wherever they may be, like unto brute Beasts'.

If so, they were the first people I'd ever heard of to do so, and many 'brute Beasts' display a level of control in these matters. I wondered if William Tabb had seen a toddler or two pee on the floor without immediate sanction and concluded that this was an unsocialized society, the kind of world that Anna Freud thought young children might inhabit if left without training in the inhibitions of civilized life. I turned to the front of the book, where there was a table showing variations in population over the centuries. The Rev. MacFarland guessed, on what basis I was not sure, that there were around fifty people on Colsay in the 1640s. It is a constant challenge to social restraint to have seven people living together on this island, even with an internet connection and a boat and more rooms than people. If there were fifty in one-room huts and they weren't fighting each other to stow away in William Tabb's boat, they knew things we don't, things about the relationship between individuals and communities.

'Are you coming to bed soon? It's nearly midnight and you said you were really tired.'

I can see no painless way of telling Giles that marriage does not preclude knocking on doors. Giving birth in front of someone is not a permanent abrogation of dignity.

'Soon I am. But if I go to sleep next thing I know Moth'll be screaming again. I get to have some time off.'

He sat down on the edge of the bath. I pulled my stomach in. 'I didn't say you didn't. What are you reading?'

I hoped the Malteser wrapper hadn't rustled. 'Oh, just a local history. The librarian thought I'd be interested.'

'I thought you hated local history.'

I once spent quite a lot of the three hours it took to drive home from one of Julia's drinks parties explaining to Giles the depth of my scorn for a retired lawyer in a brass-buttoned suit

238

who believed that his self-published work on the history of Monckton Parva qualified him to discount the development of women's history.

'It has its place. There were some great books in the '60s. By proper historians.'

Night Waking: 05:24

Not Moth but Raphael. I wait a minute. It is keening, as if it all happened long ago and nothing is better. It is light outside, light enough for anything, and the attic stairs are full of pale sunshine.

'Raph?' He's sitting up, wrapped in his duvet as if it's cold. 'What's wrong?'

I touch the tears on his cheeks but he doesn't look at me.

'Raph? Why are you so sad?'

It's as if he doesn't know I'm here.

'Raphael, love. Why are you crying?'

He shudders, stares at the wall.

'Is it the baby again?'

He nods and leans into my arms and I cuddle him as if he were Moth with a bumped head.

'There, love. It's all right. It was long ago.'

His hair smells of shampoo and he appears to be fully dressed.

'I saw the bones,' he says into my shoulder. 'I saw them in the ground and now I wish I hadn't. And one day I'll be in the ground and so will you and so will Moth and we'll all be dead.'

'Not for a long time,' I say, as if that makes any difference. In the end, I make him lie down and I sit on his bed and read *Little House on the Prairie* in the gentlest monotone I can muster, and at last his breathing softens. Then I slip along the landing and look round Moth's door. He is still there, his nest of blankets still rising and falling, starfish hand clutching his bear.

*

239

There is no point in going back to sleep after 5 a.m. I inch down the outside edges of the stairs, avoiding creaks, open the front door, which Giles has failed to lock, and step out into the morning. The shadow of the hills behind the house reaches across the garden, over the beach and out to sea, but beyond it the waves glisten ice-white. I shiver. There is someone moving down on the shore, someone running as if the Vikings are after him with drawn swords. Brian, keeping his heart in good order.

Colsay

28th Nov.

Dear Aubrey,

I violate all etiquette and advice to young ladies (for I have still
had no letter from you) under only the most pressing
circumstances: I have seen the Northern Lights! Does that not fill
you with envy for my diet of oats and seafowl, my evenings with
only a small fire and some decidedly amateur knitting to counter
the effects of the eldritch tales Mrs Barwick likes to tell, and my
work harder in the accomplishment even than your Medusa (for at
least that battle was between you and your Muse, a lady far more
open to reason than those on whose assent my achievements here
must depend)?

I was on my way to bed when I saw the Merry Dancers (a further
violation of etiquette: I am sure correct young ladies have nothing
so improper as beds when they take it upon themselves to write to
young gentlemen), and paused to adjust the curtains, which tend to
stir disconcertingly at the hands of what I do really know to be the
draught from the window. You will smile when I confess that it has
become my habit to assure myself on retiring that there is nothing
unseemly behind the drapes or under the bed, only it does save time
when Mrs Barwick's tales come to mind if I chance to wake in the
early hours! Anyway, on this occasion the precaution was justified,
for outside the window, and indeed stretched right across the sky,
were great swathes of green light, wavering and flickering as if
shaken by the hands of Atlas himself. I went out, of course,
although Mrs Barwick had already bolted the door and made no
pretence of concealing her disdain for my proceedings, and stood at

the garden wall trembling with cold and then, as the lights seemed to swoop lower and lower over my uncovered head, also with a kind of fear. It was as if the sea and the bare hillside were being swept for mortal sinners, as if the God of the Old Testament were returning with signs less ambiguous than the burning bush or even the Flood. For after all a tree may take fire and rain is not unnatural, whereas sheets of green light are decidedly – strange.

Anyway, having confided this sight I shall forthwith reassume the guise of the correctly-brought-up young lady, and cease this unauthorized correspondence forthwith. But I do think of you, Aubrey, and remain, after all,

Yours affectionately,

May

12

IRRATIONAL EMOTIONAL ATTACHMENTS

In reality it is not the absence of irrational emotional attachments which helps a child to grow up normally but the painful and often disturbing process of learning how to deal with such emotions.

– Dorothy Burlingham and Anna Freud, *Infants Without Families: The Case For and Against Residential Nurseries*, p. 50

I was not surprised when Zoe reappeared while I was still tidying up breakfast.

'Hello! Do you mind if I come in?'

'Sure.' I filled the porridge pan with water. I believe in leaving things to soak.

'Zoe?' Raph looked up from *The Discovery Guide to Space Travel*. 'Zoe, did you know that people's bones get weak when there isn't any gravity?'

She sat down beside him. 'Hello, Moth. Yes. So do muscles. We need something to work against.'

Raph watched me find my hairbrush under *Freezing Ahead* (not polar exploration but cookery), the current *British Journal of Social History* and a drawing by Moth alleged to represent a big boat and a spade.

'How do people brush their hair in space?'

'I have no idea. Moth, can you come out of that cupboard, love? No, could you put that back, please?' I gave up on the hair-brushing. 'Moth, look, play with this instead.'

'Oh bugger flour,' said Moth. He sat down, raising a small cloud.

'No, love. Not playing with flour.'

I picked him up and he screamed. Raph put his fingers in his ears and went on reading.

'Moth?' said Zoe. 'Look!' She picked up an oven glove from under a two-week-old *Guardian* and made the gloved hand chase the other one across the table. Moth giggled. The oven glove seized an envelope from Her Majesty's Tax Inspectorate and began to eat it, growling.

'More!' said Moth.

I started sweeping the floor.

'Do you know if you'll be wanting the boat again today, Zoe?'

She shrugged. The oven glove scuttled towards Moth.

'I won't. I should think if my mother thinks she can cause inconvenience by wanting it she will. You could say no, you know.'

I swept the flour into the bin. 'You're our visitors, Zoe. We advertised a ferry service. She's quite right.'

'No she's not, she's a whiny bitch who wouldn't say what she means unless you held a gun to her head. Which I would.'

'That doesn't mean she's never right.' I put the brush away. 'No, love, see if you can find the blue tractor. You seem very angry with her.'

Moth pottered off towards the toys and the oven glove wilted on the table like the dying swan.

Zoe tossed her hair back. 'She hates me. She's always hated me. She only liked me when I was a baby and she could make me do anything she liked.'

I looked into the playroom, where Moth was driving toy cars

on to Noah's Ark. Noah's roll-on, roll-off high speed Ararat service.

'You can't make babies do anything you like,' said Raph. 'You can't make babies do anything at all.'

Zoe sniffled. 'She's always hated me, anyway.'

Raph looked up. 'She's your mummy.'

'People can feel very angry with their mummies sometimes. But no, love, you're right. Mummies don't hate their children.'

'She does,' said Zoe.

I frowned at her.

'Well, she does.'

'I'd say she loves you and she's angry with you.'

Raph pushed his chair back and went upstairs, still reading.

'Sorry.' Zoe turned over the *Journal of Social History*. 'Do you need to go after him?'

'No. He'll tell me later if he's bothered.' I sighed. I was going to have to hear about Zoe and her mother sometime in the next week and at least in my own kitchen I could combine counselling with cookery.

'So why are you on holiday with them?'

I opened the cupboard quietly, so as not to alert Moth to the availability of messy play. Zoe fiddled with her hair.

'They wouldn't let me stay at home. And I don't have anywhere else to go.'

'Grandparents?' I asked. Mine were a great refuge when nuclear family life became overwhelming.

She shook her head. 'Dead or demented.'

'Oh.' I poured flour into the bowl. I wondered if she'd considered paid employment as a possibility. 'Where exactly was your gap year?'

'Clayoquot. Vancouver Island. Have you been?'

I nodded. Annual Conference of the North American Women's History Alliance, 1999, University of British Columbia. A display of eye-opening knitwear and artisanal jewellery. 'Around there.'

I ran the tap until it was lukewarm and filled a jug. I hoped Raph wasn't halfway up the stairs, listening. His puberty, it occurred to me, could be as little as five years off.

'My friend was going to go help at a school in Kerala and I wanted to go too, but Mum said they'd only pay for me to go to university if I didn't go off to "some disease-ridden Third World country with bombs going off on every corner", by which she seems to mean anywhere outside Knutsford. And maybe Wilmslow. So I was like, fine, I'll take loans instead and she said, fine, in that case you can start paying your own way now and they hadn't worked all those years so I could throw all my opportunities away and I was like some parents would be glad if their children wanted a job and she said only poor people want their children at the till in Tesco instead of revising.'

I stirred in the yeast and peeped at Moth. Noah was driving a fire engine and the animals were grazing inside the toy hospital, except the giraffe which was jammed up the lift-shaft of the garage.

Zoe put the oven glove back on. 'Sorry, am I being boring?'

'Not at all. I worry when Moth goes quiet. He's fine.' I added a handful of linseeds, said to contain vital nutrients which might compensate for my failure in sourcing organic meat for the children. 'So you went to Vancouver Island?'

She shrugged. 'Mum said I'd hate it. Because I was going to work on a conservation project in the rainforest and I don't like gardening. And she said only a spoilt teenager would imagine that manual labour could be liberating, and I was like, you think manual labour involves a trug and wellies with pink roses on them and she was like—'

'What about your dad?' I put the yeast in the window, where watery sunlight made the closest I could come to the 'warm place' required by the recipe. 'You haven't mentioned him at all.'

The oven glove undulated. 'Oh, Dad.'

Moth was talking. I peered into the playroom to see him holding *Lucy and Tom Go to School* upside down and declaiming *The Gruffalo's Child*.

'Dad just, like, works. All the time. It's like he fathered us and then plugged himself back into the office and he's been there ever since. Mostly that's where he actually is, but sometimes Mum can make him go on holiday as long as he's got the internet and he can pretend he's still at work. Mum totally fell for it, she acts as if it's him working that – that stops the sun crashing into the earth or something. It's totally just an excuse for hiding from Mum and surfing the net. He always seems to have read most of the world's newspapers. Why, were you wondering if she'd tipped him off the cliff?'

'Of course not. It's just we've barely seen him since you arrived. And you don't mention him.'

'No. Well. He doesn't do anything worth mentioning. Unless you're into the world of cardiology. Will once said it wouldn't make any difference to us if Dad was dead as long as the life insurance was good. He thinks he's so important he can't even take time to stop Mum emotionally abusing me.'

I suspect we are all guilty, of emotional abuse. I suspect most relationships between humans are emotional abuse. The alternative would be to become an anchorite. And anyway, I could entertain the idea that conducting heart surgery might reasonably take priority over saving Zoe from her mother's pressure to eat enough to stay alive until the beginning of term.

'Will's your brother?'

She shrugged. 'He's doing medicine at King's. What a good boy.'

The yeast showed a bubble or two. I reckoned it could finish rising in the dough later, when the children weren't entertaining themselves, and poured it into the flour.

'Do you miss him?'

Her hair swung down. 'Yeah. We used to fight a lot but at least he was there.'

There was a crash from the playroom. 'Oh bugger a books.'

I went through. The last few books slid off the shelf. 'Moth? Do you want to come and help Mummy knead the dough?'

I balanced him on my raised knee while I washed his hands. 'Oh bugger a water.'

'Oops a daisy water.' I put him down and he stood on my foot. 'Up, up and see!'

I picked him up again and he lunged at the bowl. Kneading bread is one of few culinary procedures I have not learnt to conduct with a toddler on one hip. 'Moth, let me mix it and then you can have a bit, OK?'

I tried to put him down and he swung from my neck. 'Ow. Moth, do you want a biscuit?'

He gripped my waist with his knees. 'No. Not today biscuit.'

'Moth,' said Zoe. 'Look, it's an oven glove fish!'

'No,' said Moth. 'Not today oven glove. Cuddle Mummy.'

I nuzzled his face, which was sticky.

'OK,' said Zoe. 'Why don't you cuddle Moth and I'll knead the bread?'

I could see all the bones in her hands.

'It's quite energetic,' I said. 'Cooks used to be great big strapping women with muscles.'

'Yeah, well. I'll burn off some calories. Seeing I can't go to the gym here.'

Moth and I rubbed noses. 'Raph's working on it.'

We put the bowl on the floor so Moth could see what we were doing and I showed her how to push and turn, push and turn, until the sticky heap became cool and silky.

'Have you always made your own bread?' she asked. 'Mum used to do it but she stopped when Will hit puberty and started eating a loaf a day.'

I held Moth's hands as he climbed up my lap. 'No. I think it's a criminal waste of time. People weren't expected to make their own bread anywhere in Europe until women got shut in kitchens in the nineteenth century. That's why there were medieval bakers' guilds, as opposed to soup makers' guilds or turnip boilers' guilds. Everyone who could bought ready-made bread because it was too much hassle to make at home. Well, and most of them didn't have ovens. But Giles won't let the kids eat the processed stuff from Spar and he's probably right about the additives, though God knows he ate enough of them at boarding school, and anyway if I can't be working I might as well make bread. At least I'm producing something. What's your mum doing for bread?'

It is the logic of amateur cake decorators and sock knitters across the land, that production of any kind is by definition a moral way of spending time. As if more stuff is what the world needs. Giles, in the days before children, when cooking could be a creative performance rather than the industrial-scale generation of spills and leftovers and was thus something he was willing to undertake at weekends, once made his own tortellini. I timed him from my desk, where I was writing an article on eighteenth-century fashion journalism and its relation to early industrial gender ideologies, and worked out that each pork-and-mushroom-filled pasta ear represented about twenty-five minutes of his time, or around £18 after tax and National Insurance, not including the ingredients. Some of them fell apart when he boiled them, which doesn't happen to the ones from plastic packets. He said that what I was doing wasn't any more useful, and may have had a point.

Zoe knelt and shoved the dough down. Her knuckles looked as if they were about to come through the skin. 'I've no idea, I don't eat with them.'

Dear Professor James

I am writing to apply for the Lectureship in Modern History recently advertised in the *Times Higher Education Supplement*. I completed my doctorate, entitled *The Unformed Clay of Humankind: theorizing British childhood from 1760 to 1820*, at Oxford in 2006, and since then have held a Research

Fellowship at St Mary Hall. I daily expect to be summarily dismissed for flashing my breasts at the Principal, an error which I have compounded by moving to Outer Scotland, and trust you will understand that the gaps in my publication record result from two episodes of maternity leave and its attendant disruptions rather than a dereliction of intellectual duty. I can assure you that I do not enjoy the practice of motherhood and would be very happy to focus my energies instead on your department, where I believe it is possible to stare out of the window and consume hot beverages at will, and furthermore that research seminars and the like may occasionally afford reason to miss the children's bedtime.

I regretfully deleted everything after the second sentence and started again. I wanted to compose a resignation letter, or maybe two resignation letters, one from college and one from motherhood, and in fact maybe one from marriage as well, although I might be willing to go on having sex with Giles. Computers have memories, somehow accessible to the police even though Computer Services have no means of recovering documents that one has not deleted but only failed to back up. I told the computer to empty the trash can, but I don't know where it empties all these cancelled thoughts and wisely unsent letters. Is there a municipal dump somewhere on the internet? Show me your deleted documents and I'll show you who you are. And who you don't want to be.

I sipped some tea and looked along the table at Giles. His face was somehow unfamiliar in the glow of his laptop, his eyes intent on something that wasn't there. His puffins, his mysteriously absent puffins. When numbers drop it's obvious to assume they have died, but they might just have gone somewhere else, in which case there is probably a reason, a reason which ornithologists imagine to be accessible to the human mind, although it seems to me arrogant to assume that we can think like birds. Fiona Firth's book says that the islanders killed tens of thousands of puffins, some for food but most for use as manure. I wonder if Giles would eat one? Sing a song of sixpence. I used to care about things like that, about the imminent extinction of tigers and the destruction of the Amazon rainforest, and you'd think having children would have made me care more. You'd be wrong. I refreshed my e-mail and found a new message.

Dear Anna, just wondering if you had plans for the evening. With much love from a secret admirer.

I looked up. He was so intent on his screen he looked as if he was reading the *Guardian* online. I e-mailed back.

For admiration, I could change my plans. What did you have in mind?

His face didn't change as he typed. I blushed. 'Giles! This is my work e-mail.'

'So?' he said. 'Turn it off. Come on.'

'Hang on a minute. I need to delete that. What if the Fellows saw it?'

He lifted my hair and kissed my neck, hard. 'The Fellows are still using carrier pigeons.' He reached round me. 'There. Gone.'

I paused on the landing. All the lights were off in Black Rock House. I imagined Judith standing on the barrows on the headland, casting spells into the dark, and remembered Zoe's dead-looking face on the boat. And Brian with the blinds down in his virtual office.

Giles put his hand on my waist. 'You OK?'

I rolled my shoulders. 'Yeah. A bit worried about Zoe.'

'Is she as much of a mess as she looks?'

'I think she's probably pretty when she's well. But yes, I think

251

she's got a bit stuck. And I'm not short of people with needs.'

He took his hand away. 'What's that supposed to mean?'

'The children. Obviously.' And Mary Homerton. And the dead baby. 'Are you going to sweep me off my feet or what?'

A baby cough came scuttling across the landing. We froze. 'Shh.' A stronger cough.

'Mummy! Moth wants a drink!'

'Ah, fuck.' I leant against Giles.

'I'll go,' he said.

'Really? You want a shag that much?'

'Go to bed. I'll be there in a minute.'

The voice of inexperience.

The clouds had cleared and there were stars, and moonlight strong enough to cast the shadow of the window frame and the fingered branches of the tree across the bed, though not, I decided, strong enough to show that white worms of elastic were hanging out of my bra straps. I pushed Giles's pillows off the bed and stretched out my arms and legs. Maybe the Hôtel de la Mère should offer double beds after all, just without the marital hint of two sets of pillows. Maybe half the room should be a bed, inviting mothers to sleep like toddlers, sprawled as they lay when the final rendition of 'The Wheels on the Bus' petered into longed-for silence. I wondered what additional services the Hôtel might offer. Not massage, no 'pampering' or 'beauty treatments'. Button replacement, shoe-polishing. Dry cleaning, to return to service all those milk-stained jackets that have padded the bottom of the laundry basket for months. Perhaps a hairdresser. Marriage guidance, divorce law, careers advice, CV workshops. Financial planning, an explanation of pensions. What do women want? (The equal distribution of responsibilities as well as rights, failing which utopia equal pay for equal work would be an acceptable starting point that oddly eluded Freud, and sadly is not in the gift of the Hôtel either.) I remembered Rebecca the post-natal depression counsellor, sitting in her over-heated office overlooking the bus stop and listening to me saying that I would never read or write again. Feminists have much for which to blame Freud but the advent of psychoanalysis does at least mean that people now sometimes listen to madwomen. When they are paid to do so.

I turned over. I could hear Moth singing 'Old MacDonald' and Giles murmuring in disharmonic counterpoint. In the name of God, shut up and go to sleep. God seems oddly plausible in the watches of the night, when we entertain the possibility that a Being immune to the despair of Palestinian children, the Ogoni nation and the grieving mothers of Bihar might intervene to our advantage in the matter of toddler insomnia. I suppose there are other beings, in Whitehall and the White House for example, who might reasonably be expected to take responsibility for the bigger cock-ups on the planet, but, as Raphael points out, it would take omnipotence to make a baby go to sleep. Which Giles does not possess. I took off the bra, whose underwires slipped their moorings several washes ago, and pulled a nightie from the dirty clothes pile at the foot of the bed.

Night Waking: 03:56

Raph, again. Making a noise that is not, or not only, a demand for attention. I slide out of bed, the memory of certain moments earlier in the night inspiring unusual solicitude for Giles's undisturbed rest. Summer is passing on and, although there is a grey brightness behind the hill to the east, there is no light in Raph's room, where I have to feel for his shoulders and hair to find his face deep in his pillow. He doesn't want to be held, doesn't respond to stroking or his own baby endearments, which haven't crossed my lips in years. I sit on the bed, the draught from the window snaking round my shoulder, and wonder if he would rather I went back to bed.

'Raph. Is this about the baby again? We have to stop worrying about her, you know. She's been dead a long time and I'm sure people cried then. She's not our baby, Raph.' Not exactly, anyway. You'll have enough to grieve for in your life. There are deaths waiting for you, and if there are not it is for a reason that I cannot contemplate. My hand tightens on the cords of his shoulders, runs over the wings of bone on his back. 'We're all alive now, and for a long time to come. Raph?' I don't know who I am comforting, if the death I am addressing is general or particular. There is no response, and I sit there, rubbing and patting his back as I did when we spent our nights walking the room and crying.

Colsay House

2nd Dec.

Dearest Allie,

The child was born last night and I was not called. Oh, Al, all
the women were there, even Mrs Barwick was there and not I! I
have not been allowed to see it – I went there with the baby clothes
you packed, as soon as I had finished breakfast when Mrs Barwick
told me – but no doubt if it is not already failing it soon will. I had
to leave the little clothes with Mrs Barwick, who was already
there, and actually came to the door to tell me that Mrs Grice
would not have my company. (I also gave the shawl I have been
making – it is no fine thing but could at least serve to ensure that
the child's few days of life are not tormented by cold as well as
pain, and no better knitter has seen fit to make a similar
preparation.) When she at last came back to the house I upbraided
Mrs Barwick, I could not help myself. She knows that I am the one
person on this island who could have brought Mrs Grice a living
child and I left explicit instructions that I was to be called the
moment her pains came on, day or night. Mrs Barwick says yes,
Miss May, I ken that, but a woman can surely choose her own
company at such a time and, forgive me, Miss May, but she did not
choose you, and not for lack of offering. I'm afraid when she said
that I left the room and banged the door. It is just wicked, to kill a
child like that, and Mrs Grice and those evil women have killed
this infant as surely as if they had strangled or drowned it. What
will Miss Emily say? And Aubrey? I did my best but I could
hardly watch every night on her doorstep in case labour began, and
if I had I could not have been sure of being admitted. All these

horrible weeks here, and to fail now! And nowhere even to hide myself, for if I want my tea I will have to go down the stairs and face Mrs Barwick again. I hope Lord Hugo sends them all off to Canada under the most unfriendly conditions; I have heard of one place near here where the people were rounded up with dogs, like sheep, and packed into the boats and not allowed even on to the deck until they were far on the way west. Even animals don't kill their own young, and what ingratitude to those who have sent me to them with no motive beyond easing their grief!

I don't know whether to cry or throw things around the room, and don't tell me, even in my mind, that neither will help. As Mrs Barwick would say, I ken that very well.

How can I go on here now?

13

THE CHILD'S NEEDS

It is the mother's task to be attentive to the child's needs (for food, sleep, warmth, movement, comfort, company), not to misunderstand them, or to confuse them with each other, and to fulfil them, not according to her own speed and rhythm, but by adapting her actions to the child's.

– Anna Freud, *Indications for Child Analysis and Other Papers*
(London: Hogarth Press, 1969), p. 591

There were two major crises on the island of Colsay during the eighteenth century. In 1724, a schooner sailing out of Glasgow ran adrift in a heavy fog on the skerries to the north-east of the island. There were rumours, persistent into this century, that the islanders' interest in the cargo of the *John Frederick* overcame their humanity with regard to the survivors and particularly to the bodies of the majority of the crew, who did not survive. These rumours are now impossible to substantiate or disprove, but what remains sure is that the people of Colsay soon had reason to regret any contact with the fated ship. Smallpox broke out—

'Oh,' said Giles. 'You're busy.'
I looked up. 'Sure am.'
'Is that the book?'

'Yes.'

'Really?'

'It's the book, Giles. I'm producing deathless prose which will change the face of eighteenth-century historiography and redeem my career from the morass of nappies and spat-out biscuits into which it has fallen.'

'Oh.'

The space hopper stopped and Raph appeared behind Giles at the back door.

'So can I come too?' he asked.

'Judith and Brian need a lift to Colla.' Giles leant on the door jamb. 'I was hoping to finish some data collection.'

I glanced up to where the rising dough was pushing against the tea-towel over the bowl. SAVE CANTERBURY CATHEDRAL, though the tea-towel did not elaborate on the threat from which Canterbury Cathedral needs to be saved.

'Judith doesn't like my driving. And the bread's going to need shaping and baking in the next hour or so, after Moth wakes. Why don't you take Raph to the library? Fiona Firth said she'd get some more space books for him. And we're nearly out of olive oil, I forgot to order so it'll have to be the best Spar can provide.'

He stood up. 'OK, OK, we're going.'

'And another pack of baby wipes, just to tide us over. And if you want a salad tonight you should get lettuce. We've still got avocados.'

'Come on, Raph. I'll take you to the pub for crisps if you like.'

'And don't get drunk and push Judith into the Sound!' I shouted after them.

and, although no eye-witness accounts survive, it is clear that there were few adult survivors. The vulnerability of small island populations to infection is well documented, the obvious comparison here being the 'boat cold', which invariably afflicted the inhabitants of both St Kilda and Pitcairn Island on those rare occasions when they had contact with people from elsewhere. None the less, the death of almost all resident adults is surprising, and particularly so when we consider that even two hundred years ago, Colsay was by no means isolated. Colsay Sound is a treacherous and unpredictable stretch of water, but only in dense fog is it impossible to see the island from the mainland and vice versa, and, although few would wish to make the crossing daily, most of the inhabitants of Colla were probably almost as familiar with the geography of Colsay as with their own outfields. This seems to have been a particularly virulent strain of smallpox, from which the people of Colla also suffered very badly, reporting a mortality rate of around 60 per cent, and perhaps deaths on Colsay were higher because the epidemic came in March, towards the end of the 'hungry season' when the people's resistance must have been particularly low.

Antonia Rivett would have given up on the Reverend. Clearly, probably, must have been, seems to have been. 'Reserve your energies for explicating what you actually know.' She had no truck with theories of history suggesting that we don't actually know anything at all, regarding this epistemological flaw – perhaps rightly – as a disability common to most human endeavour and one that, if not regarded in the proper spirit, would bring us all to stupid silence. Like death. Wilful stupidity is the basis of intelligent thought. Ignore the chasm beneath your feet.

An earlier predecessor of my own, the Rev. Adamson, who was the incumbent of Colla from 1718 to 1732, was alerted to the sorry state of affairs on the island by the arrival of James and Elizabeth Grice, aged eight and ten, in one of the community's small fishing boats. He noted in the Parish

Record that 'These Children brought a Tale so chilling that at first they were scarce believed, but they soon convinced us of the Tragedy that had visited the Island, where they were themselves but just come from interring their Mother in a shallow Grave, there being none other to do them that Service.' Reverend Adamson had some trouble finding healthy men who were willing to accompany him back to Colsay with these unfortunate children—

'Anna?' Zoe, framed by the door. 'Oh, sorry. You're working. I thought Moth would be up by now.'

14:37. 'Oh fuck. You're right, he should. He'll never to go bed now.'

I pushed the book into my laptop bag and rearranged the pile of monographs that should have been absorbing my attention. 'Sit down, if you like. Make some tea. I'll be down in a minute.'

Moth was sleeping as if far out of sight of land, adrift wherever it is that the toddler unconscious needs to go. In the end I picked him up limp with sleep and took him downstairs to be woken by the novelty of Zoe.

'I made you some tea,' she said. 'And I think the bread's overflowing; do you want me to knead it again?'

I sat down and arranged Moth on my lap, floppy as a doll. He opened his eyes and looked at Zoe as if she had just landed from Pluto.

'Yes, please. If you don't mind. And could you put the oven on? About two hundred?'

Zoe peeled Canterbury Cathedral off the dough and began to knead. I hoped her hands were clean.

'You'll need extra flour. Bottom cupboard.'

Moth took my hand and sucked my knuckle as if it were full of milk.

'Moth love. Do you want a drink?'

He rubbed his face against my jumper and I hugged him.

He won't always want to sit in my lap. I kissed his hair, and looked up to see Zoe watching us.

'It's so sweet. I know my mum never did that.'

'Zoe, I'm sure she did. All mothers do this. It's not even about love, it's not as complicated or demanding as love, it's just animal physicality.'

She sprinkled flour on to the dough. 'All my mother's animal physicality is directed towards food. And drink. You know that ice cream I bought? For the children? Well, the next day when I went to look it was gone. She hadn't even recycled the pot, it was in the bin. I suppose she thought I wouldn't look there. There's about three thousand calories in a litre of that stuff.'

I sipped tea and felt tired. Moth wriggled on my lap. 'Moth do kneading?'

'Can you give him a bit, Zoe? Just a small handful.'

Moth slid down and wobbled over to her, and then sat on the floor and pressed his dough.

'Don't worry, we won't eat that bit.' I watched her hands moving like crabs in the dough. 'Zoe, are things OK? Over at Black Rock?'

I would never have gone on holiday with my parents at eighteen. Nor would they have invited me. I could see the muscles in Zoe's arms moving like ropes between bone and skin. She tossed her hair. Another health and safety issue *in re* bread.

'No. But they made me come. Now she keeps saying I ought to be grateful when she's spent all that money bringing me here. They were paying for the cottage anyway, and it's not as if my presence in the car is going to add much to the petrol consumption. Not with her up front.'

I had a vision of the three of them on the motorway, Brian driving, Judith issuing a running deprecation of the landscape, other drivers, the lack of foresight shown by those using service stations and not bringing their own sandwiches, the weather, and anything else that came to mind, as if with enough superiority she could earn her daughter's health. And Zoe getting obstinately thinner in the back and an empty space where Will used to be. It's a long way from Manchester to Colla.

Moth threw his dough at floor. 'Splat! Squash a dough!'

'Yes, but don't stand on it, please. Look, knead it like Zoe.'

'Splat!'

I stood up. 'Sit down and have some tea. I'll do this. You don't honestly look up to the work anyway.'

She looked away. 'I'm fine. I went running this morning. It's Mum who's not fit.'

'Well, I shouldn't think that makes her happy.' I floured the bowl and began to knead. 'So do you have plans for the next year? Or are you going to see if you can go to Cambridge in October? If someone's missed their grades they might have a place for you.'

She ran her finger round the top of the mug. 'If I decide to go at all.'

'Old MacDonald!' said Moth. 'Old MacDonald had a dragon!'

'You might as well try it,' I said. 'You can always leave.' I could hear the law tutors at Trinity cursing me. 'Surely you'd be better there than at home. Are you looking forward to the work? Old MacDonald had a farm, ee-i, ee-i, o. And on that farm he had a dragon, ee-i, ee-i, o.'

'Yes. I'm not doing it for the reasons you think.'

'More dragon!'

'With a puff, puff here and a puff, puff there, here a puff, there a puff, everywhere a puff, puff. What do I think?'

'I'm doing law because I want to join the Establishment and make lots of money.'

'Old MacDonald had a leopard.'

'Old MacDonald had a farm, ee-i, ee-i, o. Not at all. You might want to work in a women's refuge or with socially disadvantaged children. I imagine that would annoy your mother. And on that farm he had a leopard, ee-i, ee-i, o.'

'I just like the idea. It's a matrix that makes sense of what

262

people do. I mean, you can be driving along listening to what-ever and thinking about whether to buy a pair of shoes and if you're doing it at twenty-nine miles an hour you're innocent and if you're doing it at thirty-six miles an hour you're guilty. It's like, we make it sound objective but it's all about telling sto-ries. Pushing people under trains is illegal but if they were trying to knife you at the time it's probably OK. Eating bananas is totally fine unless you haven't paid for them. But it looks exactly the same at the time whether you're becoming a criminal or not. I like the way law makes sense out of the way people behave. It's kind of reassuring, I suppose. Like there's something consistent.'

'Leopards say roar! Leopards on a farm!'

'With a roar, roar here, and a roar, roar there. Ee-i, ee-i, o.' Killing babies is wrong but if it is your own baby you may be mad, which is not a criminal offence. Zoe passed me the bowl and I pulled the dough apart into three more or less equal pieces. 'Yes,' I said. 'I see the appeal of that. History is also about narrative, in the end. Whether the gaps and silences might mean anything. Though the consequences of the stories you tell are much more general. Cultural memory and national identity rather than who goes to prison. And you don't get to think about individuals in quite the same way.'

'Wolf on a bus.' Moth held up his dough, grey now and with a small feather partially embedded in it. 'Moth made bread.'

'Thank you, Moth.'

'Wolf on a bus!'

'The wolf on the bus goes munch munch munch, munch munch munch, munch munch munch. The wolf on the bus goes munch munch munch, all day long.' I drank some more tea. 'Not that he's seen a bus in months.'

'People do go to prison because of cultural memory and national identity,' said Zoe. 'Most kinds of terrorism are kind of about cultural memory, aren't they? Righting the wrongs of history? It's all, like, story-telling in the end.'

'Yes,' I said. 'You know, Zoe, you'd be good in a tutorial.'

'Do you miss Oxford?' she asked.

I floured the loaf tins.

'Less than I did,' I said. 'Less than I did.'

I put the loaves in their tins and set them to rise again.

'Moth, shall we bake your bread?'

He looked appalled, as if I'd suggested wiping his nose or combing his hair.

'No. Moth looking after bread.'

He carried it off to the playroom, cupped in his hands like a baby bird or an insect, glancing back over his shoulder in wonder at my barbaric ideas.

'Come on, Moth's bread. We play with a animals in a par cark.'

Maybe Raph brings on the apocalypse and Moth plays at the nuclear winter that follows, where animals browse car parks and make nests in office buildings cracked open like Easter eggs.

I filled the mixing bowl with hot water. Zoe was picking at the skin around her nails.

'So what happened in Canada? You were on a conservation project?'

She glanced out of the window, where heavy clouds were congregating in the north. Giles and Raph should be safe in Colla, cocooned in the warmth of the library or absorbing the smell of chips and beer in the pub. The washing up seemed to have proliferated inexplicably, as it does when people won't reuse plates from which it is easy to shake a few crumbs. I poured Zoe some more tea.

'At first it was great. There were six of us. Volunteers. The others were all Canadian. And there was Bill. Bill runs the place. We slept in this wooden hut with a veranda and you could just step out into the forest in the morning. The trees were like taller than I've ever seen, taller than this house, and it's like being in a greenhouse. This ceiling of pine branches, and underneath a huge space for growing. And we could hear the sea in the night. It felt so totally far from home. It was so cool, thinking about the world and my parents right round on the other side of it. I'd never seen the Pacific before. I mean, you think it's all just sea but it was different, all the shells and things were different. Everything smelt of trees and rain. And one of the guys – Hayden – we got together. And I really liked him.'

She ran her finger round the inside of her mug's handle. From the playroom, I heard Moth singing 'Pop Goes the Weasel'.

'It sounds lovely.' I began to scrub the flour that had dried on to the mixing bowl. Gap years were still a minority pursuit when I was eighteen, Grand Tours for the rich and indecisive. Giles had one. I went to skivvy in France and told my mother it was to save some money for university.

'And then I met this woman one day. I was out for a walk on my own and I was like a bit worried about bears. They have these signs telling you what to do if you meet one but it's really obvious that the things they tell you are just ways of amusing yourself until the bear eats you. You know, make lots of noise, stay in groups. The bit I liked said, "Exercise extra caution walking into the wind or near water," but it didn't say how. And then if you do meet one you're supposed to back away slowly and talk to it in soothing tones. Can you imagine? *Don't worry, bear, I'm on my way. Don't eat me.* And if that doesn't work, you use your backpack to protect your head. I mean, wouldn't you rather it ate your head first? And if you've still got your head on you can try climbing trees, except that black bears are better at climbing trees than people are, and then if you end up in a tree with a bear you're meant to try to like intimidate it. It's not really advice so much as a manual for a messy death.'

Moth put his head around the door. 'Mummy laughing,' he remarked, disapproving as if Mummy were throwing her bra at the stage.

'Anyway, so I didn't want to be scared by these ridiculous signs but I also didn't want to turn into bear lunch before I'd even got to Cambridge, and there was no one around so I was sort of walking along singing. The signs tell you to make a noise. Jerusalem the Golden, actually. I went to that kind of school. And I met this woman so I was embarrassed and she thought it was totally funny and we got talking. And it turned out she was running a campaign group against logging and fish farming. And that was when I realized.'

She pushed her hair back. There were tears in her eyes and her voice was harsh.

'None of it's real, Anna. There's almost no virgin forest left. It's all been like logged and they've let some of it grow back because in the pretty bits by the sea they can make more money out of tourism than logging. In the middle of the island where tourists don't go, there are hundreds of miles where it looks like a nuclear bomb fell. They've just totally obliterated it. All those centuries of slow growth. They just take these horrible diggers that're designed to go up almost any mountain and they raze the rainforest. All of it. And the blue inlets I liked are full of fish farms, which fill the water with antibiotics and pesticides and poison everything else, and the fish farmers kill all the seals and bears they can get their hands on to stop them eating the farmed fish.'

She put her hands over her face.

'They don't even always shoot them. There were some baby bears – I don't want to think about it. I mean, I know it's kind of sentimental to get upset about baby bears because they're totally cute but it's not just that, it's the mountains and the sea. I mean, I went to this place because I thought it was the real thing, you know, one of those rare bits of the planet we haven't utterly fucked up, and I was wrong. It's fucked up but we're so totally good at fucking up the planet now that we can do that and still make money out of morons like me who think the cultivated bits round the edges are the real thing. And it's too late now. My parents' generation have totally screwed the entire planet beyond any possibility of redemption and when they've finished spending their retirements buying like new teak garden furniture and flying to New Zealand because sixty is the new thirty and they can still go bungee jumping they're going to die and leave the rest of us to kill each other for water and oil. I mean, Jesus, Anna, how could you have kids when there's nothing left for them because my mother's eaten it all?'

I rinsed the bowl and rebuilt the pile of wet dishes on the draining board to accommodate it. You wouldn't want to eat off anything that had been dried on our tea-towels.

'We worried,' I said. 'People have always worried that it's a stupid time to have children, even in the eighteenth century. And the seventeenth. That's where the hostages to fortune quote comes from, Bacon. We wanted them. That's the only good reason for having babies. They're people who are wanted. At least at the beginning. And you never know, they might change the world.'

She pushed her hair back. 'They might have to.'

'Well,' I said. 'If they have to, they probably will. People usually do what they have to do. I mean, Raph's working on it already. And it sounds to me as if you've got some excellent reasons there for being the best lawyer you possibly can be. Go to Cambridge and specialize in environmental legislation or work for Greenpeace or something.'

'It's too late,' she said. 'Don't you understand? There's nothing left to save.'

I watched the water pooling along the tidemark on the draining board. The bottom of the tap was encrusted with something brown. The problem with the logic of despair is that it is right, only not useful.

'There are six billion people, or whatever it is. And you'll need to do something with your life. You can't help consuming, so you might as well produce something useful. You're here now.'

267

I sounded like a Girl Guide leader. I looked at the ribs poking through her sweater. There are, of course, ways of not consuming, though I'm sure full blown anorexia must in the end have a higher carbon footprint than Giles's kind of eating. All those plastic tubes, for one thing. But the moral argument for consuming less is from any point of view incontrovertible, and I do not know that I can argue that there is still time to save the world.

Rain spattered the window. Those clouds had taken over the sky. 'Remember telling your mother she's not a superior being? Well, you're not either. You've got a body and a mind just like everyone else. There are no career opportunities in being an anchorite these days.'

She looked at me. 'I'm not like my mother. She thinks she's better than everyone else. She thinks Judith Fairchild is like the measure of humanity and everyone else falls short.'

'Well,' I said. Looking at the bones in her hands, I thought there was nothing to lose if I upset her. She couldn't eat less. 'You're not the Messiah either. You might as well join in and have some chance of making a difference. On whatever scale.'

There was an alarming silence from the playroom.

'It's too late.' She twisted her fingers.

I held out my hand to her as if she were Moth.

'Come on, let's see what Moth's up to. And then I want to go down to the jetty and see if we can see the boat. I don't like those clouds.'

By the time we had bundled Moth into his puddle suit and wellies, I needed the light on to tie my shoelaces. Outside, the sky hung low and the clouds had a purple tinge. The rain was provisional, a prelude to the torrents we could see hurrying across the sea towards the island. Raph would probably be enjoying it. I shifted Moth on to the other hip.

'Down!' he said.

He ran unsteadily towards the pebbled beach. I'm sure he

wouldn't really walk into the sea. The waves crashing on to the stones were taller than he is, a more obvious hazard than a glass cliff, and even toddlers must have some residual, atavistic sense of self-preservation or it is hard to see how we reached the over-populated mess in which we now find ourselves. The boat was coming round the headland, sitting low in the water. Giles was steering for a point on the horizon wide of Colsay, avoiding turning side-on to the rising waves. I could see Raphael, a red curve in a grey seascape, kneeling in his favourite place in the bows, and the white lumps of Judith and Brian in the middle. I hoped Giles had thought to make Raph wear a harness as well as the lifejacket.

'Your parents aren't wearing lifejackets,' I said.

Zoe shivered in the wind. 'Mum probably thinks she can walk on water.'

Moth was arranging piles of small stones. Choking hazards. I went over to him, keeping an eye on the boat.

'Moth, do you want to see the boat? With Daddy and Raph on it?'

He looked up. 'No. Moth building a train. Where Moth's bread?'

Damn, the bread. Forgotten again. I looked out to sea again. Giles had changed direction and was making for the landing stage. Raph waved.

'Hold on to the boat,' I muttered. 'Never mind waving.' I waved back.

'Moth, do you want to wave to Raphael?'

'No.'

My watching wouldn't keep the boat afloat, but on the other hand if they foundered close to land I could jump off the rocks and save Raph. Assuming Moth stayed put while I did it. Assuming Raph wasn't harnessed to the boat. Assuming I could get through the waves. And back. I decided the chance was worth letting the dough spill over. I stood there on the beach with Moth at my feet, poised to save one child from choking and the other from drowning, while Giles brought the boat to land. The rain gathered strength and began to hiss into the sea. I thought Zoe said something.

'What?' I shouted.

'I don't feel well. Do you mind if I go in?'

I picked up Moth and went towards her.

'Down! Moth in a rain!'

'Wait a minute,' I said. 'Go see Zoe. Zoe, are you OK?'

She applied a smile. Her face was bone yellow inside her hood.

'I think I need to lie down.'

The boat was inside the bay, almost within shouting distance. Within swimming distance.

'Go lie on the sofa,' I said. 'I'll be there in a minute. I'll bring your dad.'

She walked slowly across the grass, bent into the rain, hunched and stiff as an old woman.

'There's boat!' said Moth. 'Hello, boat!'

He wriggled. I put him down and we walked hand in hand along the landing stage, built and rebuilt by the villagers over a couple of centuries until the last families left. I smiled at Giles, helped Raph on to the stones and put my arm round him.

'Brian,' I said. 'Zoe's just gone back to the house. She said she needed to lie down. She didn't look very well.'

Judith snorted. 'She was all right this morning. I hope she hasn't been bothering you all afternoon.'

Moth tried to push my hair back into my hood.

'No,' I said. 'She helped me make bread.'

'I'll go,' said Brian. 'I'm not surprised.'

We stood back as he jogged towards the house with the loping gait of the long distance runner.

'Is she OK?' asked Giles.

I squeezed Raph against my side. 'I wouldn't have let her go back alone if I thought she was about to collapse. Not that I'd know. Come on, let's get you two warmed up.'

I left Giles to tidy up the boat and took the children back to the house. Judith followed.

'Did you have fun, Raph?' I asked.

He nodded. 'Lots. Daddy bought me some chips in the pub and Fiona Firth told me to say hello and she'll see you soon.'

'See me soon?'

He shrugged. 'That's what she said.'

Zoe was lying on the sofa reading *The Lighthouse Keeper's Lunch* with Brian perched at her side like a seagull. His hand, hairless as my own and tanned, lay on her shoulder. I put Moth down and started taking his boots and suit off.

'You OK?' I asked her.

'She says she won't let me take her blood pressure,' said Brian. 'Zoe, please will you eat something. Or drink something.'

'I've been drinking tea.' She didn't lift her eyes from the book. 'Ask Anna.'

'Lapsang without milk,' I said.

'Zoe,' said Brian. He stroked her hair. 'If you collapse, we'll call out the helicopter. And they'll take you to hospital, where they'll put you on a drip. With sugar in it. I really don't want you sectioned and I really don't want anything to happen to you without your consent. You're running out of options, sweetie.'

Yes, I thought, but she needs a reason as well as a method for staying alive and in my understanding Freud himself can offer nothing more convincing than convention. Or maybe love, which is insufficiently sophisticated for a bright eighteen-year-old.

'Is that what you want?' Judith stood in the doorway with water dripping from her cagoule on to the floorboards. 'Well, Zoe? You'd rather be in hospital than with us, would you? How do you think I'd feel, coming to see you on some filthy NHS ward with tramps and schizophrenics and drug addicts? When you could be at Cambridge? Don't think we'll go private this time. You'll get bedpans on a mixed ward instead of Trinity

271

College. And God knows what the admissions tutors will think, I doubt they let people straight into Cambridge out of the psychiatric ward.'

Zoe's face reddened but she flicked the page. She will need to have her own children to learn that mothers' fears speak in anger, anger that life does not recognize our children's glory, that every step into the fallen world is a step away from the inhuman perfection of the newborn's ten new wrinkled red fingers and new eyebrows sketched on a new face. Her eyes scanned the page. Every morning, Mrs Grinling made a delicious lunch for the lighthouse keeper. And there is freer passage than Judith imagines between psychiatric wards and Oxbridge colleges.

Brian looked tired. I should perhaps have felt sorrier for him from the beginning. 'Judith, that's not helpful.'

She sniffed. The smell of alcohol, tentative on the cold air, reached my side of the room. Moth came over and held his arms out. 'Up!'

'I'm going away,' said Raph. 'I don't like this.'

Zoe turned another page. Mrs Grinling sent the lunch out to the lighthouse in a basket.

'Oh, you know what's helpful to the children, do you?' said Judith. 'Because I must not have noticed you around helping for the last twenty years.'

Moth hid his face. Sometimes marriage seems like an alternative to self-control.

Brian stood up. 'In case it escaped your attention, I've "helped" by buying you that house and paying the fees for the schools you chose and clearing your credit card every month. Oh, and saved a few people's lives every week or so. You've kept Zoe dependent on you all these years because otherwise you'd have to face the fact that you've done nothing with your life except spending what I earn. And now she can't handle it any more and you're drinking because you've got nothing else left.'

Judith's face darkened. Her voice shrilled and I knew she'd lost the argument. 'You think you know what I've done with my life? Raising your children and scrubbing your shit off the toilet and picking your socks off the floor year after bloody year?'

Brian pretended to laugh. 'Wrong script, darling, you forget you've had a cleaner for the last twenty years.'

I checked to see what she might throw. There was nothing irreplaceable immediately to hand. Moth grasped my hair as if he were falling through the branches. I kissed his head and took him upstairs to find Raph. Voices rumbled through the ceiling while I answered questions arising from Raphael's perusal of the World Atlas and eventually allowed jumping on the bed as an alternative to a ringside view of family break-down. I kept wondering if Zoe was able to get off the sofa, and whether the helicopter could land here in the dark. At last the front door banged and there were footsteps on the stairs. Giles came in as the children bumped into each other and collapsed into a giggling heap. I established Moth on top and looked up.

'Have they gone?'

'Judith has. Brian says can Zoe stay here tonight. But that's not why I came up. There was a letter for you at the post office.'

He held out a crumpled white envelope. A fat, crumpled white A5 envelope from Glasgow, containing more pages than it takes to thank someone for their interest in your vacancies and regret that on this occasion they have not been shortlisted.

'Oh.' I took it out on to the landing; I couldn't face the three of them watching me open it. Dear Dr Bennet, I am writing to invite you— I felt my face flushing.

'Giles! Giles, I've got an interview. At Glasgow. But it's next week.'

He appeared round the door. 'See, I told you you could do it. Well done.'

'I won't get it,' I said. 'They probably just have to include at least one woman on the shortlist.'

'So they thought they'd pay your expenses from here and hotel there as the cheapest way of ticking the equal opps box?'

Giles has served on Oxford appointments committees and therefore, I suppose, must be assumed to know about ticking boxes.

'I can't go overnight,' I said. 'What about the children?'

Raph came out to join us. 'What about us? Where are you going?'

'Mummy's got a job interview,' said Giles. 'In Glasgow. And if she gets the job, which she will, we can all move up here.'

Raph looked from Giles to me and back. 'But she said she wouldn't live here. Can we really? Please?'

Moth came and put his arms round my leg. 'Where Zoe gone?'

I picked him up. 'I won't live here. Not on the island. Well, not unless Daddy wants to stay here with you while I commute to Glasgow.' I could be the one with the pristine flat. I could use it to eat ready meals and have a clean bathroom and spend my salary on cut flowers that are actually supposed to die and get thrown away and replaced.

'You can't do that!' Raph came to hold on to me too, as if it might require physical restraint to stop me running for the metropolis.

'No.' Giles ruffled Raph's hair. 'Mummy's teasing. No, we'd find a house for all of us. Bigger than in Oxford. And a new school for you.'

'Moth new school too.'

'And a new nursery for you.'

'If I get the job,' I said. 'Remember I probably won't. Anyway, I can't go overnight. And I haven't anything to wear.'

Giles grinned. 'Then you'll have to go overnight, won't you, to buy yourself a suit. We can cope, you know, for thirty-six hours.'

There were footsteps downstairs. 'Hello?' called Brian.

274

Giles leant over the banisters. 'Sorry, Brian. We got distracted. Down in a minute.'

He ushered us all back into Raph's room. 'Anna, is it OK if Zoe stays with us tonight?'

'She can't sleep in here,' said Raph. He climbed on to his bed and opened *The Way Things Work*, which is not as useful a book as the title suggests.

'Is that because she's too weak to get to Black Rock House or because he can't face having her and Judith under the same roof?'

Giles frowned. 'The latter. He says he thinks she might eat something if she doesn't have to deal with Judith. He says if he could send her away from Judith without putting her in hospital, he would, but she's in no state to go anywhere on her own. It sounds to me as if they've got a lot to say to each other that Zoe really doesn't need to hear.'

The last thing Zoe needs is to feel more powerful than she already does. Medieval women who starved themselves were revered for their holiness, their miraculous ability to live without food, which must have made it hard to start eating again. I sighed. The ethos of the Hôtel de la Mère does not encourage taking responsibility for other people's dysfunctional adolescents. In fact, taking responsibility for other people's dysfunctional adolescents may well entitle you to a very long stay there. I thought of Zoe walking through the rainforest, singing 'Jerusalem the Golden' and deciding that she'd rather be eaten head first. And lying on our sofa because she no longer has the energy to stand up. Judith could probably use a couple of weeks in the Hôtel as well. 'Oh, all right. I'll make her some hot chocolate or something. But she has to come to the table like everyone else. I'm not playing handmaid to Zoe's decline on the sofa.'

'I'll go tell Brian. You should look in your wardrobe and think about booking train tickets.'

I already knew what was in my wardrobe (in fact very little;

most of my clothes get put back on before they have quite dried and the remainder are draped damp over chairs and heaters in a spirit of quaint optimism). More pressingly, I thought, I should think about what to say, which was more or less compatible with cooking.

The children thought that if Zoe was allowed hot chocolate just before dinner then so were they, and having conceded that point the only reason I could see for not having it myself was that we'd run out of milk sooner and have to brave the Sound again. The wind had risen and rain whipped the windows. We'd probably have to go back to Colla in the next couple of days anyway, to facilitate Judith's exhaustive investigation of the distilleries of the West Coast. The bread had overflowed again, so I masked it with tinned tomatoes, garlic and some cheddar from which I cut the blue furry bits to construct a form of nourishment inspired by the idea of pizza. Zoe ate more than Moth.

I woke to daylight: 07:08. Moth must be ill. Maybe something fell on him in the night, maybe the ceiling fell in. Maybe he scorned the 'pizza' because he was in the early stages of meningitis which got worse while I slept like a pig. Maybe he did wake and cry and I was too sodden with sleep, too pleased with myself, to hear, and maybe he tried to get out of his cot and fell on his head. Maybe I hadn't sewed that ribbon on to his bear as firmly as I thought and it got round his neck in the night. Giles was still asleep, as if he didn't care that it was morning and his own son had been silent for nearly eleven hours. I flung the duvet right back and Giles grunted and felt about.

'Giles! Did you get up to Moth in the night?'

'What?'

'Did you deal with Moth in the night?'

He pulled the duvet back around himself, leaving a tuft of hair poking out.

'No. Don't think so.'

I pushed the duvet back down and touched the floor with my toes. The last few minutes of normal life before I'd have to find Moth and face what had happened. I went slowly to his door. He was breathing. I went in. He was lying on his front, legs tucked under his bottom as usual, one thumb fallen from his open mouth and the other hand clasping his bear. I touched his cheek. No warmer than it should be. I opened the curtain so I could see if he was pale or blue around the mouth.

'Mummy. Porridge now?'

He sat up, pink-faced and damp with sleep.

'Hello,' I said. I scooped him up and hugged him. 'You slept all night.'

He frowned at the grey sky.

'Morning now.'

'I know,' I said. 'Come and tell Daddy.'

I plopped him down on to our bed. He giggled.

'Jumping on Mummy's bed?'

I sat down and tucked my feet under my thighs, feeling the cold seeping through the folds of my nightdress. 'Find Daddy.'

He crawled over the pillow, pulled Giles's hair and burrowed under the duvet.

Giles sat up. 'Bloody hell, what time is it?'

'Seven o' clock,' I said. 'He slept through. I had to wake him.'

'You had to *what?*'

Moth pulled Giles's nose. 'Beep!'

'Wake him. I was worried. Anyway, he wouldn't sleep after lunch if I let him sleep now. Or go to bed before midnight.'

'Daddy, beep!'

'Beep,' said Giles. 'Well, are you going to get him up, then?'

I lay down and held out my arms. 'Cuddle Mummy. No, I thought you could do that.' Moth crawled over my stomach and rubbed his nose on my shoulder, leaving a shining trail. 'You'll have to, won't you, if I go to Glasgow next week?'

Giles looked down at me. 'You are going to Glasgow. And of

277

course I can get him up. What are you worried about? You went off to that conference, didn't you?'

I stroked Moth's head. 'They were at school and nursery. And I left you lists.'

'Do you really not believe I can look after my own children for thirty-six hours?'

I haven't, I thought, seen any evidence that you can.

Moth poked my eye. 'Mummy got blue eyes.'

'I'm sure Zoe will help.' I intercepted Moth's next poke. 'Raph really likes her.'

Giles got out of bed.

'Mummy not going away,' said Moth. 'Moth come too.'

There was a knock on the door while we were having breakfast. Zoe was still asleep in the spare room, on Julia's old bed with its horsehair mattress and blankets and a silk counterpane that slides off every time you move. She was also still breathing, appropriately coloured and warmer than my hand, although life is, I know, more complicated than that when you're eighteen.

'I'll go,' I said.

The newspaper rustled. He must have scored a *Guardian* in the pub yesterday. 'It'll be Brian.'

It was Judith, in the Liberty peacock skirt and her cagoule, her eyelids painted the steel grey of the battleships that sometimes pass through the Sound. I stood in the door. Putting Zoe up for the night didn't seem sufficient reason to deal with Judith before breakfast.

'I just wanted to check Zoe is all right.' She looked behind me, up the stairs. 'I kept worrying about her in the night.'

'She's asleep. I checked. She's warm and pink and breathing evenly. I expect she needs the rest.'

'Did she – did she eat anything?'

'Yes,' I said. The sun was breaking through the cloud and shining white on the sea, and there was the smell of warm grass. A breeze slipped past Judith and stirred the pages of a book about whales that Raph had left open on the floor.

'Mummy!' called Moth. 'Down! Find Mummy!'

I gave up. 'Do you want to come in? We're having breakfast.'

Judith shuffled her feet in their heavy boots. 'Did she eat what you cooked?'

'Yes,' I said.

'Mummy! Where's Mummy gone?'

'Come in, Judith.'

She put her hand on the door. 'I'm sorry. About Zoe.'

Don't tell me, I thought. 'Not to worry. Families are messy things. You can't control children.'

She started to say something and then stopped. 'Thank you.'

I left her in the hall and went back to the kitchen.

'It's all right, love. Mummy was just answering the door.'

Moth held up his arms to me. 'No door. No answering.'

The *Guardian* flapped like a flustered seagull. 'Where is she?'

Judith appeared in the door. She was wearing pink towelling socks, worn at the toes.

'Oh God,' said Raph. 'Not her again. I'm going upstairs.'

'Raphael!'

He looked round. 'Excuse me.'

Moth stroked my cheek. There was porridge on his fingers. 'Raph gone away.'

'He'll come back,' I said. 'Judith, tea?'

She looked at the teapot as if it were a hand grenade. 'Do you have any Earl Grey in?'

'No,' I said.

Giles put the paper down. 'I've got work to do. See you later.'

'Not so fast. I've got work to do too.'

He stood up. 'I need to observe the birds.'

'I need to write the book. And my presentation.'

Judith was reading a bank statement. I reached out and turned it over.

'Don't you have a filing system?' she asked.

279

'No,' I said. 'Too busy writing books.'

'I find it saves time.'

'No doubt. Giles, I'll do the morning if you'll take over at lunchtime. That way you get the nap.'

'No nap,' said Moth. I frowned at him.

'I never expected Brian to look after the children.'

'No,' I said. 'Well. It was different for your generation, wasn't it? You could manage a mortgage on one salary. And no student debt.'

She sniffed. 'We were careful with our money.'

'I'll be back later.' Giles left.

I hugged Moth a moment, letting time pause as it does when adult conversation leaves the building.

'Moth, will you help Mummy tidy up?'

He looked disbelieving. 'Tidy up?'

'Oh, never mind. Can you find the ark? And the animals?'

'No.' He clung to my leg.

'See if you can find a fire engine. A noisy fire engine.'

'No.'

I reached over and unhooked the steel pasta pot.

'OK, play at cooking. Here's a spoon.'

He sat down, turned the pan over and began to bang it with the wooden spoon. If toddlers didn't have such an uncomplicated relationship with anger you'd have thought he was engaging in some kind of primal therapy. I reckoned even Judith wouldn't compete with that. The house is so solid it seemed unlikely to wake Zoe.

Judith was reading our post again.

'Sit down,' I shouted over the din. 'Or go wake Zoe.'

She sat down. I stacked plates.

'Anna?'

'What?'

'What did Zoe eat?'

I ran the hot tap.

'Some hot chocolate and some dinner.'

'What dinner?'

No wonder the girl starves herself.

'A kind of pizza thing.'

Judith frowned.

'Can you get mozzarella from that shop?' she shouted.

Moth redoubled his efforts.

'No,' I shouted back.

'What, frozen pizza?'

'No.'

She frowned again.

'What kind of hot chocolate?'

I put the scrubbing brush down.

'Judith, do you think she might be happier if you were less . . . curious?'

'What?'

I crouched by Moth. 'Moth, love, can we take that in the playroom? It's noisy.'

'No playroom.'

'If you take it in the playroom you could use the jingle bells as well. Come on. And the maracas.'

I came back. The cacophony was greater but further away.

'Don't you think if she's anxious about what she eats, feeling watched all the time will make things worse? I mean, I eat more when I'm on my own. Don't you?'

Wrong rhetorical flourish. Obviously she does or she wouldn't be the size she is.

'No. I can't say I do.'

I went back to the washing up. 'Well, maybe Zoe would. I would.'

Judith jabbed at the pad of her forefinger with her thumbnail.

'I don't know why she came back from Canada. If I'd had my way, she'd never have gone.'

'Have you asked her?'

The sun was stronger. Shadows appeared on the grass outside.

'She says I wanted her to fail all along.'

'And did you?'

'Of course not. But I knew she wouldn't cope and I told her so.'

I waited, but Judith was not alive to the advantages of self-reflection.

'And now she's got herself into such a state I'm not sure she'll cope with Cambridge either.'

'She might be better there,' I said. 'I've certainly taught students who've been more settled at university than at home.'

'There's nothing wrong with Zoe's home life. My son is doing very well indeed. Reading medicine, at King's.'

'I know. You told me. So did Zoe. Look, Judith, I'm not trying to upset you. I thought you were asking what I thought.'

I finished washing the plates and started on the knives.

'She was a lovely little girl,' said Judith. 'So pretty. We used to go shopping together. Now she says I was dressing her up like a doll but she doesn't remember what it was like, she loved every minute of it. And everyone used to say what good manners she had.'

'You said.' I wondered where she had learnt the manners. 'She's lovely,' I said. 'She'll do well at Cambridge. She's old enough to go to Canada and come home and go to university and be rude or polite all on her own. She has good qualities, even if they're not the ones you wanted for her. She'll be fun to teach. But maybe you'll have to let go of her.'

Judith looked up. 'Hardly. She won't eat enough to stay alive. Her clothes are awful, I had to force her into a suit for her Cambridge interviews. She couldn't cope with Canada and she's appallingly rude. Honestly, Anna, she's not ready to leave. I'm amazed she could even manage the flights on her own. We got one of Brian's colleagues to pick her up in Vancouver. God knows what people in Cambridge will think.'

I dried my hands. Moth had gone quiet. 'Maybe you need to trust her. Or at least behave as if you do.'

'She'd kill herself,' said Judith. 'She'd be dead in six weeks.'

It wasn't clear to me that Zoe's life expectancy was significantly longer than that under the current regime. There were slow footsteps on the stairs, as if the ghost had finally decided to make an appearance.

'Here she comes,' I said. 'I'm going to find Moth.'

He was sitting on the floor, leafing through one of Raphael's more basic science textbooks.

'Moth, love, are you all right?'

He looked up and held out the book. 'Mummy sing a stars.'

Many of the stars that you can see in the sky at night are actually bigger than our sun. They are so far away that we measure their distances in light years.

'Mummy sing twinkle twinkle.'

I took him on my knee and began. He joined in, and behind our disharmony I heard Zoe greet her mother.

'What do you think you're doing here?'

Judith's chair scraped.

'I was worried about you. Zoe, I just want you to be well, and happy. That's all I've ever wanted for you.'

That's all any of us want for our children, but since we can't achieve it ourselves it seems an unreasonably heavy burden to place on the next generation.

'Come on,' I said to Moth. 'Let's find Raph and go see how those apple trees are doing in the garden.'

Since I am hardly about to ask Mrs Barwick the favour of sending this at the moment, I have kept it open. Well, the child is sick. I tried to visit again today and was again denied at the door, but when I met Mrs Gillies at the stream and questioned her she agreed that the babe, a girl, cannot feed and lies screaming as if in the throes of pain, which it no doubt is. I could hear the screams from the 'street' outside, and when I peered through the door the child lay in a box on the table with no one near. It appeared to be wrapped in a meal-sack and I saw no sign of our layette.

I meant to walk on up the hill, perhaps along the clifftop from where it is sometimes possible to see the ships bound for America and Canada, but although the morning was clear enough I soon found the wind so hard that I was forced to turn back. I had thought that winds strong enough to strike an adult to the ground were a mere figure of speech, or at least a reality known only to those who make a point of presenting themselves to the least hospitable climates on the globe, but it is not so; I turned back when a certain gust laid me flat on the turf, albeit with more damage to my dignity and my hooped petticoat (frequently, I find, closely related to each other) than any other part of my anatomy! It was as well that the local people have more sense than to offer themselves to such inclement elements and so my disarray went unwitnessed, though from the look Mrs Barwick cast towards me on my return you would think she had spies in the very rocks to report on my foolhardiness and its consequences.

You can imagine Mrs Barwick and I are living on fine terms now. I have had no clean linen since the confinement and not even the luxury of a bannock to vary the dried fish and oatmeal – think of me as your Christmas preparations progress! (Don't fret, I am not really hungry, only bored by a monotonous diet which will do me no harm and probably much good in the general scheme of life.) I would write to Miss Emily in complaint at Mrs Barwick's insolence – except that it is beginning to cross my mind to doubt whether my letters to her are being sent.

14

THIS HAPPY PARTNERSHIP

But this happy partnership between mother and child is not destined to last. As the child grows older, the mother's attitude changes, often very abruptly, the child's exhibitionist advances are rebuffed, and nagging and criticism often take the place of the former admiration, which is then shown to a younger member of the family. Consequently the child itself turns against its own wish to show off, represses it or turns it into the opposite.

– Dorothy Burlingham and Anna Freud, *Infants Without Families: The Case For and Against Residential Nurseries*, p. 66

There was still some light in the western sky at ten o'clock, and no movement in the branches of the tree outlined against it. I stretched, and wondered about going out again, wandering up over the turf, now sequinned with dew, to visit the anchorite for a while. When we get back to Oxford, I will probably wish I'd spent more time up there with her and less failing to write my book at the kitchen table.

It had been a windless afternoon, and we'd spent all of it outside, with the sun glittering on the sea and the turf buzzing with insects, but being out alone at night is quite different. The scents on the air are layered: sea, and flowers, but cold stone also, and an Arctic breath on the wind, an intimation of winter.

If you travelled west in a straight line from here, you would land not in Boston or New York but Greenland. Our summer afternoons are brought by the Gulf Stream, a warm ocean current cheating our real latitude. For now. Raph alternates his prophecies of a frozen or a burning end to European life.

My screen gave up waiting for me to add to my book. I flipped through to the Elastoplast I seemed to be using to mark my place in the history of Colsay.

The arrival on the island of the families from Inversaigh seems to have passed remarkably smoothly. The Rev. Adamson, who organised the transition and allocated the orphan children among the incoming families, records that 'at the end of the Weeke I did conducte a Service of Thanksgiving whiche all attended with good Hearte'. Land at Inversaigh was poor and there was little fishing because the nearest safe landing in most winds is at Colla, which is now a ten-minute drive from the site of the Inversaigh village (which was cleared in 1838 and is now one of the more atmospheric sites in the west Highlands), but was then a difficult climb across hard terrain. The new islanders may well have been grateful for the relative plenty of Colsay, for at the end of the first year there the McColl estate received full rent for the first time in nearly a decade.

Antonia Rivett would not have thought much of the Reverend's writing, but I was grateful to be reminded that the Cassinghams were not responsible for all the hardship and misery on Colsay over the centuries. Giles's great-great-whatever-grandfather bought it from Julius McColl, who was selling everything to pay off his dead father's debts. There are still McColls living locally, and I wondered if they too felt their bloodline tainted by their great-grandparents' greed. We would all rather be descended from victims, whom we confuse with the innocent, which is inconvenient because it is aggressors who

287

tend to survive. The last innocents on British soil were (possibly) the Picts, who leave a few place-names to the language and no distinct trace in the population. Guilt runs in all our veins.

The dead baby was a Cassingham, her oppressors' DNA infusing the Colsay ground in which she lay. But she was not, of course 100 per cent Cassingham. Even Cassinghams are not capable of parthenogenesis.

'Giles,' I said. 'Did the police ask you for a DNA sample?'

He looked up. 'You're meant to be writing your presentation.'

'Yeah. But I'm not. Did they ask you for a sample? Because they didn't ask me.'

He saved his work and looked out into the night. We'd taken the children into the garden in their pyjamas to see the stars come out and Raph had told me three things I didn't know about astrophysics.

'I wondered if you'd ask that.'

'I'm asking.'

Giles fiddled with the flex for his laptop. 'It's not terrible. I mean, it's not my dark secret.'

There is, of course, the national database of DNA. Which includes, as far as I can remember, everyone who has been arrested since the early 1990s, even if they were not prosecuted or were found innocent. I remembered reading about it and being outraged on behalf of my sons, who, being boys in an urban environment, are very likely to come into contact with the police sometime in the next fifteen years. I've also read about women who discover their partner's violent history only when he repeats it.

'Giles?'

'Before we met. I'd just left school.'

'Gap year?'

He nodded. I waited. 'Jesus, Anna, I'm not about to tell you I'm actually a convicted murderer.'

'Good.'

'I came here with some friends. A kind of last fling before we all went off.'

'To find yourselves,' I murmured. 'Which friends?'

'Bertie's the only one you've met. And someone called Charles.'

'Of course.'

'And – and a couple of girls.'

'Careless not to bring one each.'

He grunted, the public school way of expressing annoyance with one's wife.

'Thank you. Mostly we stayed on the island. It was good, actually. Good weather. We swam, a bit. Had bonfires on the beach. Bertie had been here before, he came with us a couple of times for summers. Pa sent a case of wine. And then we decided to go to Colla. One of the girls thought it would be fun to meet the locals.'

My computer whirred and went to sleep.

'And it wasn't?'

'We went in the evening. You know, it was light so late. We had a couple of drinks in the pub. I mean, I knew people were listening but we weren't being loud. Only Pippa—'

'Pippa?'

'Pippa thought the accents were sweet.'

'Bet that went down well.'

'Yeah. So we were trying to get her away. She was – you know, kind of blonde and she had that sort of laugh and she kept laughing. She didn't usually drink but she was – she was kind of trying to show Charley and she'd had a few. Anyway, we got her down to the harbour and we were getting the boat and she sort of sat there doing this impersonation. There was no wind. You know how voices carry. We were trying to shut her up but it was sort of funny and we'd all had a couple of pints. And we'd had some wine earlier. And Bertie'd brought some weed.'

'So you shouldn't have been in the boat anyway?'

Giles rubbed his foot against his trouser leg. 'If it's the worst our boys do I'll be happy.'

I saw Raph and Moth, formed in my womb and held in my arms and fed with my milk and tucked up nightly by me, trying to cross the Sound in a small boat while high and drunk.

'No way. Not my babies.'

'We weren't babies. And our parents were hundreds of miles away.'

'I'm not letting them go anywhere until they've got enough sense not to do that.'

Giles looked at me. 'Isn't that what Judith said?'

The Milky Way was scribbled across the sky, a sign of human insignificance. But my children on my island on my planet in my solar system are still the centre of the universe.

'Then what happened?'

'Some boys came. Younger than us but more of them. It got – you can imagine. It got a bit rough. Someone fell in.'

'Someone?'

'One of the boys. He was drunk. The lifebuoy was missing. You know. They always are.'

'So he drowned?'

Giles looked up. 'No, of course not. Charley jumped in and held him up and someone went for help. But the police came. We all got arrested. Drunk and disorderly, breach of the peace.'

'Locals too?'

He shook his head. 'Pa got really cross about that. No. Just us. They took us to the station at Inversaigh. Kept us in overnight. And then Pa and Bertie's dad arrived next day and took us home. No charges.'

'Bertie's dad the QC?'

'That helped. Kind of. But I didn't come back for three years. And I didn't go back to the pub until we started renovating.'

I've been into the pub only to use the ladies', which has the

290

swirly carpet and cigarette-scarred toilet seats of unrecon-
structed pubs across the land.

'And how was that?'

'Fine, actually. I mean, it went a bit quiet when I went in. I
bought a round and asked some people's advice. When I took
Raph in the other day they let him pull pints.'

'Giles!'

'He liked the hoses. Don't worry, I let him taste some and he
hated it. Put him off for years.'

'What if he'd liked it?'

'He didn't. No one likes beer first time.'

'Doesn't stop them trying again.'

'Pa was giving me port after Sunday lunch from when I can
remember. He's not about to start on a career of pre-teen
boozing.'

'Then don't give him alcohol. I'm serious, Giles. He's too
young.'

We looked at each other. I shouldn't have been tired, having
once again slept for seven unbroken hours. I'd imagined since
Moth's birth that sleep would transform me back into the slim-
line research machine I vaguely remembered from before the
kids, but it didn't seem to be working. Maybe the brain damage
of childcare is permanent.

I yawned.

'Just remember this isn't the '70s and he's not going to Eton.
I'm going to bed.' I went over and put my arms around him.
His jumper was rough under my cheek. 'And I'm glad to know
your dark secret.'

He stroked my hair. 'How do you know that's my only dark
secret?'

I patted his bottom. 'How do you know I haven't got one?'

'Because your DNA isn't on the police database. QED. Go
on, get some sleep. I've just got a bit more work to do.'

I went slowly up the stairs. There is nothing to gain by telling
him now.

Night Waking: 02:05

Something woke me, but there is no sound. I sit up. Wind under the eaves, and the roar of the sea. My own heartbeat, Giles's slow breathing. And then the creak of a floorboard on the landing, and a shuffling noise, as of something brushing along the wall. I get out of bed and go to the door. There is fast breathing on the other side. I open it.

'Raph. Whatever are you doing?'

He is shivering, goose-bumped. He must have been out of bed for a long time.

'Come on, love. Back to bed.'

I take his hand and lead him back down the dark passage to his room, and step on something warm and furry. I squeal, which is not helpful. He grabs me.

'Mummy, Mummy, what is there? What?'

A teddy, of course. The teddy my mother made for him before he was born, the one that, lighter in colour and firmer of face, is in the background of almost all the two hundred photos of his first two weeks of life.

'Just your bear, love. Sorry.'

But there are more small furry bodies under my feet. I can't get to the light without treading on them. It is very dark.

'Raph, can you put your little light on?'

He lets go of my hand, and there is light. He huddles on the bed, shaking, and all his soft toys and several of Moth's are lying on their backs on rows on the floor, a mass of victims awaiting burial.

'Where's your pyjama top?'

He shrugs. I pick up the duvet and wrap it round him.

'Shall I put the teddies back?'

He pulls the duvet up round his face. I pick them up, arrange them more comfortably on the bed.

'Why are you awake, love? It's the middle of the night.'

I stroke the duvet where his shoulder should be. He is still shaking.

'You won't – believe.'

I try to hug him but he is stiff.

'Try me. I'll believe that it feels real. And important.'

He pulls the duvet up further and speaks from inside it.

'I'm so cold.'

'I know. I'll make you some hot milk if you like.'

He shakes his head. 'Don't go away.'

I sit and wait. The wind blows, and behind it I hear a scuffle in the attic above. Raph still has the duvet over his ears. After a while he lies down, and I hear the noise again. It's back.

'Mummy?'

'Yes, love.'

'I keep hearing that baby. In the night.'

'Oh, Raph.' I am trying to get this right. No, you don't, leaves him alone with his fear. Yes, you do, confirms it. 'I think you hear it in your mind. Because you're thinking about it a lot. When I'm away from you and I think about you and miss you, I can hear your voice in my mind sometimes. You're still at school, or with Daddy, or wherever you are, but I can think of you talking to me.'

He speaks into the pillow. 'But I'm not dead.'

'No. None of us is dead. And the baby has been dead a long time.'

'And one day I will be dead. And you and Moth and Daddy. And Grandma. Grandpa's already dead. And when people are dead they never come back and we never see them and they are just lying in the ground.'

Another long night yawns in front of me. And Raph's right, there is something in the attic again.

I had been expecting Judith or Zoe since before breakfast. At mid-morning, when Moth had started trying to turn the pages of a leather-bound world atlas from 1928 which Raph had been studying for nearly an hour and Raph had retaliated by pulling Moth's jumper up over his head while I neglected them and dragged the clothes airer outside to make the most of what was not quite sunshine, I wandered down the field towards the blackhouse. The curtains were open but I could see no lights or movement in the windows.

'Mummy, you said we could go somewhere today. You said we could make a special trip.'

I turned back towards them. Raph was in the garden, balancing the atlas on his head with one hand while Moth pulled at his T-shirt.

'Moth have it! Raph do sharing!'

'No, love. Raph's book. Well, Daddy's book really, I suppose, but Raph's looking at it. Let's come back in and I'll find you *Peter Rabbit*.'

'No.'

Raph took his hand away. I caught the book as it fell and went back to the kitchen. I looked at the clock. There was only bread and cheese for lunch, and we seemed to have been eating bread and cheese for a long time. I was not distressed by the idea that Giles might return from the puffins expecting to be served lunch only to find that I had something better to do.

'All right. We'll go over to Colla and have lunch at the pub and then you can choose what we do in the afternoon, all right? There's about a quarter of a tank of petrol in the car.'

There is no petrol station at Colla and when the petrol gauge reads empty there is not enough left to get to Inversaigh. Mrs McConnell at Spar will sell some of her emergency supply but she won't make you feel good about it.

'Can we go to the graveyard?' asked Raph. 'The proper one by the church with writing on the stones?'

His bare toes were turning blue. 'Oh, Raph. What about the playground at Inversaigh? I don't mind driving you over. We could go see the glass-blowers at the same time.'

I like the glass-blowers more than he does. I am a medieval

peasant to whom the actions of heat on melted sand remain a spectacle of transubstantiation, while to Raph the scientist these hot bubbles of light are as predictable as water running downhill or copper turning peacock blue. And I will admit that there is little overlap between the responsible parenting of a curious toddler and proximity to glass-blowing.

'I'd rather go to the graveyard, please, Mummy.'

'I'll take you to the bookshop in Inversaigh.' It's not Blackwell's of Broad Street, but people read a lot up here and it's much better than you'd expect. Than I expected. I could think of a couple of things I might buy myself.

'Moth have a book?'

'No.' Raph stood up straight, frowned out of the window as if what offended him was peering in. 'You said I could choose. And I've told you what I want to do.'

'Moth go a playground?'

Maybe it would be cathartic in some way. Maybe it was what he needed.

'All right. If you'd really rather look round the graveyard of Colla Church than go to Inversaigh and play in the playground and go to Bramley's and the bookshop then it's up to you.'

They make fudge at Bramley's. The smell of butter and sugar glides along the High Street, and even Giles will permit an occasional artisanal sugar high.

'I'd rather go to the graveyard.'

We stopped at Black Rock House on the way, to see if anyone wanted a lift to Colla, and to make sure they were all still alive, although if they weren't I thought I might creep away and invent a plumbing problem for Jake rather than be the official finder of more bodies on Colsay. I knocked and waited.

'Moth play a washing machine and press buttons?'

'No, love.'

I knocked again. Oh God, maybe something really had gone badly wrong. You can't just be 'out' on a small island. I turned to scan the shoreline for Raph, who wanted to wait by the boat and had given a more or less reliable promise not to climb in or touch the mooring ropes until I came.

A shadow appeared behind the frosted glass panel, a tall male shadow. Brian, whom I'd had down as the most likely victim, opened the door.

Not for him, thank you, he was working on a paper, but he believed that perhaps – no, he hadn't seen either of them this morning but he had been working since very early. He would ask. He went inside. Brian, I thought, must have a gift even greater than Giles's for ignoring his family while working if he could really lose two people in the blackhouse.

'Now Moth see a washing machine?'

'No, love. Not now.'

Moth began to jiggle up and down, the dance that precedes a tantrum. 'Zoe share a washing machine!'

Brian reappeared. 'My wife says Zoe is still asleep and she doesn't want to leave her. But thank you. And – ah – sorry about – well, the other day.'

'Oh well.' Moth was beginning to kick me. 'No problem. I mean, we've all had rows.'

He looked as if I'd stamped on his toe. 'Yes, I suppose so. Well, don't let me hold you up.'

'No. Of course. But Brian? Is Zoe OK?'

He looked tired. 'It's good of you to be concerned. Obviously, I don't think she's at immediate risk. Yet. She's sleeping. She's getting very tired these days.'

'Mummy! Stop it!'

I couldn't see a way of saying that it was her mental health I was interested in.

I put Moth down and held on to his hand as he lurched towards Brian.

'Washing machine!'

'OK. Tell her I said hello. And if she'd like to come round later I've got lots of hot chocolate.'

'Moth wants chocolate!'

'Thank you, Anna. Goodbye.'

I could see Raph sitting on the edge of the jetty. He swims well, or at least did when we left Oxford, but he knows about the power of waves only in theory.

'Come on,' I said to Moth. 'Let's see how fast we can run.'

He sat down. A disadvantage of Danish rainwear for children, lovingly sourced over the internet when I should have been working, is that the under-fives can enjoy the great outdoors without moving much while the adult minder develops hypothermia and suicidal impulses. I picked him up and tucked him under my arm.

Moth remained irate on the boat and along the harbour and up the main street. He was not mollified by two small dogs behind a gate, nor by Raph's invitation to jump in a coffee-coloured puddle by the postbox, nor even, except momentarily, by my offer of an old train ticket from my pocket to post. I picked him up again, strode into Spar and returned to Raph and the puddle with a packet of chocolate buttons.

'What would Daddy say?' asked Raph, holding out his hand.

The day Daddy takes the pair of you out for lunch while I work will be the day he qualifies for an opinion on the subject. 'I don't know,' I said. Moth dribbled melted chocolate on to his Danish raingear and reached out for more. 'How does he deal with Moth having a tantrum?'

'Not having a tantrum,' said Moth. 'More.'

Raph dabbled his boot in the puddle. 'I think he calls for you.'

I ate a couple of chocolate buttons. My grandmother used to allow me to sandwich them between ready-salted crisps, making one of the best mouthfuls of the 1980s.

'Well then. Have another.'

*

The church in Colla is nineteenth-century, made of sandstone for people who regarded aesthetic pleasure as a form of gluttony. No rambling path through ivied life stories on weathered stone here, but suburban rows of red marble gleaming like slabs of pâté in aspic, with inset metal letters as a garnish. There were plastic flowers on some of them, dead carnations on others, and the overall effect reminded me of the large garden centres with piped music enjoyed by my mother.

'Pretty flowers,' said Moth, squatting down to smell.

'They're nylon.' Raph nudged one with his foot.

'Don't do that. Someone put those there to remember someone they loved.'

Raph nudged it again. 'Why?'

I supposed this was the conversation we'd come here to have.

'Hello, blue flower.' Moth stroked it with a chocolatey finger. 'Would you like a caterpillar?'

I decided Raph's interest in rituals of grief took higher priority than Moth's misapprehension of the relative positions in the food chain of flowers and caterpillars. I shut the gate, which clanged behind us, echoing off the hillside.

'See if you can find a caterpillar, Moth. For the flower. I don't know exactly why, Raph. I think it's traditional in most places where flowers grow to bring them to graves. I suppose because flowers grow from seeds, and they bloom and then they die, but when they die they rot and make compost for their own seeds, which grow and bloom and so it goes. So they're pretty and they smell nice, but they're also a way of thinking about being born and living and dying as how the ecosystem works.' I hoped the Judge of Motherhood was taking notes.

'But these won't die and rot. They're made of plastic.'

'Well, I suppose in this weather fresh ones wouldn't last long. Or maybe whoever leaves them can't come very often but likes to think of them looking nice.'

He scuffed at the grass with his foot. 'And they don't have

seeds. You can't even recycle them, they'll end up in landfill and take about two hundred years to decompose and the PCBs will go into the soil and stop other things growing.'

Moth crawled behind the next row of stones and I moved so I could follow his progress, as if I thought a pâté slab might fall on him. As if I thought I'd be able to catch it if it did. Raph kicked the nylon flowers over. Pellets of white gravel trickled on to the grave.

'No, Raph. Put them back. Those are important to some-one.'

He kicked the gravestone. Andrew McConnell, 1933–2001.

'Raphael, stop that. Or we're leaving. You can't stay in a graveyard and behave like that. Put the flowers back.'

'No. They're stupid. And the stone's stupid and Andrew McConnell's stupid.'

Moth came running. 'Mummy, Raph saying stupid!'

'Put the flowers back, Raph. Now.'

He threw them at the gravestone. The plastic pot cracked and the rest of the gravel spilt. The flowers blew away, and Moth scampered after them.

'Right. Out. Now.'

I grabbed Raph's shoulder and pushed him towards the gate. He stumbled, resisting, and I shoved him against the wall.

'Ow,' he said. 'Stop it, Mummy.'

'Now you stand there and you don't move one muscle, is that clear? I'm going to pick up the mess you've made of that poor man's grave.'

'He's not poor, he's dead!' shouted Raph. 'And it's stupid to feel sorry for him because he's rotting into atoms and he doesn't even know it!'

I took one of the deep breaths recommended by the par-enting books, which had no more specific advice for a mother fighting her seven-year-old in a graveyard, and went back to Moth. We reassembled the flowers as well as we could. The sky was clearing and there was watery sunlight on the heather above us. My hair blew into my face and Moth pushed it back and touched my cheek.

'Raph said stupid. Mummy cross.'

I hugged him. In some ways, people who lie on the floor screaming when the world does not conform to their expectations are easier to live with than people who brood privately on death.

'Come on. Let's go make Raph feel better.'

But Raph was talking to someone, or at least being talked to by someone. An old lady, holding some leafy pink roses and a pair of secateurs and wearing a scarlet plastic headscarf which would leak as many PCBs (whatever they are) and take as long to decompose as any artificial plant, stood in front of him. I took Moth's hand and hurried over. The headscarf was matched by a raspberry-pink jumper and red cord trousers.

'Hello,' I said hopefully. Moth ducked behind my legs and clung on, pulling worryingly on my waistband.

Raph scowled at me and kicked at the wall behind him.

'He doesn't say much, does he?' She gestured towards him.

'Oh dear. I hope he hasn't been rude. He's – he's ...' Congenitally anti-social? The product of maternal negligence, not to mention emotional abuse? A bit upset?

'Acting up? Aye, well, it's not really the place for a wee boy, is it, in the graveyard? I suppose you're looking for someone? The Cassinghams don't bury here, you know.'

Moth peeped out. 'Hello.'

'No,' I said. 'Raph wanted to come. I offered to take them to the playground at Inversaigh. It's his choice.'

She turned back to Raph. 'And why would that be?'

He kicked the wall again. 'I just wanted to see it. That's all. But it's stupid. It doesn't make any difference. They're all still dead.'

She looked at him. Moth peeped out again.

'Hello, you,' she said. She tucked her secateurs under her arm and held out the other hand to Raph. 'The graveyard's for

300

the living. It's not all just flowers and old ladies, though. If you want I'll show you Henryson's grave.'

Raph looked up. The patch of sunlight widened down the hill towards us and there was a slight warmth on my face. I tilted it and shut my eyes. Get the vitamin D while you can.

'What's that?' he asked.

'It's where a lot of people got really angry. It was said – come here.' She bent down and whispered. 'It was said people came from miles around to piss on his grave!' She smiled and nodded, as if she'd just told us where they were having a big sale on tea-cosies.

'What?'

'I'm sure they didn't, not in the kirkyard. But they wanted to.'

'When was this?' I asked. I'd like to be that kind of old lady.

'Back in the 1880s. He was Hugo Cassingham's man, in fact.'

Raph looked confused. 'Grandpa Hugo?'

I picked up Moth and opened my mouth to rescue Raph from the sins of his ancestors. The Hugos. She stood between us.

'No, not your grandpa. Long ago. The family lived in London then, isn't that right, Anna? And came up here just for their summer holidays, like you're doing. Only they owned more than just the island then, and they kept a man to get the most out of it for them while they were away.'

'Excuse me,' I said. 'Mrs . . .?'

She raised a hand, like the Queen Mother. 'I'm just telling him, now. And this man, Henryson, he bled the people here dry. The children were going to school with empty bellies and the little ones, like your brother there, crying for brose, which was all the food they knew, and not getting it. And a bad business trying to have the place cleared and everyone sent off on a boat to Canada and enough places round here left deserted already. Anyway, what I'm telling you is when at last the old bugger died and they came to bury him, the people said they wouldn't have him here along with those he'd starved to an early grave and thrown out of their homes. And the Rector

301

said he was a Christian man and he'd lie in Christian soil like the rest of us and it would be up to the Lord to pass judgement on his life.'

'Old bugger,' said Moth appreciatively.

'Only they wouldn't hear of that in Colla, and come the funeral there was a bit of a shindy in the kirkyard, and old Virginia Grice from the island, she made a curse and she said that people would come from miles around to piss on his grave. So you'll see, young man, it's a place where you can be angry as well as sad.'

'Were people angry with Hugo Cassingham?' asked Raph.

'It was different then—' I said.

She interrupted. 'Aye. They were. He stayed down there in London and knew nothing about what was being done in his name up here. Or worse yet, he did know. His sister knew, from what I've heard.'

'Emily?' I asked, remembering the family tree. Had Emily Cassingham spent time here, in Colsay House? Before she married?

'Emily. Terrible interferer, my gran used to say.'

Moth pulled on my hand. 'Moth wants a snack. More chocolate?'

'We don't usually give them chocolate. It was just a treat, wasn't it, Raph?'

'Can I see the grave? The one people peed on?'

'Moth pee on a grave?'

'No,' I said. 'Certainly not.' I am quite adequately embarrassed by Cassinghams already.

We followed her round the corner of the church. Henryson's grave was the incarnation of another type of Victorian bad taste, the kind with flying buttresses and stalagmites of fungal stone.

'It looks like one of those loos in Paris,' said Raph. 'Remember, Mummy? The ones just for men.'

'*Pissoirs*,' I said. 'They were more restrained.'

Our local sybil laughed. 'I've seen them. My nephew lives

302

there, Paris. I'm off to my Robert's grave now. You can say hello to your dad from me. He came to my house once, you know, when he was about your age. Though he'll not remember it now.'

'Thanks,' I said. 'I'll tell him.'

'You do that.' She glanced down at Raph, who was tracing engraved letters with his finger. 'I heard you've been finding things in your garden.'

'Bones,' said Raph. 'People bones from long ago.'

'We had to call the police out.' I stroked Moth's hair. 'It must happen a lot, round here. Archaeological remains.'

'Aye. Not usually the bones, mind. But you keep an eye on what comes up when you're building. Giles will have told you about Andrew MacDonald?'

'Andrew MacDonald?' I asked.

Raph turned back to us. 'Who's your Robert?'

'Robert a pig,' muttered Moth, remembering a fictional pig who falls into a duckpond.

'Robert was my brother, Raphael. Dead four years and I've still things to say to him.'

'Oh.' Raph wandered round the other side of the stone.

'Your Giles pushed Andrew MacDonald into the harbour. Ten years gone. Or more like twenty. Did he never tell you?'

'Is Andrew MacDonald related to Ian? To the policeman?'

'Brothers,' she said. 'I wasn't sure you'd know. I doubt Giles knows who's who. Bye-bye now.'

So it wasn't about me, or my mothering, at all, only a battle in which I have been caught. Another battle in which I have been caught. I don't find the harbour-pushing incident very likeable, either.

I straightened my back and took hold of the children's hands. 'Come on, now. I'll buy you chips in the pub, OK?'

Raph rubbed my hand against his cheek. 'Sorry I kicked the flowers, Mummy.'

I kissed his hair. 'I'm sorry I pushed you. Chicken or burgers with your chips?'

That's what abusers do, they apologize and buy treats and then do it again.

However, within a generation the population of this small island suffered another serious blow through shipwreck. One of those lost was James Grice, one of the children who had rowed across the Sound after helping his sister to bury their mother, and the loss of fourteen of the twenty-one men between the ages of sixteen and fifty was a serious blow for the island.

The summer of 1769 was glorious. Iain McColl, writing from Inversaigh to his sister in Edinburgh in June of that year, recorded, 'The People say there is no memory of such Fishing in these Parts these Ten Years and more, the Herring almost leaping from the Water into the Boats, and the Fishing stopped at Nighte lest the Boats founder under the Weight of their Riches and the Women working all Daye and Nighte at the Salting.' The people of Colsay, not traditionally fisherfolk because of the lack of safe landing place, participated in this bounty, leaving the farming even more than usual in the hands of women.

The Reverend Mitchell, who had taken over from Rev. Adamson the previous year, noted that he had twice had to reprove the men of Colla for taking their boats out on a Sunday, and on 3rd July he devoted his sermon to the subject. He appears to have been a fire-and-brimstone preacher of the old sort and the sermon was no doubt stirring to hear, but regrettably not as stirring as the thought of the schools of herring churning the water below the old church.

The following week, most of the Colsay men rose in the early hours of that bright summer night, before their more devout elders left their well-earned rest, and took the larger of the island's boats some way north of the usual range of these small craft, where the more practised fishermen of Inversaigh were reporting huge catches of mackerel. The men of Inversaigh were beginning to take their sixeens far out beyond sight of land, navigating by cloudscapes and the course of seabirds in flight and occasionally finding themselves within sight of the Norwegian coast, and perhaps the Colsay men were inspired by travellers' tales heard at ceilidhs on summer evenings. No one survived to explain what the men were thinking when they left their sleeping wives, mothers and children.

The weather on Colsay remained calm and clear as it can sometimes be at that time of the year, and hope lasted for some weeks; perhaps the men had been blown off-course (supposing them to have had a course in the first place) and were making their way back down the Norwegian coast, or perhaps they had been picked up by a westbound ship and were working their passage home. As the autumn storms began some families could no longer deny their concern, although there were other cases where men returned years after going missing, and indeed the mother of Matthew Dunnet went to her grave twenty-two years later murmuring that 'Matty will be home soon.' But in fact nothing more was ever heard or seen of any of the men who set out that day, and the consequences for the island are still felt today.

I sipped my wine. The clouds were turning pink and the hill glowed in the evening light. The more I read about the island's past, the more it seemed an insult to be installing a rain-mist shower and slamming doors when the electricity went off, like the woman I once heard complaining about the quality of the coffee in the café at the museum of the Jewish ghetto in Venice. Well, said Giles, they do sell coffee and actually it's not cheap coffee, and why would drinking nasty coffee in any way counteract historical anti-semitism? It's an offence against aesthetics, that's all, and you, Anna, take those much more seriously than mere violations of the commandments. Admit it, now, you would sooner commit adultery than own a big television or a lace curtain. That would depend, I said, looking up at him, on whom you are proposing as my accomplice, and after a little more conversation along those lines we went back to the hotel, he apparently forgetful of the fact that he was taking to bed someone who grew up with lace curtains and whose mother had recently bought the big television. And he has been very careful, Giles, to commit no aesthetic offence in the renovation of the blackhouse, much more careful than any of his forebears were about not stealing land and starving children ... I stood up and rolled my shoulders, wandered over to the window. Zoe was sitting on the beach.

She looked round as my feet scrunched over the pebbles.
'Hi.'
'Hi.' I sat down next to her. The waves were dark blue, their foam catching the sun's pink. A fleet of white birds surfed the breakers. The stones weren't arranged for sitting on. 'Don't the pebbles bruise your bottom?'
She shrugged. 'No.'
'Medieval monks and nuns used to put stones in their shoes and beds to mortify the flesh.'
Zoe watched a raven flap across the sunset. The flowering grasses running down to the water were back-lit and a path of copper light began to form, leading west over the sea. 'Like the opposite of the princess and the pea.'
'Yes. Though some of the holier ones started off in rich families. I suppose self-denial's less fun when it's compulsory.'
The raven drifted on to a rock and stood surveying its domain with a critical eye.
Zoe pulled her sleeves down over her hands and shivered. 'You think I'm a princess.'
Her shoulder blades poked through her stretched jumper. I touched her arm. 'I don't think you're a holy woman. Did you have a good day today?'
She shook her head. 'I fought with Mum. I'm cold. Can we go back to your place?'

I cast a last look at the sea and sky. 'Come on. The kids are in bed. I'll make hot chocolate.'

She nodded. 'Thanks.'

I tipped half a pack of gingernuts on to a plate and put it between us. The cocoa was too hot to drink and I dribbled it from my spoon back into the cup, watching the reflection of the overhead light break into concentric rings as miniature chocolate waves spread across the mug. I took a biscuit and dipped it.

'Have you been thinking about what you're going to do next year?' I sound so much like a parent these days.

Zoe's hand moved towards the plate and then back again. She warmed it on the Bird Mug. 'I'm not going to Cambridge.'

I heard Giles's tread on the stairs. Giles refuses to creep around the house like a burglar, has no map of creaking floor-boards and clicking door-handles engraved on his heart.

'Hi, Zoe.' He peered into my mug. 'Did you make any for me?'

I looked up. 'I thought you preferred more sophisticated refreshments.'

He stroked my hair. 'If you're offering.'

'It's in the playroom. Behind my laptop. Would you bring my glass?'

Zoe was eating a biscuit.

'But you don't want to stay at home, do you?' I asked her.

She shrugged. 'Do I have a choice?'

What I would do with a free year. Grape-picking, with the sun on my back and the smell of the dark leaves on my hands. Paris: ladies in scarves with small dogs under manicured trees in the park, and the way even the rain falls differently there. The overnight train to Venice, not for the golden menagerie of Piazza San Marco but for the mist oiling the stones along the back streets and the frescoes flaming out high in dark churches. And then on, why not, to Prague, Budapest, Istanbul, Sana'a, as the leaves in Vienna and Munich turn gold and the trees of London and Paris stand naked under streetlights.

'Oh, Zoe. You could do anything.' Giles handed me a glass of wine and I drank most of it.

'Zoe? Half a glass?'

She shrugged again, sipped her chocolate. 'Maybe later.'

Giles sat down and took a biscuit, which he turned over as if it might have the mark of Satan on the underside.

'It's from Spar,' I said. 'Own brand. Glucose and hydrogenated vegetable fat and some e-numbers.'

He bit it. 'So, Zoe. How's it going?'

Giles, of course, has students too, and I am probably wrong in imagining that fledgling ornithologists are less given to complicated distress than our hair-flicking historians.

She drank some more cocoa and took a second biscuit. Her shoulders had relaxed and her skin tone was that of someone more recently alive. 'Anna was about to tell me what to do next year.'

'No, no,' I said. 'No such thing.'

Giles finished his biscuit, grimaced, and drank some wine. 'What do you want to do?'

'I wanted to go to Canada.'

'You did go to Canada,' I pointed out. 'Do you mean you want to go back?'

She shook her head. 'Never.'

'What are the parameters?' asked Giles. 'You're going to Cambridge next autumn, I take it, all being well. Do you need to earn some money?'

'Dad was going to pay for Canada. I think he'd probably cough up for anything that keeps me away from Mum.'

Giles and I exchanged glances.

'Where would you really like to go?' I asked. 'If you could do anything at all, anywhere in the world?'

She put her mug down. 'I know I'm supposed to be excited about all these opportunities and I'm really lucky and everything, but I mean, just look around you. Open any newspaper. What am I supposed to do that will make anything better?'

308

I finished my hot chocolate. Found an institution, I thought. Ban the Bomb or Stop the War or End Poverty Now. Votes for Women. Decide what matters most and work out what you can do about it. That's how people abolished slavery and extended the franchise and provided universal education and healthcare. Maybe Zoe's problem, and even Raph's, is satiety. I hoped I wasn't going to spend my old age answering to committees of despairing youth for my carbon footprint in years gone by. 'Well, it might be fun. More fun than waiting for the apocalypse with your mother.'

Giles refilled my wineglass. 'Anna, do you remember Peter Freidmann?'

'Your Keble physicist?'

When I first met Giles, he used to get up in what felt to me like the middle of the night to cycle off to the river and row up and down while a bird-like Austrian woman called Clara shouted instructions at him and seven other men with beguiling shoulders (long since, at least in Giles's case, gone the way of my flat stomach and upward-looking breasts). Perhaps, I thought, Zoe could be a cox. Peter Freidmann was Clara's husband, thin from a vegan diet and vague from long hours in a field of physics that was never adequately explained to me.

'He's just got a Chair in Vienna. I was in touch with him because they're building a house that's meant to be carbon-neutral. Growing their own fruit and veg, and I think hens. They've got three kids and Clara's just gone back full time. It's a bit of a struggle.'

Zoe was watching him as if he'd just galloped in with good news from the western front. 'Do they want an au pair?'

Giles drank some more wine. 'He said they were wondering about it. I can find out, if you like. But Zoe, I have to tell you that no reasonable family is going to want an au pair who passes out from hunger on a regular basis.'

She looked down and her hair swung across her face. She pushed it back. 'I didn't pass out. Please ask them. It sounds totally cool. And I'm OK with kids, aren't I? I did German. I'd like to speak German again. Can you e-mail them? Or call? You can use my phone.'

So maybe a carbon-neutral house outside Vienna was less totally fucked than wherever her mother happened to be at the time.

'What would your parents think, Zoe?' I asked. 'Would they approve?'

'Oh, Mum'll say it's like skivvying or something. Probably that your friends want cheap childcare. And that I wouldn't know one end of a vacuum cleaner from the other and can't be trusted with kids.'

'But would they mind my making enquiries for you?' asked Giles.

She finished her third biscuit. 'I'm over eighteen, aren't I? I don't need their consent to ask someone to e-mail a friend. Please. Honestly, I know I'd be better there.'

'OK,' said Giles. 'OK. I can ask. But two conditions: I'm going to be up-front with them about the food issues and if Peter and Clara are interested you negotiate directly and you sort it out with your parents, OK? And if they've got any sense, which they do, and if they take Anna's and my advice, which they will, your going and staying will depend on your health. So you'll need to address that, Zoe, if you don't want to end up back home with your mother.'

She brushed the crumbs from her fingers. 'OK. It's a deal. Promise.'

'You don't know anything about it yet,' I muttered, though I remembered quite well setting off for my year in Paris knowing even less about the people to whom I was confiding my welfare for the next ten months. There must be an annual tide of teenage girls sweeping across Europe in the belief that other people's families are kinder and more reasonable than their own. And who knows, maybe some of them are right; I was.

The screaming has stopped now, which is no good sign, and still I am not permitted to attend. Of course it is too late for me to intervene in any way, and has been almost certainly too late since the 'knee-woman' cut the cord, but I have laudanum and could ease the sufferings of both mother and child while they await the inevitable end of this sorry tale. I have not left the house and have made no effort to see anyone – there is really no point when they are so set on death and destruction. Really, that 'knee-woman' is no better than a witch. I do not know if it is the same person, but apparently there is also a woman here who will sell 'good winds' to anyone about to make a journey and cure people of certain sicknesses by means that my informant would prefer not to describe. For all there is the church at the end of the street and they spend three hours huddled there being shouted at by the minister every Sunday the weather lets him over the Sound, these people are really barely so much as medieval.

Did I tell you that in olden times here, rather than burning at the stake which would, no doubt, have been a waste of precious wood, witches, and also women taken in adultery, were tied up and sewn into sacks weighted with stones and dragged into the sea? Not even taken out by boat and dropped over the side, just dragged into a rising tide while the villagers watched from the beach. Some of Mrs Barwick's tales revolved around their reappearance.

Midnight—

Mrs Barwick just came to my room, the candle under her chin giving her an uncanny resemblance to the weirder beings from her stories. I was already in bed and hardly in a state to receive friends, much less enemies, but I already knew that she has had occasion to

311

forget many of the finer points of etiquette since she left her position with Miss Emily. I sat up and asked what she meant by disturbing me at that hour and she said that she was come to tell me a story. I said I was in no mood for stories and she said that was no matter – really, if I had had a veil at the end of the bed I would almost have expected her to start rending it before going off to set the house on fire (I can certainly imagine Aubrey leaving me sponging blood off someone with a maniac lurking nearby, in the blithe conviction that he was offering a compliment to my good sense, though in other ways I would call him rather more elegant than Mr Rochester). Anyway, after we had established that she was not to be allowed to perform this scene seated on my bed I allowed her to continue. She had come, it seemed, to tell me about a Lady Sands, *floreat c.* 1750–1770.

Lady Sands was a fine Edinburgh lady, finer than any Manchester nurse even if she is of good family, and she made a fine marriage. She was known to have a temper on her right from a bairn, and they say before the wedding her father took the young man aside and told him if he had to treat her harshly for it he'd hear no complaints from them. Anyway, at first all went well – they made a bonny pair and of course a rich, beautiful woman can always do what in plainer folk might be taken badly. (You must imagine our prophetess raising her candle towards the mirror at this juncture, as if to remind me that I share neither of Lady Sands' indemnities.) Her clothes were the envy of the town, and if it was said she went to church just as often as she had something new to display, well, she wasn't the only woman of whom that might be said, then or now, and better than her lord, who rarely showed his face at all without his mother was visiting. Anyway, after a year or so there was a child, a boy, and rejoicing as if it was the Lord himself come again, and nothing in the land her ladyship couldn't have for the asking, forby there was beginning to be word his lordship was getting through the money faster than it was coming in. (The old story, I suggested, and the candle was raised again. Maybe so, but not, she thought, one I knew yet.)

312

And then Lady Sands announced herself in the family way again, and this time, what with her sick and pale and money maybe not quite so free as it had been, his lordship wasn't quite so quick to jump when she wanted peaches and another maid and a new carriage when she had to stop riding. A few of the servants were turned off and said they'd heard her screaming sometimes late at night and bruises on her arms and maybe other places too when the morning tea went in, but of course they'd a grudge against the house by then and her skin was always smooth enough by candlelight.

They say by the time the child came Lord Sands was openly escorting Mrs Mitchell to dinners as well as the theatre and whatever. She had the midwife all right at the birth, and a hard time she had and her not strong to begin with, and then a few days after it was given out that she'd taken a turn for the worse and died. Well, there was a big funeral and everyone very sad, the infant sent out to nurse, which was what she'd done with the first one anyway, and an English governess brought down for the boy, who'd have been maybe three. And that was the end of that, except (the stage directions call for a pause and the raising of the candle; the audience begins to feel that another prop would lend variety to the performance, which is none the less excellent of its kind, even remarkable under the circumstances) – well, I know of the roofless hut out near the church, do I not? (It is in fact hard to tell one hovel from another here, and since the vicar has come but twice from Colla since I arrived, neither occasion in any way edifying to me, I have not frequented the church, but I agree as the script indicates that I should.) And I know that house is known as the Scold's Bridle? (I do not.) It is so called because Lady Sands was bridled there; she did not die in childbed but was taken to her brother-in-law's house outside the city, from whence, after the 'funeral', she was brought, by stages and at night, gagged and bound, to Colsay, where she passed the seven or eight years that remained to her until she died in the smallpox which killed all but five of the islanders. (The speaker gazes piercingly at the audience.) And how do I think she passed those years? (I shrug; there is an icy

313

draught snaking around my shoulders and I have not been indulged with a fire in my bedroom since our words over Mrs Grice's labour.) Doing just nothing. She had no books or papers, none of her embroidery, nowhere to go. Lord Sands told the islanders to feed her when they could spare the food and hide her if anyone came to the island; he wasn't specific about how and where but he made sure to leave a rope and a witch's bridle, and they say she was so changed by then that it wasn't likely anyone who'd seen her in her prime would recognize her anyway. He said if she got away or got a message to anyone he'd clear the island and burn the houses over the heads of anyone who couldn't or wouldn't go, and just to make the point he evicted the McConnells and fired the roof before they'd been able to get the beds out, and as it happened she was such a wildcat and acting like the queen herself, for all she'd suffered, after the first summer no one was feeling much sorrow for her however bad her plight.

When Esther Grice died the women offered Mary Sands her quern stone and even her spinning wheel, thinking she could find work for her hands and earn a little money for some handspun to replace the clothes on her back, and got slapped and spat at for their troubles. Well, after that she might live or die for what we cared, and you may be sure when the fever came and the bairns, hardly grown enough to raise a spade, had to bury their own parents, no one was worrying much what became of her ladyship. They say she lies in the old churchyard but I doubt anyone troubled themselves much over a Christian burial for the likes of her and there's some have heard crying from the old hut of a winter's night. (NB: You can hear all the voices of hell crying in the storm-winds here, in the prosaic mid-morning just as well as in darkness.)

The curtains stirred and the candle flickered and she fell silent, waiting for the next cue. I pulled my shawl around my shoulders and remarked on our good fortune to live in the present day when such outrages are quite impossible. Maybe they are, she said, and maybe they're not. Good night to you.

Al, I think I may come home now. Not because I really think

Mrs Barwick is going to tie me up in a stone hut for the rest of my life, nor even because I believe in the past or present presence of Lady Sands, only that I have failed here. I cannot tell if a different woman would have succeeded; I suspect a more circumspect manner might have achieved more, but I have failed. If the infant Grice is not this moment dead, it will be in the next day or two, and it is not really conceivable – nor, to be honest, worth another four months of my time and my absence from the Society, where I know that my energies are well spent – that I will be allowed to direct the next birth. I do not know what I have done wrong but I know now that my longing for home has deeper foundations than the self-indulgent wish for the company and fellowship of those I love best. There is better work for me to do.

May

15

THE NEXT GENERATION

The therapeutic analyses of adult neurotics left no doubt
about the detrimental influence of many parental and environmental attitudes and actions such as dishonesty in sexual
matters, unrealistically high moral standards, overstrictness
or overindulgence, frustrations, punishments, or seductive
behaviour. It seemed a feasible task to remove some of these
threats from the next generation of children by enlightening
parents and altering the conditions of upbringing . . .

      – Anna Freud, *Normality and Pathology in Childhood*, p. 14

What follows below is surely the darkest chapter in the history of this area. Between 1800 and 1860 the population
of Colla, Colsay and Inversaigh dropped by 74 per cent,
and even this statistic masks the complete desolation of
most of the smaller settlements, left burning and roofless
as if in the aftermath of war. Some communities removed,
or were removed, *en masse* to the New World, although the
mortality rate on those transatlantic crossings was little
lower than in the slave ships whose evil passages ceased
during this period; there are stories of reluctant families
hunted like foxes out of caves and mountain fastnesses to
be carried bound and struggling on to these transports.
Other villagers were forced into townships already over-

316

crowded and hungry, where the sanitary arrangements were wholly inadequate for the distended populations and there was no visible means of support. The shifts to which people were reduced to feed and clothe their children bear comparison to the desperate ingenuity which the present author saw in Eritrea in the early 1970s, and both cases illustrate Sen's thesis that famine is a consequence of relative rather than absolute shortage; it is not that there was no food, but that there was no food there. The problem was more to do with distribution than supply, a fact tacitly acknowledged by the Cassingham family's response, which was to offer bowls of soup in exchange for labour on the new stone jetty.

The Reverend in Eritrea? Voluntary Service Overseas, I supposed, or maybe some post-war version of missionary work. He would have been the right age to kindle and burn in the liberation theologies of the 1960s, whose promise to combine divine reassurance and radical politics even I find appetizing. Perhaps I might in time find friends here after all, except that I am on the wrong side of this war. In Oxford, being a mother, state-educated, the product of lace curtains and roll-up garage doors, I can, when it suits me, raise the banner of my presumed inferiority. Here, I am Marie Antoinette, righteously menaced by those whose rightful inheritance keeps the roof of the Oxford terrace over my children's heads. Even though the blood of Viking invaders, who also burnt the roofs over the heads of Celtic children and dragged their mothers into slavery on the black beaches of Iceland, runs in the veins of those cleared. And indeed, even though those who survived eviction and the emigrant ships and the howling winters of Manitoba founded their new lives on the genocide of thousands of Native American cultures and communities. Zoe is right: in moral as well as practical terms, we're all fucked. I didn't feel like reading any more.

317

I was cold. Put another jumper on, Giles would say, and enjoy it while it lasts. There will be no woolly jumpers in my grandchildren's lives, if the world continues long enough for me to have grandchildren, certainly no knitted vests, nor those tights that seemed to have been made from the untreated wool of some particularly hardy brand of Greenland sheep. I went out into the hall, listened for the children's voices upstairs where Giles was meant to be supervising the changing of sheets, a task which with enough ingenuity on the part of a parent who has no desire to go out in the rain can become a morning's camping game. Moth giggled and I could hear Raph and Giles singing 'The British Grenadiers' as if it were the last night of the Proms. I went upstairs.

'I thought you were writing your presentation?' said Giles. He was sitting under a duvet cover draped over two chairs, outside which Raph stood at attention.

I looked around. 'Where's Moth?'

There was a flurry under Raph's duvet. 'Moth camping. In a bed.'

Raph stood at ease. 'Mummy, Daddy says we can go camping.'

'Does he? Daddy can take you camping if he likes.'

'Really? Daddy, will you? Please?'

Giles peered out. 'I didn't say we could, I said ask Mummy.'

So Mummy can be bad cop again. 'I just don't think it's my kind of thing,' I said. Moth crawled back into his burrow. 'Maybe when Moth's out of nappies. And sleeping through the night. I don't think anyone else on a campsite would thank us for taking him at the moment.'

Giles crawled out and stood up. 'You don't have to stay on a campsite, you know. It's more fun to camp wild.'

I was beginning to wish I'd stayed downstairs reading about man's inhumanity to man.

'Not in northern Scotland with a toddler in nappies it's not.

318

It's more fun to have hot and cold running water. And central heating, and floors to play on, not to mention a roof over your head.'

Raph had gone very still.

'What is it, love?'

Moth reappeared. 'Peepo!'

'Peepo!' said Giles.

'Raph?' I asked.

'It's that thing in the attic. Listen.'

'Oh, Raph—' Giles began.

But Raph was right. There was something brushing along the wall, chattering. Giles left the room and ran up the stairs.

Raph came for a hug. 'It's been there ages and you never believe me.'

I put my arm round him. 'We can all hear it now. Daddy will see what it is.'

Moth scrambled off the bed. 'Cuddle Moth too!'

I picked him up. Raph pushed his head under my arm. 'It's the baby. Or the baby's mummy.'

'Not in the middle of the morning,' I said, as if there are times when one should expect reunions of long-dead families in the attic.

'Anna?' Giles called down the stairs. 'Can you get me a torch?'

Raph and I looked at each other as if Giles had confirmed an outbreak of fire or a hole below the waterline. Then Raph reached under his pillow and handed me his wind-up torch, which also has a small compass and a mobile phone charger in case the apocalypse happens in the night.

'I'll mind Moth,' he said. 'But come straight back.'

Moth clung like a koala so I took him with me. Giles was kneeling on the boards by the chimney breast, tapping the ventilation panel. Something flustered and went still. I stood as far away as possible and handed him the torch.

'Thanks. There's a bird in there.'

319

My skin crawled. 'Oh God, trapped. And fluttering about.' Moth's legs tightened on my waist.

I swallowed. 'How – how long has it been there?'

Giles aimed the light through the metal louvres. 'It's still pretty lively. Rooks can get in and out. Doesn't mean it's trapped.'

I hitched Moth up. 'It's been there for weeks. Raph's been hearing it.'

He was still peering. 'Rooks come and go. The same one won't have been there for weeks.'

'And is it a rook?'

Giles shrugged. 'I can't tell through a chimney breast. It's about that size.'

I remembered Raph, waiting. 'Are you going to let it out?'

Not in my house, not a bird dashing itself—

'We'll give it a few hours and see if it finds its way out.' He turned the torch off and stood up. 'Do you want to do any more work or can I get off to the puffins now?'

I thought about the bird all afternoon. I couldn't see how it could be in there without being hurt, how it could move without breaking its wings on the sooty brickwork. It was trapped, panicking, in darkness. In my house. I would rather have had a ghost, but Raph went out on his space hopper for the first time in many days and made several forays to the attic, coming back to assure me and Moth that it was still there and still making a noise. If the noise stopped, it occurred to me, we wouldn't know if the bird was dead – rotting above Raph's sleeping head, parasites teeming off its cold skin – or free.

'More reading, Mummy!'

'"You may go into the field or down the lane, but don't go into Mr McGregor's garden: your father had an accident there; he was put in a pie by Mrs McGregor. Now run along, and don't get into mischief. I am going out."'

'Mummy?' Raph was swinging around the door handle.

'Mummy, do people eat rabbits?'

'Mummy, reading!'

'Then old Mrs Rabbit took a basket—'

'Mummy, I said, do people eat rabbits?'

'Yes. Grandma Julia makes rabbit pie.'

'Rabbits have a pie?'

'No, Moth, rabbits eat grass, and vegetables. The Flopsy Bunnies eat lettuces, don't they, and Peter's going to find some cabbages.'

'But then I am not a rabbit,' Moth quoted dreamily. 'More reading.'

'—and went through the wood to the baker's. She bought a loaf of brown bread—'

'You mean she makes them out of rabbits?' Raph stood still.

'Of course. Rabbit pies.'

He looked green. 'But I thought it was like gingerbread men or – or those horse things with raisins.'

'Prunes,' I said. 'Devils on horseback.'

'Not dead rabbits.'

'More reading! Not talking, Mummy.'

'—and five currant buns. Flopsy, Mopsy, and Cottontail, who were good little bunnies, went down the lane—'

'Where does she get the rabbits?'

There was a knock on the door.

'I'll go!' shouted Raph, and Moth struggled off my lap to follow him.

I stood up and rolled my shoulders, stretched my arms. I couldn't hear the bird from the playroom, but I knew it was there.

'Mummy! It's Zoe. Can we have biscuits?'

I went into the hall. 'Hi, Zoe. No, Raph, no biscuits. I think there are some crumpets in the freezer you could have when it's snacktime.'

'Moth have a biscuit?'

'There aren't any biscuits, love.'

321

Raph frowned. 'There were yesterday. I saw them.'

Zoe and I exchanged shifty glances.

'Well, today there are crumpets. It's not good for people to eat the same things all the time.'

'Is Giles with the puffins?' asked Zoe.

The knife I was using to prise frozen crumpets apart grazed my palm.

'Again. Though to be fair he changed the sheets this morning.'

Zoe fiddled with the wrapper of the block of butter on the table. 'I don't think my dad's ever changed a sheet in his life.'

I deposited a crumpet in each slot of the toaster. 'Without in any way condoning biological determinism, I have yet to meet a man who can put a duvet into a duvet cover. But I expect it's just social conditioning. Or coincidence.'

'Daddy tried but he ended up in the duvet cover himself,' said Raph. 'Mummy, if there isn't any honey can we have golden syrup like when you were a little girl?'

I told Raph once that I used to have margarine and golden syrup on white toast when I got home from school and he has never quite got over the thrill.

'There is honey. Look.'

Moth came in with *The Flopsy Bunnies*. 'Mummy read it sleepy lettuce?'

'Mummy's making your snack.' Zoe held out her arms to him. 'Zoe read the sleepy lettuce.'

'Did you know people eat rabbits?' asked Raph.

'I don't.' Zoe lifted Moth on to her knee, the muscles in her arms standing out like ropes. 'I don't eat meat at all.'

'Really?'

'It's bad for the environment. If everyone was vegetarian, no one would be starving.'

'Really? Not the babies in Africa?'

The crumpets popped up, but they were still cold as death.
I pushed them down again.

'I wanted to do that,' said Raph.

'Sorry.' I forced the lever up again and he came to press it
down.

'It's not that simple,' I said. 'There are more than enough
calories in the world for everyone anyway. There's a global food
surplus. It's about distribution, not supply.'

'It takes ten times as much land to produce a beefburger as
it does to produce the same amount of protein in beans,' said
Zoe. 'Not to mention the methane.'

Raph stood on tiptoe to see into the toaster. I have been
known to set crumpets on fire. 'Daddy doesn't let us eat beef-
burgers. Mummy, can I be vegetarian?'

'Oops,' said Zoe. 'Sorry. I didn't mean that.'

'Zoe read it sleepy lettuce!'

'When Benjamin Bunny grew up, he married his Cousin
Flopsy. They had a large family, and they were very improvi-
dent and cheerful.'

'Yes, if you want to,' I said. The crumpets reappeared, only
a little black at the edges.

'What, really can I?'

I ran a jammy knife from breakfast under the cold tap.

'As far as I'm concerned. I don't like cooking meat anyway.
You'll have to push the environmental argument with
Daddy.'

'I do not remember the separate names of their children;
they were generally called the "Flopsy Bunnies."' Zoe sniffed.
'He needs to think globally.'

I started rubbing lumps of cold butter into the crumpets.
'No salami, you know. No ham or sausages, or roast chicken.'

Raph scooped a globule of butter off one of my burnt offer-
ings and ate it. 'I don't mind. I don't like things being dead. I
don't like them in my mouth.'

I offered the plate to Zoe and she took one. 'Things will still die.' I fanned the air with a crumpet, to cool it for Moth. 'Only you won't eat them.'

The population of Colsay, like that of many other marginal communities along this coast, was in fact swollen by the Clearances of the 1840s. The island itself was not cleared – at least until the last permanent inhabitant left in the 1960s – although threats and the rumours of threats persisted throughout the nineteenth century. Half the families from Rothkinnick were rehoused on Colsay in the wake of the loss of the *Helga*, though within ten years four of the six households had left for Glasgow and Canada. Three or four landless cottar families came to stay with crofting relatives on Colsay after evictions elsewhere and stayed for many years, apparently accepted into the broadly egalitarian life of the community there. Other settlements forced to accommodate the dispossessed in this way suffered very badly for it as hunger became endemic rather than seasonal and what we might now call environmental health problems relating to sanitation became acute, but on Colsay these consequences were to some extent offset by what some outsiders felt able to call a divine limit on population increase, 'ordained by God that the people of this sea-girt isle might never exceed its bounty'. For most of the nineteenth century, infant mortality on Colsay was well in excess of 50 per cent, peaking between 1865 and 1880 at around 85 per cent.

There has been no modern research to confirm the views of unqualified Victorian observers, but comparison with the histories of other North Atlantic islands (particularly the Westmann Islands to the south of Iceland and the Faroe Islands) as well as contemporary anecdotes suggest that the likely cause was infant tetanus. The majority of infants affected died in the first eight days of life, being unable to feed, listless and then racked by muscle spasms which left their bodies unnaturally distorted. The islanders seem to have been schooled to accept these losses as God's will, although the nearest thing to a contemporary record of their views is contained in the report of the Highland Commission, which heard the testimony of a generation who had lost the majority of their cousins and siblings within days of birth but had no first-hand memory of these brief lives, nor of the characteristically ham-fisted response of the Cassingham family.

The Highland Commission records suggest that Emily Cassingham, the unmarried sister of Lord Hugo, visited the island and felt the need to intervene in the ways of birth and death. Emily, who remained childless herself, became increasingly devoted to charitable endeavour in later life and sponsored three child health clinics in Edinburgh. Even at this early date, she seems to have taken maternal and infant welfare as her pet cause. Rather than having a local woman trained in nursing and midwifery, Lady Emily chose to send an English girl who had no Gaelic at all. The islanders were placed under great pressure to accept this unknown outsider's participation in the most intimate moments of their lives in the name of progress and modernity, threatened with rent rises and even eviction if they continued in the old ways.

Perhaps fortunately for all the islanders but the hapless infants at the centre of this conflict, the nurse did not stay long. She drowned with three of the six men whom she bribed to row her to the steamer, against their better judgement, for her passage home for Christmas in December 1878, and no births took place during her time on Colsay. If they had, it seems possible both that the women would have refused the alien nurse's attendance and that the Cassingham family would have carried out their threats, setting a new standard for the shameful behaviour of English landowning families in the Highlands. Sir Hugo and later

Hartley Cassingham were convinced that the islanders were mired in foolish superstition and needed, for their own good, to be forced into the modern era.

If we consider the Victorian habit of comparing Highland people to 'savages', the roots of this attitude become easier to understand; the people of these islands were merely another group of ignorant natives to be bribed and threatened into the industrial age. Neither can we exonerate the patronizing charity of Lady Emily, a Victorian lady who, without a young family of her own, devoted much of her life to interference with the home lives of those less fortunate than herself.

I pushed the book away and stared out into the night. A full moon hung over the sea, and the garden wall and the rocks on the shore reflected its stony light. Lady Emily was only trying to help, I found myself thinking, and who is the Reverend to say that she had no life of her own, just because she didn't marry? In any case, there was no reason for burying any of those babies in our garden. Especially if it was a mark of orthodoxy to refuse the care that would have saved them, the children would have been laid to rest in the graveyard with whatever passed for full honours under the Nonconformist ministry of the day. If I had been allowed to choose at the time, I would certainly have sent away the midwife who oversaw most of my first labour, who held my legs down with her elbows as I twisted and cried out on the bed and Giles turned away in embarrassment. Who left me afterwards for half an hour still splayed and helpless in stirrups with a drip in my hand, unable to reach the baby, while she ran some errand, Giles slept in a chair and a cleaner wandered in and out. If I saw her drowning now I would watch and smile. It is no wonder women's careers collapse after childbirth; the image of ourselves exposed and whimpering on hospital beds reappears in our minds as we ascend the podium or open the meeting. I had no trouble understanding why the women of Colsay would send an English nurse packing. I remembered also the final weeks of my own pregnancies and the conviction, which took root and grew in my mind until my head was as full of death as my belly was of life, that I or the baby would die, that the reality I could no longer postpone was the end and not the beginning of life. And when the moment came the second time and I began to labour, it seemed at last that birth and death were not that different, that perhaps in the best of both cases one would know what one was doing and submit, as grass submits to wind or sand to water.

Maybe it was like that for those mothers, maybe their babies' deaths were the same elemental process as their births. There must have been an interim period, a few days when those small beings, not yet human, hung between the womb and the grave. Would you, I wondered, make little clothes, prepare a cradle? Or would you wait awhile, gathering your strength, to see if God wanted the new creature now or later? I did not let Giles assemble the cot until each baby was old enough to have presents, middle names, guests, the outline of a place in the world, and even then it seemed that these things were there to keep the baby with us, to stop it turning back to its own place among those who are not alive. And there were moments in the first weeks of both children's lives when I believed I would have been happy to see them die, to restore a world that did not revolve around the baby's mouth. The newly born and the dying are not like us, and our love and hate for them are stories we tell ourselves to help us through the night. Only anchorites find a way of getting through life that does not depend on the daily and hourly denial of death. I saw, for a moment, out of the corner of my eye, why the mothers on Colsay might have chosen their children's deaths, and their reasons had nothing to do with ignorance or stupidity. But they also brought no need for secret burial.

There were footsteps on the stairs.

'Hi there,' said Giles. 'They're both asleep. Or at least silent. What are you reading? I'm afraid that bloody bird is still in there, I'm going to have to take the ventilation plate off and get it out.'

I felt as if someone had switched the light on while I was still dreaming. 'What?'

'The bird. It's quieter but it's still in there. Can't really leave it another night.'

Wings beating the brickwork, reptilian feet scrabbling against plaster.

'No. I'd rather it was gone. But Giles, what if it gets out? Flies around the house?'

Bashing itself on windows, banging against lights, spattering faeces on beds and Persian rugs.

He looked surprised. 'Well, I won't let it, of course. Stay down here, if it bothers you. I'll shut the door.'

I opened the book again. 'And the children's doors, please.'

However strong the islanders' sense of Hugo Cassingham's failures as a landlord, there was no joy when his son Hartley took over the responsibilities of the estate as the old man began to decline in the late 1880s. There had been ugly rumours about Hartley Cassingham's conduct towards local girls in his youth, and gossip – admittedly among those who had much more obvious reasons to hate and fear the family – that he expected *droit de seigneur* in exchange for rent relief during the hungry years. It is unlikely that there was serious foundation for these suggestions, for allegations of rape would have been a grave matter even for Lord Cassingham's son, and there is no reason why the most dissolute young man with access to all the drawing-rooms and back alleys of London and Edinburgh would have found it necessary to complicate the family position by sowing his wild oats among the rigorously Calvinist and malnourished virgins of Colla and Inversaigh. Nevertheless, Hartley Cassingham was a man of whom such things could still be said a hundred years later—

The front gate clicked and Judith bulked like Frankenstein's monster in the moonlight. It was half-past ten.

'Oh, for fuck's sake,' I murmured to my laptop. 'We didn't advertise a holiday counselling service.'

Though, come to think of it, we'd probably make a profit if we did. *Tackle your compulsions in the peacefulness of this ancient isle! Let the spirit of our anchorite watch over your addled teenagers! Twice-weekly therapy sessions an optional extra.* My parents fought so intensively over planning holidays that the travelling itself became almost redundant. We would spend two weeks on a series of interchangeable Greek and Spanish beaches, where my mother followed the holiday routines described in the magazines with which she kept the doctors' waiting room supplied and my father marched the countryside as if he were part of a defeated army in hiding from the legions of women uniformed in swimwear and wielding pink novels, slinking back across the sand-scattered tiled floor sunburnt and blistered in the late afternoons. It was too late to hide, but I was still annoyed that Judith ignored the front door and tapped at the window as if she were Catherine Linton, who is allowed to behave like that only because she is fictional and dead.

'I saw you were still up,' she said. 'Is it all right if I come in for a quick chat?'

'I was working.'

She looked in at the laptop, my glass of wine inky in a pool of light, the tower of monographs on eighteenth-century history. 'Sorry.'

It was the second time I'd heard her apologize. 'Never mind. I'm not making much progress anyway. Go round, I'll open the door.'

I drank the rest of my glass and hid the bottle in the flour cupboard before I let her in.

'Thanks.' She stooped to take her shoes off, and noticed that I was wearing mine. 'Should I take them off?'

'Not to bother. Come in, Judith.'

'Sorry. Your evenings are precious, I remember that. Though of course Brian was out at work all day.'

I followed her into the kitchen. She didn't seem drunk, smelt of nothing more sinister than pink perfume. Mutton dressed as buttercups. 'Giles is out on the cliffs a lot. That's why I work in the evenings.'

She sat down, and the chair creaked. 'I made a point of spending the evenings with Brian when the children were young. When he wasn't too busy. I mean, the marriage is the basis of family life, really, isn't it?'

I filled the kettle. Outside, the moon had moved round behind a tree and clouds were muffling the stars in the west. 'That's a very historically specific idea,' I said. Judith was picking at the dried porridge on the table. 'And I'm not sure it's done anyone much good. Anna Freud found that some children did better in intelligently run institutions than in families.'

'*Anna* Freud?'

'Sigmund's daughter. Specialized in child psychoanalysis. Wartime and post-war, especially interested in what happened to child development when mothers went to work. Or ran away.'

She turned round a letter from the Inland Revenue so she could read it. 'Not much, I should think.'

I made the tea, Giles's lapsang souchong. I had no intention of giving her a biscuit.

'How's Zoe?' I asked.

The porridge came loose. Judith shrugged. 'She's – she's still thin enough for it to be dangerous.' She looked up. 'We put her in hospital before. When she was sixteen. She won't even see a doctor now, and legally we can't force her. I'd have her sectioned.'

'She doesn't seem crazy to me.'

Judith pushed her tea away. Some slopped on to the table, over the porridge. 'Sorry. Anna, she's starving herself to death.'

Not actually to death, just close enough not to have to take responsibility for life. Rather like the anchorite, hovering on her cliff between the world and eternity, or like the nineteenth-century mothers of Colsay, who could see more urgent issues than individual living and dying. I mopped the table with one of the bibs Moth has always refused to wear. 'People can do that without being crazy. Hunger strikers. Suffragettes. People fasting for God. Maybe she needs to work out what she's protesting against. I mean, her generation have grown up being told that if they don't consume less than we did the planet will end on their watch, haven't they? And that they're all obese? It's a logical response.'

'You wouldn't say that if it was one of yours.'

Would I? Raph with every bone in his face shadowed and his jumper draped over his ribcage, Moth – but I couldn't imagine Moth as anything but his chubby, milk-scented self. 'I can't tell that. I know I'd be very anxious. I can only tell you what it looks like when she's not mine.'

'It's not about logic. It's not that abstract.'

'You're worried it's about you.'

She pulled the tea back and ran her finger round the rim. 'I gave up everything. I've got a degree, you know. Geography. I'd have liked a career. But I couldn't, not with Brian being a doctor, and they worked much harder twenty years ago. On call and up all night. He worked and I did everything else. It's not just arranging flowers. I sorted out insurance and got the cars serviced and dealt with all the house moves and bought birthday cards for him to send his mother and took her food when she stopped cooking for herself. And he did complain, if I didn't get things right. Because he was working so much and I was just at home. He expects a certain – standard.' She glanced round the kitchen, seeing it, and me, through Brian's eyes.

331

'If Giles wants the floor washed, he knows where the mop is,' I said, although actually I doubt either of us could find the mop and suspect that it would turn out to be mildewed and smelly if we did. I do not think I have ever bought a mop.

'I found plumbers and electricians and made them cups of tea and talked to them. I researched and booked all the holidays and then worried about whether he'd like them. I packed for him when he went to conferences and took his suits to be dry-cleaned. I knew when the cars needed servicing. But mostly I cooked and shopped and looked after the children. I took them to piano and painting and ice-skating and I made costumes and cakes and spent eight years running the PTA because no one else wanted to and I listened to reading and I helped with homework right up to A-level, I even taught myself German because Zoe was doing it, and I drove them to university interviews from St Andrews to Sussex and – and this is how she repays me. Trying to kill herself.' Her hand shook. 'Hating me.'

What must it be like, to be the object of twenty years of someone's daily work, left overnight under wet cloths, sculpted, smoothed, adjusted, polished until you are found ready for display? I find much for which to blame my mother but at least she never took me to a piano lesson. Perhaps I shouldn't have tried to make Raph join the chess club. I thought about the silence of the Hôtel de la Mère, the way the beds are smoothed flat and the books lie waiting to be read and footsteps in the corridor are muffled, because mothers must be protected from disturbance more assiduously than any Victorian invalid with straw on the road outside. 'Judith, I don't think she's trying to kill herself. There are more direct ways.' And I have counted them out like hoarded coins. 'Whatever she's doing, she's doing to herself, not to you. Maybe you need to find ways of letting her go.'

'I wouldn't have any problem letting her go if there were

any signs that she could or would look after herself. She's no readier to leave home than Moth is. At least he'll eat when he needs to.'

There was a bump upstairs, the screech of wood on damp wood as the old sash window in the attic opened, and, at least in my mind, the flutter of wings across the dark garden and out into the starry night.

'Giles,' I said. 'There was a bird stuck in the chimney.'

'Brian was never around to deal with things like that.'

My tea cooled. When she went, I would get the wine out again. 'Birds are Giles's thing. The idea makes my skin crawl.'

The window banged closed again.

'Have you thought about counselling?' I asked. Anna Freud blamed mothers for 'feeding disturbances', which were resolved by institutional care, but she was also keen to liberate adolescents from their parents. It sometimes seems that the best thing mothers might do for children is to stay away. They will have enough trouble, the next generation, without us misshaping their minds.

'Brian says it's nonsense. Pseudo-science.'

'Brian doesn't have to do it.'

'I suppose not. He'd disapprove.'

She had not struck me as someone who cared much for anyone else's views.

'And you can't discuss it with him?'

Giles came in with a newspaper parcel in his hand. 'Oh, Judith. Hello.'

He glanced at me, a question.

'Judith came round for a cup of tea,' I said. 'What's in the newspaper?'

He grimaced. 'Dead bird, I'm afraid. Been there a while. I let the other one out.'

I felt sick. Raph's ghost, a bird dying slowly in the dark, fluttering and fading in the wall above his sleeping head. Are birds intelligent enough to resign themselves to death? Or does instinct keep them battering dulling feathers against the wall, scrabbling yellow feet on the stone hearth, until they can no longer move? And the second bird, trapped like the victim of a Gothic novel with the rotting corpse of its fellow.

'It's only a bird, Anna. You should put guards on the chimney if they bother you that much.' Judith looked restored by the bird's death, or by my horror.

'Back in a minute,' said Giles.

'It hasn't happened before.' I turned my mug so the handle pointed into the corner of the envelope, which had IMPORTANT, ACT NOW printed across the corner in Her Majesty's typeface. 'Raph heard it. He thought it was a ghost.'

'It must have happened before. This place is full of birds, they always nest in chimneys.'

'Not in August.' I stood up. 'Judith, I'm sorry, I'm very tired. I'm sorry I couldn't help you more about Zoe.'

She stayed where she was. 'I worry about her so much. You'll find out. You think it's hard when they're little but getting up in the night is nothing to this. You'll see.'

I picked up the mugs, hers still half full. 'Maybe you should talk to someone who's been through it. There must be support groups.'

She tossed her head. 'I don't need a support group, thank you.'

'OK. Good. Judith, I'm going to bed now. Good night.'

'What?' she said. 'Oh, sorry. Good night.'

I went upstairs, and when I peered down over the banisters she was still sitting at the table, head bowed, holding on to a brown envelope as if it would keep her afloat.

'So did it fly away? Mummy, have we got peanut butter?'

I squatted down to rummage in the cupboard, and knocked my head as I saw Moth climbing over the bar of his highchair and down its stylish Scandinavian steps (made from sustainably harvested wood by people who may not own the means of production but enjoy better parental leave entitlements and childcare subsidies than anywhere else in the known universe).

'Moth helping find it jam.'

'I don't want jam, I want peanut butter.'

Zoe took a second slice from the toaster. 'In Canada people put jam on peanut butter.'

Moth pushed against me. 'Hello, jam! Hello, syrup!'

'Mummy, can we have syrup instead?'

'No,' I said. 'I've found some peanut butter. It's out of date, though.'

'Moth have a date?'

'Not that kind of date, love.'

'Can we eat it anyway? Can I try it with jam?'

'Moth have a raisin?'

'It was grape jelly, in Canada. Not really jelly, though.'

'Was it nice?' asked Raph.

'The first American conference I went to I ate peanut butter on bagels for five days.' I stood up, jar in hand. 'I had a grant for the hotel but it didn't cover food.'

'Not as nice as peanut butter with Marmite,' said Zoe, chewing. 'Though not much is. Mum says it's disgusting.'

'I can see that that would make it desirable,' I said. I opened the peanut butter. It smelt quite ordinary, and the oil on top should be preservative. 'I can't see why we shouldn't eat this. I can't imagine peanuts are very corruptible.'

'Moth up and see!'

I picked him up. 'But I think the only jam is Julia's gooseberry. You can try it if you like.'

'Yes, please.'

'Moth try a gooseberry!'

'Mum makes gooseberry jam. With elderflowers.' Zoe's nose wrinkled as if she'd smelt a bad nappy. 'She puts it in jars with like *frills* on them and *gives* them to people.'

'How kind,' I said firmly.

335

'Why?' Raph swirled his milk around in the cup with his finger.

'Don't do that, love.'

'Moth try it jam!'

I gave Moth a spoonful of jam, which surprised him so much he stopped talking. We heard the bluebottle buzz of Giles's phone.

'I'll get it!' Raph flung himself off his chair, as if he'd been in hourly expectation of a job offer or marriage proposal for some days.

The peanut butter had the texture of clay, but held together the bread, which had been dry and crumbly to start with and was now also stale. I smeared brown jam on top.

'Can I have some?' asked Zoe.

'Moth have some!'

'Zoe, of course. Moth love, you're too little for peanuts. Would you like more jam?' Recent research suggests that toddlers who encounter peanuts are less likely to develop allergies than those protected in accordance with current policy, but the consensus is still that the good mother should deny peanuts to the under-threes, presumably because despite increasing the risk of anaphylactic shock in small children this deprives mothers of one of the few sources of protein to involve nothing more housewifely than opening a jar.

Moth stiffened on my hip. 'No. Some of Zoe's.'

Zoe looked up, toast in mid-air.

'Oh, all right then.' Would you rather be bad in the eyes of an imaginary Health Visitor or in those of your wrathful toddler?

Raph came back, holding the phone out in front of him like rotting fish. 'It's that policeman. You gave Zoe my toast!'

'Actually, it's my toast,' said Zoe. 'And I'm sharing it with Moth anyway. Which policeman?'

I took the phone and looked at her. 'Raph, yours is here.'

I put my finger in my other ear and went out into the hall, trusting Zoe to call me in the event of anaphylaxis.

'Mrs Cassingham.'

'Dr Bennet, actually.'

'Mrs Cassingham, we're closing the file on the remains from your garden. I thought you would like to know that the remains are indeed historical.'

Of course they're bloody historical, even I could see that they're not prehistoric.

'Oh. Do you have a date for them?'

'They are historical,' he repeated. 'I regret the oversight, but I'm sure you understand that we have more urgent business. We won't need to trouble you any more. Unless, of course, there should be any further concerns about the boys.'

There was a small crash from the kitchen. 'Oh bugger a milk. Zoe mop it.'

'Further concerns?' I was, I found, not scared of him any more, maybe not as scared as I should be.

'Let us hope not. Goodbye, Mrs Cassingham.'

I went back to the children. It was only what I'd known all along, but I felt as if there were more room in my ribcage, as if the clouds were clearing from a rainy sky. As if I'd been absolved of some of my sins.

Zoe looked up from the floor, where she was blotting spilt milk with an old *Guardian*. 'Moth's milk fell. There doesn't seem to be any more.'

I sat down and lifted Moth on to my lap. 'There probably isn't. Raph, Ian MacDonald was phoning to tell us about the baby.'

He froze. Moth reached for Raph's toast and then pushed it away.

'That Raph's toast,' Moth told himself. 'That not Moth's toast. No.'

'We were right, Raph. She's from long ago. Way back, when things were very different.'

He pulled at his toast and the peanut butter glue along the faultlines failed. 'She still died. Even long ago.'

'Yes,' I said. 'Nothing will change that. Everyone long ago died.'

'And one day we'll be long ago and we'll be dead.'

'Yes,' I said. 'We will, one day.'

Moth rubbed his jammy face on my top. 'Moth be dead?'

I stroked his satin hair, his sticky cheek. 'One day. Yes. Not for a long time.'

Raph picked up some peanut butter. 'When you're old and you come to the end of your life. And Zoe. And Mummy and Daddy. And Grandma. Like Grandpa Hugo.'

Zoe was circling her forearm with the thumb and finger of the other hand. 'Like my grandma, too. Anna, what's this about? Which baby?'

'Raph and I found an infant skeleton when we were planting apple trees.' I kissed Moth's head. 'People do turn things up, round here. It was much more densely populated than it is now for most of recorded time. But of course you still have to call the police when it's human remains.'

'Oh,' she said. She finished her toast. 'But it's all sorted now. Can I have another cup of tea?'

I poured it for her.

'Anna?'

'Yes.'

'Uh, Anna, look. Can I ask you something?'

I looked up. How much I weigh? Why Raph's clothes are tattered? 'Probably.'

She ran her forefinger around the top of the mug. 'Could I, I mean, if I do go to Austria, could I maybe like kind of stay with you until then? I mean, just for an extra couple of weeks or something? And then I'd go home and pack and everything. I mean, sorry. I probably shouldn't have said. Dad told me not to ask you.'

'Yay!' Raph beamed at her. 'Zoe staying with us!'

Moth waved damp toast, from which he had licked the jam. 'Hooray.'

'Oh, Zoe. We'd love to have you, of course. But – listen, we can't rescue you from your parents. As far as your mum's concerned, we're just the people who run the cottage. Isn't there a friend you can stay with? You don't know that you're going to Austria yet, do you?'

She bit her lip. 'It's going to work out. I know it is. But – please don't make me go back with Mum. I mean – please.'

She sniffed. Raph was watching her unblinkingly, as if she were demonstrating some skill that he believed to be vital to growing up.

'I thought things were going better.' I scooped peanut butter off Moth's chin with my finger and offered it back to him. 'I thought she was trying to be more understanding. She was scared, you know, when you collapsed.'

'Why?' asked Raph. 'Why was Judith scared?'

'Because Zoe was ill.'

Zoe drank some tea. 'Not really. Come on, Anna. Understanding? Understanding someone else? My mother? She doesn't do understanding.'

No, I thought. No. I am not good enough at this, at relationships and nurturing people and giving of myself. And in fact, really, when I have to take sides, when push comes to shove, I'm not willing to betray Judith, to steal the daughter she's worked on all these years. Zoe needs to leave, not to be rescued by a proxy mother. Having parents may not be in anyone's best interest but we all must do it. And it is Giles's job, not Zoe's, to look after our children while I work, a fact which he may at last be coming to recognize.

I touched her shoulder. 'Zoe, in lots of ways it would be lovely for me too. I enjoy your company and of course I'm grateful for your help with the children, it's the only way I've managed any work at all since you came. But, look—' I glanced at the children, Raph listening as if memorizing every word for later analysis, Moth scraping peanut butter off his toast with his finger. 'Look, let's just say yours isn't the only family with some – some aspects that need addressing, OK? There might be other people who are also – well, negotiating responsibilities.'

'Oh.' She wilted over her tea. 'Sorry.'

'Mummy, what are you talking about?' asked Raph.

'Zoe's plans for the rest of the summer.'

'We're going home at the weekend.' She picked crumbs off her plate with a licked finger.

'Zoe, have some more if you're hungry. And come and see us in Oxford, OK, when you're back for Christmas? Who knows, maybe we'll make it out to Vienna. For the Christmas market or something.' Maybe, though since we have discussed this plan at least twice in each of the eight years the Friedmanns have been there and never got as far as looking at flights, I doubt it. We will be in Oxford, our horizons physically bounded by the railway, the river and the M40, but in fact seeing no further than the walled college gardens, for the rest of our lives.

I went up to the anchorite's cave when Moth went to sleep, leaving Zoe and Raph assembling a toy airport and taking Giles's phone. There were at least three books I should have been reading, and one I should have been writing, but I wanted to stand where she stood and see the sea and sky through her holy eyes. I thought on the way up there that it couldn't have changed much, that a thousand years were less than the flight of a sparrow in the geological life of rock and water, but when I got there I saw that I was wrong. There were three cargo ships between Colsay and the horizon, the red and white-striped lighthouse on the Shepsay skerries, the jetty with our fibreglass boat poking out into the grey sea in front of the ruined village. I sidled down the grassy slope to the entrance of her cave, which is really more of a crevice. No Stone Age family would have contemplated it as a desirable residence, and I cannot quite convince myself that she never went home

340

for Christmas or at least – mindful of my own experiences of going home for Christmas – retreated to a nearby sheepfold or one of the stone igloos, grain cists, which the islanders used as food stores for most of the last millennium.

I sat where she would have sat and peered down between my feet. The cliffs were spattered with birdshit, and white flowers waved like bunting from some of the ledges. A few gulls drifted past, but the tenements of nests were deserted, whether through seasonality or ecological mishap I could not tell, and there was no cacophony of birds, no calls between mates or infant demands or maternal upbraiding. The anchorite, I realized, had not lived alone but, at least in spring, in the middle of an avian city. Rubbish and bits of driftwood crawled like insects through the waves washing the cliffs' feet. The cave was damp, though supplied with enough fresh air that it was never going to smell of anything. She must have slept on heather, which is almost certainly more comfortable than the ancestral Cassingham horsehair mattresses, and if she wasn't supplied with the heaviest wool blankets I doubted she'd have lasted long enough to form the basis of a legend.

'Knock knock.'

Giles. 'Who's there?' I said.

'Arthur.'

'Arthur who?'

'I've no idea, Raph couldn't remember the punchline. I thought I saw you heading up here. May I come in?'

I moved over. The anchorite was debarred as much by logistics as chastity from entertaining gentleman visitors.

'Is Zoe looking after the kids?'

'No, I left them with Brian. Of course Zoe's looking after the kids. But I need to go back in a minute, it's time Moth was waking up. Unless you're volunteering, of course.'

His gaze rested on the cargo ships, which were inching towards each other like snails. 'Can't. Not today. Listen, Anna, when I was getting the birds out of the chimney?'

I shivered. 'Yes?'

'I found something.'

Another death. 'Giles, do I want to know about this?'

'It's a packet. Brown paper and string. It's full of letters.'

'What kind of letters? Why didn't you tell me?'

'Judith was there. And then you were asleep. They've been opened. With stamps but no postmarks. Penny stamps. Red. Mostly to an address in Manchester. I didn't look inside.'

The ships met, became one. 'You mean they're Victorian? Victorian letters?'

He shrugged, still watching the ships, waiting for them to draw apart and prove that there had been no collision. 'Your field not mine. Old handwriting, and red penny stamps.'

I stood up. 'Where are they? Do you mind if I go back and look at them now?'

He looked as if I'd pushed him. 'I'd like to see too. I mean, it's my family.'

'Is it?' The cargo ships uncoupled. 'Cassingham letters?'

'I don't know. They're in my box. But wait for me, OK? And we can look together.'

Victorian letters had postmarks. It sounded as if these hadn't been sent, as if they'd been aborted between stamping and posting. And then opened.

'Mummy,' said Raph. 'Mummy, are we having whole onions? And Moth's eating a worm.'

Mortality avenged. I thought I would rather let him finish a worm out of my sight than have to deal with a half-eaten one. Raph was right: I had tipped the onions from the chopping board into the pan but forgotten to cut them up. I picked them out, warm and slimy with oil.

'Well, can you tell him to stop? I hope he's not short of protein.'

'You should have given him more peanut butter,' said Raph. 'What are you making?'

342

The onions skidded about as I attacked them with one of Julia's old bone-handled knives. 'I don't know,' I admitted. 'But it usually starts with onions. I think there's a tin of chickpeas in the cupboard. If not, we're a bit sunk.'

He turned back at the door. 'We can find some more worms, I suppose.'

'Not much good if you're vegetarian,' I pointed out. 'Anyway, it hasn't come to that.'

'I was only saying.'

'I know.' There were not only the chickpeas but a tin of clams, though perhaps better not to think about worms at the same time. 'But there's always the chippy in Colla if things get that bad.' We could leave Giles to the locally harvested organic worms and go eat southern-fried battery chicken with our fingers and leave the bones in Andrex-coloured polystyrene shells.

He paused again. 'Do vegetarians eat fish?'

Yes, I thought, invariably. Fish fingers are in fact a vegetable. I found the tin opener but there were no tomatoes. 'Most of the ones I know do. Now can you run and check what Moth's up to?'

Giles's eyes widened at the sight of his plate but he said nothing, as befitted someone who came in late to find a meal on the table, and wielded his fork as one trained on the playing fields, or at least dining halls, of Eton. Moth picked out the chickpeas and ate them with his fingers and then demanded biscuits, which Giles thought we hadn't bought, and Raph objected to the murder of clams but faced the rest with more spirit than I found I could muster.

'Not hungry?' asked Giles.

'Maybe not hungry enough,' I admitted.

His mouth twitched but he took another mouthful before he put his fork down. 'Anna, my love, was there any motive but desperation for this combination?'

I poked at the mound on my plate. It looked like the vomit of some bottom-feeding fish, only drier.

'Mummy,' said Raph. 'Is this the nastiest thing you've ever given us?'

'I don't know,' I said. 'Giles, what about your thirtieth birthday cake?' Bicarbonate of soda, I demonstrated to our assembled friends on that occasion, is not the same thing as baking powder, and the eighteenth-century household manual that suggested the exchange of milk and vinegar for buttermilk was either wrong or an example of the historical specificity of certain forms of material culture. Furthermore, if you replace the butter in 'buttercream' with an olive-oil-based margarine and fail to sieve icing-sugar of uncertain vintage the result will not mask the former misjudgements. Subsequent birthdays have been celebrated by courtesy of Marks & Spencer for the children and the Patisserie Maison Rouge in Summertown for Giles, enterprises after all founded on their ability to exceed amateur culinary efforts at a competitive price. Nobody provides a cake for me, although every year Giles and Raph express their surprise and regret when one does not materialize.

Giles considered. 'No, I think Raph's right. This is worse. Darling Anna, may I make you something else?'

'Oh, you may,' I said. 'Any time, Giles. Every time. Be my guest. The question, if you look in the cupboards, is whether you can.'

'Oh.' Giles pushed his chair back and knelt at the cupboard's mouth. Raph slid down and squatted beside him, as if they were peering into the lair of a potentially edible animal.

'Mummy, biscuit!' said Moth.

'How about some fruit? A nice banana?'

'Banana hates me. Chocolate?'

'No, love. Not for dinner.'

Giles sat back. 'What's in the freezer?'

'About twenty-five gallons of your mother's home-made stock. And it's too dark to go to Colla for fish and chips.'

'I wasn't thinking of going to Colla for fish and chips. I'll make something, OK?'

'Remember to leave some stock for your mother's next visit.'

Moth yawned and I gathered him in my arms and cuddled him. It was eight o'clock.

'I might go put Moth to bed while you do that. I don't think he's going to eat anything we've got.'

I let Moth swim his plastic cows around the bath until he noticed that the water had cooled and asked to come out, and then set a regrettable precedent by reading all of *The Big Alfie and Annie Rose Storybook* as well as *The Tale of Jemima Puddleduck* and a chilling little parable about some owlets whose mummy flies away. Eight circuits of 'Hush, Little Baby' and I was free, though I hung over the cot for a while, watching his eyelashes settle on the curve of his cheek and his fingers loosen on his bear. The landing outside was already dark; you can feel the earth tilting away from the solstice here, towards the dark weeks of winter, even before the back-to-school flurries of yellowing leaves at home. I could hear the hammering of knife on chopping board downstairs (would I be a better cook if I made more noise about it?) and Raph asking a question.

I went into our bedroom. There was still a pink glow coming through a rift in the dark cloud in the west, and enough light in the room that I didn't need to acknowledge what I was doing by flicking a switch as I moved towards Giles's box. The wind moved through the tree outside, which was already losing its leaves, but the sea was quiet. I opened the lid. The package lay on top, just as he said. Worn brown paper soft as skin and sandy with soot, tied like a Christmas parcel with hard string. Giles had pushed one quadrant of string aside and unfolded the top. I slid the letters out on to the bed, about a dozen of them. The writing on the front was too fine to read in the dusk, although I could see that there were several different addressees, and I could barely tell the colour of the stamps, which were colder and shinier to my fingertips than the weave of expensive envelopes. No postmarks, and the envelopes ragged where they had been ripped open. It was unusual, in the nineteenth century, not to have a paper-knife to hand. Some were much heavier than others, fat with old news.

Condensation trickled down the kitchen window, leaving a trail of dark sky and stars. There were three pans on the stove, and the smell of fish.

'Raph?' I said. 'Raph, love, shouldn't you be going to bed?'

He looked up from the table, where he appeared to be doing the *Guardian* crossword. 'I haven't had supper yet.'

'Not much longer!' said Giles. He'd found a butcher's apron somewhere and there was an invisible chef's toque on his head.

I looked round. 'Who's doing the washing up?'

Giles sashayed past me with a device which I believe chops parsley when the handle is wound. I do not think there has ever been parsley on Colsay.

'Don't be a spoilsport. It'll all be worth it in the end.'

I began to scrape the fish-sick I'd made earlier off the plates and into the bin, which required dexterity because the bin bag had technically been full since Giles's breakfast tealeaves. I filled the sink.

'Mummy, what's a divorce petitioner?'

'What Daddy's going to be if he makes me clear up,' I muttered. 'Er, someone who doesn't want to be married any more.'

He put the pen down. 'Why?'

It seemed unreasonable to have to have this conversation without the excitement of an actual divorce.

'I suppose because – because occasionally things go wrong and people don't notice until it's too late to sort them out.'

Giles looked up.

Raph clicked the biro up and down. 'What sort of things? Why does that mean people want to stop being married?'

I went over and leant against Giles, who put his arm round

346

me. 'Oh, I don't know. All sorts of things. One person can think that things are unfair but the other person won't listen. Or one person could be very sad about something and the other person could be too busy to notice. Things like that can be sorted out if the people like each other and they see what's happening in time to make it better. But if it goes on and on I suppose they can forget why they got married in the first place.'

Giles's arm tightened and he kissed my hair. I rubbed my head against his shoulder. He smelt of Giles, clean with notes of grass and wind, and his fisherman's jersey was unravelling at the holes in the elbow. He reached round to stir one of his pans.

Raph sketched a space ship in the margin of the crossword, as if reminding himself of where he came from. 'When Rosie Roberts' parents got divorced she said it was because her dad was shagging someone else.'

'Raph!'

Giles's shoulders shook as he turned back to the stove.

'What?'

'Er – we don't use words like that. Oh, never mind. Look, put the paper away and help me set the table, OK?'

It was past eleven when Raph went to bed.

'I'll wash up in the morning,' said Giles.

'Yeah, right.'

He paused, the pile of plates unsteady in his hand. 'I always used to wash up in the morning. I used to wash up while you had your bath. Remember?'

It was true. Before any of us could really afford it, people used to bring good wine for Giles's cooking, and, before any of us had the babysitter's meter ticking away in our minds all evening, people used to stay late. Giles sometimes ran a bath for me before I woke, and by the time I emerged pink and in search of coffee our rented Formica kitchen looked like an illustration from a 1970s *Good Housekeeping*.

'*Used* to wash up,' I said.

He put the plates down and came over to me. 'I know. Sorry.'

'Sorry I forgot that your maternity leave ended months ago, sorry I forgot that you have a career too, sorry I've been systematically dismantling your intellectual life until you don't recognize yourself any more, or just sorry for making you take over the kitchen and then belittling your best efforts?'

He reached out for me and I pushed him away. 'Or maybe sorry for acting as though sex makes up for everything?'

He turned and stared out of the window. The condensation had cleared, adding to the mould round the window frame, and I could see him staring back at himself. 'All of that. Anna, I'm sorry.'

I picked up the plates and put them by the sink. I knew he would never speak to me the way I had just spoken to him. I could have counted off my next words on my fingers. 'I'm sorry I didn't care about your grieving. I'm sorry I've been rude about you to the kids. I'm sorry – I'm sorry I've been so resentful.'

He didn't turn round. 'And we're in time to make it better?'

I went and stood beside him. Our reflections gazed back from the orchard, where the apple trees stood black against the dark sky, showing signs of neither life nor death. I put my arms round him, pressed my face against his rough wool back.

'Yes,' I said. 'Yes. But it's probably time to start trying, wouldn't you say?'

Dear Lord Hugo and Miss Emily,

I write with sadness to resign my position here. The Grice child
was born five days ago, by night, and I was not called. I believe it is
not yet dead, but I am sorry to say that the coffin prepared by the
father will be of more use than the shawl that I, seeing no
preparations in hand for a living child, passed my evenings in
knitting; the infant ceased feeding three days ago and lies now stiff
and pale. There is another child expected on this island in March of
next year, but I have no confidence that the mother would accept
my ministrations even were I to pass the Spring here and devote
myself to befriending her.

Sir, if you wish to save the children of Colsay you must either
disband this people and send them into a land of progress and
forward-looking or, perhaps, send one of their number to be trained
at one of the great nursing schools in London or Edinburgh,
though I suspect the latter course, could you persuade any of these
women to pursue it and, harder yet, to return to the hardship and
filth of her native island having pursued it, would serve only to
alienate the chosen girl from her own kind. It is my deep
conviction that the only future for these people lies away from this
place.

I regret, also, that relations between myself and Mrs Barwick,
who was called to the birth, have not been friendly, and indeed I
have reason to complain of her conduct towards me in many
regards. I know, of course, that a lady's relationship with her

personal maid must of necessity be an intimate one, and further
that she must have given perfect satisfaction in that position to be
so maintained in later life, but I must inform you that, far from
being that help and support to me in this work that I had hoped,
there is all too much reason to believe that she has given to the
'knee-woman' (whose identity remains unknown to me) that
loyalty which, as your employee and even agent in this place, I had
every reason to expect.

I trust you will understand my desire, under the circumstances,
to depart immediately; I am told that the wind is such as to make it
unadvisable to launch a boat this morning but I am determined to
prevail upon the men to make it possible for me to take the Oban
steamer which leaves on Thursday, and I have yet, I believe,
sufficient means to induce them to do so.

Yours truly,

May Moberley

16

WHAT MAY BE FOUND WITHIN

In the quiet of the bedroom we raise the boxlid, and the skeletons are there. In the calm evening walk we see in the distance the suspicious-looking bundle, and the mangled infant is within. By the canal side, or in the water, we find the dead child. In the solitude of the wood we are horrified by the ghastly sight, if we betake ourselves to the rapid rail in order to escape the pollution, we find at our journey's end that the mouldering remains of a murdered innocent have been our travelling companion; and that the odour from that unsuspected parcel too truly indicates what may be found within.

– William Burke Ryan, 1862, quoted in Hilary Marland,
Dangerous Motherhood: Insanity and Childbirth in Victorian Britain
(Basingstoke: Palgrave Macmillan, 2004), p. xxx

They stood on the pavement watching as I started the car, Moth in Giles's arms looking at me as if I were chopping up Teddy or taking an axe to his cot, as if I were destroying all the things he had trusted me to protect. He was still as if sick, wide-eyed. I put the car into first gear and released the handbrake. It would have been easier if he'd cried, although when I saw a tear on Raph's cheek I thought maybe tears were worse.

'They'll be fine,' said Giles. 'You'll be fine. Don't think about us.'

I leant out of the window. 'I'll phone you, all right? Moth, love? You can talk to Mummy on the telephone. On Daddy's phone. And you'll probably be asleep when I get back on Wednesday but I'll come and see you. Giles, remember Moth needs Teddy to watch him having a bath. And you need to get milk before you head back.'

'I'll stay awake until you come back,' said Raph. He rubbed his sleeve across his eyes.

'I'll think about you all the time,' I promised. As if that would make any difference. 'Moth? You'll see me the day after tomorrow, OK? Mummy's coming back very soon.'

Moth hid his face on Giles's shoulder.

'Just go,' said Giles. 'You're only prolonging the performance. Come on, Raph, this is silly. When I was your age I was at boarding school.'

I put the gear lever back into neutral. Could the very small chance of getting this job be worth the psychological damage Giles might accomplish in forty-eight hours?

'You said you'd never say that to them,' I said. 'You said you'd never hit them and you'd never threaten them with boarding school.'

'Well, I've never hit them and I'm not threatening them. And you'll get anxious about missing your train if you sit here winding them up much longer.'

I checked the time. 'No, Giles, I'm miles too early.'

Raph sniffed. 'The car clock's still on Greenwich Mean Time, remember. You wouldn't let me change it.'

'But you do need to go,' said Giles. 'Go on. Mirrors, signal, manoeuvre. I'll talk to you later. Bye.'

Raph waved, but Moth didn't raise his head as I drove away, watching him in the rear-view mirror. I drove past Spar, between the parked cars along the village street and out past the library. The road widened, a reel unwinding in front of me across the green hillside, but I drove slowly, the engine hesitating as we came to the hill. I could feel the cord, the filament, that joins me to Moth and Raphael, stretching and thinning and thinning. It is unnatural to go away from your own children. It hurts. I changed down a gear. Maybe I didn't want the job. It is a myth, anyway, that work makes us free. Why do I imagine that paid employment is the road to fulfilment? I checked the mirrors. Because I know that motherhood is not, that's why. Because Marx, who never asked what women want because it did not occur to him that it would be any different from what men want, who saw that equality extending to responsibilities as well as rights was the basis of a just society, is a better friend to me than Freud. The road levelled out and I accelerated across the moor.

The filament lay more lightly when I got to the station. Nobody refused to get out of the car until he'd finished the chapter, nobody got stuck trying to squeeze through the gap between the front seats while I was arguing with his brother, nobody lay on the pavement screaming because I wouldn't let him write on the car with the keys. I turned off the engine and there was silence. I didn't have to go round the back of the station to find the pushchair ramp or restrain small children from leaping on to the track while we waited for the attendant to conduct us across the lines because you can't get a pushchair over the footbridge. I walked up the stairs, bought myself a tuna sandwich and a bag of crisps, went back when I remembered that it is possible for a solitary adult to carry cups of hot coffee as well as lunch and a bag, arranged myself on the platform as far as possible from the parents with a double buggy and a school-age child who was already jumping off the benches and trying to chase pigeons on to the track, and when the train arrived, auspiciously on time, boarded it without squabbles about who pressed the button to open the doors, who set his foot first into the carriage and whether the toy car had fallen down the gap. I did not have to judge close enough proximity to a toilet to allow me to leave Raph *in situ* while changing Moth's nappy and yet distant enough to prevent Raph making unnecessary visits for the sake of novelty plumbing. I awarded myself a window seat at an empty table where I intended to sit quietly with my laptop for the next four and a half hours. It was, I thought, already worth the effort of applying for the job.

The train jolted and the grey stone streets of Inversaigh began to slide away. Most of the gardens backing on to the railway had plastic slides and the sort of sandpit that cats interpret as a toilet. A more optimistic woman than I am was hanging out washable nappies with one hand while holding a baby of about eight months in the other. Alexander Buchan's mother must have had to do that, day after day, drying them over the stove most of the time. Which, I wondered, discounting such trivia as antibiotics and the welfare state, is the best invention of the twentieth century, the washing machine or the pill?

Houses ceded to fields, and then hills with the bracken already turning bronze, interrupted by a rectangle of Forestry Commission pine trees, dark and spiky as any of the woods in the fairy tales Raph won't listen to. They should be back on the island now, and should have no reason to cross the Sound again until I came back. Giles should be able to distract Moth from my absence, if he thought to try. If he didn't let his eyes slide towards the newspaper, or his computer, and ignore the children's questions. I have heard Raph ask Giles the same question, admittedly about the inner workings of a certain kind of 1970s space suit, twelve times without an answer better than a grunt, and Moth is more easily discouraged than that, might in fact give up on language altogether if left in Giles's care for too long. Where Mummy, he would ask. Where Mummy and where Mummy and where Mummy, and when Giles didn't answer he'd think I'd gone, left him as I have so often longed to do. My eyes filled and I took out my phone, dialled. I stared out of the window, waiting for Giles to pick up. If they were upstairs, he wouldn't hear it on the mantelpiece. Reception is unreliable, though I imagine it to be influenced by the weather, which was a perfectly ordinary British grey. Eight, nine. Raph usually hears it. Eleven, twelve. Hello, this is the voicemail of Giles Cassingham. I ended the call. The train was climbing, following the line

of a rust-coloured river across the heather. A tall bird rose from
the water and flapped away, legs dangling. Giles was probably
just changing Moth's nappy, or maybe they were on the beach
or – or – would a person's phone ring if it were underwater? Is
what the caller hears the actual sound made by the other handset or some kind of electronic substitution? I could send a text,
but since I refuse to write anything that doesn't have correct
syntax and punctuation it takes me longer to compose text messages than it would to catch and train a carrier pigeon, and
anyway Giles wouldn't reply. There was probably just no reception on Colsay today. They were probably fine.

I opened my laptop. The Reverend's endless citations of the
Highland Commission report had at last led me to look it up,
something I would have done as soon as I suspected that Eve
might have been born and buried in the nineteenth century if
I'd known, as any historian should, that it existed. I'd found it
online, digitized by the Gaelic further education college, and I
thought I would have a quick look to see if it included anything
about Colsay before I revised the conference paper on children
and public space which I was planning to recycle as an interview presentation. My document files were superimposed on a
picture of the children on the swings by the river in Oxford, the
only picture I've seen in which they are both smiling. I think I
chose it as wallpaper because it is the sort of picture that someone who would rather be with her children than working would
use. Maybe Giles had taken them for lunch at the pub before
they went home, in which case they might be in the boat now,
where I'd much rather Giles didn't answer his phone. I opened
the Highland Commission report, and then my phone rang.

'Giles.'

'You rang. Is everything OK?'

We were high up now, crossing the bare moor like a ship on
the open sea.

'I just wanted to remind you to bring the laundry in. Because
of the rain.'

I heard Moth singing 'Little Boy Blue' in the background.

'Oh, is it raining where you are?'

No. 'Just started when I rang you. And I remembered the laundry.'

Giles started laughing. 'Anna, the laundry's in the kitchen. Where it always is.'

'Is it? I thought I put it out.'

I heard Raph. 'Daddy, can I talk to Mummy?'

'We're all fine,' said Giles. 'Here's Raph.'

'Mummy, do you want to hear my idea. If aeroplanes flew in formation like birds, they'd use less energy, wouldn't they? And we've already got air-traffic controllers so they could move the planes from one formation to another, only the airlines would have to take turns who went at the front because that one would use more fuel than the ones behind, and you'd probably need some new safety features to keep them the right distance apart. Mummy, Moth wants the phone.'

'Moth pressing a buttons!'

The call ended.

I woke my computer. I hoped Giles knew that now mobile phones recognize both 112 and 999, the chances of a toddler calling the emergency services are even higher than they were in Raph's infancy. I hoped he knew the importance of calling someone else as soon as one has apologized to the emergency services, to prevent the toddler using redial to repeat the offence. I finished my coffee and opened my laptop.

Highland Commission, Colla, Tuesday 17th May, 1888

James McPhee, Crofter, examined

For how long have you been a crofter?
I have been paying rent twenty-eight years at Michaelmas.

Have you lived on the island of Colsay for all of that time?
Yes. Except I was away for the fishing sometimes.
Away where?
Out of Aberdeen.
You lived in Aberdeen?
I went for the winters, to earn a little.
So the crofting does not keep you and your family?
Not in itself, no. Not now.
Have you and your family ever been able to live on the croft?
Not without the greatest hardship.
How large is your family?
There are seven of us in the house, including four children under eight.
Do the children do well? Are they warm and well nourished?
They are no worse than the neighbours' children.
Are they warm and well nourished?
No. No, I cannot say that they are.
When did you last eat flesh meat in your house?
I cannot tell. We have never had flesh meat.
What do the children eat?
We can buy a little meal in the spring but it is only from Mr Dunnet's goodwill that we have credit there.
Mr Dunnet owns the store in Colla?
Yes.
And you have debts there?
We try to pay what we can.
Do the children have milk?
No. We have no cow.
Are there cows on the island?
Yes. But they belong to Henryson.
Henryson is Lord Cassingham's factor?
Yes.
Did you ever keep a cow?
My father had a cow. Before the pastureland was taken from us.

And did the children have milk in those days?
Yes. The children did better then. I remember it.
Mr Henryson took the pastureland from you?
From my father. From all of us.
And was there any reduction in the rent at that time?
Rather an increase.
He reduced your land and increased your rent?
Yes.
Why did he do that?
I do not wish to answer that. I cannot tell another
man's reasons.
*That is a shame. Do you fear any consequences of speaking the
truth here?*
I do not wish to find a fire in my house at Michaelmas.
I cannot speak to the distress of my people without
also speaking to the cruel ways of certain persons.
*It is your impression that stating your independent opinion would
expose you and your family to danger from the landlord or his
representatives?*
I have heard of others so served.
*Mr Henryson is not here, and we are not empowered to
offer you any assurances on his behalf or that of Lord
Cassingham, but I will tell you that it is our sincere hope, as
representatives of Her Majesty's government, that every man
should feel free to tell us the truth without fear of reprisals
from those with power over him, and that we express that
hope most freely to your landlord and to his agents. That
being said, do you wish to give further evidence to this
commission?*
I will continue, yes.
Do the children have blankets for their beds?
No. Not even hay, this year, for we could not grow
enough grass for an ass to bite. They are sleeping
under the sacks from last year's meal.
Your harvest is less than last year?

It cannot be termed a harvest. A three-years child
could gather it in a day.
Do the children attend school?
Sometimes. When they have clothes to their back and
the burn is not in spate.
They have to cross the burn to reach the school?
Yes. It is safe enough in the summer.
There is no bridge?
It was swept away last year.
Did the children used to be schooled more regularly?
We had no school until the Education Act.
But you are a literate man?
I can read and write.
And your grandchildren?
I cannot say that they can.

I sat back. Pale sun glinted off black water broken by grey
rock, and scree-covered slopes rose so steeply from the water
that it seemed as if the vibrations from the passing of the train
should send boulders cascading into the loch. It must be very
deep, that dark water, its surface barely rippling because the
hill blocks the wind off the open sea. I imagined groups of
people picking their way across this land towards ships waiting to take them across the Atlantic, people huddled in worn
cotton clothes because they couldn't keep sheep and spin wool
any more, toddlers whining and refusing to walk and the old
slowing everyone down until it seemed that even the young
and fit would die in the rain and wind before they reached a
makeshift shelter.

The train turned inland, along an empty valley. A bird of
prey hovered in the white sky as if hung from the ceiling of an
art gallery. There was part of a dry stone wall scribbled with
yellow lichen, and then a scattering of stone that might once
have been a habitation, for people or for sheep.

359

Alexander M'Caskill, Crofter

Do you pay road tax?

These ten years and more.

Is there a road on the island?

No.

Where is the nearest post-road?

To Inversaigh. There is no road in Colla.

So when you wish to transport goods or letters to the south, what means do you adopt?

We are obliged to carry on our backs whatever we would send, or pay the carriage.

Do you have a horse or ass?

No.

Do any of the crofters have such an animal?

No. We cannot keep cows and are not likely to try such a thing.

Do you pay for a doctor also?

Yes.

There is no doctor on the island? Is there a doctor at Colla?

No. At Inversaigh.

And you have no nurse?

No. A girl was sent some years ago, but she did not stay.

Is the doctor able to get to Colsay when you have need of him?

Perhaps. If the ground is not too wet and the weather fit for a passage across the Sound.

But you wish for the services of a doctor?

We wish for a road, or at least not to pay for a road that we do not have.

And have you expressed this wish to the landlord?

To his factor. To Mr Henryson.

What was his response?

That we might stay or go, just as we pleased. That if we thought we might do better elsewhere we were

360

quite at liberty to depart as soon as we should have
paid our debts.

How many people now occupy the land?

There are now twenty-five crofting families here, and
perhaps ten cottars.

*And have these families come here by natural multiplication or by
immigration from elsewhere?*

They were moved here from the land at Killantilloch
and Shepsay when those places were cleared.

They did not choose to come here?

No. No one would choose to come here, with the land
so poor and the living so hard. Their houses were
burnt over their heads if they did not leave. A great
many went to Canada and into the south, but those
who remained, who would perhaps be mostly the older
and weaker of the people, were sent here and our
crofts divided with them.

And your rents were not reduced at this time?

Our rents were increased.

Did you object to this increase?

Some of us did.

Did the landlord hear your objections?

He offered our passage to Canada if we did not like
our situation here.

But you did not choose to go to Canada?

We had mixed reports from those who had gone. We
want only to be able to subsist on our own lands where
we have always been.

Why would you not want to get out? He was describing people
with nothing to lose, in a situation which they themselves
acknowledged could not get worse. I would have tied Moth to my
back and taken Raph by the hand and headed for Glasgow and
then New York. The train slowed. A road cut across the bracken
on the hillside, and then there was another wall, a terrace of

361

stone houses. We stopped, the doors opened to let in the smell of outdoors, heather and diesel, and closed. We trundled on.

James Logan, Schoolmaster

You are the schoolmaster at Colsay? How long have you been there?
Five years.
Have you taught in other places before this?
Yes. I was under-master in Lennoxtown outside Glasgow.
And would you say that your scholars here are better or worse than there?
I am afraid that they are worse. They are for the most part very slow children.
Is Gaelic used in the teaching in the school?
No. I have no Gaelic.
But the children speak English?
They appear to understand it very well.
Are they able to speak it?
Most of them can say enough when they wish.
They are able to speak as they do in Gaelic?
I cannot speak to that, for I have no Gaelic myself.
Do they write in English?
A little. They are slow enough.
And to what do you attribute this?
To native habits. Laziness.
Have the parents expressed any desire for their children to learn in Gaelic?
They should rather be grateful that the children learn English.
Do you have such apparatus and equipment as you need? Maps, compasses, books and the like?
It is good enough. The children are not very apt for these things.

Do you see signs of poverty in the children's clothing? Do they
have shoes?
Their clothing is mostly very dirty.
They have shoes?
They go barefoot.
In winter also?
Yes.
In snow?
Yes.
Does this trouble you?
They are hardy enough.
Do they seem to you well nourished?
I cannot say. I do not see them at table.
They bring no lunch to school?
Perhaps they may. I suppose they must, for it is too far
for them to go home to dinner.
But you do not see their food?
It is not my position to meddle with such matters.
Would you say that they are, in material terms, better or worse
off than the Lowland children with whom you are familiar?
The Lowland children are not so hardy as these and
could ill endure what these have been accustomed to
from birth.
You would not have your own children live as these do?
I could not say. I am not a married man.

There were more houses now, concrete bungalows scattered
along a single-track road, some of them edged with barbed-wire
fences to contain rusting bits of agricultural equipment, car
chassis and barking dogs. Sheep grazed between the lots.
Giles, I think, might understand crofters' relationship with 'their
own land' better than I do. They had an alternative. Why, for
their children's sake, did they not take it? There is something
about land and human rootedness that I am not equipped to
understand.

363

John Barwick, Crofter

You have been delegated by your neighbours to attend this commission. You have heard this morning's evidence; is there anything you would like to add?

Only about the jetty or slipway. And I recall the nurse. It was my mother was charged with her board and lodging.

What is it that you wish to say about the jetty?

Only that there is a place where one could be built so we could be landing the fish. Many a time the men have spoken of it.

And have you discussed this with the landlord?

With his factor. And we were told it would not be worth the money.

Were the villagers offering to pay or were you asking the landlord to fund the works himself?

We were offering our labour. There are stones enough, it's only the cement would be wanting.

It would cost something to bring the cement in, would it not?

Yes. But we would bring it from Inversaigh ourselves if we must. It is not much we are asking for. And the fish would help us all to live.

You wanted to speak of the nurse?

Only to say that she did not help us. My mother, who is something of a nurse herself, although of course not trained in any way, spoke of her sometimes. She did not visit the women.

She was sent by Miss Cassingham, is that correct?

Yes. But she left after a few weeks and could not tolerate island life. She was drowned out in the Sound, along with the men she tempted beyond their judgement to take her across for the steamer.

Did the people call on her at all? Were her services required during the period of her residence?

I believe not. She was sent mostly to help the women in childbed but my mother told me that there were no births while she stayed.

She was never asked to treat any injuries or tend any sick children?

She did not stay long. There was little sickness that year, and of course the people preferred to consult my mother who had tended to them for many years.

It was suggested that the people's reluctance to avail themselves of her services resulted from the landlord's threatening rent rises or eviction if they did not comply. Have you heard anything about that?

My mother used to say so. It was believed the nurse was sent partly to see if we should be cleared to Canada or Australia. To report back.

And did she in fact make any such report?

No. Not that we knew on the island. If she had told Hugo Cassingham we should be evicted, I doubt we would all be here now.

So is it the belief of the present islanders that they would now welcome a trained nurse?

I cannot say. It is often the doctor is needed and cannot get to us.

It would perhaps be better to have a trained nurse living among you?

Perhaps if it were one of the island women. Not someone sent among us from outside.

You want the landlord to pay for the training of a local woman?

No, Sir. If we had our own crofts and our own land we could choose and pay a girl ourselves, do you see? Sir, we no more want to be always asking for things than Mr Henryson wants always to be giving; we want only to run our own affairs and spend the result of our own labours as we find best.

You wish to be able to buy the island from the landlord?

365

Of course we cannot do that. We would never be able
to do that. We only wish to say, that we are not
wanting to be given things for free, only to live on our
own lands in our own way as people do throughout the
kingdom.

Outside the window, the fields gathered speed.

'This service is now coming into Glasgow Queen Street. Please
make sure you take all personal belongings with you when you
leave the train.'

I looked up. My back and shoulders had stiffened as they
used to stiffen when I was regularly allowed to sit still and work
for hours at a time, and I realized the last landscape I'd
admired was somewhere west of Fort William, when I'd eaten
the last of the crisps. I slid my laptop into my bag, checked
that it wasn't crushing the padded envelope full of Victorian
letters that I shouldn't have brought with me, and stood at the
door watching as the city slowed down around me. People
stood waiting on the platform, people with whom one could
have conversations, people with heads full of ideas and worries
and hopes and wild imaginings, people carrying computers
that were also full of hopes and fears and fantasies, and books
written by old people and young people in Paris and New York
and Istanbul and Dakar, people listening to music from Detroit
and Delhi and Iceland, eating food grown in China and
processed in America and shipped through Germany. I
threaded through the crowd, brushing suits, silk jumpers, football strips, and out to the road where buses jostled in the sun,
taking people home to high-rise flats with lino floors, Victorian
terraces gentrified and otherwise, 1960s concrete bunkers
whose desirability is yet to be recognized in north London,
bay-windowed '30s semis where, thirty years ago, mothers in
aprons and fluffy slippers threatened their children with inven-
tive forms of violence and humiliation which were legal at the

366

time. I pushed my sleeves up, felt sunshine on my skin, and inhaled the dusty smell of the city in summer. Somewhere out there, also, was the house we would live in if I got the job, an eventuality that seemed more probable than it had when I boarded the train. They had sent a map with the letter inviting me for interview, as if the candidates weren't expected to have the kind of mobile phone that makes such skills as map-reading redundant, but I was in no particular hurry. I turned left and set off, following the crowd, who presumably had reason for going that way.

I found my hotel in good time to shower, change and lie on the bed watching television before going out to meet the interviewing panel and the other candidates over dinner. Oxford is useful for some things: the idea of competitive dining held no particular alarm. There was suddenly no further pleasure to be gained from standing in silence under hot water paid for by somebody else, even inhaling the shower gel that someone else had chosen for my use, and I climbed out on to a clean bathmat to wrap my hair in one clean towel and dry my body with another. I dropped both of these towels on the floor, choosing clean linen of one's own over polar bears every time, and then, remembering that the chambermaid probably never had her laundry done for her either, picked them up again. It would perhaps be even worse than being the only woman if the other candidates were child-free women who came from places with hairdressers. I wandered round the room naked, cooling down. Is it worse to meet or imagine the competition? I turned off the lights over the mirror and reminded myself under no circumstances to mention the children at dinner. The Hôtel de la Mère will have few mirrors, perhaps none at all.

There cannot have been many mirrors on Colsay, at least until the final decades of habitation. Our house probably contained the only one in the nineteenth century. Probably the

367

same mirror now over the fireplace in the sitting room had reflected the deeds of Giles's great-grandfather and his factor. I looked at the bedside clock. Giles should be getting the children's supper ready. I had left a pasta sauce in the fridge to save Giles having to juggle cooking and childcare. I picked up my phone and put it down again. Later, so he doesn't try to answer the phone while draining the pasta and answering questions about where Mummy and the software required to move 757s around the Himalayas in formation. I took my new, tissue-wrapped clothes out of their string-handled paper bags and decided against taking the tissue paper back to Colsay for arts and crafts projects. They were the kind of clothes to which price-labels are attached with thin satin ribbons rather than plastic tags, and I couldn't bring myself to throw away the ribbons. I stroked a cream silk shirt, which could never be worn within twenty metres of a child. I will, I thought, put my make-up on and straighten my back and imagine myself suspended by a hook on my head as instructed by the Pilates teacher, and perhaps I will not be invisible, will not be erased by the ghost of the pram in the hall. I had even bought a new bra, as if planning adultery rather than employment.

I wandered back into the bathroom to blow-dry my hair for the first time since the Canadian conference, hairdryers being, like vacuum cleaners, rather more distressing than ethnic cleansing in Raph's cosmology. Then I turned back the bedclothes and lay back to watch an episode of *Sex in the City* which I thought I might have seen the first time around, when laptops had square edges and mobile phones were big enough to make a plausible weapon. The lighting in the bathroom had also shown some faint scribbling at the corners of my eyes and the blow-drying revealed wings of grey under my temples that weren't there when we left Oxford. I opened the complimentary biscuits and thought that anyway, being middle-aged would probably be more fun than my early thirties have been;

368

I couldn't possibly have less sleep, our marriage would either get better or go away, and the children would without doubt get older. And perhaps I was about to usher in a new era of financial equality, which I would use to leverage all kinds of bargains. The wrinkles were not unbecoming and it is possible to have very elegant long grey hair. I would, I decided, standing up, taking my new tights out of the packet – the first tights for two years that would not have me hobbling with the astonishing pain of a big toe protruding through a hole all evening – without doubt rather go forwards than back. Which was just as well. I slid my arms into a charcoal coat-dress with black ruffles at the wrists, a dress so serious that it came with its own padded hanger and a silk lining that felt like scented oil on skin accustomed to Shetland wool and the scratching of irate children, met my own gaze in the mirror, and went out.

Next morning, I followed the secretary down the corridor. My heels on the wooden floor made a grown-up sound effect that I wasn't sure I could fulfil. I touched my hair, which I had pinned up in keeping with my decision to age with the grace of Virginia Woolf. Having abandoned my PowerPoint presentation, I had placed myself, wrinkles, new tights and all, in the spotlight. I was perhaps trusting too much to my hairpins. Virginia Woolf's knickers, I reminded myself, once fell down on Oxford Street and she stepped out of them and kept going, perhaps in the same spirit as, thirty years later, she walked into a fast-flowing river and did not swim. I tugged on my skirt, which was not tucked into my tights, and walked through the door and up to the lectern.

'I had planned to give you a version of the paper on children, class and social space that I gave at the History of Child-hood conference in London last year. However, during the summer I have found myself working on a different and unex-pected project, and as it came to fruition in the last few days it

369

seems to me now that this work, albeit unpolished, is the best example of my future research.

'I want to talk to you about an episode in the history of Colsay. As I know most of you know, Colsay is a small island to the south of the Inner Hebrides, inhabited from far prehistory until the early 1960s. The island was never cleared, but relations with the English family who have owned Colsay since the mid-nineteenth century have always been vexed. Colonial arrogance and native superstition have both been blamed for the practices that killed eighty-five per cent of the babies born on Colsay between 1860 and 1880 before they were a fortnight old, and the fact that both readings are possible offers a sharp illustration of the impossibility of untangling history and ideology.'

Zoe was right; there is nothing that has more impact on the terrors of the next generation than the way we tell the stories of the past. I heard myself talking about the politics of Scottish historiography. They were listening, though I hope I look as if I'm listening when I'm actually wondering if I should pick up more nappies on the way home. The head of department was making notes, though I sometimes write shopping lists while casting attentive glances at the speaker. Maybe it was a mistake, not to use PowerPoint. Too late now.

I told them, avoiding the first person, about how Eve's body was discovered, about the DNA test and the historical limits of the police investigation.

'The Cassinghams maintain a family tree which did not produce a baby of the right age at the right time, suggesting an illegitimate and perhaps covert birth. Nevertheless, there were a great many dead infants on Colsay during these years, as a result of infant tetanus, which was endemic on Colsay, as on St Kilda, the Westmann Islands to the south of Iceland and some villages in the Faroe Islands. All of these remote North Atlantic communities endured infant mortality rates in excess of sixty per cent for periods of several decades between 1840 and 1900. The two medical historians who have investigated this phenomenon remain unsure of the cause; these were all societies that relied heavily on the harvesting of seabirds, which were stored and butchered around the home, and the first doctors to work with these communities believed that the instruments traditionally used to sever the umbilical cord were contaminated with blood from the birds, or that the cord stump might be anointed with fulmar oil, but in fact testing of artefacts and dwelling sites found no tetanus from these sources. The best we can say is that something that was done at birth, almost certainly involving the treatment of the umbilical cord, on these islands and not elsewhere, caused the disease from which up to ninety per cent of newborns died slowly and painfully within the first ten days of life. The Parish Record shows a burial immediately following every birth on the island from 1871 to 1878, when a baby lived until the influenza outbreak of 1881.

'None the less, these were public tragedies, resulting in public burials in the churchyards. There was no reason why, in the ordinary course of things, a child who died of neonatal tetanus should be interred in an unmarked grave in the landlord's garden. Further research uncovered later tragedies involving babies on the island, but nothing that could plausibly result in this particular body in this particular place. And then a parcel of letters was found, hidden in the chimney of Colsay House.'

I reached into my bag and pulled out the envelope, gently tipped the letters, the envelopes flapping open, on to the white plastic table in front of me. They looked dirty there, like a display of evidence from a crime scene. Everyone craned forward, not at all like people who had been writing shopping lists and counting nappies. I held up the first of May's letters. *Dearest Allie, I had hoped to find a letter from you at Inversaigh.*

'These letters were written by May Moberley, the younger daughter of the artist Alfred Moberley and Elizabeth Sanderson, an early feminist campaigner who became a friend of the Pankhurst family. It is surprising that Faith Stanley's biography of Alfred Moberley makes little reference to May's adult life beyond stating that she trained as a nurse and practised in Manchester for several years, for the final events of May's life as they appear here are colourful. Most of these letters are addressed to Alethea, May's sister, who had just decided join the small band of British women training as doctors in Edinburgh, but several are to Aubrey West, a protégé of her father who had spent the summer of 1878 travelling in the Hebrides and whose paintings of Colsay featured in the Royal Academy exhibition the following year. West, who was intimate with the Moberley family, seems to have made the acquaintance of Hugo Cassingham and his sister Emily, and persuaded them to employ May, who was experienced in urban welfare work, to resolve the infant tetanus problem. There is some basis in these letters for the idea that May assented out of loyalty to Aubrey West rather than any sense of calling to Colsay; certainly she did not find out much about her destination before leaving Manchester and made no effort to learn Gaelic while on the island. Evidence given to the Highland Commission ten years later, after the deaths of all the main participants in this episode, suggests that Sir Hugo had prepared the way for May by telling his tenants that they would be evicted if they refused her attendance. And that, I think, is why this particular baby was not given a funeral and buried in the churchyard; as long as there was no official record of her birth and death, Sir Hugo had no reason to implement his threat. Childbirth had become the locus of the tension between modernity and tradition, between metropolitan and peripheral ways of understanding the world. If they had accepted May's support and attended the lectures she offered them, the women of Colsay would have been accepting an alien and colonial intervention in the most personal and also the most political life event, the birth of a new islander. In refusing, they would expose themselves to the anger of a man who had the power to end their life on the island. By burying the baby in secret, they were able to conceal their non-compliance, and because in the event May died at about the same time as the child she failed to deliver, no one need ever know the full story of May's failure on Colsay. There was no attempt to replace May, and life on the island continued to become steadily harder relative to life on the mainland until the last permanent resident left in the late 1960s.

'There seems to have been local gossip to the effect that Sir Hugo showed little interest in the infant death rate until a relationship between his son, Hartley, and one of the local women resulted in a pregnancy. May's suspicions about the dates of the pregnancy she attempted to oversee, and the DNA of the bones found in the orchard, would seem to confirm that the child in question was the result of such a liaison.'

And then I told them the story of May, Eve and Mrs Barwick, no longer quite sure whose story it was. I could imagine Mrs Barwick out in the garden in the days after May's death, standing where Raph and I had stood, forcing the spade into the matted roots of turf as I had forced it, a bundle in a badly knitted blanket lying on the ground beside her. Would she have said something, made some ceremony, before shovelling the earth back over the baby's dark hair, watching it trickle down the folds of pale wool? I told them about the Highland Commission, and about the reports of May's shipwreck in the *Oban Times*. And that what was probably May's body appeared on the beach at Invercarron in the first of the big storms in the new year.

The head of department had stopped writing and was watching me as if I were about to chant Mrs Barwick's spell for raising storms. Spell for getting a job. Would Virginia Woolf have supported May or Mrs Barwick? Which is really the heroine?

I looked up, gathered my papers. I was finishing exactly within the allotted time. 'I cannot say why the baby was buried

373

in her father's garden rather than elsewhere on the island. It is easy to understand that Virginia Grice would want to know where her daughter lay. Perhaps the location was Mrs Barwick's choice, perhaps it was meant as a private insult or revenge on Hartley. The other question I cannot answer is what would have happened had May survived the passage across the Sound that day, and been able to tell her story to the Cassinghams; despite the loss of their own men, it must have been a shipwreck that was not unwelcome to some on Colsay at that time.'

I bought myself a copy of the *Guardian* for the train home, and settled down in another window seat of my own with the third cup of hot coffee in three days and the new Booker Prize winner, the first time I had bought a new hardback for myself. In my bag, with my laptop and the padded envelope, I had one of those plastic pots of fruit, air-freighted, peeled and chopped by other people for my convenience. The city, silenced by the thick windows and air-conditioned hum of the train, rushed past. Colsay lay waiting for me at the end of the day: the sound of the sea, the ghost of the anchorite watching over us all, the children with their sticky hands and night wakings. The newspaper showed a woman's torso emerging from concrete rubble, although the headline I could see was about the arrest of an American singer for attacking his girlfriend with a baseball bat. I do not know if there is a good reason to read the news.

We crossed a motorway and suburbia began outside. Rain spattered diagonally against the window, as if thrown in anger, and my coffee slopped under its plastic lid. Raphael tugged at my mind, as if he were thinking of me, willing me home to him. He is not all right, Raphael, not really. He needs help of some kind, from someone. And Moth, riding through the day on my hip, poking his fingers in my ears and resting his satin head under my chin. Moth, I think, barring accident, barring illness and addiction and the treachery of strangers, barring most of the things that can happen in a life, will be all right. We were leaving the city now, me and the man in the suit watching television on his laptop, and the woman fiddling with her iPod and staring out into the rain as if the song were about to make her cry, and the boy texting some urgent thought with the hyper-evolved thumbs of the generation born more than five years later than me.

I will never learn to write with my thumbs. I will never bake cookies and keep baby wipes in the glove compartment. My stomach will never be flat again. I will never do Voluntary Service Overseas, not even if there is an impoverished and oppressed community whose problems could be resolved by the application rather than the undoing of nineteenth-century history. I will never recover the lost innocents, those who in dying as children took the only way of not doing harm, not even my own.

My phone rang. The rain was heavier now, rivulets racing across the window, behind which the heather on the moor was bowing under the wind. I pulled the handset from under the papers in my bag. It was not Giles telling me that something had gone wrong, that the children needed me now, but the head of department in Glasgow, calling to offer me a different kind of servitude, and an institutional room of my own. The train carried me onwards, across the moors, towards the island and the cliff.

SELECT BIBLIOGRAPHY

Colsay is a fictitious island, but some readers will have recognized similarities between the history of Colsay and that of St Kilda. A lot has been written about St Kilda, and there is a comprehensive bibliography on the island's website. These are the standard texts:

Mary Harman, *An Isle Called Hirte: A Culture and History of St Kilda to 1930* (Waternish, Skye: Maclean Press, 1997)

Charles Maclean, *Island on the Edge of the World: The Story of St Kilda* (1972; rev. ed. Edinburgh: Canongate, 2006)

Martin Martin, *A Late Voyage to St Kilda* (London: 1698)

Tom Steel, *The Life and Death of St Kilda* (London: Harper Collins, 1988)

I found specialist research on neonatal tetanus in:

Peter Stride, 'St Kilda, the neonatal tetanus tragedy of the nineteenth century and some twenty-first century answers', *The Journal of the Royal Collage of Physicians of Edinburgh*, April 2008; 38(1): 70–77

E. J. Clegg and J. F. Cross, 'Aspects of the neonatal death in St Kilda, 1830–1930', *Journal of Biosocial Science*, Jan 1994; 26(1): 97–106

The history of the Clearances is well known and well served; I found the following useful for an anecdotal approach:

David Craig, *On the Crofters' Trail: In Search of the Clearance Highlanders* (London: Jonathan Cape, 1990)

Derek Cooper, *The Road to Mingulay: A View of the Western Isles* (London: Warner Books, 1992)
Eric Richards, *The Highland Clearances* (Edinburgh: Birlinn, 2002)

My sense of life on Colsay in the late nineteenth century was informed by:

Lynn Abrams' book *Myth and Materiality in a Woman's World: Shetland 1800–2000* (Manchester: Manchester University Press, 2005).

Some readers will also have recognized the reports of the 'Highland Commission' as inspired by the Napier Commission, the full record of whose proceedings can be found at the website of Lochaber College in Mallaig: http://www.lochaber.uhi.ac.uk/links/napier-commission

ACKNOWLEDGEMENTS

I thank everyone who gave me permission to quote from their work, and especially Nyree Findlay, who also corrected my archaeology, and Julia Donaldson, who let Moth have *The Gruffalo*.

I thank my colleagues at the University of Kent and at the University of Iceland for their support and interest as I wrote this book. At Kent, my especial gratitude to Jennie Batchelor and Scarlett Thomas; in Iceland to Peter Knutsson and Messiana Tomasdottir, Maeja Gardarsdottir, Mads Holm and Matthew Whelpton, and all the students in my writing courses. Sinead Mooney's reading and comments were much valued.

Thank you to my agent, Anna Webber, to everyone at Granta, and especially my editor, Sara Holloway, for her bounteous patience and for the gift of her discernment, and to Amber Dowell for good cheer (and pink drink) when I needed it.